Th

~

"An unflinching assessment of the ragged edge between good and evil, tolerance and intolerance, Ms. Ross's debut novel offers a solution that can mend hearts and patch together lives that have been torn apart—*faith*. Three stories braid and ravel through the pages, mysteriously but ineluctably connected, until they finally come together in something very like the illumination. Throughout, suffering itself emerges as both the content and the conduit of the stories we must tell to make sense of it all. A deeply moving and memorable narrative journey across the landscape of loss and faith."

—Lynn Stegner, author of *Because a Fire Was in My Head*

~

"In a novel with aspects of magical realism, the horrors that Jewish people suffered sit side-by-side with a timely story of a modern society in which antisemitism is on the rise, resulting in an emotional and compelling tale."

—*Kirkus Reviews*

~

"*The Bones of the World* feels terrifyingly familiar in its portrait of a contemporary America riven by political resentments and prone as always to find someone—the same someones as always, alas—to blame and banish the purge. But despite its well-rendered settings of agony (the Holocaust, the Inquisition, a mother's inconsolable grief for her son), Betsy Ross's novel succeeds in winning through to a hope that's not beyond suffering but that is *composed* of suffering. By making anguish into story, the novel implies, those who are scapegoated and victimized may not only preserve bitter experience but transmute it into a kind of salvation. Vivid, moving, intricately structured—*The Bones of the World* is an excellent debut."

—Michael Griffith, author of *Trophy: A Novel*

~

"A book about returning to the heart over and over and how to access the courage to return, Betsy Ross's debut novel dives head-first into the darkest regions of human suffering and breathes life into every part of us we thought we may have lost. *The Bones of the World* offers us a choice—we can either let grief calcify and haunt us, or allow it to initiate us into a secret world governed by an ancient, forgotten language that connects us all. A brave, beautiful work."

—Rachel Nagelberg, author of *The Fifth Wall*

~

"Among the astute historical and social inspections that move Rachel from past to present are thought-provoking questions about the choices her Jewish people have made to survive, and the costs they may have unwittingly incurred as a result. This gives the novel an added layer of social and philosophical reflection that will lend to book club debate."

—D. Donovan, Senior Reviewer, *Midwest Book Review*

~

"I devoured *The Bones of the World* in 36 hours. Rachel, Sariah, and Jakob became my friends and my heroes: I felt instantly woven into the fabric of their stories. Betsy L. Ross is a master world-builder thoughtfully crafting not one but three immersive worlds in which true loss, true love, and true redemption fight, fail, and flourish. Clear your calendar and read this book."

—Jerry Rapier, Artistic Director, Salt Lake City Plan-B Theatre

~

"A profound spiritual meditation on the human reaction to atrocity and if any meaning can be found in great suffering."

—Erica Ball, *Independent Book Review*

~

"*The Bones of the World* is a prolific account of why we must 'never forget' what history encourages us to learn."

—Feathered Quill

~

"... A captivating mystery novel that leaves readers pondering long after the book is read. There are no answers but rather an offering of important personal and philosophical questions to think about as the reader is guided through the intricate maze of intertwining personal stories of the characters. This is definitely a highly recommended read."

—Literary Titan

~

THE BONES OF THE WORLD
BETSY L. ROSS

atmosphere press

For the disappeared around the world whose stories must be told.

There is only one thing that I dread:
not to be worthy of my sufferings.

Viktor Frankl, *Man's Search for Meaning*, quoting Dostoevsky

Do you not see how necessary a world of pains and troubles
is to school an intelligence and make it a soul?

John Keats, *Letters of John Keats*

1
RACHEL

The room was small and dark though the sun had begun to light the sky, projecting patterns of roses onto the walls through the cotton-chintz curtained window. Before Rachel's sight grew clearer, while the morning interplay of sun's rays and dark merged, she was reminded of a room from those magic tricks in which the walls slowly move closer, threatening to crush the magician within as the space becomes smaller and smaller, or, no, to protect, becoming increasingly womb-like, until the magician breaks out of the chains and finds the nail on the floor with which the inexorable grinding of the motor animating the walls could be halted. That, Rachel decided, was what it felt like to wake up each morning. The room smaller, the constant temperature-taking to determine if today her quarters were jail or womb.

She can't remember exactly when the room had begun speaking to her. Not in words exactly, but in patterns she found in niches and corners. Three cracks in the plaster of the ceiling above her bed. Some nights, as she lay observing them, they were the branches of a tree; one night, a laurel, and she imagined herself Daphne, metamorphosing just in time to elude Apollo's lustful advances. Another night the sacred

Kalpa, through which she prayed to the divine, and another, the dignified olive, whose branches promised peace. But sometimes the trees disappeared, and the cracks appeared more sinister, as asps, and she feared herself Cleopatra.

How long had it been? Days, weeks, months even? Time was a concept for the outside. For her, there was only the interminable present. Often, she found herself replaying memories of arriving at the mansion.

"But Henry, who're we visiting? Why're we here? Why'd we bring a suitcase?"

Something she'd had to drink. Something making her head foggy.

"Don't worry, Rachel. Everything is planned. You'll be safe here. Eloise, take this bag and put it in the room, won't you?"

Who was that woman? How did Henry know her? Why can't she make sense of this?

"Let me help you up the stairs, Rachel; you're a bit unsteady."

"But ... but ... why?" Why were they here? Why this mansion? She remembered the feeling of danger. But why?

"I'll explain everything to you after you've had time to rest. Here," Henry said as he opened the heavy oak door with the large brass handle, "this is where you'll be for a little while, until things are safer outside."

She must have slept a long time, and when she awoke, she was alone in a dark, unfamiliar room and remembered she was supposed to feel safe but, in fact, felt far from it. She looked out the window at the cemetery below.

———

Inside the high stone walls, oaks just visible from Rachel's second-story window reached for the heavens, dreaming of the selfless beanstalk that gave its life to provide for Jack and his mother.

"Oh, if only the Children could climb *our* branches and be

saved," they murmured among themselves.

But what could they have meant, for the Children were already dead.

"We are, after all," reminded the Oldest Oak, "in a cemetery."

Nevertheless, the oaks dreamed of a role even larger than the noble one they now played as protectors of the graveyard, their full, unclimbed branches providing cover from the sun and peering eyes. But not from those eyes. Not a mother's eyes.

Inés walked along the gravel paths weaving in and out among the tombs in the old city's cemetery that she'd tended her entire life. Inside the tombs were the bones of the Ancestors. Now they shared the space with the Children.

The night it happened, Inés, who lived close by, heard the Ancestors before hearing the ruckus itself. "Come quickly, Inés," they called to her. Others had entered upon the sacred ground as though climbing planks of a harbored ship, depositing "cargo" to be sealed up for the voyage into eternity. But as with cheap cargo valued only for its dollars' worth, dead bodies were thrown into tombs, two here, three there, with no concern for folding arms over chests, untangling limbs, or other civility. However cowardly the killings, secreting them away in such a manner was even more so. They were children kidnapped and killed by a government intent on hiding its deeds. This Inés heard from the Ancestors. The Children cried and the Ancestors cried. The tears of the Children for their shortened lives and families left behind. The tears of the Ancestors for the unbearable injustices of the world. Still.

Inés knew then, even before the Keepers spoke, that her role had changed. Not only was she bound to honor the Ancestors by caring for their tombs, leaving offerings, and supplying herbs they may need, but she now had the Children to care for—dead though they might be. The Children's lives may have ended, but their stories were yet to be told. Their mothers still cried at their absences, still held hope in their hearts, unknowing. The world could not bear the weight of that silence.

The summons from the Keepers arrived shortly after the Ancestors' call. Five Elders met at the cemetery's exedra, sitting in a semi-circle on the high-backed stone benches among the softly scented magnolias, and waited for Inés. Though a member of the Keepers of Story for many years, Inés had never been called to meet with the Elders. To quell the anxiety she could feel rising within, she sat on the wooden porch steps of her worn-down shotgun home with Homer purring in her lap and took a few moments to compose herself. Passing her hand reflexively through his fur again and again, she couldn't fathom what use she could be to the Elders but knew she must be ready to do whatever might be asked of her.

As if to hurry Inés along her way, Homer climbed down and settled off to the side of the steps, posing sphinxlike, preparing to protect the home in Inés' absence. She stood, shook off the clicks and clacks of old age, and began the short walk to the cemetery, uncertain she'd had the time to ready herself as she wished or, for that matter, that any amount of time would have made a difference.

The first time the teenaged boys, festooned in red, white, and blue, appeared on the streets of the old city with automatic rifles, Rachel had been returning from a night at the opera. She and Henry had four season tickets and had invited along her mother and her mother's friend, Maura. Rachel's father had begged off with a headache, and David raised him one with an earache, the onset of which was certain to correspond to the first notes of *Die Fledermaus*.

"Let's stop for dessert around the corner. I've heard they have the best—" But Maura didn't finish her sentence. Had they not almost been run over by a truckload of armed teens, she would have lavishly praised the eclairs.

"Quickly," Henry spoke calmly but with authority, giving his arm to his mother-in-law, Eva, for assistance. "This way ... to the car."

The cracked sidewalks reeled with chaos as others who'd been enjoying a night on the town also ran for safety. There had certainly been hints, murmurings, but the impulse to trust in the social fabric has always been, alternately, a human forte and a foible.

"What in God's name was that?" Eva asked after hopping into the car's back seat next to Maura.

"I'd heard this might be happening," offered Maura. "While at the Café this morning, Marco warned he might have to close early, that all the business owners on the street had been tipped off the government-sanctioned Righteous were planning a show of force."

Henry drove as fast as he safely could, taking back streets to avoid the trucks. They encountered the inevitable leak of anger and disorder in those taking advantage of the fear in the air by breaking shop windows and looting them. Though shocked and afraid, none of them spoke again until arriving at William and Eva's.

"Rachel, you and Henry stay with us tonight; it makes no sense to go back out," Eva suggested. "You, too, Maura. Please stay here tonight. We wouldn't feel comfortable leaving you alone in your home."

Maura looked toward Henry, who hesitated a moment before agreeing. "Of course, Maura. You must stay the night."

There was a moment in which Henry and Maura's eyes connected, and an understanding that passed between them was lost on Rachel and Eva, who had gone into the kitchen to prepare some hot chocolate to calm their overworked nerves.

Rachel awoke early in her parents' home, revisiting the horror of the night before. *Here we are again. How can it be that we don't learn, that we clutch at low-hanging branches of wrongs and misunderstandings from the past, fearful always of difference? Why this continuing predisposition toward creating otherness?*

Walking down the stairs to make a pot of coffee, her mind raced. *Couldn't Jews themselves be indicted for creating an off-putting insularity? Might the Jewish history of practicing exclusion by "circling the wagons" have contributed, and continue to contribute, to a perceived sense of otherness? And don't Jews—why did she have such a difficult time saying 'we'—actually perpetuate this—call it what it is—discrimination against others? This refusal of some to assimilate, isn't this begging for trouble?* Her thoughts were interrupted by stirrings in the house. She remembered that Maura had spent the night and heard whispering in the parlor.

"You may not be a Jew, Henry, but you *are* married to one. Last night was not the first act of antisemitism, and we both know it won't be the last."

"I don't know what can be done, Maura."

"You know I can protect you and the gallery, even if I can't protect Eva and William. I, after all, am a good Christian," Maura continued.

"You said nothing about Rachel."

"Would you even *want* me to protect her?"

"That's a dandy question, Maura. What do you expect of me? And this isn't something to discuss here ... now. For God's sake, Rachel is upstairs."

Rachel opened and closed the cupboard loudly, replacing the washed mugs from the night before. She didn't like what little she'd overheard, wasn't sure she understood, and didn't have the emotional bandwidth to hear more. She called out to the other room so they'd know she was in the kitchen.

"Is that you, Henry?" She stuck her head through the doorway. "I thought I'd fix some eggs before heading home. Would you like some? Could you turn on the TV and see if there's any news about last night? And would you check in with David and make sure he's okay?"

Rachel knew her mother and Maura had become friendly, if not close, since Maura had married her father's friend, Herb. Her parents had been wary of the age difference between Herb and Maura, but Maura had been there for Herb during his lengthy illness, which had ended in his death only, what, two years ago? Rachel would have to reflect on what she'd just heard in light of those facts … later. Right now, she just wanted to get home.

Weeks after what had come to be known as the Night of the Ascent, David was in his bedroom trying to focus on a project but kept thinking about the signs that had begun popping up around campus not long after that night. His parents had nearly been caught in the middle of the violence. While the Righteous claimed no harm had been intended, that the parade of trucks was just a celebration of our great country, that the deaths had been caused by America-hating Jews and dirty socialists, some questioned—though only in private and then only in whispers—why the Righteous had been armed with rifles and why the shooting had occurred only when the trucks passed by the synagogue on a Friday night during Sabbath services. Twenty-three inside the synagogue had been shot that night; five had died. No weapons were found inside the synagogue. Soon after, the American flag with the stars replaced by a swastika that his mother had seen on the trucks began showing up at the Student Union and in many of David's classroom buildings.

Over coffee at the Campus Rest Stop a few days later, Eli remarked to David and Caroline, "You weren't in our History of Architecture class last week when we had to wait for Dr. Marcus to show up. After fifteen minutes, someone I'd never seen before walked into the room, stood at the lectern, claimed he was from the department, and told us that Dr. Marcus would no longer be teaching, and our new professor would be arriving momentarily."

"But what reason did he give?" asked Caroline, with concern.

"That's just it," replied Eli. "He didn't give one. We all shouted a lot of questions at him, but he just walked out of the room. We were kinda stunned, and then in walks some new guy in a suit—a *suit* of all things!—who tells us to sit down and then just jumps into a lecture on the profligacy of the Bauhaus movement in 1920s Germany. I have the notes if you need them, by the way."

"So ... Dr. Marcus," David prodded.

"Yeah, right," added Caroline. "Did you ever find out what happened to Dr. Marcus? How come we haven't heard yet? We're in her class, too."

"So that's the scariest part," answered Eli. "You know her daughter, Abby?"

"Sure," said Caroline. "She's just a year behind us, right?"

"Right. Well, word is, she hasn't been back in school since that day either."

David jumped in angrily. "So, it's a mystery ... but it's not. They're Jewish! Remember studying about Argentina in the seventies when people were being disappeared? There've been too many instances of spontaneous vacations and dying relatives in other states. Soon, the excuses will all be used up. I think it's pretty clear that Jews are being disappeared here, now, all these years later."

"But that's impossible," Eli remarked.

"Oh my God, David," Caroline added.

"That's exactly it," David replied, biting his lip.

"And I just thought, of course, it's always been so obvious, but the prevailing attitude of political correctness just wouldn't allow any of us to say it out loud ... What? ... Of course, there's so much misinformation all over the internet these days. I just think it's horrible the way the media puts its liberal spin on things. Well, when you can't rely on facts anymore, you just have to rely on your instincts. Wait, I think that's someone at the door. I'll have to call you back, Kate. Bye."

Henry walked into the foyer and hung his hat and raincoat on the coat rack—damn the pervasive rain; the city was likely to flood again if this weather continued.

"Oh Henry, I'm so glad you're here." Maura walked over, took his hand, kissed him on the lips, and led him to the bedroom.

Afterward, she said, "I'd just finished making a pot of French onion soup when you walked in. Would you like to have some before you have to leave?"

"That sounds wonderful."

Henry enjoyed Maura's cooking almost as much as Rachel's. He sometimes wondered what he was doing with Maura, but always came back to that moment with William at Herb's bedside when Herb had asked them both to look after Maura until she settled into life without him. William had promised, and the next thing he knew, he'd promised, too. And then, well, Maura was so damned inviting! He hated himself for this indiscretion and the lies necessary to keep Rachel from getting hurt. Or, at least, he thought, he ought to hate himself and hated himself for that equivocation.

"Kate was just telling me about recent studies she read on the Internet that prove once and for all the Holocaust never happened—"

Henry immediately cut her off. "Maura, I can't believe you'd be hoodwinked by that kind of propaganda. There are too many accounts detailing Nazi barbarity. There is simply no question that the Holocaust occurred."

"Now, Henry, I know this is sensitive for you, but wouldn't you feel better knowing Rachel's ancestors hadn't *really* gone through all that horridness made up for God-knows-what purpose? The fact is none of those who provided those supposed eyewitness accounts is alive. Why would we believe the testimony of people we can't question?"

And there it was. The always-inevitable argument. Yet it was absurd to believe that all history, therefore, was suspect. What could Henry say? He knew William and Eva had spent numerous vacations with Herb and Maura, and never had they told him or Rachel that religion had been a subject of conversation, much less a point of contention. Maura was a practicing Catholic, which had proved valuable when they'd visited churches along the Mediterranean coast. But now it was apparent the proverbial antisemitic cat was out of the bag.

"Let's not talk about that right now, shall we, Maura? It's been a lovely afternoon, and your soup is delicious." Henry tried an old defense: deflection by flattery.

"I'm glad you like it, Henry. But there's no good time to discuss what's happening now, is there. We were just witnesses to the direction of current events, and it becomes more and more obvious that you're going to have to act unless you want to go down with the ship."

"What are you trying to say, Maura? Act in what way?"

"Well, as we discussed briefly at Will and Eva's after *that* night, the gallery is at risk. Haven't you heard the rumors of a law to be passed allowing Jewish businesses to be confiscated by the government and sold off? As difficult as it will be, you're going to have to distance yourself from Will and Eva at the very least."

"And Rachel? Her too? I don't know how I would possibly do that."

"Don't worry, Henry," Maura cooed. "I'll be here to support you. I'll always be here for you."

———

"Welcome, Inés. Please make yourself comfortable; we have much to discuss."

Inés sat on the bench left for her so she would be facing the five Elders. They were dressed in white robes, each with a different colored sash signifying their degree of seniority. The exedra exuded solemnity, and Inés hoped she could comport herself with the same air. She sat quietly, counting her breaths, waiting for the explanation of why they were there.

"I am Ryu," the Elder with the gold sash began. "I could introduce the others, but our names do not matter. We are all here to support you in the task you are being assigned. It will behoove you to listen well. We will respond to questions, but have no time to coddle."

Inés nodded to show she understood, though she felt such sternness was unnecessary.

"It is your time. You are to help prepare a chosen one to become a Teller. Few of us feel ready for such a task," Ryu continued preemptively, "but you can trust in our faith that you are."

Inés remained silent, knowing she could contain the fear best that way. Seeing her discomfort, Ryu softened, her voice echoing now with strength and kindness both.

"The stories of the Children in the cemetery must be told. The Teller is being prepared even now, but you, along with Eloise, are charged with completing that preparation. The Teller's name is Rachel, the mother of a son who will come under your care in the cemetery soon, with a story of his own to be shared." They paused to allow their words a place to settle before continuing. "For her to be an effective Teller, she must come to terms with the role of suffering in a holy world. It will be your job to guide her in her submersion into suffering."

The Elder to Ryu's left continued. "To help you, we will make two of Rachel's previous lives available for you to share with her when you deem most appropriate." The Elder handed a small bag to Inés, continuing, "Place these herbs in her tea and she will begin the dreams of her past lives."

Another Elder, one with a blue sash, added, "We leave you with this most important principle to guide you in your task: Suffering's meaning is as vast as the compendium of its stories, though the paradox is its greatest power is not in the many, but in the one."

Inés, hear my tale. I, Benjamin Noah, was taken on a Saturday morning on my way to the synagogue by classmates and their fathers. Two boys approached me on the street before I reached the synagogue. I knew them, having been to their houses after school. We'd played soccer together, shot at birds with slingshots together, and traded baseball cards. We were friends.

The Children's Chorus: Oh, this is too hard to hear. Why such betrayal?

They suggested I skip out on services and go with them to the park for a pick-up game of soccer. The temptation tore at me. I'd soon be thirteen and knew at that time I would become a bar mitzvah and be accountable for my actions. But I was only twelve and so believed I could wriggle my way out of my synagogue responsibilities. And so, I went with them.

The Children's Chorus: Wrong! Wrong! But who among us

might not submit to such a temptation?

The park was not too far away, but one of the fathers drove by and offered us a ride. The three of us got into the back seat. On the way, we picked up another father. Now, there were two adults, two boys and me. Still, I wasn't worried. Of course, I'd heard stories of the disappearances of Jewish families but considered them to be urban folktales.

The Children's Chorus: What our minds won't do to protect us from the unbelievable, the wicked.

But only too soon, I began to sweat, to shake with fear. I knew the way to the park, and we'd turned away from it. Still, afraid of being disrespectful, I spoke softly to the boy on my right.

"The park is the other direction, I'm sure."

At that, he and the boy on my left each grabbed an arm and turned to their fathers. "Hurry, he knows."

I thought to scream, but one of the fathers said, "Scream and you won't see your family again. We're only going somewhere to talk."

The Children's Chorus: Oh, the lies! Who are we to trust?

I remembered at that time the biblical story of Satan, who went to God jealous of all that Job had and suggested to God that Job only loved Him because of the wealth He had given him. God agreed to test Job with torments. In one day, Job's houses and lands were destroyed, his cattle stolen, and his children carried off in a whirlwind. Stunned by these calamities, Job nevertheless dressed in a sackcloth, shaved his head, and continued his worship. Though deserted by all, Job turned from the temptation to rebel and remembered the many miracles God had performed for his Chosen People. Yet I, succumbing to such a simple temptation as a reprieve from religious services, rebelled and suffered for my lack of faith.

The Children's Chorus: You are too hard on yourself. Faith comes with challenges. It grows over years and years, and even then, it is the few who are equal in faith to Job.

Inés had in her hands a stone she had picked up along a cemetery path. She took out of her pocket some herbs and rubbed them on the rock while mouthing a silent incantation. When she spoke aloud, she said, "Your story is locked in this stone, Benjamin Noah, where it will not be lost."

The Children's Chorus: There will come a time when it will be shared.

Following the Night of the Ascent, Jewish synagogues closed. There were interrogations. Jews were arrested for minor violations—parking tickets or barking dogs that disturbed neighbors—and taken to government facilities where they were never heard from again. Laws, created as a basis for the peaceful coexistence of citizens, were used as a cudgel against Jews. Most laws were simply ignored, the vacuum left filled with frightening silence. What you thought you knew about the existence of a missing son was denied, and if you offered proof of any government involvement, your daughter might go missing as well.

How could one survive under such a regime? They each had a different answer. Henry implored David and Rachel to keep low profiles. David should go to classes and return home. No extracurricular activities that might be a cause of irritation to others. Rachel should stay away from the gallery and work from home on her art and writing; Henry would get Maura's help at the gallery.

David petitioned the university for a semester's sabbatical

in order to follow his conscience. He knew Eli and Caroline were already involved in the Resistance; he decided to join them in the fight, courting images of the hero. The first test came quickly, though, and it was all too real.

Caroline and Eli looked David directly in the eye to gauge his reaction as Caroline explained, "I received word that we're to plant a bomb next week at the hotel where the government is holding a meeting with members of the Righteous. We're to plan it ourselves; the fewer people we involve, the less likely any trouble."

David started at the concept of harming others. "Whoa, Caro. A bomb? That's pretty extreme. Doesn't that make us just like them?"

Eli jumped in. "Unfortunately, the cause of justice will always have to be balanced against harm. Collateral damage is a part of the war for justice."

"Now we're talking war?" David asked, even more certain he was getting into something he wasn't ready for.

"Don't be naïve, David. You know this is a war now. How many of our Jewish acquaintances, friends, and family have disappeared? Do you think they're enjoying deluxe stays at five-star hotels or all-expenses-paid cruises to Caribbean islands? We've all heard some of what's been going on—do you need to be reminded? I'm happy to regale you with the tortures they've been employing. You've heard of the waterboarding, I'm sure. That's what I'll pick if provided a menu in my cell because that's got to be a million times better than having my fingers lopped off."

Their discussion had become heated as the reality of how their world had changed came home to roost. David shoved Eli as if it were his fault. "Quit it, Eli; you don't have to talk about it like that. Besides, whatever happened to the commandment 'Thou shalt not kill?' Do the Commandments mean nothing to you?"

Eli contemplated how to respond. A theological discussion

was not what David was after, but Eli could have answered that the correct translation of the Hebrew *Lo tirtzakh* was "You shall not murder." The difference between *murder* and *kill* was everything. But Eli only answered, "Of course they do, but that's not the point right now."

David shook, not solely out of fear, but also out of an emotional buildup. Should someone have told him to buck up? Be a man? The times no longer allowed such sentiments, and even if they did, David would prove himself in the end. He knew he would. The discussion turned to planning. Eli assured David, "I understand your concerns, and you know both Caro and I share them. We'll do our best to limit injuries. I promise you that."

Still, David couldn't help but wonder. If this act could be justified in the name of defeating an enemy, what act could not be? Truth be told, David feared becoming a cog in escalating violence, co-opted by the insidious attractions of power and authority. It was one thing to study the philosophical underpinnings of power, to read Schopenhauer and Nietzsche, and quite another to live them. But he would continue to assist in the Resistance even with these misgivings because, really, what choice did he have? The government was not just repressing Jews; it was actively annihilating them.

As it turned out, the use of existing laws to harass Jews was not enough. Shortly after the Night of the Ascent, the government proposed the passage of new laws that would create two classes: Americans and Outsiders. Primary among the "Outsiders" were Jews, though it included all others whose existence was not sanctioned by the tastes of the Righteous. Lacking the creativity to produce more trenchant laws on their own, the government turned for inspiration to the Nuremberg

Laws. They commissioned a study—with a predetermined outcome—that came back with the following "recommendations":

1. There should be enacted a law for the protection of
"American Blood and Honor" focused on racial pollu-
tion that would criminalize sexual relations and marriage between Americans and Outsiders.

2. There should be enacted a Law stripping Outsiders
of their citizenship.

3. There should be enacted a Law barring Outsiders
from all jobs in education, politics, and industry, preventing government contracts from being awarded to
Outsider businesses, and forbidding Outsider doctors
from treating American patients.

4. The consequence for any person violating any of the
Outsider Laws, including Americans who aid or abet
Outsiders, is imprisonment or death.

David tore a copy of the laws off a neighborhood grocery's
bulletin board and showed it to his parents. Rachel and Henry
had been aware of the discussions but had yet to see anything
in print, though soon there would be fliers everywhere not
only to inform Jews but to warn "Americans" who might be
sympathetic to their Jewish neighbors and, yes, family. There
would no longer be such a thing as an American Jew, an American Black, or an American queer. Those were all Outsiders;
the regime had created a new definition of *American*.

"My God, Henry, what are we going to do?" asked Rachel,
aghast at the first law, which threatened the freedom of all
persons in existing mixed marriages, making Henry and Rachel criminals.

"I don't know, Rach. We'll have to talk to others, figure out
how far the government is really prepared to go."

David jumped in, amazed at his parents' naïveté. "I can tell
you how far they're prepared to go. I've heard what happens

in the interrogation cells; you don't want to know. It's incomprehensible!" David's face grew red with the anger over how far the government, in cahoots with the Righteous, had already gone, but also over the denial in his parents' attitudes. What is it that made us all think America would be different?

***

Eloise took out her key ring and placed the skeleton key into the lock on the solid wooden gate of the cemetery. She had no need for the key as the cemetery was protected, but Eloise did so love the feel and sound of the key's introduction and mingling with the inner workings of the lock. The gate's heavy metal hinges creaked as the door swung inward, allowing Eloise to push it open by pressing both her large shoulder and larger hip against the door just enough—which was more than it used to be—to slip through. Inside, she found Inés replacing flowers at many of the tombs. Eloise called out softly so as not to awaken any of the elderly Ancestors.

"Hello, sister."

Inés turned around, startled, and swallowing her impulse to chastise her sister for sneaking up on her, handed Eloise half of her bundle of flowers.

"Hello, sister. Here, would you take these and help me replace the old flowers at the tombs while we talk?"

They walked side by side, placing flowers by the slate, marble, and granite tombs that were styled in a mixture of Greek, Egyptian, Gothic, Romanesque, Renaissance, and Byzantine revivals. The flowers wouldn't survive long in the desperate, moody heat, which is why Inés was forced to change them so often.

Inés continued. "I must speak with you about Rachel. There is much for her to learn before she can fulfill her destiny. We must quicken our pace; the Keepers are relying on us. Rachel is already facing pain and confusion—and there is so much more to come, as you know." Inés rubbed her hip as she stood up from placing a few rosebuds on a new headstone not yet inscribed. "It is time for the dreams." She dropped her hand into her capacious pockets, withdrew some herbs, and said to Eloise, "Here, take these and place a pinch into her afternoon tea each day for a week. That should do it."

Eloise pocketed the herbs in silence. She knew there was more she could do. She would not force it but would make herself more available to Rachel, who, after all, had no one else to talk with these days except for very occasional visits from Henry. Yes, the pressure was on.

The sun's final rays lingered along the closed edges of the room's curtains as Rachel sat at the small antique desk that doubled as her dining table. A knock on the door interrupted her thoughts, and in walked Henry. Before he could say anything, Rachel jumped up angrily and challenged him.

"Where have you been? Eloise has told me it's too dangerous for me to leave! What's going on, Henry? Why am I still here?"

"Hello, my dear," Henry said too nonchalantly as he walked toward her and past the table on which he saw she was reading Philip Roth. Never liked him. Could only make it halfway through *Portnoy's Complaint*.

He gave her a peck on the cheek and, raising the bag he had with him, said, "I brought you a new tea and almond macaroon that I thought you'd like from the Crescent." He placed it on the table next to the book. "You're looking lovely. How are you feeling today?"

How did she feel? She wanted to hit him, take out on him all her growing frustrations. At the same time, she craved his touch and conversation. But how could he pretend that all was normal? Nothing could be less normal in her life! She'd been stowed away—that's really what it was, wasn't it?—with only Eloise's sidestepping references to danger and promises that Henry would return when it was "safer."

Nevertheless, she answered him curtly, "Never mind all that. Just tell me about David and the gallery."

"Well, you'll be happy to know that we received a consignment from a wonderful young photographer who is being touted as the next, albeit conservative, Annie Leibovitz. He's quite talented and is being commissioned to do some photos of our new governor. That will surely be wonderful advertising for us! I think we'll be able to have a show ready in the next few months. I'll be certain to bring you the brochure."

Henry knew Rachel would likely never have agreed to such a show at the gallery. Her interest had always been in the more abstract, what *she* would call more intellectual fare. But that wasn't what was selling these days. *Appropriate* representational art had made a resurgence, keeping with the political philosophy of the times. Edward Hopper–style realism with a nationalist slant.

"So, I shall be here for months? What about David? Is he safe? When will you tell me more of what's going on?"

"David remains safe." Henry, tired and resistant to going down this road, hoped to keep it short. "You're still here because you're still being hunted."

Eloise had told her the same thing, foregoing any details. Henry must know more.

"But what do you mean ... hunted? Hunted by whom? Why me?"

"You must remember that night we were with your mother and saw the trucks with the armed Righteous members? You remember the attack on the synagogue? Many Jews are now in hiding." He hastened to add, "But all of this will end soon. I see more and more opposition to the current political scene every day. Soon we will all be together as a family again."

The Children's Chorus: Beware!

In a sudden change of topics, Henry said, "I brought some legal papers for you to sign. Your signature will remove you from ownership of the gallery and allow me to retain ownership for our family. This will prevent the government from taking the gallery under the Outsider Laws."

"Oh, Henry, no!" Rachel exclaimed, understanding finally sinking in. "Has it really come to this?"

"It's why, my dear, I've been adamant that you stay here. It won't last forever. It can't. But we must be careful to make sure that when the times change, we'll be able to be a family again and able to return to our lives together managing the gallery. I understand how you must feel here, Rachel. But you must also remember that we have reason to fear and that your safety, and David's, are paramount to me."

Something nagged at Rachel as Henry said this. A memory fighting its way to the surface. Henry placed the papers on the desk on his way out and said, "I'll leave these here for you to sign."

Rachel stood up and glanced at the papers but had no appetite for reading them just yet. She took a sip of the warm tea Eloise had left her and strolled over to the window, looking out at the world that was off-limits to her, watching as the sun, in its downward dog, spied into the cemetery next door, alighting upon a pile of stones she'd not noticed before. Suddenly she felt sleepy, so sleepy she climbed into bed still clothed.

2
SARIAH

The landscape boasted gently swaying flowers of a burnt um-ber hue and scrabbly hilltops off in the distance. The breeze was hot and suffocating. Barefoot, Rachel felt the bottoms of her feet burn as the grasses and flowers gradually transformed into loamy dirt and then crystalline sand.

Dressed in a long skirt and long-sleeved blouse, with a beautifully and intricately embroidered scarf tied around her head, she marched a short distance behind a wooden wagon filled with large barrels of fruits and grains. "Sariah, you're falling behind," came a woman's voice, not unkindly, from the front of the wagon. "Forgive me," she responded, raising her gaze from the ground just in front of her to the wagon, noticing it was farther ahead than she intended, and picking up her pace. She'd been daydreaming, remembering earlier days in Portugal before the Inquisition had irrevocably changed her life.

The Lisbon streets were busy as Sariah made her way from her home just above the family spice shop to the market in time to pick up some fish and over to the Rocha family home to procure some kosher wine for Sabbath dinner. She knew to be circumspect, to keep her eyes on the ground in front of her, to attract no unwanted attention. She had worn a white blouse and dark skirt, with a dark shawl over her head. This, also, to prevent any unwanted attention. At fifteen years, Sariah was of marriageable age and attractive. But she had no wish for marriage, and circumstances conspired to grant her that wish.

She'd been an only child until a month ago, when God had blessed her mother and father with a baby boy, Baruch, *blessed one.* Her mother's pregnancy was a surprise, though a joyful one. Her parents had been married for ten years before having her and hoped desperately for a boy who would run the family shop when her father could no longer. She awoke each day to the taste of their disappointment that she was a girl. When there were no more children, she tried especially hard to please her parents in all things, knowing the burden she was and feeling responsible for the sadness that lived in the shadows of every moment. And so, with the birth of little Baruch, Sariah learned something of joy. She loved him fully even when she could have been bitter that what love her parents had been able to invoke for her was now showered on him.

Sariah knocked on the door of the Rocha home. "Senhora Rocha, it is Sariah de Lopez. May I come in?"

"Yes, my child, do not linger on the doorstep. One cannot tell who may be watching."

"Senhora, I have come for some Sabbath wine."

Senhora Rocha told Sariah to wait while she went into the basement and brought up two bottles of wine. "You should come earlier next week. When you come each week on Friday, it is dangerous. I know your family is taken up with dear Baruch right now, but that should be no occasion for lessened vigilance. The Inquisition is quick to seek evidence that we *conversos* are backsliders. May God keep you and protect you and your family."

Sariah was anxious to return home as her parents would

be awaiting her to begin Sabbath prayers. Walking into the kitchen with the bottles of wine, Sariah could hear Baruch's cries in the other room, then the blessed suckling noises that coincided with the delicious quiet of feeding time. Babies were noisy creatures, she had decided, and though she adored her brother, the smell and noise further supported Sariah's distaste for marriage, which she knew to be the precursor to children.

"Thank you, Sariah," her father said as he walked into the room, kissing her on both cheeks. "Just in time for lighting the Sabbath candles. Your mother is busy with Baruch, so you must light them."

"Yes, Papa." Sariah pulled the shawl over her head and covered her eyes with her hands as she welcomed the Sabbath, waving her arms over the candles three times. Time disappeared as she intoned the sacred prayer spoken by Jews throughout the centuries and all over the world: *Baruch atah Adonai Eloheinu melech haolam asher kid'shanu b'mitzvotav, v'tzivanu l'hadlik ner shel Shabbas. Blessed art Thou, oh Lord our God, king of the universe, who has sanctified us by Thy commandments and commanded us to kindle the Sabbath lights.*

Tomás was eight years older than his wife, and to have the blessing of a son—a son!—at almost 55 years of age, when others his age were being blessed with grandchildren, was a miracle he had long prayed for. He had thought it too much to ask of God, but his was the God of Abraham, Isaac, and Jacob. There was nothing that could not be asked, nothing that would not be given the faithful, and Tomás was faithful. His family had become New Christians after arriving in Portugal from Spain, but their conversion came with an unspoken proviso. They would accept Christ outwardly, but inwardly Jesus would remain their brother, another Jew subject to the laws of Yahweh as they were.

While the birth of Baruch in itself brought joy to the de Lopez household, it was, for Sariah, an even greater blessing as it provided her independence. Sariah's father was often away on trading voyages to procure the spices and herbs they sold in their shop. That left Sariah and her mother to the everyday work of maintaining the home and tending to customers at the shop. Because her mother spent most of her time at home with Baruch these days, Sariah worked at the shop alone. While the family's business afforded the means to hire help, they could not afford prying eyes and ears.

Sariah enjoyed her time alone in the shop, time she could address the questions in her heart natural to a fifteen-year-old but perhaps not to a fifteen-year-old *girl*. Sariah's antipathy to marriage was more than a fear of growing up, of being an obedient wife, of bearing children. There was something additional she had never had the time to explore. Something that made her feel ... different.

The afternoons were quite busy, and Sariah felt the confidence her father had shown in allowing her to manage the shop alone begin to grow. The Judaism she had experienced, as practiced in secret, had very separate roles for men and women, roles that grated within her. While her mother, and now she, could recite the Sabbath blessing over the candles, only the boys were allowed to study scriptural texts. Reading itself was a male privilege, but because Father traveled so often and there was no son to manage the shop in his absence, Sariah had been given more latitude than other girls. She had been taught to read to help with the tracking of inventory and writing receipts.

One day while Sariah was in the back room of the shop, she heard the clanging of the front door's bell. She hurried out to welcome Senhora Pessoa, a frequent Old Christian customer who was always friendly and did not act towards

Sariah's family with condescension or aversion.

"Hello, Sariah. How is your dear little brother doing?"

"He is fine, Senhora Pessoa, though he seems to cry quite a lot."

"Ahh, yes. That is normal. You'll find out for yourself one of these days, I'm sure."

"Yes, ma'am," Sariah replied, though she believed otherwise.

"I expect your mother is upstairs, but is your father in the back? May I speak with him?"

"He is also upstairs with Baruch. I am the only one here."

"Oh. Well, I have a short list of spices. Would you see if you have them all?"

Sariah looked at the list and knew immediately where each spice was and knew the jars were full. She filled the Senhora's bags with joyful confidence while the Senhora made conversation.

"I understand there are church officials in the streets today searching for heretics," she began gently. "Of course, that would have nothing to do with your family," she quickly added. "It may be wise, though, for your father to return to the store."

Sariah knew what the Senhora meant, and it made her shiver as she finished filling the jars for her order. The Inquisition had been instituted in Lisbon shortly before Sariah's mother had been born. Sariah knew to talk with no one, even other *conversos*, or as they were also known, New Christians, about what occurred within their home on the Sabbath or on Jewish holidays. Her family attended church each Sunday, and she had learned Christian prayers as well as any other young woman her age because of that faithful attendance. If asked to recite the Lord's Prayer, Sariah would have no problem. Given the atmosphere in Lisbon, however, the tricks of an obedient dog might very well not be sufficient.

Soldiers poured into the streets late in the day as many

shops were full of customers purchasing food and wine for the evening's meal. The soldiers went two by two from shop to shop, asking questions, fingering the merchandise—whether women's clothing or plump, ripe figs—and taking bribes. They laughed among themselves, enjoying the cooler temperature as the sun began to set and the respite from the harder work of previous days when they had been tasked by the Inquisition with building a *quemadora* for the Auto-da-Fé planned for the coming months. High spirits prevailed as they enjoyed the power they had as representatives of the Inquisition. Operating at the order of priests, they enjoyed more respect than they had as mere soldiers of the Portuguese army.

Tomás returned to the shop, hearing of the potential for trouble. Herta came with him, Baruch in her arms, and began talking with Senhora Pessoa.

"He is beautiful and appears so well-behaved. How old is he now?" Senhora Pessoa inquired of Herta.

"Two months today. It is the first time I have brought him to the shop, and I believe he is taken with it. He must know that someday it will be his to run, and he is anxious to learn all he will have to do," Baruch's mother laughingly said.

"I have been watching his eyes, and they do seem to be looking here and there and taking everything in. He will be a wonderful son. Have you had his baptism yet?"

Herta answered carefully. "We have spoken with the priest and scheduled it. Baruch has had some problems eating, so we have kept him inside for fear of exposing him to sickness in his weakened state."

"Oh, but he looks so healthy now! It will be a blessing to have his baptism. And, of course"—the Senhora lowered her voice—"one cannot be too careful as a New Christian."

As they were talking, two soldiers entered the shop.

"The owner, where is the owner?" one of them bellowed, a bit too loudly. He had, perhaps, been plied with bribes of excessive wine at Senhor Altua's store. The shop became silent and customers began slipping out.

"I'll be back for my order, Tomás," assured one customer. "It is getting late, and I have to get this food to my wife if I have any hopes for a meal this evening!"

"Senhor Tomás, is it?"

The other soldier went up to him to inquire, as they had in all the shops in this New Christian quarter, whether he sold any Jewish items and when his family had last been to church. Tomás was accustomed to such an interrogation and was ready with appropriate answers: he sold only spices and herbs that could be used for cooking, and he and his family attended church every Sunday.

The first soldier interrupted them. "Wait," he said to the other soldier. "What's this here?" And he picked up from the floor a child's top.

Tomás answered him quickly, attempting to control his voice as he saw what it was, "It looks like a child's toy. It must have been dropped by one of the customers."

"But what do I see here? These look like Hebrew letters."

Tomás experienced the first blush of fright. He had seen that it was a dreidel, a toy that Jewish children played with at Chanukah. He had no idea how it had come to be on the floor of his shop ... but he knew it could cause him to be taken in for interrogation. He also knew that, too often, those taken away never returned.

"I believe it is a Jewish child's toy. But I have no children who would play with such a toy."

"Come outside with us, Senhor, and we will get to the bottom of this."

"No, no!" pleaded Herta, still holding onto Baruch (sweet little Baruch), who, feeling his mother's fear, was beginning to cry. "Please, it cannot be ours. We are faithful Christians. Our daughter can go get the priest, and he will tell you."

The soldiers laughed, drunk with power as well as wine. They grabbed both Tomás and Herta to pull them outside the shop. Those customers left in the shop were silent, knowing that interfering could threaten their own safety and that of their families.

Once outside, the soldiers' good humor subsided. It had been a long day, their own meals were waiting, and now they saw they were stuck with two New Christians who were likely backsliding Jews—and a baby, no less—that they were charged with taking back to the Inquisition offices. There were too many witnesses who could cause them trouble if they did nothing now. Sariah followed them out the door and tried speaking with them.

"Please accept this gift of some very rare and expensive spices for your wives. If you return home with these spices now, they can likely be used for your meals this very evening. You will be pleased with their delicious flavors."

Sariah's father and mother (still holding dear little Baruch) were standing passively just in front of the soldiers when one of them said, "We don't take bribes from dirty Jews," agitated by the public nature of the bribe. Sariah had been too bold.

One soldier grabbed Tomás by the arm while the other grabbed Herta, causing her to lose her grip on Baruch (dear one) and scream, "Wait, my baby, my baby!" The soldier who had his hands on Baruch's mother let her go and grabbed the baby.

"Enough!" he said. "I have him." Before she could sigh with relief that Baruch had not fallen to the ground, the soldier holding him walked over to the shop, held (sweet) Baruch by his feet, and swung him violently against the shop's stone wall, bashing his head against the stones that were, now, splattered with blood and brains.

Herta stood, watching, for only the briefest of moments before falling to the ground. Tomás, seeing his own future destroyed, groaned, deep guttural sounds emerging from the depths of his soul, and calling on the name of the God of Abraham, that Abraham who had been willing to sacrifice his own son Isaac at God's command, grabbed the soldier's knife and plunged it into his own breast.

3
RACHEL

The pitch of emotions grew with each day. The unthinkable, unbelievable became rote occurrences. In addition to the disappearances, homes suspected of housing Jews were searched to uncover items that might implicate the inhabitants in a sympathy for Judaism. This meant Jews had to scour each room of their houses to find and remove offending objects: the mezuzah on the doorframe—including taking it off, filling in the nail holes, and repainting without leaving evidence—the Chanukah menorah, or Sabbath candles. It was easier for Reform Jews; Conservative and Orthodox Jews likely also had yarmulkes in their dresser drawers, dishes and pots separated in the kitchen to enable the practice of keeping kosher, and phylacteries with leather thongs. Even a proliferation of modest dresses could cause a family to be brought in for interrogation.

And then there were books. Entire collections of Jewish scripture and commentaries had to be removed. Of course, they could not be destroyed—God forbid such a thing—and so they had to be hidden. Count on Jews to create a business for just such a need. For enough money—price reflecting risk— you could find a place for your library of religious books, but what about novels by Jewish authors? Philip Roth, Arthur Miller, Cynthia Ozick, Nathan Englander, Nicole Krauss, Saul Bellow, Michael Chabon, and on and on and on—was there a race wordier than the Jews? Of course, there was a *Catch-22* here—yep, Jewish—these books were not *only* read by Jews. The question then became whether you would be more or less likely considered a Jew if your library contained no Jewish authors at all.

The ten pm curfew was upon them as David and Eli walked home from the University. They were not far from David's parents' home and were planning to spend the night there.

"We'd better hurry, David." Eli was looking around him as he walked on the uneven sidewalk and saw not far up ahead, maybe one hundred yards, a large group of people in a partial circle. They could hear a male voice over the stunned quiet of the crowd. Should they see what was happening or hurry to the safety of David's home? The times were conducive neither to bravery nor curiosity but instead to fear and self-protection. Nevertheless, they continued toward the crowd as it grew louder. They could hear voices pleading with someone to "put something down," to "not give in to hopelessness," to "be reasonable." But these were far from reasonable times.

As they reached the outer edge of the circle, David nudged the girl in front of him and asked, "Hey, what's going on?"

"It's horrible," the young woman, about the same age as David, could barely get the words out. She was shaking and rubbing her arms as if she were cold. "Please, don't let him do it. He can't. He just can't!" She sobbed softly and stumbled off, unable to bear whatever it was that was going on.

"Wait," David called after her, "what's he going to do?"

The boy who had been in front of her turned around to answer, "He just poured gasoline over himself. He has a lighter."

"Oh my God, no!" Eli shouted. "Someone stop him!" Eli

started to push his way through the crowd that seemed all too willing to allow the immolation but was grabbed by a man in uniform. "No, you don't. Stay where you are. Let him take care of this for us."

Eli and David had gotten close enough to see that the young man in the center of the circle was drenched. They could smell the gasoline. They could also see that his face was covered in bruises, his nose askew, and one of his eyes was either closed shut or, the way it was sunken in, it could be missing. My God, what had he been through? They had no time for speculation, nor could they risk assisting the young, broken man as the uniformed guard Eli had run into was accompanied by several others, all of whom were holding the crowd at bay.

"Do it," the guards taunted and laughed. "Do it, or we'll bring you back to the cell for more *conversation.*"

No one dared say anything. Even the ones who might have were thinking of their mothers and fathers, their siblings and friends. Bravery had far-reaching consequences. And so, they all watched, many of them covering their ears but unable to tear their eyes from the spectacle as the young man lit himself on fire. He stood first in defiance, exhorting the gathering crowd to stand up to the Righteous, but, ultimately, fell to the ground screaming and writhing for much too long. Then still.

4

SARIAH

Senhora Pessoa quickly grabbed Sariah's arm and pulled her away from the scene. The guards didn't notice the stealth, busy as they were ordering those still standing where both Baruch and Tomás had died to wash the blood and other matter from the wall and stone street outside the shop. Herta they took with them. It was the last time Sariah saw her mother. Her entire family wiped out in moments in the place to which they had fled for safety. Was there any place in the world that Jews were safe? Sariah cursed not the soldiers who had been following orders, nor the officers who issued the orders, nor the King of Portugal, Philip I, nor Isabella and Ferdinand who had forced her family to leave Spain in the first place, nor the Christian God behind it all—but cursed the fact that she had been born a Jew.

"Quickly," Senhora Pessoa urged her. "We must get you away from here. You will come with me to my house. Senhor Pessoa will not mind. You must forget what happened today. It is horrible, but there is no changing things. Your father and brother are in the arms of Christ now, and, I am afraid, your mother will soon be, too."

Hiding at the Pessoa home where she was safe from the soldiers' searches, Sariah was empty, a shell with no feelings, no hunger, no language. As much as she could, she eschewed the outside world. For a time, it was allowed her. Ana Pessoa was gentle with her. Ana had seen. She understood. But she also believed, as Sariah did not, that this world was a place of pain and useful only as a gateway to a more glorious future. Because of that belief, Ana found Sariah's grief out of proportion and an insult to the promises of eternal life in Christ. And so, she prodded Sariah in moving beyond her grief with busyness.

Ana's husband, Martín, learned that the local church officials had usurped the shop and were preparing to sell it, so went to clear it out before the sale could occur. It was a dangerous step, perhaps, but the Pessoas were confident in their status as Old Christians. Were they to be found clearing it out, they could say they were ensuring the contents were not stolen by the Jewish friends of Sariah's family. If they were not discovered, all the better. There was a store of herbs and spices they would be able to use on their journey to Peru, as Martín had decided it was time to leave Portugal for the opportunities offered in the New World. He had heard the silver mines in Peru promised to be very lucrative and wanted to be one of the first to take advantage of the opportunity, using what he considered his prodigious people skills to become a successful trader in moving silver from the mines to nearby port cities for export.

Ana spoke with him about bringing Sariah with them. She was not certain how he would react, as Sariah had been less than appreciative since coming to their home.

"Martín," she began furtively, "the trip to Peru will be very strenuous, and, of course, once we are there, establishing a comfortable home will take some time and work. It would be helpful to me to have Sariah come along and take care of the girls so that I am freed up to do other things."

She was surprised how quickly he responded, expecting him to have balked at the additional mouth to feed. But he said only, "As you wish, my dear. But she will be your responsibility. You must make sure she follows your orders and does not make trouble for us."

And so it was that Sariah had no choice but to leave her home and what might be left of her family.

5
THE CHILDREN'S CHORUS

Please tell us why you revile us so.

6
RACHEL

Maura found herself in a situation she would never have anticipated. First, she was having an affair with a married man, though that wasn't what surprised her, as she had had other affairs when her husband, Herb, was still alive. No, that didn't cause her a moment's concern; it was that it was with *Henry*. All those trips together with Henry's in-laws, Eva and William. Even she had some sense of propriety, and an affair with their daughter's husband might just be the other side of appropriate. Henry *was* a good-looking man, but he was also—well, admit it—he was married to a Jew. The friendship hadn't bothered Herb, who had known William since they'd attended MBA school together and who had become William and Eva's private banker. Let's face it: if you're a private banker, you have to at least pretend broad-mindedness, as a large portion of your clientele was bound to be Jewish.

She'd gone along and had even become friends with Eva, though they weren't good friends, were they. And now? Well, initially, it was Henry's loneliness that reached out to her. Rachel often seemed distant, somewhere else. Maura offered Henry attention and sex that reminded him of earlier years. But now, it was appearing as if the initially illicit nature of their relationship might evolve into something more. If she played her cards right, and with the announcement of the Outsider Laws, the future was looking more and more promising.

"Of course, I shouldn't be telling you this, Kate, and I *know* you'll keep it to yourself, but … I had this idea, and I needed to run it by someone, just, you know, to make sure I wasn't going to get myself into any trouble." Maura had met Kate for a glass of wine at a popular wine bar far enough away from Maura's neighborhood that no one she knew would see her. Not that she was really worried about being seen. She wasn't, after all, branded with an "A" on her breast … but the affair was the least of her worries if she followed through with the plan she was cooking up.

"Oh, do tell, Maura. You live a much more exciting life than I. Old Douglas has become so boring."

Kate and Douglas had celebrated their thirtieth anniversary earlier in the year and had spent it on a cruise to the Caribbean. Maura and Herb would ordinarily have gone with them had Herb not up and died. And under the current circumstances, Maura was unable to bring Henry … but that was the plan she had called Kate to discuss over wine.

"Well, this is what I was thinking. You read about the Outsider Laws recently passed?"

"I heard something about them. I felt horrible, you know, poor Eva and William."

Maura interrupted before Kate could simper further, "Oh, hush, Kate. You know you don't really feel sorry for Eva. It's not *our* fault that she's Jewish or that she's promoted immoral art at the gallery or cheated so many of her customers with her exorbitant prices. You know you agree with me."

"Of course I do, Maura, but it just doesn't seem right when we're talking about a friend."

"If that's the way you feel about it, I don't think I should be discussing this with you at all. A Jew is a Jew is a Jew. Friend or not. They're dangerous, Kate. You believe that, don't you?"

"Well, I haven't really thought about ..."

Again, Maura interrupted. "That's just it. No one is thinking. Well, I am. And I'm thinking I should report Eva and Rachel to the authorities for promoting an exhibit at the gallery of photographs of nude homosexuals. Henry told me about it. Robert Maplesyrup or something. Even Henry is worried it might create a stir. I know he spoke with Rachel, who became indignant and defensive, thinking the government had no right to intimidate their artistic choices."

"But Maura, I've heard the government has been taking Jews who've been reported for one reason or another to a building they've called an Interrogatorium. Just the name frightens me!"

"Perhaps it should frighten *them*. This isn't the first time in history that Jews have caused trouble. You know what they say: where there's smoke, there's fire."

"I just think, Maura, that you shouldn't act hastily. You've heard about the disappearances. How would you feel if, because of your information, Eva and Rachel disappeared?"

Maura's answer was swift. "I would feel that Henry and the gallery both could be mine."

7
JAKOB

Rachel had always thought more solitude would enhance her creativity, that disentanglement from obligations would free her to write and think and dream! Her life as a business-woman, wife, and mother had kept her from realizing her now-dim aspirations as a writer. Yet in the room, the solitude she'd so craved lent itself only to frustration and dreams, day and night, and those were as confusing and disturbing as the rest of her life. She sipped the tea Eloise had brought her and dressed for bed.

Rachel recoiled at the scene before her. Screams of such terror, the chaos of people running, making an already grey and smoky day appear even bleaker. Wearing only a threadbare open coat with a too-well-worn shirt and pants underneath, she was horribly cold. While she was not barefoot, her shoes were at least two sizes too big with what looked like brown, dried blood on them, likely taken from the corpse of an older boy. She saw everything as if through a clouded lens—foggy, out of focus. But what caused her uncontrollable shaking was not the cold but the boy with so much dark, dried blood gluing his head to the ground, his eyes open wide in rebellion as if to show the act causing his death had not been done in secret, could never remain secret. There were, there would be, witnesses. She closed the dead boy's green eyes with dirty, trembling fingers. That simple act released a wash of color over the world, if only for seconds.

It was September 8, 1939, when the *szkopi* entered our beautiful city of Radom. The first week of the occupation was difficult for my family. My father owned a butcher's shop that served mostly our Jewish, but also a few of our Christian, neighbors. My mother worked in the office of our shop doing the paperwork and handling the accounting. That first week after the German invasion, though, a Christian neighbor came to the shop accompanied by German soldiers with an order that the shop be turned over to them. I wasn't there, but I knew my father. He would have tempered his words out of wisdom but would have been unable to hide his anger. When angry, his cheeks would redden as though it were the middle of summer and he had stayed out in the sun all day. Mila and I were home when our parents returned in the middle of an argument about what had happened.

"They can't do that to us, Sol. I have never been so humiliated in my life. And that Jan. I'll have a word with his wife, I will. That she would not be ashamed to benefit from our misfortune!"

My father spoke softly and slowly. "Yetta, we will do nothing. We can do nothing. What we will do, is survive. And that will be its own test. You will not speak angrily to Jan or his wife. Remember, right now, it is the Germans who wield all the power; we cannot hold our Christian neighbors responsible. We must wait. The God of Israel, blessed be His Name, will not let us down. The Holy One can see, and the scales will be balanced."

"Tata, Matka, what happened? What's wrong?" My sister Mila's voice shook. The bombings hadn't affected our home. The Germans hadn't yet treated us poorly, though others may have suffered at their hands. In her mind, we were all going to continue as if nothing had really changed.

"Come with me, Mila," my mother said. "We must fix some dinner."

I was left in the parlor with my father. He began, "Jakob, I want you to take a note to the Rabin for me. You will do it tomorrow in the daytime, as there is a curfew now. He must know that the shop was taken from us. This is only the beginning, and we must be ready."

"But how can we be ready? Do you mean we must pray to God for His protection?"

"We always pray, my son; we are Jews. But, sometimes, we must use means other than words. Remember that David used a slingshot and, with God's help, was able to fell Goliath. The Germans are Goliath. We must find our David."

The Rabin bade me enter. He was just taller than I, though I was only twelve, his black hair flecked with white, a pock-marked face, large, sad eyes—eyes I would have described as sad even before the Germans invaded Radom—and a long beard that signified his pact with God.

"I have come with a note from my father, Rabin." My voice and hands trembled as I spoke and handed him the letter. I didn't know whether to stand there while the Rabin read the letter or quietly back out of the room, as my father had left me no instructions beyond delivering the letter. Consequently, I stood there shifting nervously from foot to foot, conscious of wringing my hands and therefore shoved them into the pockets of my pants. The Rabin had been providing me bar mitzvah lessons and had treated me like the man I was about to become; nevertheless, I felt nervous in his presence, forever afraid that my unworthiness would leap out and reveal itself at the most inopportune of moments. This would be one of those.

"Thank you, Jakob. Have you discussed this letter with your father?"

"No."

"Well, as you are about to become a man, you should know what is going on. I am sorry to hear about your family's shop. Your father is not asking for help in getting it back. What he seeks is to spread the information to all Jews that our livelihoods are at risk, that those who argue the Germans will treat us fairly must open their eyes, must see with the eyes of King David, that is, with wisdom. He is a wise man, your father."

I experienced a moment of pride before asking, "How will we tell the others? There are eyes watching us everywhere."

"At times like these, there are always those seeking an advantage. It will be important to act quickly. We will meet as a congregation tomorrow morning. That is the message you are to take back to your father. We will meet and discuss what God would have us do to answer the German aggressions."

"But what could that be, Rabin? How can we confront the German army?"

"I did not say 'confront,' Jakob. I said, 'answer.' There are many ways to answer aggression. Jews must always trust in our God that He will provide a way out of our difficulties even when there seems to be none. We must make sure that as many congregants as possible are at the meeting. Some may fear coming, but we must never be afraid of doing what is right. You will go door to door and make certain that all will be there; that will be your *tzedakah*."

I first went to my father to tell him of the Rabin's orders. It was as he expected, though I could tell he was concerned for my safety in fulfilling the Rabin's instructions.

"You have been given a man's job, Jakob. Hurry, but be aware of your surroundings. Do not spend more time at any house than is necessary. Go, and make sure you are back before curfew."

I knew where most Jews lived, but if I was ever uncertain, I would look for the mezuzah on the doorframe, as there was no observant Jew who did not have one. As I was returning home, I was stopped by a Christian neighbor, someone I did not know.

"You, boy. What are you doing out ... it is almost curfew," the man warned me.

"I'm returning home now, *proszę pana.*"

"I have seen you going door to door. Are you trying to incite some trouble?"

"No, *proszę pana*, I was just ... I was inviting our friends to our home for a birthday celebration."

"I know you. Aren't you the son of Sol the butcher? Hasn't your family just lost your business? Why would you be celebrating? I don't trust this. You Jews keep causing us trouble. Go home now before I decide to take you to the Germans to explain to them what you have been doing."

"I'm going," I answered, hurrying away.

My heart was in my throat as I ran as fast as I could the rest of the way home. Upon arriving, I opened the door, closed it quickly behind me, and locked it at once. My mother saw me enter, saw my fear, and took me in her arms as she hadn't done since I was a little boy. At another time, I would have been offended; now, I melted into her warmth, wondering if that meant I was not yet the man I was hoping, shortly, to become.

The next morning, Tata and I left later than we wished as Mila was ill, and Matka decided she would remain at home with her. The synagogue was already half full when we arrived, and filling quickly.

"Welcome all congregants," began the Rabin. "Let us begin with the Shema, the prayer that is our strength and the foundation of our faith.

Shema Yisra'eil Adonai Eloheinu Adonai echaud.

Hear, O Israel, the Lord our God, the Lord is One.

Baruch sheim k'vod malkhuso l'olam va'ed.

Praised be His name, whose glorious kingdom is forever and ever.

We have much to be thankful for, as the Lord our God has protected us for centuries from evil and distress and will continue to do so in consonance with the covenant we have entered into with Him. We must always remember that we are his Chosen People—"

"Rabin, forgive me," came an interruption from a man two rows behind me, "but how can you say that now, now that God has allowed the Germans into our city?"

I had never heard the Rabin interrupted during a service. Order disrupted by those outside the synagogue was one thing. What did it mean for that to happen within our sacred spaces, in front of the Torah—though, thanks be to God, it was closed. The fright I'd experienced yesterday deepened as all that was normal slipped away.

"Do you question the God who saved our ancestors from the Persians through His vehicle Esther? Do you have no faith in the God who saved the Israelites from the Philistines through His vehicle David, the David of blessed name who became the wise King David? Do you not believe in the power of our God who declared in Exodus 20:2: 'I am the Lord thy God, who brought thee out of the land of Egypt, out of the house of bondage,' through His vehicle Moses?"

The Rabin's voice had become louder and louder as he listed the miracles performed by our God for the Jewish people. There was silence in the synagogue.

The Rabin continued, "What is the same in all these acts of God? It is that He uses one of us as His tool, one of us who has the faith to believe not just in God's power but in man's power to do the biddings of God. Who is our Esther, our David, our Moses?"

He let that sink in for a moment, the silence in the synagogue deafening, before answering.

"I will be that sword in God's hand. I will go to the Germans and entreat them to deal with us fairly. I will go with faith in God that He will strengthen my resolve and put the right words in my mouth. I will tell them that we wish only to remain faithful to our God and wish them no harm. I will plead with them to allow us our professions, our livelihoods. God be willing, it will be enough. *Baruch sheim k'vod malkhuso l'olam va'ed.* Praised be His name, whose glorious kingdom is forever and ever."

At that moment, the silence gave way not to cheers of support and thanksgiving for a magnanimous God and a brave Rabin, but to the heavy footfalls of soldiers' boots entering the back doors of the synagogue, which were not locked, for who would lock the doors to the House of God, which is welcoming to all?

In the flurry of activity, amid shouts of "*Heraus, alle heraus*" from the German soldiers and screams from my Jewish brothers and sisters as we were herded out of the synagogue and into the street, I remember two things, and only two things, which would be a blessing were those two things not so horrific. One was the desecration of the Ark, where the sacred Torah lay in the front of the synagogue. God forgive those who knew no better. The second was the Rabin, who had set himself up as the one who would be the sword of God and save us from the Germans' wrath. Two soldiers each grabbed an arm and dragged him out of the synagogue first. A third soldier laughed as he pulled at the Rabin's beard and cursed him, calling him a Jewish satyr. I felt the pain the Rabin must have felt, though I did not yet have full whiskers to know what that pain might be. Nevertheless, I imagined it to the depths of my soul and cursed those under my breath who would treat a holy man so. Fortunately, I did not feel the fire consuming his beard, the beard that was proof of the Rabin's piety, the beard that the soldier lit with gasoline and a torch. Nor did I have the chance to imagine the pain of the bullets that I learned tore through his body, as I had already fainted.

8
SARIAH

The home built for the Pessoas in Arequipa was small, though there were plans for a larger home once the silver mines produced more prodigiously, something Sariah heard outside the parlor door while Senhor Pessoa discussed details with his crew chief. Sariah could hear the stress in the Senhor's voice. Over the past year, she had come to understand the home dynamics well and was frightened by them. The Senhora—Ana as she preferred Sariah to call her—could be sharp with her for little reason, Sariah felt. She began to see the pattern, though, of bruises on Ana's body corresponding to the sharpness that followed.

The children, seven-year-old twins Marta and Chloé, were sweet enough but not accustomed to the hardships of living in the arid countryside in a home that did not allow them more than a single room for their beds, their toys, and a cot for Sariah. Sariah was constantly shushing them at night when she was most exhausted and needed to sleep. Marta and Chloé were never touched in a disciplinary way by Sariah, yet they knew when she had had enough, and even at seven, they understood the boundaries necessary for their coexistence. Sariah was their *de facto* mother, tutor, and playmate. The only role she did not fill was religious as, though appearing to all as a faithful convert, she was nevertheless considered a heathen when it came to Christian education. She could not outrun her New Christian status.

Sariah's dark curls had thickened, often hiding her even darker eyes that sometimes shone with the promise of a large life, though the one she had led her first seventeen years had been small and painful. Still, she felt gratitude to Ana for taking her away from her life in Lisbon after the losses of her father, mother, and brother, Baruch. And she also felt sorry for Ana and wished to provide as much comfort as she could, for Sariah knew that Ana, too, suffered.

"Ana!" Sariah could hear Senhor Pessoa calling for his wife from his parlor, where he was meeting with businessmen from Spain, working out a deal for the export of silver. "Ana, bring us some cups for wine." As a request, it would not have been notable. Again, Sariah could hear from the Senhor's voice that it was not a request but an order. She heard Ana's hurrying steps to the kitchen and ran there herself to offer help.

"Ana, let me bring the cups. The Senhor should not be ordering you around so," offered Sariah.

"You must not criticize Martín, Sariah. He has a lot of pressure on him to provide for all of us, you included. We all must be grateful and do our part quietly and with love."

It was not a rebuke but a reminder to Sariah of the hierarchy in the home. Ana would remain loyal to the Senhor regardless of bruises or belittling conduct. It was not conduct Sariah had experienced in her own home, and so she did not fully understand it. The family, as Sariah remembered it, was a unit in which respect for each person's unique role was paramount. Even though she was not a boy and knew that had made her something less in her father's eyes, he nevertheless loved her and valued her as any girl was valued. Perhaps this was why she stood up for Ana: she still felt the pain of disappointing her father for being a girl. The Senhor's treatment of Ana reminded Sariah that being a woman was the equivalent of being something less.

———————

That evening after telling the girls a story and waiting until they had fallen asleep, Sariah tiptoed out of the room and headed to the kitchen, where she hoped for a glass of warm milk that might help her fall asleep. Recently, the nightmares of her father's and brother's deaths had returned, keeping her up and making it so the next day with the twins was more arduous than usual.

She had also, recently, found herself remembering biblical stories her father had told her at bedtime when she was the twins' age. One lately frequented her thoughts. It was the story of Lot's wife, who had not even a name in the Bible. Two angels had arrived in wicked Sodom to save Lot's family, for Lot was a good man dedicated to the Lord. The angels urged Lot to flee with his family so they would avoid being caught in God's destruction of the degenerate city. Lot, his wife, and two daughters were told that in fleeing the city they were not to look back, but Lot's wife disobeyed and, in looking back, was turned into a pillar of salt. The story disturbed Sariah. Why, she wondered, were they told not to look back? And why did Lot's wife disobey? She must have had a good reason, for who disobeys an angel of God? If she did have a good reason, why was God so hard on her? Why did it seem that women were treated so harshly wherever Sariah looked, even in her deepest thoughts?

While in the kitchen warming her milk, Sariah heard heavy steps heading toward the kitchen. Her heart quickened as she imagined having awakened the Senhor and his anger. His footsteps came not from his bedroom but from the parlor. Sariah knew the visitors from Spain had left, after drinking much wine with the Senhor, to return to Lima. The Senhor must have fallen asleep in the parlor.

Entering the kitchen, he spoke loudly enough that Sariah feared he would wake the girls, who had taken much too long to get to sleep that evening. "What are you doing in here this late in the night, Sariah?" His speech was slurred.

"Nothing, Senhor, only getting a warm glass of milk. May I get one for you also?"

"Aagh, no. 'Twould not mix well with the wine. But come with me to the parlor. There is a mess to clean up that I would not like the Senhora to have to attend to in the morning."

Sariah followed the Senhor into the parlor but saw that Ana had likely already cleaned whatever mess had been there. She spoke, "It appears that the Senhora has already cleared the room of any mess, Senhor." She turned to leave the room but was interrupted.

"Stay with me a bit, Jewess," the Senhor answered. This was, of course, an insult and one Sariah had never heard from his lips.

"Senhor, please speak more softly so that the girls do not awaken." She realized she was chastising him, which would certainly only anger him, but was more worried about being caught alone with him in the parlor. Having started, though, she could not stop and went further, saying, "And Senhor, you know I am no longer a Jew ..."

"You will not speak to me in that way ... s-s-slut!" Between the slur and the word *slut*, neither of which she had heard from him before, Sariah became agitated and turned to run out of the room, but could not, as the Senhor immediately grabbed her arm and slapped her face with his open hand. Sariah fell to the floor, and the Senhor fell on top of her. She could feel him loosening his pants, and though she had never thought of the act that was to come, much less experienced it, she knew what was happening and kept silent, as much to protect Ana as herself, though it felt as though she were being ripped apart. In her mind, she shut out the parlor, the Senhor, her life with Ana and the girls, and thought again of Lot's wife.

Why hadn't God even given her a name?

9
RACHEL

The bomb was ready. To get it into the hotel, Caroline had had to use Resistance contacts with a catering company hired for the meeting. She hadn't wanted to do so, as the more people who knew their plans, the greater the chance of being caught. The government's interrogations were effective; few were able to resist the persuasive tortures. In this case, however, they needed help to get the bomb past the dogs. They would hide it in a box with one of the lemon cakes to be served, brought in through a kitchen entry. Caroline and Eli were betting on two facts: the caterer was trusted by the government, and the kitchen entry would not be guarded by dogs. David would act as an employee of the catering company and would be the one to clear the area before giving the signal to detonate the bomb. Eli had promised that the bomb would not be too powerful; the intent was to make a statement, not kill.

They'd all spent the previous night together, going over and over the plans, this pushed by David, whose nerves would not let him sleep.

"We've done this before, David," assured Caroline. "I can promise you that this is almost routine now. We just want them to know they can't act with impunity. We're not going to lie down, as our ancestors did, and allow them to destroy us."

"I hear you, Caroline. I believe in your good faith, and in yours, Eli. I have to wonder, though. *Were* our ancestors so wrong? Is violent resistance preferable, especially when consequences can't be predicted or managed?"

Eli laughed. "Caro, we have another Gandhi on our hands!"

"Boys, boys. I'm tired and we must get some sleep. We're ready. Let's go to bed."

David awoke early the next morning and rushed to the bathroom, closing the door tightly behind him and trying to throw up quietly. Very quickly, Eli and Caroline were knocking at the closed door.

"David, are you alright?" Caroline was able to squeak out just before Eli burst into the bathroom to find David kneeling in front of the toilet.

"I just felt a bit sick to my stomach. Must have been last night's dinner."

"But we didn't eat dinner last night. You wanted to fast, remember, as an offering of some kind to ensure our success today," Eli retorted.

"Right, right. Well, I feel better now."

"Good," said Caroline. "Then let's go over the plan one more time before we head out."

Just two hours later, they were on their way. The three of them headed over to the catering company with the bomb. Caroline's job, having set up the connection, was to make sure all was *go* with the caterer. Eli would handle the bomb, placing it into the box with the cake, and then turn it over to David, who would bring the cake into the hotel as the other catering staff brought in the rest of the food. The bomb would be detonated by Eli when the catering staff retreated to the back of the room and David gave the signal, which was to take a cigarette out of his pocket and light it. Simple.

David was visibly shaking so that Caroline and Eli weren't sure they shouldn't pull him, but he found a steady voice with which to reassure them. He wanted to participate, wanted to stand up for right ... he just wished he could be writing political tracts, something he was pretty sure he was good at, instead of planting a bomb. But there was no backing out now.

The first hurdle was getting into the hotel. The group of caterers, six of them in total, all dressed in the uniform of the catering company—black shirt with the name of the company, Good Times Catering, silkscreened on the top—arrived an hour before the officials, giving them all time to set up. Caroline had asked for another uniform and came along, both to steady David but also to provide a diversion. When they arrived at the kitchen entrance, Caroline had a box with slices of cake that she shared with the guards. David eased in with the others without incident.

The catering staff was taken to the meeting hall and began to set up, having brought along with the cake some mini muffulettas and boiled shrimp. Caroline joined them when she'd finished with the guards. The plan had not included her at this point, but she figured it was her plan anyway, so she had the right to improvise.

In no time, both government officials and Righteous members began entering the room. David could feel sweat dripping down his forehead and covering his palms and hoped the others wouldn't notice. It was time. As he headed to the back of the room with the catering staff, he felt dazed. He knew he had only one job left, and that was to give the signal. As they all stood far away from the banquet table, next to a window through which Eli could see him, David slipped his wet hands into his pocket and took out a mashed cigarette, putting it to his lips. He slipped his other hand into another pocket to pull out a lighter. It was then that he noticed Caroline still at the front of the room, no more than fifteen feet from the cake, caught in a conversation with one of the Righteous officials. Caroline was a beautiful woman, really, often attracting unwanted attention.

Eli had seen the cigarette and lighter and, likely due to nerves himself—after all, it wasn't so many years back he'd been playing capture the flag, and now here he was, whether for the first or fiftieth time, setting off a bomb in a hotel ballroom—detonated the bomb prematurely.

In the chaos that ensued, bodies on the ground, much more blood than David could ever have imagined, dense smoke in the air, and police swarming, David and Eli were unable to find Caroline and were forced to flee without her.

David was all but a zombie when he staggered out the back door. He left the hotel running with Eli, but after they'd made it four or five blocks and it appeared they were not being chased, they slowed to a brisk walking pace and spoke very briefly.

"We need to split up here," said Eli, in a daze but still able to consider which strategy would best protect them. They didn't know if Caroline was dead, or alive and had been captured; God knows which of the two they should pray for. "Go home, clean up, and get some clothing and food, then meet me at the bookstore. Don't take too long at home. If they captured Caroline, we don't know how long we may have before they find us."

David immediately countered, asserting, "Caroline would never betray us."

Sometimes David was exasperatingly naïve. "You do know what they do to get information, don't you?" Eli asked rhetorically. "It'll take you about thirty minutes to get home from here. Walk, don't run, as you don't want to attract suspicion, but use quiet streets as much as you can. If you take an hour at home, you should be able to make it to the bookstore in two hours. Enter through the back door by giving one knock, pause, two knocks, pause, then one knock. If I'm not there already, I'll be there shortly after you. Watch for anyone following you and if there is someone, enter the bookstore by the front door and tell whoever is at the checkout. Be safe, my friend." And with that, Eli turned left and headed for home.

Arriving at his parents' house, David ran around to the back door, opened it quietly, and slipped in. He remained still for a few moments, listening for unusual noises. It would be unlikely, but he worried the Righteous had already figured out he'd been involved in the bombing and were waiting in the house somewhere to kidnap him and take him to the Interrogatorium. At this thought, David shuddered involuntarily. God forbid Caroline might already be there. If she were even alive.

After a few silent minutes, David heard his mother on the phone with his father. Her voice was normal, so David felt safe for the moment. He hurried up the stairs to his room and began packing a large backpack with extra clothing. Rachel heard him and, after she hung up, came upstairs.

"David, I'm so glad you're here! Did you hear what happened ..." she began but then caught sight of him, disheveled and dirty as though he'd just climbed out of a chimney. And was that blood? "My God, David, are you alright? What happened to you?"

"I'm okay, Mom. But I can't stay. I have to pack some clothes and food and go away for a few days."

"What have you done, David? I was just talking with your father about a bombing at the downtown hotel. Please, please tell me you had nothing to do with that!"

"I can't talk about it, Mom. Don't ask me anything. If anyone comes looking for me, tell them you haven't seen me ... that I've gone somewhere for a week—I don't know where, just tell them something."

"Oh, David. I can't believe you've gotten yourself involved with the Resistance. Why would you do that? For God's sake, we're secular Jews at best; it's not our fight!"

"*They* don't make those distinctions, Mom, so why should we? Now, please, don't ask me questions. If you could just put together a bag of food for me, I'll be out of here quickly."

"I can't believe we're having this conversation. What have we done to merit this hatred?"

David lingered just a moment so he could answer. "I don't know all of it, but whether we choose this fight or not, it chooses us."

"Go, then. But please, please find a way to let me know you're okay."

When Caroline awoke, she was alone and in darkness. But sight was the only sense deprivation she experienced. There was a familiar taste in her mouth. Iron? Yes, that was it. The taste of blood. She explored her mouth with her tongue for the source and found that her whole lower left jaw was toothless. Next, her sense of smell kicked in. Shit. Not an exclamation, but the actual substance. Feces. She was uncertain whether her own clothing was soiled or if the entire area in which she found herself was covered in it. She had not yet unfurled her body to discover if she could walk. Later. Then there were the sounds. Screams actually. Somewhat faint, either far away, or the source no longer had the energy to produce anything louder. Then she knew. She remembered. They'd all been at a hotel with a bomb. Somehow it had gone awry, and now she was here, in what she believed to be a cell, alone.

Don't panic, she told herself. First things first. She went through the list of steps they'd been taught by the Resistance. Check your injuries, then investigate your surroundings. Caroline tried sitting up. Yes, that she could do, but the effort caused a searing pain along her left upper trunk. Broken ribs, she thought. Nothing to do about those. Doing her utmost to ignore the pain, Caroline next tried to stand. Her legs, though wobbly, supported her weight, and she could walk. So, she must have been thrown by the bomb onto others who'd acted as a cushion, or she would likely have had greater injuries. Eli must have underestimated the charge.

Accustomed now to the dark, Caroline surveyed her surroundings. Indeed, she was in a cell with a bucket in the corner, whence the smell of shit. Someone else's who was no
longer in the cell, she thought, as she couldn't remember using
the bucket herself. In other times, the thought of another's feces would likely have made her gag. Here, it was almost soothing evidence that she was not entirely alone. She hadn't had
much time to really consider her circumstances, yet she already most feared being alone. She'd read Robinson Crusoe as
a young girl and was always frightened by his eight-and-
twenty-year solitude on the island. One could go crazy alone
for so long. Please, not that. On the other hand, her thoughts
racing as fast as her pulse, there were worse possibilities. In
fact, where *was* the shitter? She limped over to the bucket and
felt the exterior. Still warm. If not in this cell, then where
might they be? No, Caroline, don't let your thoughts go in that
direction, though the screams wouldn't leave her ears. Having
tired herself out with her pacing, she lay down on the cold
floor and fell asleep.

"Up, Resistance bitch!" were the words she awoke to,
along with a kick to her torso that lit up her broken ribs. Two
soldiers grabbed her by her arms and lifted her to her feet. She
groaned in pain, causing one of the soldiers to grin and punch
her in the gut.

Through the pain, she had the presence of mind to challenge her description as a Resistance member. "What? Why do
you say that? I have nothing to do with any Resistance," she
demurred. For that, she was given another punch, this time to
her head, and hearing the pop was certain it had broken her
nose.

"You'll have a chance to talk with the interrogator. Right
now, you listen, you obey, and you shut up, or you'll regret it,"
one of the soldiers threatened.

They carried her by her arms to another room, dropped
her into a chair, and left. She was alone again, but this time

there was a light. Her fear of the dark notwithstanding, this room was even more frightening, for there was a long table with leather straps attached to it and a shorter side table with instruments she didn't want to inspect further. This, she knew, had to be the Interrogatorium. How long she waited in the chair, she wasn't certain. Fear was a powerful weapon, and they were using it to its maximum.

She was just drifting off, exhausted from the day's activity, or had it been two … or many days ago? Caroline really had no idea how long she'd been in the cell or how long ago the bombing had been. Finally, a doctor—or so he appeared to be, dressed in a long white coat, frighteningly (purposely?) decorated with smears of blood—entered the room and greeted her with a smile.

"So, young lady," he spoke, settling in a chair across the room, "we find ourselves here together. I am Dr. Kurtz. Tell me, how are you?"

Caroline remained silent, not certain yet that speaking would not have its negative consequences.

"Come now, you can talk to me. I'm here to help you."

"I'm fine," Caroline answered.

"Really! I'd contest that description, to be honest. I had a chance to look you over when you were brought in, and you have quite severe injuries. Why, if one didn't know better, one might think your injuries the result of a bomb. But, of course, we don't live in a society where bombings are *de rigueur* now, do we?" The doctor had been speaking almost cheerfully, but at Caroline's silence, his demeanor quickly shifted, and he walked over to where she was sitting and slapped her face on the left side. He was quite aware of her vulnerabilities and wanted her to know he was prepared to make use of them. Caroline swallowed a scream as she guessed the missing teeth had hidden the more severe injury: a fractured jaw.

"Yes, you see, I know your injuries better than you do. And I know how to make use of them, and how to inflict others, if necessary," he spoke menacingly. But then he changed his demeanor quickly again and asked with a smile, "So, who were the naughty people who planted the bomb at the hotel? You know, there were deaths; such a sad thing. So many relatives to inform, so many tears! We've promised all of them that we would find those who were involved and, of course, put them on trial. So, tell me, purely so we can keep our promises to the heartbroken relatives, who else was involved?"

Caroline didn't know what she could say. Deny her role? She could do that, but they would still ask for names. If she gave them names, those individuals, her friends, would receive the same treatment she was receiving. And even then, from what she'd heard, she would still be killed. Trials were a thing of the past, the act of lawful regimes. She could try confessing that she'd acted alone, but they wouldn't believe that such destruction as must have occurred could be accomplished by one person. She would be tortured until giving them names, with, again, the result that she would betray her friends. And then be killed.

So, she was a dead woman. The only question was whether she would drag others into the same grave. She'd like to say she wouldn't, but then she looked at the instrument tray next to the table. On it she saw surgical knives, what looked like instruments to crack crab claws and a cattle prod. She knew the cattle prod from flyers that had floated around the city, likely distributed by the Righteous to stoke fear. The story that went along with the prod was that it would be used to inflict electric shocks to the most sensitive parts of the body. The crude joke was that it was an electric-powered dildo. Enjoy!

No, she didn't think she would be able to resist such torture. Then an entirely different thought shook her broken body, a complaint against God—Why does God allow this again? What do we Jews have to prove; must our devotion to our covenant continually require us to suffer? As the *doctor* began his work, as she tried to keep her fellow conspirators safe, in between screams, she prayed, and then, after the third surge of electricity through her anus, she saw God and had the opportunity to take her complaints to Him directly.

The Children gathered around the Oldest Oak, some lying with their heads in another's lap, others bracing against each other, back-to-back, one child, little Isaiah, lounging beneath the oak, which had one of its lowest branches, a thin, scraggly stick with very few leaves, resting on his head. All in all, they adjusted themselves so they were all contented, and Harold began.

Inés, hear my story, though it is a sad one, for not only was I killed but two of my friends as well. I hope someday to learn where they are and apologize to them for their deaths, for it was truly my fault.

We were all seventeen years old when we died. Eric, Maria, and I were taking an AP Chemistry class at the college, the three of us having made a vow to each other to become doctors and attend to our communities of origin. There was one day of lecture and one lab day. Lab days could go very late, as we were given a tube with a liquid and had to perform experiments to determine what the liquid was. I loved lab because I felt like a police detective accumulating clues and solving a crime.

"That sounds just like what my dad does," came the interruption from Phillip, whose father was, indeed, a detective, though a private one, having lost his job on the police force when the Outsider Laws were first passed.

"Children, what have I said about respecting the speaker?"

"Oh, right. I'm sorry, Harold," Phillip apologized.

"Continue, Harold."

One evening, later than usual, as the liquid had been particularly difficult to determine, I told Maria and Eric they could leave while I finished up, as they were anxious to go to the varsity women's basketball game. I learned only later that they never made it to the game. Their parents came to our home the next morning to ask if I knew where Maria and Eric were, as neither had returned home the previous night. Of course, I had no idea. They seemed skeptical, though, and pushed further until my parents intervened and invited them to leave our house. My mother was angry.

"What did they mean by 'We believe you know something and aren't telling us'? Were they accusing Harold of being in on whatever happened? Surely they are as aware as the rest of us of the disappearances occurring, though God forbid that is what happened to their children," she made sure to add.

"Calm down, Astrid," my father spoke gently. "They're just upset. You would be, too, if Harold went missing."

"Oh Gerald, don't even say that out loud! It's a bad omen!" my mother exclaimed.

"I'm fine, mom. I just wish there was something we could do to help."

"Don't you even think of doing anything, Harold. Can't you see? They believe that as a Jew, you would do horrible things. Christians have always believed that about us. You must lay low and not bring any attention to yourself. This isn't our fight." My mother believed we could wall ourselves off and thus maintain our safety, but that has never worked.

Nevertheless, I did lay low, staying home from school for the next few days with the "flu." It was only two days after I returned to school, Eric and Maria still missing, that I, too, was kidnapped, pulled out of my mother's car—she had allowed me to drive to school, believing it would be safer than my walking—beaten with a baseball bat, and thrown into a cell in what I now know was the Interrogatorium. When I awoke, I was alone and frightened and could see dried blood everywhere. I'm almost embarrassed to say the chemist/private detective in me wished I could have been in the lab and able to suss out the blood types of those stains. But at least such thoughts were a diversion from other, heavier thoughts of what might happen to me.

I didn't have to wait long to find out. Very soon, I was taken from the cell and brought to an office and made to sit in a chair. This was encouraging, as I'd feared being brought into one of the torture rooms we'd all heard about. In the office, I was told Maria & Eric had "volunteered" information about me as a leader of an Outsider plot to kidnap American children and kill them for their blood, which I was supposedly going to use for chemistry experiments. The official who told me this didn't give me a chance to confirm or deny it. It seemed he simply wanted me to hear the accusation and the sentence as he pro-nounced it: I would be flown over the Gulf and dropped into the water. Whether the fall or sharks got me was immaterial.

The Children's Chorus: Oh, no! Not sharks! Oh, the horror!

Inés had in her hands the stone that would hold Harold's story. She took herbs out of her pocket and rubbed them on the rock while mouthing the silent incantation. When she spoke aloud, she said, "Your tale is locked in this stone, Harold Rosen, where it will not be lost."

"Surely you're joking, Maura, though even as a joke it's beyond the pale of belief. No one could be that stupid ... that vindic-tive."

"No, Henry," Maura felt righteous, even patriotic, in hav-ing reported Eva, William, and Rachel for promoting immoral art at the gallery. "It's not a joke. I went into the Ministry of Christian Culture and filed a report about the recent exhibit of homosexual nudes at the gallery. You don't have to worry; you simply handle the financial side of the business. The choice of exhibits is left to Eva and Rachel. I don't even know what William does. I was very clear about your role and, not incidentally, your religious affiliation, though I made sure to inform them you regretted the mistake of marrying a Jew at a very young age."

"That's all preposterous, Maura! I'm appalled by your audacity and the extent to which you've been willing to go to destroy my life."

"But Henry, dear ..." Maura tried to grab Henry's hand, but he pulled it away and turned to leave the room, though not out the front door, but into the kitchen. "You don't understand. I did it all for you. This way, William and Eva and Rachel will be out of the picture, and the gallery will be safe."

"And what made you think the gallery was more important to me than my wife and, not incidentally, my son? Do you really know so little about me? Did you think our tawdry affair— which is all it's been—meant more to me than my family? Did you think I would applaud you for putting William, Eva's, and Rachel's lives in danger? You do know what happens to Jews reported to the authorities? They disappear. Goddammit, Maura. And *disappear* is the official word for God-knows-what. Tortures, murders ..."

"Oh Henry, you don't believe that propaganda, do you? They'll simply be interviewed. None of those horrible things really happen. That stuff is all made up by the media. It's all an attempt to make the government and the Righteous look bad. If people really disappear, it's because they choose to leave, and good riddance!"

"Maura, I don't know if that's naïveté speaking or if you are truly that stupid. You and the rest of your kind. You're making me take sides here, something I probably should have done long ago. I've allowed myself to be distracted from the prevailing evil in our community." He looked at her with both anger and fear in his eyes but, again, did not walk out.

Maura shrugged at that description. Her instinct was to fight back with words twice as hateful as the ones he'd just used against her, but she sat down instead, counted to ten, and answered only with, "I've acted only out of my love for you, Henry. I know you'll see that in the days to come."

Henry glared at her as he finally turned around and walked to the front door. "You have no idea what you've done, Maura." He slammed the door behind him.

Henry drove straight to the gallery, where he knew he would find Eva at that time of the day. Rachel would not come to relieve her for another two hours. Arriving, Henry went inside to find Eva sitting on one of the couches in front of a black-and-white photo of two well-muscled men, side by side, each with an arm around the shoulder of the other, completely naked. It was a tasteful photo, though there was no controlling people's imaginations. The show itself was intended to question predispositions and prejudices. Interpretation is all in the eye of the beholder.

"Eva," Henry began haltingly. He knew he was going to have to tell her more than that she, William, and Rachel had been betrayed by Maura. The worse betrayal was his, and it was certain to be played out in the next moments. He was not ready for many reasons, some of them out of concern for Eva and others more self-serving. He could blame Maura, but deep down, he knew the devastating events of the day were entirely his fault.

"Eva," Henry began again, looking around the gallery and seeing no customer. "Are you expecting anyone in the next hour or so?"

"Why do you ask, Henry? Anyone could come in at any time, and God knows it would be wonderful if that person would come in not just to look, as if we were a museum. But, no, I'm not expecting anyone."

With that response, Henry walked back to the gallery's front door, closed the shade, and locked the door.

Eva jumped up and walked toward the door to unlock it. "Henry, what are you doing? We're not closed! We can't afford to close this early."

Henry led Eva back over to the couch. "We have to talk."

"Oh, no ... please tell me Rachel and David aren't in any trouble!"

"No, no, it's not that, Eva. But you won't like what I have to say any better; nevertheless, I have no choice but to say it."

Eva allowed herself to be led to the couch and sat down quickly. Henry didn't know if he should sit down next to her or if he should keep some distance between them. He opted for sitting on the chair next to the sofa.

"Eva, I've just come from talking with Maura ..."

Eva interrupted him, "What reason would you have to be talking with Maura? Where did you run into her?"

"I will explain the circumstances in a moment. More important right now is what she told me. You know that Maura has changed since Herb died. She's become very ... let's say self-interested—"

Eva interrupted again. "How are you an expert now on Maura?"

"Eva, just let me get through this without interruptions. I'll answer all your questions afterward. Maura also seems to have bought into the government's version of the times, including the threat Jews are to the societal good. I know that, in itself, is shocking and hurtful. Let me not belabor this. Maura has reported you, William, and Rachel to the authorities."

Eva couldn't be silenced at this. "That's preposterous! What for, Henry? What have we done to her?"

"It's nothing you've done, Eva, but something I've done. For the past few months ..." Here, he hesitated, but no amount of hesitation would prevent the pain he was about to impose on the woman who was the mother of his wife, who'd welcomed him into the family with an open heart even though he was not of their faith. He continued, "I've been having an affair with Maura." Eva looked at him in shock as Henry continued. "I've been stupid and risked my marriage with Rachel over a few months of boosting my ego. I'm telling you, Eva, when I haven't yet even told Rachel because ... well, I'll tell Rachel tonight. But I had to tell you, so you knew how important it is for you and William to take steps to protect yourselves. Please forgive me, Eva, as I've unthinkingly and self-centeredly put you all in danger."

Eva felt as though she'd been hit in the head by a bat, stunned, unable to think or react or speak. She stood up shakily, attempting to create more distance between herself and Henry. Poor Rachel. She was certain Rachel had no idea. How cliché, the unknowing wife. More importantly, what did this mean for the future? But Henry was not finished with his news.

"I will hope someday to get your family's trust back, but there isn't time for that right now. We must talk about what steps to take to dilute the harm Maura has done by reporting you all. She told the authorities that you scheduled the current exhibit, which she termed 'immoral.' Maura, of course, has no artistic sensibility and sees only pictures of nude men. Whether right or wrong, it's what she reported. That means you and William must go into hiding for a bit. I'm certain someone from the Righteous will come for you, and I don't want to think about what they might do. Please, let's talk about where you and William can go."

But Eva was not ready to talk. She went to the back room, grabbed her purse, and rushed out the back door where her car was parked. Henry ran after her, but she wouldn't be stopped.

"Let me be, Henry. Let me be," she almost screamed before driving away in a haze, unable to make sense of what Henry had just told her, unable to think of anything but how everything seemed to be falling apart. She reflected on her marriage with William. When he wanted to go into business for himself, opening a model train store, she'd been happy he'd found something to make him feel productive. She unreservedly supported his leaving the gallery in her hands and pursuing his own business. And when that business failed, she sympathized with him, congratulated him for giving it a try because, as he would say, if you don't swing at the ball, you'll never know if you're a home-run hitter, and then told him how much she could use his business knowledge back at the gallery. None of those ups and downs could compare with what was going on between Henry and Rachel, though. How would Rachel respond to her husband's infidelity? How could any of them look Maura in the eyes again?

What was she to do now? She, William, Rachel, and likely David would have to go into hiding somewhere. She had no appetite for challenging the resolve of the Righteous; she knew they would not be kind. Just then, Eva realized she didn't know where she was headed. She'd jumped into the car reflexively, not knowing what else to do in her desire to get away from Henry. It was dark, and the rain had started a few minutes ago, beginning to come down now in torrents. Even with her lights on, she had a difficult time seeing ahead of her on the windy road that bordered the levee, taking her away from the busier parts of town. That was a good thing, she decided, as she would have time to calm down.

Suddenly, she could see the flicker of lights behind her. A car signaling that it wanted to pass, she thought. Eva tried pulling over to her right, but there was very little shoulder, and she could see a ditch up ahead. Before she could do anything to avoid what, perhaps, she didn't even want to avoid, she felt a jolt, heard metal hitting metal, and was pitched forward and then to the side as her seat belt drew her back, causing her head to strike the metal attachment connecting the seat belt extender to the car. She blacked out as her car flew into the ditch.

Henry hadn't known what to do when Eva sped away, so he called William and told him Eva had left the gallery in an emotional state—later, he would have to explain why, but now wasn't the time. William was home and told Henry he hadn't heard from Eva but would let him know when he did. He didn't seem worried, but then, he hadn't heard the news that Eva had.

Knowing he had to tell William what had happened and hoping he would have the opportunity before Eva did, Henry drove to their home after closing the gallery earlier than normal. When he arrived, Eva wasn't there. William told him he'd tried to call Eva several times, but her phone seemed to be dead. They both sat in the parlor where William took out a bottle of Chateâu Montrose 2020 Saint-Estèphe that they finished, leaving the empty bottle on the side table. Henry paced, wondering if he should call Rachel. William had drifted off when a loud knock woke him.

"Mr. William Latter?" the policewoman asked when William had opened the door. "May we come in?"

"Tell me what this is about," William demanded without answering her question.

"We'd rather talk with you inside, Mr. Latter. Please."

William opened the door and showed them into the living room, wishing he'd removed the bottle of wine, but then thinking, dammit-all, this is my house. I can certainly drink as much as I want in my own home.

"Here," William said, motioning to the sofa. "Have a seat." He motioned to Henry, "This is my son-in-law, Henry."

Both officers gave a nod to Henry, and the female officer continued as they all sat. "Mr. Latter, we've just come from the hospital where your wife was brought after an automobile accident."

"My God," William exclaimed. "Is she alright?"

He turned to Henry. "I have to get to the hospital!" Jumping up unsteadily, he stumbled and almost fell to the floor.

Henry rose quickly and helped him sit back down in the over-stuffed leather chair.

"That isn't necessary, Mr. Latter. I'm sorry to tell you your wife passed away."

William looked first at her, then at Henry, his countenance empty, as though he hadn't understood the import of the officer's words. Then, suddenly, he dropped his face into his hands and began sobbing. Between the liquor and the guilt that he had not been with her, he gave in to the tears. Henry went into the kitchen and brought back a glass of water for William. Henry's face was white as he absorbed the weight of his responsibility for Eva's apparent death.

"We're so sorry for your loss, Mr. Latter. We have a few questions for you, though, if we may. Where was your wife going in this downpour?"

William explained he hadn't been with her when she'd left the gallery, but Henry had. When questioned, Henry said only that Eva had left in a hurry and hadn't told him where she was going.

"Had she received a phone call before leaving?"

Henry answered, "No, not to my knowledge."

"Was it usual for the two of you to be there at that time of day?"

"Not really, but I'd stopped by to talk with Eva about Rachel, my wife."

"Are you having issues with your wife that would have disturbed your mother-in-law?"

Again, Henry responded, "No, but I really don't think these matters are your business."

The second officer interjected, "Anything that might help us learn what happened to your mother-in-law is our business."

The first officer continued, "It's getting late now, and you've both had a shock." She handed Henry her card. "Please call this number in the morning, and we can set up an interview." The officers handed William a card for the coroner's office, where he would go the next day to identify Eva's body, and left.

Henry grabbed a blanket from the hall closet, went over to a broken William slouched in his chair and walked him to the couch, where William allowed Henry to cover him. "I'm going home to ask Rachel to come stay with you tonight, William. Will you be okay until she gets here?"

William had strength only to shake his head affirmatively. Henry walked out to face telling Rachel about her mother, wondering how he could have been so daft and how he could ever make up for his mistake.

Henry helped William arrange Eva's funeral, contacting the rabbi and the funeral home. It would be a private event, as the times would allow no more than that. While waiting for the funeral home director to return with paperwork for William to sign, Henry told William almost everything, specifically about Maura's report of Eva, him, and Rachel to the Righteous.

"But how could she?" was William's first response. "She was Eva's friend. Perhaps not best friend, she was so much younger, but they … we traveled together. I had no inkling of bad blood." Henry could see that William was overwhelmed with his grief, and processing culpability now, if ever, would do him no good. William was also preoccupied with his daughter and grandson's safety, as, of course, was Henry.

"I know, William, I know. At the forefront is yours, Rachel's, and David's safety, though. We must act now to protect you all. David is already out of town, interviewing for jobs in Atlanta. I'll make sure he doesn't return until the danger has passed." Henry told the *official version*. "Rachel will be a different story. I'm afraid she doesn't quite understand the danger of the times. But then, disconnectedness has always been part of Rachel's personality." If this was Henry's parlay for absolution, it was pathetic. But that, too, could be worked out later. They needed to focus now, as there were brazen threats every which way they turned. Henry continued, "If you'll finish with the arrangements for the funeral, I'll find a suitable place for you and Rachel to stay temporarily."

"I won't leave our home, Henry. It's all I have left of Eva. I'm too old to play the role of a fiddler crab. Find a place for Rachel; I'll take my chances."

Henry had no idea how difficult it would be to find a place for Rachel. He *did* know how difficult it was going to be to convince Rachel of the need. He rushed out and headed back home. Was that a car tailing him? It was hard not to be paranoid, he thought, as the 'suspicious' car turned into the school pick-up zone. He parked his car in the garage next to Rachel's and ran inside. Rachel was in the kitchen, sitting with a cup of tea in her hand, staring into space.

Henry repeated to Rachel the story of Maura's contact with the Righteous and her reporting of her and her mother. He left out that he had heard the story directly from Maura. How would he have explained that? Henry couldn't think of how it could be important for Rachel to know the chain of evidence, so to speak, and could only imagine that it would devastate her. That he was a coward occurred to him peripherally.

"But Henry, why would Maura do such a thing? She and Herb have been friends of the family for years and years!"

"Who knows what motivates another person," Henry equivocated. "Here's what I do know—we've got to get you into hiding for a while. The Righteous will likely be looking for you, too."

Rachel didn't want to admit such craziness but had little wherewithal to oppose him. It might, in fact, be nice to get away for a week or two and have some space to process the loss of her mother.

"We have to get you into hiding immediately. I have a contact who may be able to help us. Let me just go to the other room and make a phone call. You stay here and stay off your phone. We would be wise to trust no one."

"You're scaring me, Henry." Rachel's voice wavered.

Though time was precious, Henry turned around and walked back to Rachel, putting his arms around her. She didn't allow this very often—strong, independent woman that she was. He spoke into Rachel's hair, which was better than looking her in the eyes.

"I'm sorry, Rachel." At that, she broke down for the first time in years.

While Henry was out, Rachel received a cryptic text from an unknown number that said only "Spicy chai, two pm." It had to be David! Was he coming to the house for a cup of tea? No, he wouldn't come to the house. Not now, not when the Righteous would be looking for him. No, he must be referring to meeting him somewhere. "Spicy chai." He must mean the Tea Room, a local tea shop where they purchased their teas and would occasionally meet for a cup of spicy chai when she needed a break from the gallery, and he had a gap in his schedule. It was noon now. She'd have to hurry out to get there in time. It was risky, but she wanted to believe it was him, had to tell him about his grandmother. She dressed in pants, took one of Henry's blazers, and threw it over her shoulders, adding a hat under which she stuck her shoulder-length, dark hair. If anyone was watching the house when she left, they might think she was a young man, perhaps someone who'd been at the house offering condolences. She'd have to pay close attention; if she were being followed, she'd be putting David in danger. In what world was she living, she thought. How had she become a character in a spy movie, needing to move about clandestinely, worrying about tails or, worse, ghost surveillance, a term she remembered from an old John Le Carré novel.

Rachel left Henry a note that she'd gone out but would return by five pm and purposely left out any information about where she was going or who she was meeting just in case the note fell into 'enemy' hands. She went out the front door and began walking at a brisk but not suspicious pace—so she thought—checking behind her now and again on her way to the Tea Room, a mile or so away. The distance allowed Rachel time to think about her circumstances. Her son was in hiding after participating in a bombing targeting the Righteous, a right-wing guerrilla movement in cahoots with the government to rid the country of all who were not white Christians, especially Jews. Her mother had just had an accident while driving away from her home after finding out her friend had reported her to the authorities. She was being targeted after having been outed by the aforementioned *friend* as a Jew who foisted immoral art upon a pure public. Her own husband was out right now looking for a hideout for her.

What was wrong with this picture?

When she arrived at the Tea Room, she looked all around her before feeling comfortable enough to open the door. The bell announcing her entry was quickly followed by a hand grabbing her wrist, pulling her through a curtain into a back office. At first frightened, Rachel calmed down upon seeing David sitting at a table in the office. They were alone.

Rachel ran to David, who stood up and gave her a tight hug while whispering in her ear, "Shhhh. Speak in a whisper only. I don't have long, but I wanted to see how you were after Mimi's death and to warn you." Rachel stiffened at the mention of a warning. She stepped out of the hug and looked hard at her son. He was thinner, and he looked tired, but otherwise, he was David, her only child, the boy she and Henry had prayed for, each in their own way, the young man who had astounded them with his intelligence and purity and who now had taken a moral stand that put him, and she supposed, them by association, at risk.

"What is it, David? How did you hear about Mimi's accident? It was so hard not to be able to tell you ourselves."

"I know, Mom. I'm in hiding but still have ties with the outside world. I'm so sorry about Mimi. Are you okay?"

"I was shocked, to be sure, David. But we don't know when it will be our time, and accidents happen without warning."

David was silent for a moment, gathering the courage to say what he was there to say. "But, Mom, that's just it. Mimi's death wasn't an accident. I wanted you to know so you'd know not to be careless in anything you do from here on out, not to underestimate the forces around you."

David's words startled Rachel. What did he mean "wasn't an accident?" The police had specifically told Henry just that … that it was an unpredictable, unavoidable accident. And what did he mean by "the forces around you?"

"What are you saying, David?" she asked as he sat her down in a chair across from his.

"I'm saying the Resistance found out that Mimi was forced off the road by another car. That the Righteous followed her when she left the gallery that night with the intent of killing her. She just made it easier for them by driving erratically in the rain. It wasn't hard to force her car into a ditch."

"But why, David, why would they care about Mimi? What was she to them? What don't I know about my own mother?"

"There is nothing to know, Mom. She was Jewish and the target of a complaint."

A moment of silence ensued, during which Rachel absorbed the transmutation of this commonplace fact into one that could support homicide.

David looked down at his hands, stalling before explaining further. "And she was my grandmother. I have the great distinction of being at the top of their 'wanted' list at the moment. Which means that you, as my mother, are likely on their list, too. It hurts me to say that. I am the one who chose to put *my* life at risk, not yours. But the Righteous are smart and use the families to manipulate the Resistance fighters. As a result, we've spent time and effort creating safe houses for family members so we can continue our work with some confidence. We won't be silent. We can never again afford to be silent. But you must go away as I have. Dad can be the only one who knows where you are."

David couldn't tell if his mother understood all that he was admitting. That he was still actively involved in the Resistance and that never again could Jews assent to their persecution.

10
JAKOB

I found myself pulled along the current of bodies fleeing the bullets and imprecations of the Germans and the screams of my fellow Jews. I couldn't look back to see where my father might be, for to do so would likely have resulted in my trampling. I could hear panting, the whizzing of bullets flying past my head, and sometimes the hollow thump of bullet hitting body, a sound I couldn't accurately describe but would never forget. That sound was almost always followed by multiple thuds, as the fallen body was followed by others tripping over it. It had the feel of a track and field event, in which speed and hurdling were equally important and for which the winners were awarded not a medal but their lives. Briefly, I thought of Jesse Owens and the 1936 Summer Olympics that had been held in Germany. I had begged to be able to go see the famous American sprinter, but it was already too dangerous for Jews to travel to Germany. And now, it seems, it was too dangerous to stay in Poland. Where could Jews find safety?

I made it back to my house and pounded on the front door for Matka or Mila to open. There was blood on my clothing, and I was covered in sweat and the blown ash of the burning synagogue. Matka opened the door and, seeing me, screamed, quickly pulling me inside as if she could erase the outside world by closing the door on it. If reality is what we can see, can we alter it by closing our eyes?

"What has happened," Matka asked, with urgency. "Where are you hurt?"

"It's not my blood, Matka. I'm alright. But Tata, is he here? We were separated when the soldiers came."

"Soldiers?" Matka's eyes opened further in shock and fear. "What soldiers? Your father isn't here! Oh, Jakob, he could not be ..."

I tried to comfort my mother. "I'm certain he'll be here soon; we were separated, that's all. Let me go outside and see if I can find him."

"No! You mustn't go back outside. I couldn't bear the thought that you might get lost in the furor."

"Brother!" Mila had entered the room and was taken aback by my appearance. "What has happened? Where is Tata?"

I related what I could while we all silently prayed for Father to return. By the time I'd gotten to the Rabbi's burning beard, we heard a heavy thud against the door.

"Sol, Sol!" Matka screamed and opened the door. As she did so, a body fell into the foyer.

"Pull your father into the house," she spoke in a determined voice and then searched my father for holes in his clothing and blood. Blood, she found plenty, but no injury.

"Sol, have you been hurt? Can you speak?" Matka cupped Tata's face in her hands, fearing the meaning of his closed eyes. Had he been harmed, or were his eyes still closed so that he would not see what should not be seen, what should never be seen: the hatred that could cause men to kill their brothers.

Father's physical injuries were minor, but his spiritual ones were much graver. There was no time to lament injuries, though, as only months after the burning and plunder of the Radom synagogue and the death of the Rabbi and many of our fellow Jews, the Germans began a program of evicting families from the nicer Jewish homes and placing German soldiers in them. We were given one night after being notified our house was being requisitioned to each pack a single suitcase to carry our belongings. Matka was heartbroken and angry.

"How can they do this, Sol? What about our family heirlooms? How will we fit those into the four suitcases we are allowed along with the clothing we will need to stay warm? My great-grandmother's silver tea set? Your grandparents' wedding wine goblets? And what about your books, Sol? Your library of Jewish commentaries?"

My father spoke softly, "Those are things, Yetta. Things we treasure, yes, and things we will surely miss but, nevertheless, things. We must remember what is important: that we have each other and that we have our God to protect and guide us. Look around you at other Jewish families. Few have not suffered a loss of life. We are lucky! We will pack what we can this night, each of us adding to our clothing one item that will sustain us when we fall into moments of despair. Decide what that is and feel the joy of being able to bring it with you. For me, it will be my copy of Abraham Abulafia's commentary on the *Pentateuch*. Each of you will find your own."

As we packed, I thought about what mine would be, the item that would sustain me through the difficult times to come and found myself reaching for a novel I had read and reread, *The Golem* by Gustav Meyrink. I packed it with my clothing, along with writing materials thinking someday, who knows, I might write my own golem novel.

The following day we were taken away from our home and forced to walk a long way to an apartment building in another part of town along streets still sporting blood stains and spent bullet casings. If one looked up—which we rarely did, fearing the gaze of the German officers accompanying us to our new location—one could see buildings almost decoratively pricked with bullet holes. Arriving at an old, run-down building in a part of town that, before the war, we would never have entered, we were led into an apartment of two rooms already inhabited by another Jewish family we did not know. The possessions we'd left behind in our own, now-majestic-seeming home, we later learned were seized by the Germans and those items of lesser value used to offer to our Christian neighbors in return for information of hidden lucre.

One might have thought Jews would look out for each other, that we would call each other brother and sister, each of us descending from Abraham, each of us bearing the mark of the Chosen. I found out first, through Adam Behrman, his wife Marta, and their three small children with whom we were sharing the tiny two-bedroom apartment, that even among Jews, self-interest often prevailed. At first, they, who had been moved into the apartment before us, refused to clean out one of the rooms so that we could have a private space.

"Why should we be inconvenienced even further by these people we don't know?" Marta complained to her husband in front of all of us.

Her husband, tired of having to placate her, barked, "Quiet, Marta. Grab the baby's things, and the children and I will get the rest. We will do fine in the larger room." He did not look us in the eye, nor did he apologize.

11
THE CHILDREN'S CHORUS

Whether we choose this fight or not, it seems to choose us.

12
RACHEL

Some time had passed since Eva's funeral, which Maura had attended, though Henry had asked her not to. There was no way she was going to accede to the version of the facts that made her the villain. Why had Eva gone out driving in a rainstorm anyway? If only she hadn't done that, she'd be alive, though Maura had to admit, in the most horrible corner of her heart, that things were easier for her now with Eva out of the way. *So, crucify me,* she thought. *I never pretended to be a holier-than-thou person, anyway. I've had to fend for myself for too long already. I deserve this break.* Maura believed in God, particularly when she could cast God's plan in such a way as to benefit herself. Why would God have allowed Eva to die if he did not want Maura and Henry to get together? Why would God have allowed the government and the Righteous to join forces to weed out the Jews if it was not an invitation for Maura to put Part II of her plan into motion?

Maura initiated it all with a call to her contact at the Office for a Salutary Society.

"Hello, Peter? Yes, it's Maura Fitzgerald. You remember we talked about a Latter family not too long ago? You told me you needed more details of their anti-government acts and to

get in touch with you if I had any. Well, I have that information. Would you like me to pass it on over the phone, or
should I drop by the Office? ... Now is fine? Well, I know the
grandson has been involved with the Resistance, and it was
his grandfather and mother who introduced him to it. ... Yes,
I will sign the complaint against all three, but you must promise me you will not reveal publicly who the informant was. And
in return, I'd like something from you. Just a simple thing. The
grandfather and mother are part owners of an art gallery.
Once you have apprehended them, I would like to become
their replacement as co-owner along with the innocent—and
may I remind you, Christian—father. ... Yes, that does comport
with the intent of the Outsider Laws. ... Yes, the very purpose
of the Office for a Salutary Society, I know!" And so, Maura
proceeded to gut the entire family of her once-good-friend Eva
by ratting on William, Rachel, and David.

The next morning, she awoke quite self-satisfied. Yes, she
thought, today would be a wonderful day. It would likely take
a bit of time for William, Rachel, and David to be rounded up
and for her to discuss the ownership issue with Henry, but she
had the time. She looked out her bedroom window and could
see the magnolia trees beginning to bloom. There was nothing
she loved more than magnolias! Maura had not been back to
the gallery since Eva had died, wanting to give Henry a bit of
space to get over his anger at her. Next week, she felt, it would
have been long enough, and she was excited to return. It
would be a new beginning! She and Henry were the perfect
partners! They would build the gallery into what it always
should have been: a showplace for the Righteous. She would
bring grace into Henry's world and erase the blemish Rachel
had introduced into his life and his bloodline. Maura regretted
that she was too old to give him the children he deserved, but
she would bring him happiness, she just knew it.

When she arrived at the doors of the gallery the following
week, she was surprised to see they were locked. There was a

sign on the door that read: "Closed temporarily by order of the Office for a Salutary Society." Her heart jumped as she realized that was the office she had contacted. But this wasn't part of the deal. What were they doing? What do William and Henry know? They hadn't contacted her, so she assumed her name had not been mentioned. Maura hurried home, frustrated but knowing that she had to remain calm. It was important that she contact the Office and find out the latest information on what had transpired at the gallery.

Arriving home, she found her front door unlocked, though not ajar. Had she forgotten to lock it? Not like her, but then, these weren't normal times. She walked in and turned the bolt to lock the door behind her, then headed into the kitchen, where she took a wine glass from the upper cabinet and grabbed an open bottle of Chardonnay from the refrigerator. Herb would have been appalled at the wines she was drinking these days, this one a Kendall Jackson Vintner's Reserve. He had been a Francophile and would have spurned these California imposters. But Maura felt no need to explain her choice of wines to anyone.

She headed into the parlor, looking forward to kicking off her shoes and sitting down in her oversized velveteen armchair with her glass—or perhaps even two—of wine and relaxing with a magazine. Then she'd take care of business.

She entered the parlor and walked to her left over to the desk where she remembered leaving the magazine that had come in the mail only yesterday.

It was then that a man's voice startled her, interrupting her peaceful solitude with a gravelly tenor, barking, "Maura! Who are you?"

Maura turned around quickly and saw William standing on the other side of the parlor at the bar, having poured himself a rather large scotch and water. She could see the bottle, an expensive Laphroaig that Herb had bought, and that she had been saving for a special occasion since Herb had passed.

Well, it looked like this was it, though the "Who are you?" was ominous.

"William, how did you get in here? What are you doing here?"

"I have news, Maura." Maura looked over to the bottle to see how much he'd drunk. "The gallery has been shut down. What do you know about this?"

"Why, nothing, William! What makes you think I would know anything? In fact, I just returned from there looking for you."

William was confused for just a moment, hesitated, then continued. "I received a note from the Office for a Salutary Society. What kind of a name *is* that? Would you like to hear what it said, Maura? Or did you write it for them?" He walked towards her menacingly. He was a large man and, even in his 70s, strong as a bull. But why would he want to hurt her now, Maura thought? The Society had promised not to tell who the informant was. It could have been anybody. That's what she'd tell him. Nevertheless, she moved behind the desk.

"Of course I have nothing to do with the gallery closing. I was coming to work there today. You know I love the gallery. I'd never do anything to cause it harm."

"No, you wouldn't, would you? Not the gallery. But what about Eva? What about Rachel and David? Them you would harm. Here, take this and read it. Read it out loud. I want to watch your face while you read it." William handed Maura an envelope that had a government seal on the outside. She opened it and read.

Mr. William Latter: We have received a tip about the involvement of your daughter Rachel Latter and grandson David Latter-Reid in seditious activities. In order to investigate these serious charges, we will have to employ many man-hours at the cost of up to $1,000,000. Before spending such a large amount of money, we offer you this alternative. Pay $150,000 for each of your relatives and for yourself by Wednesday of *next week, and we will turn a blind eye to your circumstances. Until we receive the cash, the gallery will remain closed.*

Maura stopped there and looked up. She was shocked. They hadn't said anything about extortion. "Oh, William ... I don't know what to say! How could they!"

William went over to the leather armchair, the one where Herb would sit for hours reading his political magazines and smoking his pipe, and plopped into it, spilling his Laphroaig in the process. Maura did her best not to calculate the dollar amount of that slosh.

"What am I to do, what to do," he murmured to himself. To Maura, he said, "I can't get that kind of money together this quickly." This he said gruffly, but then, almost pleadingly said, "Can you help, Maura? You must help. You must have that kind of cash somewhere."

Where was this headed? Maura thought. She could have stock sold, but she didn't want to do that. Besides, the Office certainly wouldn't want *her* hard-earned dollars. Her family was an early settler of the state and of an impeccable blood-line. But how would she get out of this now? She could see that William was desperate.

"But, William, I don't," she answered. "How did they know about Rachel and David? Who could have told them about David's involvement in the Resistance?"

William quickly jerked his head and looked in her direction. The letter had said nothing about the Resistance. It referred only to nebulous "seditious activity." By the look on his face, Maura knew she'd made a grave mistake. She shimmied over to the right-hand drawer, where she kept a loaded gun. Surely it wouldn't come to this.

William jumped out of the chair and threw himself toward Maura. "It *was* you. You've destroyed me and my entire family!"

Before he could get close enough to stop her, Maura pulled the revolver out of the drawer, pointed it at William's large torso, and pulled the trigger. Her next actions were a blur. She didn't care about William, but neither had she ever killed a man. Her nervous system revolted, causing almost epileptic-like spasms. To be honest, she had no idea if he was alive or dead but couldn't bring herself to go over to him to find out.

William had just been murmuring, "what to do, what to do," and now it was her turn. She did the only thing she could think of. She called Peter at the Office for a Salutary Society. He came over within thirty minutes with two men. While Maura explained to Peter what happened again, somewhat more calmly this time, the men confirmed that William was dead and began the clean-up process. Peter assured Maura that all would be okay. Suicides happened all the time these days.

Henry entered the room and found Rachel sitting at her writing desk.

"Hello, Rachel," Henry always began spiritedly. "It's good to see you and to see you writing. I hope you'll allow me to read what you've written, when you're ready to share, of course. One of the things I miss these days is our discussions of your work."

What could she believe and what couldn't she? The distance between them emotionally had grown in direct proportion to the physical distance. Sometimes she wondered what his life was like. She didn't remember him to be the type of man to be alone.

"Thank you, Henry, but I've no desire to share these days. Perhaps better to wait until I leave here for good."

"Of course, Rachel. I may be more anxious than even you to have you home. Things are not better outside, though. In fact, I come with bad news, and I'm not sure how to begin."

"What is it? Something to do with David?" The possibility

that something had happened to David erased all of Rachel's reserve.

"David's fine, though I'm always concerned about his involvement with the Resistance. He's told me that he and his friends are posting anti-government rants—my word, he calls them infograms—on these temporary video sites. He claims it's entirely safe, as they last only a short time before they're deleted and can't be traced."

"If not David, then what is the bad news?"

Henry sat down on a chair next to Rachel, near enough to grab her hand and hold it in his. This scared Rachel, and she pulled away. They hadn't touched in quite a while, each withdrawing over time and doubtlessly harboring grievances against the other. Rachel was still suspicious of the need to be sequestered as she was. What Henry had to gain from it, she'd not decided, though at some point, she'd confront him about Maura. She knew only that she was lonely and afraid for her family, above all for her son. For his part, Henry was tired of all the accusations that he saw in her posture, in her eyes, when he visited. For Christ's sake, he was doing all this for her. The charade wasn't easy on him. He still wasn't sure the government believed him when he said Rachel had run away after her mother had died, fearful for her own life. After all, what mother would willfully leave her child behind? Why did he feel only blame? Caught in the deepest folds of his brain was the unsayable, the thought he couldn't acknowledge: did she doubt him for not being Jewish? Had it all come down to that?

"I'm afraid it's your father, Rachel. There's no easy way to say this. He's committed suicide."

13
SARIAH

A month after the rape, Sariah, who had taken care of her mother through her pregnancy with Baruch, knew. She also knew to keep silent. Since that night, the Senhor had avoided her, neither treating her worse for being the cause of his slip nor better to show his remorse. It was obvious he was remorseful, though, as he fell into a stupor of depression that Ana remarked upon, asking what was ailing him. Rachel, who was listening while picking up the girls' toys from the next room, stood by silently waiting to hear what he might say.

"It is nothing that concerns you, Ana. Business is not what I'd hoped, that's all."

"But why, then," Ana knew to tread lightly here but continued nevertheless, "why have you been seeing the priest at his home so often lately? Is that also because of business?"

"Must I answer to a woman? I have said it is business, and so it is."

"I know you, Martín, and I know when you are not being entirely truthful. I understand that business is difficult now ... but you knew it would be. I have tried to be attentive to your needs, noting this is a difficult time for the whole family. But there is something more now. I can feel it."

"So now you're a witch, my love?" Martín used the word "witch" threateningly and "my love" with barely hidden disdain. The Inquisition had made its way to Peru almost the same time they had and had come upon native heresies, answering them with swift action, as was appropriate. Those women who claimed healing powers beyond healings accomplished in Christ's name were branded witches and were subjected to the ultimate punishment.

"You know I am no witch, my husband. But you are also no longer acting as my husband in bed. For that reason alone, I know something is amiss."

"Perhaps you simply no longer interest me," Martín countered in an attempt to wound his wife but, sensing things going too far, apologized. "No, Ana, that is not right; please forgive me. I have no wish for our little argument to escalate. You must give me some space to work out my thoughts. Father Garza is helping me. You and the girls are my life, you know that." Martín fell to his knees in front of Ana as his head sunk to his chest. "Thus, do I prostrate myself before you, my wife, and proclaim my love and dedication." He looked up at her, seeing tears in her eyes.

"Rise, my husband. It is not right that you should kneel before me. Let us both proceed as faithful Christians, and the love of Christ in our hearts will heal any wrongs between us." She held out her hands to Martín, who accepted them, stood up, and led her away to the bedroom. Passing Sariah along the way, Ana said only, "Please take the children outside to play, Sariah."

Sariah did as she was asked, grabbing shawls for the girls and taking them to the meadow. She told them to gather grasses, and she would teach them to make the grasses into a beautiful necklace that they could give to their mother. This excited the girls, as they could tell their mother had been sad lately and thought a necklace would make her happy again.

Sariah picked some grass and found a log to sit on. While beginning to weave the strands together, she thought about her situation. What were her options? She could tell Ana now that she was pregnant and claim she was raped by a mineworker, but all the mineworkers were natives, and when the baby was born, it would be obvious none were the father. She could tell Ana the truth, but she could not be certain how Ana would react. Would she support her? If she did, might Ana want to keep the baby and raise it as her own? That Sariah could never allow. If a boy, her baby must be circumcised as the covenant with the God of the Jews required. Though in practice she had abandoned her heritage, Sariah was yet fearful of the power of the Jewish God who had once turned the entire world into an ocean because of his anger at the wickedness of mankind. Ana would never allow circumcision.

More disconcerting was the thought that Ana would blame her and send her away. To where? Sariah had met no one in the time she had been in Peru. She felt the depth of her loneliness as she absorbed that fact. She had lost her own family, her home, and her community of support. While Sariah had grown fond of the girls, and Ana had been friendly, she was frightened by the Senhor, and though he ignored Sariah for the most part, she never knew if he might repeat the act of that night. She would tell him of the baby, that intercourse might hurt it, but perhaps that is what he would want. She did not know how he would react to having impregnated her.

As she considered her dilemma further, she wished her father were alive. He would know what she should do. For the time being, at least, she decided, she would tell no one of the baby. She was far from showing now, but she remembered how big her mother's belly had seemed before Baruch was born. It would be difficult to hide the baby at that point. Perhaps by then, she would have developed a plan. Perhaps by then, she could find some other Jews who would help her. She knew she could not be the only New Christian here, but how could she find another, given the need for secrecy?

How alone she felt.

14
RACHEL

David had the perfect situation for hiding his mother. He called his father and told him where to meet later that night.

Upon arriving, David hid behind the Ligustrum bushes and waited. Because of the cloud cover, it was so dark he couldn't see if he'd been followed; it had nevertheless felt prudent to take evasive measures, and he'd taken so many turns and gone down so many dead-end streets only to have to turn around and retrace his steps that he was later than he intended. But soon, he heard the footfall he recognized as his father's. David had told his father to park at least two blocks away and walk to the front gate of the cemetery where David met him.

"Dad, this way," David whispered as soon as his father was in earshot. "We have to make this quick." They hurried inside, and as soon as the gate was closed, David's father took David in his arms and squeezed him tightly.

"David, I've been so worried about you."

David allowed the hug but pulled away quickly, unwilling to return to the role of his father's little boy. He was a man now, making adult decisions that harbored risks no child should ever be acquainted with.

"I know, Dad. I'm so sorry for the silence. The reality is the less you and Mom know, the safer you are." He pulled his father by the arm further into the quiet cemetery, so he had a view of the house next door. "But let's talk about Mom. I've found a situation for her that should be perfect." David pointed in the direction of a second-story window. "See that window? That's an empty room Mom can stay in for as long as needed. The house belongs to a family that has resided in the city for too many decades to count. They no longer live there but have hired a house sitter who does. Her name is Eloise, and she lives in a room on the second floor just down the hall from the room that will be Mom's." David took a deep breath, realizing he'd imparted a lot of information and giving his father a chance to react.

"Who are these people that they would risk hiding someone at odds with the government? Can we trust them?"

"You mean why would they risk hiding a Jew, Dad? Mincing words helps nothing. If we can't deal in truth, we are all the more lost." David looked his father directly in the eye as he said this.

David knew his father had been raised without religion, though he never knew his father's parents as they'd lived on the other side of the country and on the other side of their son's goodwill. Someday David would hear the whole story, but presently all he knew was that his mother had been a thorn in their collective paw.

Seeing the hurt caused by the implicit accusation of his words, David continued gently. "You'll have to trust me on much of this as I don't have time to go through all the details, and even in a cemetery, there can be eyes and ears."

The Children's Chorus: We will not tell!

"I can tell you the owners have ties with the Resistance, but it would take quite the research to discover those ties.

Eloise will prepare Mom's meals in the kitchen downstairs and bring them to her room, as well as pick up her laundry and wash in the laundry room next to the kitchen."

"It appears you've thought of everything. What an adult you've become. What can I do?"

"You will have to prepare Mom; I imagine that won't be easy. I can provide you a light sedative that will make it easier to obtain her cooperation." Henry almost wanted to laugh at this. David knew his mother well. "Let's plan on meeting again on Thursday at ten pm to move everything and introduce Mom to her new, temporary home." David had no idea what temporary meant but felt it would be important to emphasize it, especially to his mother. "We can talk about all the rules necessary to everyone's safety later, but for starters, you'll want to visit no more than once a month. This situation will only work if no one is made to suspect anything. If you ever feel you're being watched, you shouldn't come, and Mom will have to understand that from the beginning."

"David, is this all really necessary?"

"You know about Mimi, don't you? That it was no accident? That's your answer. The Righteous will stop at nothing to cleanse this city of its Jews."

His father had no response to this. They left the cemetery and promised to see each other in two nights.

15
JAKOB

For six months, we lived like overcrowded rats. Not long after we'd settled in with the Behrman family—whose three young children were forever a nuisance, though if I were only more compassionate, I would realize how much harder for ones so young to keep occupied than for those of us who could read and converse with each other, or so Tata continually reminded me—others were brought to stay with us. Now we were in a real bind, as we knew that the Behrmans, though in the larger room, had no appetite for sharing theirs, and our smaller room was already cramped to the limit with the four of us. There was, luckily, in addition to the two bedrooms, a small living room without furniture, having already been scavenged by the Germans or Christian neighbors and perhaps being used as fuel, and a room that we could tell had been a kitchen by the outlets that would have served to provide electricity to large appliances like a stove and refrigerator. Of course, neither existed, which also made it difficult to save any food. The Markuses chose the living room for their space. They were an older, white-haired couple with no children and so were a respite from the Behrmans. Additionally, Mr. Markus had been a cantor and could help the rabbi who lived in the building with religious services. All in all, we found them to be a pleasant addition to our everyday lives, though I doubt the Behrmans felt the same.

We might have been able to continue as we were for some time except that food had become quite scarce, and my father's position heading up one of the food details opened him up to jealous accusations of hoarding. One evening there came a loud knock on our apartment door, and in burst four German soldiers.

"*Wo ist der Jude Sol Michnik?*" they demanded, and the Behrmans quickly scuttled to their space and closed their door. My father rose from a chair made from boxes and introduced himself.

"I am Sol Michnik."

The senior German was taken aback by my father, whose erect posture belied any fear he might be feeling. The Nazi captain had an almost softness about him that surprised me as I watched him look around our surroundings, seeing no real furniture, just boxes that we had made into chairs and tables. He looked my father directly in the eye and said, "Your fellow Jews have complained that you have taken home food and are hoarding it in defiance of the rules of the detail that you command. Can you answer these charges?"

My father responded with quiet dignity, "*Herr Kapitän*, I have taken no food. Please feel free to search the apartment; you will find nothing here."

The Kapitän motioned to two of the soldiers who had accompanied him to search the apartment. We all heard the children's cries as the soldiers entered the Behrman's room. They returned shortly after going through the entire apartment and indicated to the Kapitän that they had found nothing.

"What, then, have you done with the food," the Kapitän asked, further pursuing what I am convinced he knew was a lie.

"*Mein Herr*, as I said, I have taken nothing. I am an honest man."

"There is no such thing as an honest Jew," spat out another

of the soldiers.

"Silence," the Kapitän said, glaring at the soldier.

Suddenly, Mr. Behrman came out of his room and joined in the conversation. "I can tell you where he has kept the food."

"What?" came my father's stunned question, turning his head to look at Mr. Behrman.

The Kapitän turned to Mr. Behrman. "Continue."

"He brings food back almost every night and refuses to share with any of us. I have seen him store leftovers in the snow outside."

My mother, incensed at the suggestion that my father was dishonest, blurted out, "You are a liar!"

The kindness I thought I had seen in the Kapitän's eyes disappeared. "Silence! All of you." He turned to the soldiers and told one to take my father and one Mr. Behrman. "We will go to headquarters and determine the truth."

Mr. Behrman saw then that his lie was more likely to get him killed than provide him any advantage and attempted to backtrack. "But why must I leave my family? I have little ones who need me ..." Before he could complete the sentence, the soldier whose rifle was pointed at him used the butt of it to hit him in the head. Mr. Behrman fell to the ground but quickly jumped back up to avoid the kicks the soldier administered while he was on the ground. Mrs. Behrman began crying, causing all the children to cry, as the Germans hurried out of the apartment with my father and Mr. Behrman, escaping the hubbub and recriminations that followed.

"How dare your husband accuse Sol of thievery? You both know it is not true. If they are killed, it will be your fault, and then what will we all do?" My mother was in tears, lashing out in anger.

"You and your family have treated us like inferiors since you arrived here, taking *our* space. Your husband deserves to be brought down a notch! But God is good and will not allow them to be taken from us." This was Mrs. Behrman's way of apologizing; my mother was having none of it.

"Have you looked around you at all, or are you only interested in your family's travails? Many have lost members of their families. Do you think God loves less those who have lost loved ones?"

Mrs. Behrman gathered the children and herded them into their room, slamming the door behind them. Mr. Markus put his arm around my mother to calm her and told us all to sit down; he had a story to tell.

"It is the story of Joseph and his brothers," he began. "Joseph was the favorite of his father, who gave him a coat of many colors, but no such coat to his brothers. His brothers were jealous that they were not loved as well. In addition, Joseph had spoken to his brothers of a dream he'd had that they were all binding sheaves in the field when his sheaf rose and stood upright, and their sheaves bowed down to it. His brothers were not happy with this dream and were so jealous they conspired to kill him, throw him into a pit, and say a fierce animal had devoured him. Instead, they sold Joseph into slavery. Before handing him over, though, they took his coat, smeared it with an animal's blood, and brought it to their father, telling him that Joseph was dead. In doing this, they could have ruined many lives: they broke their father's heart, put Joseph in harm's way, and risked their own souls by lying. This is a reminder of the harm and suffering jealousy can cause. But Joseph's story has a good ending, with Joseph becoming a powerful man in Egypt and bestowing upon his family many favors despite their treatment of him. Let us pray now for such an ending here."

Three long days later, my father and Mr. Behrman returned. As they walked into the apartment, the Markuses, my mother, Mila, and I were in the kitchen area sitting on boxes, trying to pass the time. I could hear Mr. Behrman walk directly to their room and open and shut the door. We all hugged Father, and Mr. Markus shook his hand, thanked God, and asked what had happened.

"The Kapitän was quite fair. He knew he would have to keep us a few days for appearances' sake, but I think he also knew the complaint was false and, as such, not worth his time, although God knows he could simply have shot us both and been done with it. Mr. Behrman and I were put in a cell together, which forced us into conversation. He claimed he thought he had heard someone talk about thefts and perhaps had heard my name, but he apologized, he said, if he was wrong. Not the apology I had hoped for, but an apology that we could build upon that would allow us to acknowledge our connection rather than our individual interests."

"So," Mr. Markus said, "we are Jews again, and not enemies. If we all are to survive this time, we will have to remember our covenant with God and therefore with each other and dispatch all thoughts of selfish interests."

"May it be so," answered my father.

Not long after that event, word came to us that the Germans were establishing a ghetto, and we were to be moved again.

"But why," my sister Mila whined. She'd become friends with a boy in our apartment building, and though work was hard and food scarce, the sting of life's hardships was lessened by her relationship with Menachem. Mrs. Behrman had also noticed the time Mila was spending with Menachem and teased that she would probably never see him again.

"I've heard the ghetto will hold twenty-five thousand Jews. It will be a city large enough that you might never run into each other again."

At that, Mila began crying—and not softly—and ran into our room, looking behind her just as she was about to close the door and yelling at Mrs. Behrman, "You old witch!"

Matka jumped up more quickly than I had ever seen before

and ran after Mila. Just before entering the room, I heard Matka say, "You will apologize, young lady," and as the door closed, I heard, "To that witch."

Unfortunately, the rumors were true, as we heard from Uncle Nat, my mother's brother, who'd been selected for the very special position of Jewish Ghetto Police, that we would be given ten days to gather up our belongings and walk to the ghetto zone. It appeared that this time we were on our own and would have to find our own living space once we arrived there. As much as I had hated living with the Behrmans, I was not looking forward to this move. It's strange, but we—all humans or just we Jews?—seem to adapt quickly to undesirable circumstances, and I had come to feel that things could be worse.

Uncle Nat stopped by during the week before we were to move and told us he could get us in a day early so we could find good living quarters, though he could not assure us that we, the Markuses, and Behrmans would be able to stay together. Mila and I looked at each other with the barest of grins that were, nevertheless, observed by Tata, who would reprimand us later. Mila squealed as though we were heading to a fancy hotel and not to a ghetto and whispered to Matka, though loudly enough for me to hear, "Maybe we can save some space for Menachem and his family! Oh, Matka, can we? Can we?" My mother didn't answer, though I could see she wasn't opposed. Neither was I, as keeping Mila happy would make *all* our lives that much easier.

As we prepared for the trip to the ghetto, we were more considerate of each other than we had been the entire time we'd lived together. I hoped we would still see the Markuses and hoped equally we would *never* see the Behrmans. I helped the Behrmans and the Markuses pack their belongings after

I'd finished with my own, taking to heart Mr. Markus' lesson of treating each other as fellow Jews and not enemies; God knew we had enough enemies around us.

There were two ghettos: the main ghetto in the central, Śródmieście District, and a smaller one at Glinice District. Uncle Nat directed us toward the larger ghetto saying it would be easier to stay out of trouble there. Rations would be small in either ghetto, no more than three and a half ounces of bread per day, he told us. I was already quite skinny as I'd hit another growth spurt, but Mrs. Behrman could use the diet, I thought.

On April 3, 1941, we arrived at the ghetto and were directed to a large apartment by Uncle Nat. He couldn't spend a lot of time with us, as he was being watched by both German and Polish police, but he helped us settle in and then said to Matka, "I will stop in when I am able, Yetta. Safety I cannot promise, but we can pray for it. There will be others to share the space—you will not be allowed such a large space for only four of you—so if you have any friends you can trust, they will make the best flat mates. Now I must go. God willing, the war will be over quickly, and life here in the ghetto will be a blessing for us all."

16
SARIAH

Martín's meetings with the priest soothed his soul. The priest had suggested to him that Sariah was a Jew sorceress who had access to demonic wiles that had tempted him beyond his ability to resist, and God would not find him at fault. Martín was open to the suggestion and thanked the priest with silver coins.

Aware of Ana's bond with Sariah, Martín had to come up with a reason to send Sariah away, fearing her wiles might entrap him once more. Using the pretext of their financial difficulties, Martín spoke to Ana about Sariah as they went to bed that night.

"Ana," Martín began, after they had dressed in their sleeping gowns and prepared to blow out the evening's candle. "May we discuss Sariah?"

Ana was caught by surprise, not knowing where such a discussion might go, but answered, "Certainly, my husband. Has she done something that troubles you? Have you seen her act with unkindness toward the girls?"

"No, no. I believe she has been a worthy help for you."

"Indeed, it is so. I don't know how I would have managed the traveling and setting up a new home without her."

"I am hopeful," continued Martín, "that times have changed so that your need is not so great. Our finances are such that it would be a help to relieve Sariah of her duties and allow her to find other work in the area."

Ana reacted with immediate resistance. "But, no, my husband. Surely, we cannot be in such bad straits as that! I truly do not know how I would manage without Sariah. And the girls love her so. There must be another way. I can save some money by fixing simpler meals and buying less expensive cloth for the girls' clothing. After all, they grow out of everything so quickly."

Ana was prepared to continue, but Martín, seeing that he would have to be more forceful to attain his end and being unwilling to engage in another argument so soon after the last one had been forgotten, relented. "Let us return to this another time. We are both tired now. I will consider your arguments." For the time being, then, Sariah was safe, though Martín had not given up.

For her part, Sariah struggled with what to do. Perhaps leaving would be the best thing, except that she had nowhere to go and would all too soon have another mouth to feed, with no prospect for work. It may have been better to have been sent away. Surely there was another family that could use her help, and Ana and Martín would give her wonderful references; Martín would if for no other reason than to be rid of her. But how could she *ask* to be sent away? What reason would she give?

Adding to the peril of her situation, Sariah was feeling tired and sick much of each day. On a recent trip to the market, Ana had noticed Sariah's lethargy. "Are you feeling well, Sariah?" Ana spoke with concern in her voice. "You have seemed particularly tired lately, and I have noticed a paleness to your face."

What could Sariah say? She wanted to tell Ana the whole truth. Lying was not something she was either familiar or comfortable with, but there was so much in her short life that was not familiar and so much discomfort to which she had had to become accustomed. This, Sariah determined, was just one more such thing, answering, "That is kind of you to notice, Ana. I believe I may have had a touch of something, but I am better, and I have watched the girls very closely and do not believe they have caught anything from me."

The months passed as Sariah hid her growing belly beneath as much clothing as she could; the cooler weather was a help. She was feeling better, though her energy was yet an issue. Blessedly, she was able to keep up with the girls. The Senhor continued to keep his distance, though not in a way that would attract his wife's attention. He had given up, for the time being, on sending Sariah away, and did what he must to counter her sexual advances, as he saw them. That meant more time away from the house and more time away from Ana. Where he might spend his sexual energy was a mystery, one Ana began to think she ought to attempt to solve.

For her part, Sariah became more and more anxious about the future. It had been a long time since she had thought of praying for some guidance. Forgiveness toward God had begun warming in her breast once she had let go of some of the anger and grief she had gathered and stubbornly embraced after the deaths of her father and dear little Baruch in particular. Such pain cannot be carried forever, and a grudge against God was sustainable only at the cost of feeling like an outsider. Sariah was alone enough. As good as Ana had been to her, she was not kin. Sariah began to understand that she must seek out a community of New Christians who could help her find her way in this new land. The deepest part of her cried out for her fellow Jews. She missed the shared rituals of the Jews that provided her warmth and feelings of safety. But of course, she reminded herself, there was no safety in those rituals these days. The Inquisition had followed them to this new land.

Finding even a community of New Christians could be dangerous. Nevertheless, she would pray to find them. She yearned
for others who would understand and for a place to go before
the baby was born, but she was running out of time.

The next market day, Sariah went alone as Ana had planned a
special picnic with the girls. Though close to eight months
pregnant, Sariah had curbed her appetite, eating only as much
as she imagined the baby required and no more. As a result,
and because it was her first pregnancy, she had been able to
keep the baby a secret. She knew it would be harder the last
month, the ninth being the month of greatest growth for the
baby, and hoped to be elsewhere by that time. But still, she
had no plan. Her prayers had been more and more insistent,
though she had no experience to know if God listened closer
to such prayers.

As she strolled among the chicken and grain vendors,
Sariah heard someone calling out her name: "Sariah ... is that
you?" Sariah turned around and saw behind a grain stall Lina,
a friend from their neighborhood in Lisbon! But it couldn't be,
she thought. Lina ran toward her, grabbing Sariah's arms with
both of hers and pulling Sariah toward her in a hug. Sariah
quickly spoke in Lina's ear, "Say nothing, Lina. I will explain
later."

"But you're pregnant!" Lina exclaimed when they'd found
a quiet spot at the market away from others. "Tell me everything! It is so good to see someone from Portugal. It often feels
so alien here. Where is your home? How long have you been
here?"

Seeing Lina brought back the memories of her final days
in Lisbon. Sariah both did and did not want to relive those difficult days. She did, as the memory of good times brought her
joy and a sense of belonging. She didn't because the difficult

memories, the memories of loss, were still like handling hot coals and burned through her. So much to tell Lina. Along with her family, their friendship was one of the things she missed most, especially here, where she had no friends, especially now, when a friend could make all the difference.

"I mourn for my family still, Lina," Sariah cast her eyes down, not wanting Lina to see the tears that fell when she talked about this loss, not wanting to see Lina's tears that must surely be falling as they would only serve to make hers heavier.

Lina placed a hand on Sariah's chin and lifted her face so she might look into the eyes Sariah had wanted to hide. "There is no need to hide your feelings from me, sweet sister. We have been friends too long. But I must go back to our stall and relieve my mother-in-law. Would you be able to come to our house tonight? We have a parlor that just you and I can sit in and catch up with some leisure."

"I will first have to put the girls to bed. If you do not live too far, I can walk to your home afterward." Sariah told Lina where she lived, and Lina assured her the distance to her home would require only a half-hour walk. And so, it was settled. Sariah would visit, and the timing could not be more perfect. Was this her answer to prayer?

It had not been difficult to get away after putting the girls to bed. Ana asked only where she was going and was happy Sariah had found a friend. Ana knew of the family, knew they were New Christians, and so only warned Sariah to be careful, as there were those Jews who converted only out of necessity and not from their hearts. Such Jews were dangerous to be around, as they were honey to the flies of the Inquisition.

Sariah enjoyed the coolness of the air, feeling as though her troubles were soon to come to an end, forgetting the trials ahead when she would be raising a child without the help of its father and with the burden of finding food and shelter sufficient for two. But her spirits were high because there was now one she could truly call a friend in her new home and a community to which she hoped to belong. The difficulty of leaving Ana and her girls, whom Sariah had come to love, was absent from her thoughts as she walked the path along the outskirts of the city to the Aragon family home.

Soon, Sariah knocked on the door of the small home, which Lina answered.

"Oh, Sariah! Please come in; I am so happy to see you. Let me introduce you to my husband and in-laws."

Sariah walked into an immaculate home that smelled of recently baked bread and was immediately hit with questions about her family history back in Spain and Portugal and profuse expressions of condolence for the loss of her parents and baby brother. They had also had many losses, which was why they, too, had fled for these parts where, at that time, the Inquisition had not yet planted roots.

"But, of course," Daniel, Lina's husband offered cautiously, "they are here now."

Sariah could tell he wanted to continue, but his father grabbed Daniel's arm to stop him, saying, "Daniel, that is not a topic our guest would be interested in, I am sure. Am I not right, Sariah? Let us leave you some time with Lina, as you did not walk all this way to be accosted by her family."

As they left the room, Lina took Sariah by the arm and sat her down on a comfortable sofa. "There, I am sure you were waiting to get off your feet. I mentioned nothing to Daniel and his parents about the baby, and you truly do not look as though you are anything but healthily plump! But now, let us talk."

And so, Sariah began the story of Ana's invitation to join the Pessoa family as they moved to Arequipa and of her life there, isolated but happy until the night the Senhor went mad.

"But what happened that night?" asked Lina, putting her

hand in Sariah's to give her the courage to speak. Sariah felt her heart jump at Lina's touch.

"I don't wish to tell the details, Lina, but I have to say that I did nothing to encourage the Senhor in that way ... ever! It was late and Ana was already in bed. The Senhor had had too much to drink, and I should have stayed upstairs but came down for a warm glass of milk to help me sleep. He told me to follow him into the parlor, which I did out of obedience. He did not ask but threw himself on me there. Lina, you have participated with love in the act he forced upon me. I wonder, can it be desired? For I remember it only as horrible in every way."

Lina answered her softly, "It can be the source of great comfort, Sariah. I hope one day you will come to know that."

"But I have no desire for that experience, even within a loving relationship, ever again. I'm not sure I ever desired it, even before the Senhor's indiscretion."

Lina interrupted, "Do not call it that, Sariah. To call it that does us all a great disservice. Call it what it was—rape, for which the Senhor must be held responsible."

"Oh, no, Lina! I am not here to ask for help in obtaining justice of any kind. You must know that justice is not something a New Christian can afford. Since leaving Lisbon and my family behind, I have also left our faith behind and am grateful I do not have to fear the Inquisition any longer. Nevertheless, I am not so naïve as to believe that Old Christians see us, *conversos,* with the same eyes they see other Old Christians."

Lina kept silent, still uncertain how much she could reveal. How much could Sariah be trusted?

"What I could use, though, is advice on what to do now that the baby's birth is only one month away. Neither Ana nor the Senhor knows of the baby. If I stay and the baby is born under their roof, I do not know what will happen."

Lina spoke up. "Of course, you must have the baby here. Go to your Senhor and Senhora and tell them our family has offered you a good position in our shop that you cannot pass up. The Senhora may be upset and may look upon you as ungrateful, but you must harden your heart to anything hurtful that might be said, knowing it is best for your baby. Come here as quickly as you can. We will work it all out once the baby is born, you will see."

17
RACHEL

Many months had passed since Rachel had moved into the mansion, yet the situation in the old city was only worsening. Rachel knew nothing of the goings-on in the outside world. She'd often ask Eloise, but Eloise's answers were at best unreliable. It seemed she didn't want to give Rachel any reason to want to leave, knowing that outside the mansion and cemetery, Rachel would be unprotected. Eloise was similarly cryptic when it came to discussing herself. Well, either cryptic or, at times, nonsensical. Things that had seemed so plain and clear *outside* had disappeared in the room, and in their place was an expansive array of seemingly crazy possibilities, enough to keep Rachel constantly off-kilter. She decided to remedy that as Eloise was bringing in her clean laundry.

"Eloise," Rachel began, "I'm curious about the stones I can see in the cemetery next door, and I wonder if the woman I sometimes see in the cemetery knows anything?"

"The woman you see is Inés, the cemetery caretaker. She has also spoken of you and would like to meet you. Let me finish a few things, and we can walk over. How does that sound?"

"Wonderful," Rachel said with surprise in her voice. "But haven't you said it's dangerous for me to leave the mansion?"

"It is, but the cemetery is safe. Let me go about my chores so we can get there and address your questions before the rain begins." Eloise looked up at the sky through the window. "It looks like a storm is brewing."

Rachel was excited but couldn't help being a little nervous. So absorbed was she in her thoughts it seemed only minutes before Eloise returned, appearing with two umbrellas in hand. She was so sensible, the perfect protector, Rachel thought, for that's what she was really, wasn't she? "I'm sorry I took longer than I thought, Rachel. We'll have to hurry to miss the worst of the weather." She handed Rachel one of the umbrellas, a bright—and tasteless—purple, green, and gold one. "Here, take this just in case."

Eloise led the way outside the garden gate, walking slowly to keep Rachel close. When they reached the cemetery gate, Eloise took out her key once again. Rachel was silent as Eloise opened the gate and motioned to Rachel to enter, following closely behind.

Inés walked towards them, a rag and an old silver bucket in her hands. She approached Rachel and welcomed her by name, then addressed Eloise with a "Hello, sister." Before Rachel could even begin to work out the meaning of that greeting, Eloise interjected, "Yes, Rachel. Inés and I are sisters."

Inés took Rachel's hand and led her to the Oldest Oak, under which the stones were piled next to a bench. "I know you have many questions," Inés began. "We'll have time to discuss them all." She lifted the folds of her cotton skirt and settled on the bench with an audible sigh.

Rachel began, after sitting on the far end of the bench. "What do you do here, Inés? I see you here almost every day from my window and have wondered."

"I care for the graves, as well as those inhabiting them," Inés answered simply, as she pointed at the bucket and rag that she'd put down. Inés paused to give Rachel a moment to take in that pregnant tidbit.

So much in Rachel's world was baffling now. She'd prided herself on how orderly her life had been, how beautiful in its precision. Terror was a strong word, but what she was feeling now bordered on it. Nothing made sense. Caring for the dead? Come now!

"It's too much to ask you to understand it all right now, Rachel. Let's start with this." Inés reached out, picked up a stone from the pile, and handed it to Rachel. She and Eloise looked at Rachel expectantly. Rachel wanted to throw it, to use it as a weapon against all she didn't understand! Instead, she found she felt somehow connected to it. She could feel heat and an undeniable vibration. She rubbed its burnished surface, measured its weight, and noted its speckled colors of grey and tan. She held it up to her ear as though a seashell, as though it could take her away into some unknown universe.

But nothing. Of course, Inés hadn't given Rachel the herbs needed to rub on the stone to allow it to speak to her. They both watched Rachel, however, to see if she could *feel* the voice contained in the stone. Rachel knew there had to be something special about the stone; she just didn't know what. For now, it was just another mystery. Another unanswered question. Another frustration.

18

JAKOB

It was morning, and my father and I, along with the other three men in our apartment, patriarchs of families who found their way to our flat, dressed in the dark and stood outside in the street waiting with other men to be escorted by soldiers to the weapons factory outside the ghetto. The air collected the acrid stench of sweat, dirt, and fear, heavy with its grit. Each of us had a work pass to show as we exited the ghetto boundary, exempting us from the frightening consequences we were reminded of daily by the prominent signs along the borders of the ghetto: "Exit forbidden on pain of death." Wartime thrifty as they were, the Germans had printed on the other side: "Entrance to Aryans forbidden. Beware of infectious diseases."

That morning, as we created two lines at the ghetto boundary policed by one German and one Polish soldier, to my left was Nahum, a young father living in our flat. We each reached into our pants pockets for our passes as we neared the front of the line. I took out mine to show the Polish soldier, who happened to be Jorg, a customer of our shop long ago for whom we would save cows' hooves for his two large German Shepherds. As I approached Jorg, I noticed out of the corner of my eye that Nahum was talking to the German soldier at the head of his line. I could hear him saying he couldn't find his pass, that he must have left it in the apartment. He pleaded with the soldier to allow him to return to the apartment to get it, that he would be back before they had passed everyone through. Jorg saw what was happening but pretended not to as he pressed me for my pass. Quietly, I petitioned him ... couldn't he do something?

"Do nothing that will cause the German to notice you," Jorg said, grabbing my arm and my card in one motion. "This one has no heart. I know."

The German was enjoying his power, playing with Nahum, now his prey. "So, you want me to let you return to get your pass? Sure. Why not? It could happen to anyone. You hurry back; we'll wait for you."

We'll wait for you. That should have been the giveaway, but Nahum—who, just one moment earlier could think of nothing but his six-year-old son, whose green eyes were just like his, his father's and grandfather's, may his memory be for a blessing, and whose red hair was like Nahum's mother's, his son, who had been born in the worst of times to give Greta and him something, some*one* to live for—was so grateful for another chance, that he thanked the German politely, quickly, and ran back toward the apartment.

He had taken only five or six long, bounding steps when the shot rang out. Instinctively, I ran to his side, cradling his head in my arms as he died. Jorg ran after me and lifted me up, calling me "Jew dog," which was enough for the German soldier not to intervene. Jorg likely saved my life. I tried to look him in the eyes to thank him, but he looked away.

The day at the factory went quickly. All of us worked harder to pick up the slack in the line left by the absence of Nahum. At noon, as we waited for the bell that signaled our break for soup and piece of bread, it was announced that we would not receive our noonday meal as punishment for the disobedience of our Jew brother. We were used to this. The

Germans punished all when one offended, making each individual responsible for all.

Of course, there were times when the individual fell short. When your child or your mother or your husband or wife was starving, could it be wrong to want to bring them food? Was there anything in Jewish law that could answer such a question? There was a commandment brought down from God on Mt. Sinai by Moses, "Thou shalt not steal." But was that commandment absolute? If you could steal a pass and sell it on the black market for food that would save your child, might the theft, though a literal violation of the commandment, be justifiable? If the commandment could so easily be cast aside, what if the result of the theft caused the one whose pass was stolen to be shot? Could the very same act of stealing, arguably justifiable in one moment, become unjustifiable in the next? How did God balance the value of two lives?

I realized I knew little about how God sees and how He metes out justice.

Spirits in the ghetto vacillated daily. No, minute by minute. One minute, hunger was all one could think of. That is until the next moment when the itching caused by the lice was overwhelming. But then, in an unexpected moment, a violin's song filled the air, its melody reminiscent of times before ... before, when you knew you were a human being. It was hard not to fall prey to the Germans' version of you, not to think: It is true, I am no longer human.

We awoke the next morning to Mila's moans. Mila had been adjusting better than I believed she ever could—given Menachem had gone to a different area of the ghetto—but I recognized I was her brother and perhaps a little hard on her. She and Matka had been assigned to one of the ghetto's kitchens, baking bread and making potato soup. It was called potato soup, but I'd never found a single piece of actual potato in any bowl I'd ever had. Mila explained to me once that they were only allowed to use peels for our soup. Potatoes were for the soldiers and sometimes members of the Judenrat. A piece of potato peel, though, was a delicacy as it could at least be chewed, reminding us of real food from before. It was hard not to think of *before* and *after*. *Before* we were in this ghetto. *After* the Germans had come and taken away our lives—whether literally or figuratively. Such thoughts did us no good, though, only inviting suffering, and one needn't invite suffering, as it could find you on its own very well, thank you.

Mila's suffering began in earnest the morning of her moaning. Matka went over to where Mila was *not* sleeping and placing her hand on Mila's forehead, could feel the heat and see the beads of sweat. Matka turned to me, handed me a piece of cloth, and told me to go outside, gather some snow and place it in the folds of the cloth. Though it hid well in the overall dreariness of the ghetto, spring must be coming, I thought, as it was not easy to keep the snow from melting when placing it in the cloth. I returned, having done what I could, and handed the dampened cloth to my mother, who placed it directly on Mila's forehead. My father was now also awake and looked down upon Mila with a creased brow. He took my arm to lead me out of the room. Once outside, he told me to find Uncle Nat and see if he could arrange for Mila to see a doctor. We had heard rumors that typhus had invaded the ghetto, bringing with it many deaths.

It was early in the morning, giving me time to find Uncle Nat before leaving for the factory. I ran all the way to his apartment—which, because he was a member of the Judenrat, his family did not have to share—and knocked on his door.

"What ... what? Who could it be at this early hour," I could hear him remarking to Aunt Ruth. I tried to whisper through the door.

"It's me, Uncle Nat, Jakob. Can you let me in?"

The door opened, but Uncle Nat did not invite me in. "What is it, Jakob? It's very early. You should not be out in the streets at this hour."

"I know, but Tata sent me. It's Mila. She's ill. She needs a doctor." Hearing this, Uncle Nat seemed even less willing to let me inside.

"Go back to your apartment, Jakob. Tell your father I'll see what I can do. In the meantime, don't let Mila leave your family's room. Even if it's just a little flu, it is dangerous, given our weakened states. Now, hurry. Many more soldiers will be up and about soon."

I saw only one soldier on the street as I headed back to our apartment and was able to hide in a doorway until he passed. I returned safely and relayed Uncle Nat's messages. Mila's moans, in the meantime, had given way to coughing spasms. The good sign was that there was no rash, something they had learned was a giveaway of typhus.

Returning from the factory that evening, my father and I came home to an ugly scene. All sharing the apartment with us were up in arms over Mila's coughing fits.

"She has the typhus! She cannot stay here—we are all at risk with her here. We don't care where you take her, but she must go." Our roommates were standing in what served as the common area of the apartment. A vestibule, really. It was obvious that they'd been talking with each other and had coordinated a response. My mother was in our room with Mila, thank God; she had enough worries without having to observe this untoward behavior.

My father, as usual, was calm and attempted to defuse the situation. "Please, let us all sit down and talk."

Mrs. Gold blurted out, "No! There's no time for talking. Every moment we talk, the disease takes up more and more of the air we are breathing. Mila is a dead girl—but our own children are not yet. She must be removed ... *now!*"

"I understand you are all frightened. I, too, am frightened," my father continued. "But let's be wise in this matter. Let's discuss as we Jews have always done. Mila may or may not have typhus. She has a fever and cough. That could be many things. We could all be creating a situation in our minds that does not play out in reality."

"Of course, that may be so. But then again, it may not. And it is always better to be safe than sorry, wouldn't you say?" offered another of those in the room who was also ready to put my sister out on the street.

"I understand that typhus is not an airborne disease. If that is what Mila has, God forbid, you cannot get it from her. You would get it from the same lice that infected her. Also, we have gone to a member of the Judenrat with Mila's condition, and he has promised to move her to the hospital," my father responded.

"I will pray for your sake as well as ours that it is not typhus, for we all know the treatment the hospital offers Jews is no treatment at all unless you mean the care with which a body is thrown into a mass grave." The grumblings continued.

"In these dangerous times, we must remember that we are God's Chosen," my wise father taught. "We are a *community* above everything else, people who worship the same God, who look out for each other. Throughout time, we have only survived because of our God and because of each other."

"I no longer believe that," interrupted our oldest apartment mate, whom we called Uncle Isaac. He was alone, his wife gone, his children and grandchildren somewhere in Germany. "We have not survived as Jews *because* of our God, but *despite* our God. If we are chosen, for what are we chosen? To suffer and die? I would rather *not* be chosen for such an exalted purpose."

I could tell Uncle Isaac was not the only one of that opinion. The silence revealed scared Jews. Guilty Jews. Weakened Jews, whose strength was challenged each and every day.

"I understand we are all frightened," my father continued.

"I also understand feeling God has abandoned us. But even if He has, we cannot abandon each other. We cannot abandon ourselves. We each must take individual responsibility for living the moral life." He continued, quoting from Exodus 23:4-5:

> *If you meet your enemy's ox or his donkey going astray, you shall bring it back to him. If you see the donkey of one who hates you lying under its burden, you shall refrain from leaving him with it; you shall help him to lift it up.*

"If it is our responsibility to do these things for our enemies, is it not even more important to aid our fellow Jews? If we are instructed to come to the aid of others during normal times, is it not more necessary in times such as these? I beg you to find it within yourselves to do what is right."

My father stood up and, in the quiet that followed his speech, grabbed my hand and led me into our room, where my mother embraced him with loving gratitude for such a husband, and I glowed with the pride of being my father's son.

Uncle Nat came to us two days later. "I'm sorry I could not come sooner; please forgive me," he apologized as he entered our room. "Mila," he said, addressing my sister directly, "how are you feeling?" In the two days since I'd run to his apartment building, Mila had deteriorated, showing sure signs of typhus, including the rash that began on her chest and was now spreading to her arms and legs. She had been sweating throughout the day and night even though the cold in the evening hours forced the rest of us to sleep in our coats. She could not answer Uncle Nat's question, as she seemed unaware of her surroundings, as though she'd taken a deep dive into herself and coming up for air was no longer something she desired or was capable of.

I could see my mother was struggling between slapping Uncle Nat for having allowed Mila to descend to this state in the days since we had gone to him for help and grabbing his long arms, wrapping them around her for the comfort she associated with him and with being a child, a younger sister, in their happy family home. Uncle Nat came to her of his own volition and wrapped her in a hug, saying softly into her hair, "Oh, my Yetta, I am so sorry. So very sorry." He looked up at my father and me and indicated with a jerk of his head that we were to go with him into the other room. My mother returned to Mila, wiping her brow and softly singing to her the Polish lullaby she sang when we were little.

"Thank you for coming, Nat," my ever-gracious father said before stating the obvious. "It is too late for Mila, though."

"I see that, Sol; may you and God forgive me."

We returned to our room, held our wife, mother, and sister and wiped her tears as they fell. Then my father took our hands and motioned for my mother to take mine so that we formed a circle around Mila's head as he chanted the 121st Psalm:

> *I lift my eyes to the mountains—from where will my help come?*
> *My help will come from the Lord, Maker of heaven and earth.*
> *He will not let your foot falter; your guardian does not slumber.*
> *Indeed, the Guardian of Israel neither slumbers nor sleeps*
> *The Lord is your guardian; the Lord is your protective shade at your right hand.*
> *The sun will not harm you by day, nor the moon by night.*

The Lord will guard you from all evil; He will guard
your soul.
The Lord will guard your going and your coming from
now and for all time.

I must have slept the sleep of the exhausted, as Father had to wake me up in the morning to go to the factory. I could see Mila's bed was empty and felt ashamed I had slept through the worst hours. Tata came over to me, put his large hands on my face, and tilted my head so he could look into my eyes. His hands felt different, and I realized age did not obey time in this ghetto. We had been here only two years, and he had aged ten. His hands were bony, the skin wrinkled, with a grayish pallor. They were cold, but everything was always cold. His gaze frightened me. There was anger in it. My father, who was always calm. He, to whom we all went to be uplifted, was angry.

"Your sister has gone to God, my son. May her memory be for a blessing."

I pulled away and rushed outside our apartment. No! It wasn't fair! Until now, my devotion to God hadn't really been tested. I'd seen death and accepted it. What else could I do? I had justified my indifference. Now I couldn't be indifferent. God had taken our Mila! How would I ever bow my head in worship to Him again?

19
THE CHILDREN'S CHORUS

If God is love, as so many say, how are we to understand suffering?

20
SARIAH

Sariah returned to the Pessoa home, committed to asking Ana for a release from her employ. She had not thought of what she would do if she were denied, being certain that any reluctance Ana might feel would be countered by the Senhor. More difficult would be telling the girls, but she hoped to avoid that, coward that she was, and leave that task to the Senhora, which she assumed is as Ana would want it.

All these worries and presumptions yielded to something much worse. Only two days after returning, while preparing for the difficult task ahead, Sariah awoke in the middle of the night with terrible stomach pains. As she began to feel the skin of her abdomen tighten against the form of the baby, she knew what she most feared was happening. While the pain was still bearable, she struggled to focus her thoughts on a plan that would allow her to give birth somewhere else—anywhere but in Ana's home.

Sariah gathered a blanket and wrapped within it another blanket, some water, a knife, and a loaf of bread. She packed it as tightly as she could so she'd be able to carry it, stopping to fight the pain when necessary, clenching a rolled-up washcloth with her teeth in order not to scream. Then she tried to tiptoe down the stairs and out the kitchen door, willing to have her child in a neighbor's barn if necessary and if she could make it that far. If she couldn't, then her child would be born in a field under the stars.

As she reached the last step of the stairs, the largest wave of pain she had yet to experience hit, and she was unable to squelch the cry that accompanied it. At the same time, she missed the last step and fell to the floor, hitting her head against the stone surface and passing out.

When Sariah came to, the next pain thrusting consciousness upon her like a bucket of cold water, Ana was standing over her, calling for Martín. As Sariah began moaning again, feeling as though a sword was plunging into her, she heard Ana tell the twins, "Go back to bed and do not leave your room until I come get you. Sariah will be alright, don't worry." She spoke more calmly than she felt, in the throes of the shock of the moment. Sariah was having a baby! Sariah, who had seemed to have no interest in men at all. The pain momentarily over, Sariah opened her eyes to see Martín putting his arms underneath hers, attempting to raise her.

"Can you walk, Sariah? We must get you to the parlor. Ana is there making a bed for you." These were the first words he had spoken to her since ... She did not answer him but complied with his request, walking with his help along the hallway leading to the parlor. He stopped her for a moment. "Sariah," he stumbled with his words, as if afraid of what might come out of his own mouth next, "Sariah ... is the baby, then, mine?"

Sariah could imagine no fitting response to such a question. There was no answer that did not disgust her, yet she knew, nevertheless, that she loved the baby desperately. Martín did not wait for an answer but pleaded, "Please, don't tell Ana. Please, it will destroy her." Sariah looked up at him without hatred but with pity, pity that he could read in her eyes.

"Here, Martín, place her on this blanket and go for the doctor. Hurry!" Martín did not want to leave, fearing a conversation between Sariah and Ana, but had no choice, hearing the urgency in his wife's voice. He could sense Ana's forcefulness and yielded to it. He knew now that she would make this work out, that she was the strength of the family, not him, and though it pained him to admit that to himself, he felt hopeful for the first time since that night some eight months ago.

"Sariah," Ana spoke with a gentle force, "We must remove your underclothing. Can you help?"

Responding, Sariah lifted her hips as Ana pulled down her petticoat that had been torn, another panel of cloth sewn into it to allow for her expanding waist. Sariah found herself embarrassed by her condition, believing Ana would have no idea what to make of it. At a different time, Sariah would have been angry at being forced to suffer in every way for a man's expression of power, but now Sariah had no leisure for anger. Now the forces of childbirth overtook her, and between the pain of such heft that she felt she could not bear it and the mere moments of relief, Sariah was borne along a river of oneness with life itself. It felt right to feel such pain, its rhythm akin to the world's heartbeat, the swaying of grasses, the swell of tides, the very cycle of birth and death.

Martín had not yet returned when Sariah heard Ana ordering her to push. "Push, now. I can see the baby's head." Sariah summoned all her strength and pushed, and in her pushing was a prayer for the little one to accept the gift transmitted through Sariah's pain. Such immense pain was not for naught. It had a purpose. All of it. And this purpose the child would hold in his heart, and in his mind, and in his soul. *He*, for she had been certain it would be a boy, would be strong *because* of his birth, and *because* of his mother's strength, and *because* of his heritage, not despite it. As he came into the world, Martín and the doctor arrived in time to clear out the baby's airway and cut the cord. All the rest Ana had done but asked for no gratitude. Women were made for such service and rendered it with the same natural force as breathing. As Ana placed the baby in Sariah's arms, she briefly smiled and whispered, "A boy, Sariah. You should name him Baruch."

He was a beautiful black-haired baby, with a large birthmark along the side of his face in the shape of an almost perfect elongated rose, as if a promise from God that he would be a peacemaker and bring with him love to all who encountered him. Or so Sariah wished to think, though it became clear very quickly that he might be more a lightning rod in the household. Her conversation with Ana began very carefully, as Ana questioned first only how she was feeling and whether she could use any advice on nursing the baby. Sariah would have loved to have confided in Ana. She wanted nothing more than her own mother now, but lacking that, she wished she could have that connection with Ana. Of course, that was unlikely, for there was a gulf now between them, not of Sariah's making, that would be impossible to cross. And that conversation was certain to occur sooner rather than later.

"He is so lovely, Sariah, and, it appears, perfect in every way. Even his birthmark honors him," offered Ana. "The girls are so anxious to see him and to hold him, but we will let both you and him rest a few more days before introducing them to each other. Would you mind, though, if Martín came in to see the baby? He does so love babies."

Sariah was caught off guard at this request but knew she could do nothing but assent, for anything else would seem strange. "Of course, Ana," Sariah answered quietly. "But he just finished suckling and will sleep, I am hoping."

"Perhaps just a few moments, then, before he goes to sleep. The Senhor is in the kitchen. I hope using the parlor as a nursery, for now, is convenient, at least until you're well enough to climb the stairs to your room. I sent the girls outside a little bit ago and must go check on them. I hope you won't mind being alone with the Senhor for just a few moments." Ana did not wait for an answer, as she left the room almost before finishing her sentence. Sariah could hear her tell her husband that he should not stay long, as Sariah needed her rest.

Before she could compose herself as she would have liked, the Senhor was in the room. "What a beautiful little boy, Sariah. How lucky you are to have a son."

Thus, he began, and Sariah wondered if he would ignore the obvious—that this was his child. Or had he convinced himself of her promiscuity and his innocence? She would have none of that! While Sariah would have liked to keep the Senhor's complicity—no, say it, his rape of her—a secret, she could do so only at her own expense, at the expense of everyone assuming her harlotry, convinced that Jews, even converts, were dirty and immoral for, after all, while they may pretend to accept Christ now, it was they who had killed him.

"Yes, Senhor, he is perfect and innocent of the events that brought him into this world."

Martín's brow creased and his eyes darkened. Mention of that night, the night for which the priest had assigned him penance that he had carried out with vigor to erase the sin quickly from his heart, brought him back to feelings of guilt and shame, feelings that would make him appear weak in the eyes of others, something he could not afford as a husband, father, and master.

"I believe we are all innocent, as it was God who orchestrated the events of that evening for a purpose we may not understand now but will in the life to come. Sariah, I must ask you again ... is the baby mine?"

Sariah had known the question would, at some point, emerge from his lips again and had not decided how to react. When she first thought of this conversation, before Baruch was even born, she was incensed at its implications—that there was another with whom she, without the sanction of marriage, had engaged in sexual activity. But she understood that it was likely coming from a hope that the fated evening could be forgotten. And perhaps, without the birth of Baruch, it could have, as many other such nights with other Jewish servants and their masters likely were. The plight of woman-hood was heavy.

"He is the fruit of that night," answered Sariah, unable to call him the Senhor's son.

Martín sighed and took a moment, looking at Baruch but not touching him. Sariah wondered what his thoughts were. Could he love this baby who was destined to ruin his life? How could anyone not have a profound reverence for the miracle of life and, therefore, love Baruch with the same effulgence as she?

"Does Ana know?" he asked, his voice breaking with the weight of the question.

"She does not," Sariah answered in a steely tone, words freighted with the power of her position.

"Must she?" he asked, almost penitently, acknowledging the shift in the balance of power between them.

"She must."

Again, Sariah answered, keeping her words to a minimum. She did not know what the future held for her and Baruch but believed it was within her purview to determine the path and would cede none of her authority to this man who had taken so much from her. Baruch was God's salve for her wounds.

The Senhor did not answer but held out his finger to allow Baruch to grab it with his little hand. It was not lost on Martín that here was the son he did not have to carry on the family name and the family business.

A month passed without further interaction between Martín

and Sariah, though she had seen him sneak into her room when she was not there and Baruch was sleeping. At first, it frightened her, fearing the Senhor might do the baby harm, and she stayed close and listened for the baby's cries. They never came, and life returned, in all other ways, to normal. Sariah recovered quickly, returning to the comforting routine of tending the twins, though she often had Baruch with her, swaddled in a many-colored woven shoulder cloth that she tied at the front, a gift from Ana. Sariah thought of the story of Joseph and the coat his father had given him and the trouble it had caused. She hoped to spare Baruch the pains of jealous brothers. Though she could not imagine life without Baruch, so quickly had he inserted himself into her heart, she had no desire for the kind of life that would lead to another baby. She was different and knew it.

Ana had not asked questions of Sariah, giving her time to come to terms with her new situation. But word had gotten out, and there was much gossip within the community, wild stories about impregnation by the devil or that secret Jews had brought to life a golem to impregnate Sariah so as to create a beast that, when it grew to maturity, would kill all Christian babies. And so on and so on. There was never a dearth of stories about Jews undermining humanity.

Ana was not one prone to indulging in such fantasies. She believed that Sariah was a sincere New Christian. She attended church with the family, and Ana had seen her praying the Rosary. Nevertheless, the time came to question Sariah about Baruch's father. One afternoon, when the girls were playing with their dolls in their room and Sariah had just put Baruch down for a nap before going into the kitchen to prepare a bottle for a late-night feeding, Ana approached her.

"How is little Baruch doing, Sariah?" Ana began.

"He is well. But it would be wonderful if he could sleep longer." Ana laughed at this, remembering how tired she had been, even with help, when the twins were young and so hungry.

"I understand, Sariah. But you seem to be doing very well. You are a natural." The compliment was meant sincerely but also as an entrée to the difficult subject close to Ana's heart. "Sariah, I have not asked until now, but surely you have known that I would. There are many rumors going through the community about Baruch's conception. I have been surprised that his father has not been here to hold his small son. What father would be so disinterested?"

Sariah had known this moment could not be avoided forever. She had enjoyed the month of relative peace, living in the rhythm of new life, caring for Baruch without thinking of the consequences his birth would set into motion when she was forced to tell the truth. But perhaps they could continue to live as they were. Maybe Ana would welcome knowing Baruch was related to the girls and, thereby, to her as well. Might she not want Sariah and Baruch to stay close, though she would surely be angry with the Senhor? Perhaps, maybe, might, surely ... the uncertainty compounded each day it was not addressed. Now.

"Senhora, the father *was* here for the birth and *has* held his son."

Ana looked at Sariah as though she were possessed. "You are making no sense, Sariah. Why are you speaking riddles?"

Sariah looked directly into the Senhora's eyes and said only her husband's name—Martín. It was the first time Ana had heard that name from Sariah's lips and was as taken aback by the vocalization as the meaning it portended. But it couldn't be. In her own house. Had they been carrying on an affair that she knew nothing about? Did she know so little about Sariah? About Martín?

Seeing the thoughts through Ana's eyes, Sariah spoke again, bravely, though naïvely, "The Senhor raped me one evening when he had been drinking."

This was too much for Ana to hear. She slapped Sariah across the face saying, "You will never use that word in relation to my husband. Who are you to accuse the man who provides you a home, who ensures that you are fed, and who protects you, a Jewess, from the slander of others?"

Ana took a step back and was silent for a moment as she looked at the mark her slap had made on Sariah's face. Ana believed herself a generous person, one who took the requirements of a Christian life seriously, which included obeying the Golden Rule. She thought about what that meant under these circumstances. She knew she would want to be believed. Could she go that far, believing that her husband had broken his marital vows? Not without at least hearing Martín out on the matter first. And so she said to Sariah, "Please forgive me for slapping you; I had no right. I don't know why you would make such an accusation against Martín unless it were to hide the shame of your relations with another. I will talk with Martín to discover the truth, and then we will decide what to do. I would give you a chance, before I speak with the Senhor, to recant," Ana offered, believing it to be the Christian thing to do.

"I have been brought up believing truth is important, and so, Senhora, I cannot unsay what I have already said."

"So be it," answered the Senhora. "I will speak with the Senhor."

Holding Baruch in her arms after feeding him, looking into his dark and happy eyes, Sariah could not imagine being without him. Whatever the Senhor told the Senhora, Sariah hoped it would be the truth, though her belief conflicted with that hope. Not a pessimist at heart, Sariah felt it her responsibility to Baruch to consider all plausible possibilities. If the Senhor were to lie, how could she then protect Baruch? What would happen to her and, by extension, Baruch under such circumstances? On the other hand, if the Senhor were to tell the truth, might the outcome be worse?

Ana found Martín in his office, writing at the desk. Though the anger still coursed through her, she prayed to be able to approach him with equanimity, as she knew any other way would not yield fruit.

"Martín, we must talk."

"This is not a good time, Ana; I am working on our bills."

Ana pressed, "It must be now, my husband."

He looked up, saw the resolve in his wife's face, and relented. "What is it, then?"

"There is no way to ask this question save quickly, with little prelude. I have heard that Baruch is your son. Tell me, is it so?"

She laid it out without bringing Sariah into it at all, without mentioning the charged word *rape*, hoping to minimize raising his defenses. As she spoke, Ana looked directly into Martín's eyes, believing she would see the truth there.

Martín was caught off-guard, though Sariah had said Ana would have to know, and so he knew this day would arrive. He had thought about his response, had even prayed about it, but now that it was before him, any strength he had found in prayer emptied from him. He could not tell Ana the truth.

"Where have you heard such a thing, Ana? Have you now become one of the gossipers you have always proclaimed to despise? Look at the baby. Do you see any evidence that he could be mine?" Thus far, he had not had to lie directly, but Ana would have none of it.

"I do not wish to discuss who provided the information. Nor do I wish to engage in aspersions against my character. I am not on trial here. In fact, no one is on trial. As your wife, as the person who has supported you and bore your children, I am asking whether the occasion exists to repent together for any sins against the marriage."

Giving him the out that might encourage the truth to emerge from his lips, she looked up into his face, her own eyes shining intently through tears.

"I am innocent of wrongdoing, Ana."

He had endeavored to believe it to be so. He justified his taking of Sariah by believing it was the drink, or it was her lack of propriety, or whatever other excuse he could imagine. And perhaps he believed by not saying directly, "Baruch is not my son," that he had preserved his soul. Or, he may have decided that if it was a lie, it was to spare Ana pain. But with this response, he harmed himself as well as Ana, for she had seen the truth in his eyes.

———

Any hope Martín may have held deep within his breast that he and Ana could raise Baruch as their own, that he could be the son they had not had together, was shattered the following day. It began with Ana taking the twins down the road to spend a few days with their cousins, though they protested, as they had grown fond of spending time with Baruch, watching all the funny little things he would do, like turning his head toward their chests when they would hold him, as if their flat chests could provide him any nourishment. What a funny little boy!

When Ana returned, she pulled Martín aside to tell him of her decision. They went into the parlor and shut the door behind them. Sariah was upstairs nursing Baruch, but still, Ana spoke softly. Today was not going to be easy. She had gone over things in her head, again and again, sleeping little, refining her plans to ensure all would go as it must so that healing could begin. For all of them.

"Martín, I have determined our course. You may or may not agree; it doesn't matter. If you agree, we will continue as a committed family in the eyes of God and of the Church. If you do not, you may leave today and pave a new way for yourself. I will raise the girls, and you can begin a new family in a new place. I have learned enough to be able to continue the business without you."

"Ana, you are speaking nonsense! Of course we will remain a family. As a woman, you would never be able to take on the business. The workers would not obey you. Our creditors would take advantage of you. But it is not necessary in any event. I would never abandon you or the girls."

"Do not underestimate me, Martín. While in your eyes, I may be weak and frail, I believe in my strength and in the strength of my gender. The truth is you would be lost without me ... though I have faith that you would find another to play wife. But that is your choice. Here are my terms. Sariah will be sent away from our home with a stipend that will help her resettle."

"But Ana, the business has no money to spare right now," Martín interrupted. This was trifling on his part. He could not abide having a woman make the decisions.

"Do not interrupt me, Martín. I have thought this through, and these terms are final. Your role is simply to accept or reject them." As she spoke, Ana grew in her conviction that what she was planning was correct. "We will place Baruch with the priest to find a Christian home for him. You will see neither Sariah nor Baruch again."

Martín was surprised at the cruelty of Ana's plan. Not that he would never see Sariah again—that he understood. But his son?

"I have no quarrel with never seeing Sariah again," Martín offered. "But the boy, why must we give him to another Christian family? We are a Christian family, are we not? We will be able, over time, to afford raising another child ... and the girls already love him so." As he spoke, Martín grew more certain that this was the path Christ wanted for them.

"That will never happen, Martín. I will not raise your son

by another woman. Another, more Christian woman might, perhaps. But that woman is not I." Her stare stopped the denials from exiting his mouth. They were at a crossroads; he could choose only one path safely.

With his silence, Ana continued. "I will tell Sariah that she has two days to get her things together and make her plans. She must be gone before the girls return."

Ana went directly upstairs and knocked on Sariah's door. She had seemed so resolute, but that belied her feelings at the moment, for Ana believed Sariah. While Sariah had reason to lie, she supposed, she nevertheless knew Sariah well enough and knew her husband as well. Though it pained her to believe that Martín had taken Sariah by force, she had to accept it. This made sending Sariah away both more urgent and less just at the same time. And to take away her baby ... As a mother, Ana knew this to be the most unjust act of all. But, she told herself, justice was determined by Christ. Ana had prayed for confirmation that the path she had chosen, the path out of the unjust situation created by her husband, was the most just thing she could do. And while praying, she may not have felt the answer as a true burning in her breast, but she did feel lighter, as though a weight had been lifted, and this she interpreted as a sign from God. She also prayed that God would take the pain of the loss of the second Baruch from Sariah.

Ana steeled herself as she stood outside the door to Sariah's room. She was remembering the day the first Baruch had been thrown against a stone wall, the sound of the baby's crying and then nothing, immediately followed by the wailing of Sariah's mother and the moans of her father. It had been difficult not to return to these thoughts occasionally, especially seeing Sariah now with a healthy baby. How could she take this baby away from Sariah?

Hearing the knock, Sariah covered up her breast, having just finished nursing Baruch, and answered, "Come in."

Ana walked softly into the room and sat down on a chair

opposite Sariah. She could not bear to look at the baby now, knowing it to be Martín's, the boy she had so wanted to give him but had not.

"Sariah, I have come to a decision. You will not like it, but there is no other way." Ana stopped to gather her courage. Sariah said nothing, just looked down at the floor, waiting for her sentence, for the penalty that would come for being a woman, for being enticing to a powerful man, for the suffering that was the consequence of being a Jew. Ana took a few deep breaths before continuing, praying for the ability to be soft, to convey understanding and her own grief at being forced to this end.

"You must leave, Sariah, and you must do so before the girls return. It would be too upsetting for them to say goodbye. I will tell them you had a family emergency and may not be able to return, but that you told me to hug them both for you, which I will do."

Sariah looked up at Ana in shock. She had expected some punishment though knew she deserved none. She looked into Ana's eyes to see if there was room in them for forgiveness, for understanding. Seeing none, Sariah looked back down at the floor, her tears falling onto Baruch's head. It would be hard to leave the girls. But she had Baruch and would make a new life for them both.

"I understand, Ana," was all she said.

Ana had hoped for anger, for hatred, for some foul words that would help her justify what was to come next. Without it, Ana felt her heart beating rapidly with the injustice of what she had to do. But she knew the path had been set. She continued.

"The Senhor has authorized me to give you some money to help you get started in a new life. So, it is done. You will, of course, leave the boy here. Your uncertain path is not one for a baby."

At this, Sariah looked at Ana in horror and clutched Baruch

tighter in her arms. Words filled her head and her throat but would not leave her mouth. They had no right; this could not ... would not be! She began hyperventilating as she attempted to calm herself enough to respond. Ana became frightened that Sariah would perish in front of her and longed to jump from her chair to put her arms around her in comfort and support. But, of course, compassion was not allowed her. She was the cause of Sariah's suffering and would have to live with that always.

21
RACHEL

Back at the mansion, Rachel sat with a letter Eloise had handed her. She looked at the bottom and saw it was from Henry. Why would he write a letter? Why not just come over? She read.

Dear Rachel,

First and last, and probably always, I will ask your for-giveness for all the ways I've failed you and David. There is, and has been, so much unsaid between us over these 25 years. I've loved you as best I could, and know you did your best to love me as well. Already you can tell something is amiss as I am writing in past tense. So let me get it out up front, then try to answer the questions that I know you'll have. I am leaving. I can hear you saying that I have the tense wrong. That I left long before today, and you're right. A discussion for another time, if we are lucky.

I am not leaving for another; I am not leaving be-cause of any distaste for our marriage. But I won't let myself off the hook that easily, don't you worry. I am leaving out of fear and an inability to face the present circumstances with its myriad consequences any longer. So, yes, I am likely the coward you always thought I was.

I am most the coward for not telling you in person what I am about to write you in this all-too-impersonal letter. But it is the only way I could emotionally handle this. Do sit if you're not already, Rachel. And forgive me.

David is dead.

Our son, who brought such light and joy into our lives, who caused us worries, yes, but who taught us so much and allowed us to be a mother and a father, is gone.

I received the news via a note from Eli. A simple, short note that said only, "I am sorry to inform you of David's death. Please know he was a strength to all of us until the moment of his passing. That is all I can share now. When all this is over and we can begin to live civil lives again, I will find you and tell you more. But for now, please accept my sincere condolences, and know we, too, are mourning. Eli."

I have nothing left here except you, Rachel. With the help of the Righteous, Maura has taken over the gallery, which is the only thing she ever really wanted. I expect they will come for me anytime, and in coming for me, they have access to you. I doubt I could resist their efforts to learn where you are from me. Again, I know myself for who I am and am not proud of it.

I have provided sufficient funds to Eloise for your support. I am leaving no one a forwarding address. This is no longer a country I know; no longer a country I want to know. When all is over, though, I hope to come looking for you. I will even retain the hope we can, against all odds, someday be together again.

*As I said in the beginning of this letter, please for-
give me for not being stronger. You will be safe with
Eloise. Listen to her; she is quirky but wise. Love,
Henry*

Eloise walked over to the cemetery with two cups of chicory
coffee while the early morning dew beaded on blades of grass,
and kicked at the gate. Inés had been expecting her sister and
opened it, inviting Eloise in. Together they walked down a
path toward the back of the cemetery where they could sit on
a bench hidden from the upper window of the house next
door.

"How lovely it is to sit with my sister and enjoy this delicious cup of coffee," said Inés. She sighed, a deep, cleansing
sigh.

"It's just as enjoyable for me," echoed Eloise. "We don't do
this enough. Just sit, that is." She held the coffee cup in both
hands, enjoying the warmth, though it was warm enough outside for iced coffee, to which Eloise would switch soon. She
looked at the ground as she and Inés relished their first few
sips in silence. Just beyond her feet was a soldier's battalion of
fire ants bringing food back to their hill. Eloise touched Inés
on the leg and pointed to the ants as they both pulled in their
feet. Both had been bitten in the past and understood well the
phrase "Caution is the better part of wisdom."

Eloise then shared with Inés, "I was just reading about a
species of red ants that raids other anthills, steals the pupae,
and carries them over great distances to their home hill where
they install the pupae and raise them as slaves. When born,
the foreign ants don't realize they're serving a different species
and simply do what they are programmed to do, but for a different master."

"Fascinating," Inés responded, with no hint of sarcasm in

her voice. "You do know so many interesting facts."

"Well, I've been around a while," Eloise joked, and both she and Inés enjoyed a giggle. "How are the Children today?" she inquired.

Inés reprised her sigh. "We've had two new ones in the past few days who are having a difficult time adjusting, but we're all doing our best to bring them along. It will take a while, I believe, before they will be ready to share their stories."

"My, my, the stream just flows and flows, never abating," Eloise lamented. "I keep hoping for the inevitable transition of power to happen sooner rather than later, but history has its own momentum, doesn't it."

"It does," agreed Inés. "But speaking of readiness, did you come to speak to me of Rachel?"

"Oh, thank you for the reminder! I was so enjoying our coffee and chat I had forgotten."

"Really, Eloise," Inés spoke in a gently scolding voice, "you must be more vigilant. The Keepers are relying upon us, you know."

"Yes, yes, of course. I know. Please forgive me a little lapse." Eloise frowned penitently, or perhaps it was a bit of little-sister annoyance. "I just brought Rachel a letter from Henry in which he tells her of David's death. I left so she could have time alone to struggle with her emotions; I thought she would need that. But I'll return shortly and see how she is."

"Use your judgment, Eloise. I imagine she will have questions. Rachel has already endured the deaths of her mother and father, and has been having the dreams of past lives that are unsettling her. David's death will be the most difficult. Her suffering, while not a path one would choose ..."

The Children's Chorus: Oh, never! What pain! Unimaginable! Inexpressible!

Inés continued. "Rachel's suffering is necessary for her growth as a Story Teller. But we must be careful she does not get lost in her grief."

―――――――――

Rachel spent two days in her room, refusing entry to Eloise. She'd lost the ability to breathe easily. Her pupils fought the light coming in through the window. The thought of food made her stomach twist. In short, her body was in shock. Why wasn't it she who had been there when her son died? Why hadn't she been the one to wash his body, to softly stroke the capsule of his soul? Why hadn't she, the chrysalis protecting her son before his allotted time for emergence, been the one to usher him into whatever was next, something she didn't know but for which the evidence grew stronger each day she glimpsed the activity in the cemetery.

On the third day, Rachel could handle no more of the room whose walls were closing in on her. She left with the letter in her hand and headed down the stairs to find Eloise, who was sipping tea in the parlor.

"Please, Eloise, I can't take being here anymore! I must find Henry! I must leave this wretched place!" She threw herself on the sofa and broke down yet again. Her tears moved Eloise, who placed her teacup on a table, stood, and sat next to Rachel a moment before taking her hand, saying, "Would you like to sit in the garden, Rachel? Come with me; I'll show you the way."

They entered a gate and walked past two newly budding lemon trees before reaching a bench. Rachel preferred the ground, to feel a connection to the organic world. She sat near some pink Ligustrum bushes while Eloise sat on the bench nearby, silent, waiting for Rachel, in her own time, to speak. Finally, Rachel looked up, her eyes red from crying, her cheeks blotchy.

"Do you know, Eloise? Do you know?"

Eloise replied quietly, reverently, most sadly, "I know."

At this answer, Rachel threw the letter away from her and began sobbing anew.

"When did you know? Why did you know before me? Doesn't that seem wrong? Doesn't this all seem so terribly wrong? I am his mother! Or I *was* his mother? Damn it all, which is it when your child is dead?"

Eloise sat on the ground next to Rachel but did not initially touch her. "You *are* his mother, and in this life, you will always be his mother. That cannot be taken away. I'm so sorry you're having to bear this pain, Rachel. Please believe me."

Rachel stiffened, not yet ready to be comforted, not yet ready to acknowledge the truth. Eloise allowed her to feel whatever it was she was feeling in silence. Then, as if it had just occurred to her, Rachel turned to Eloise and challenged, "Henry didn't say how David died. I must find Henry! Or do you know that, too, Eloise?"

Eloise knew, but it wasn't her place to share that story, so she avoided a direct answer. "Henry did not tell me."

"Where is he? How could he simply abandon me? I have nothing, no one left. He knew that and yet still left me. What kind of man does that?"

Rachel jumped up angrily and began pacing as if her body could no longer restrain itself, as if she needed to enlist the entirety of her physical being to express the kind of pain and anger she was feeling. She was full of self-pity, her anger poison-tipped arrows aimed at all targets within emotional range. Eloise knew this and knew she had to help bring Rachel back to the source of her pain, which had nothing really to do with Henry.

"It's not my place to defend Henry, especially not now. But, Rachel, let me suggest this: You've experienced a great loss in your son's death. Allow yourself to acknowledge and embrace that pain."

"It's too much! What have I done to bring all this down upon me? I've loved my mother and father, perhaps not as fully as I could have, but I tried. I've been a faithful wife to Henry and accepted the times he faltered. I loved my son with all my heart, protected him ..." Upon pronouncing these last words, Rachel stopped as it sank in that she had been unable to keep him safe when it most mattered. Why had Henry made her leave when her protection of David was most important? She began to sob again, but the tears quickly dried up.

"I want to go back to my room," she said abruptly.

Eloise could see Rachel shutting down, afraid of such great pain. But, of course, this grief would be a process, the duration of which could neither be guessed at nor controlled. Walking together back to her room, Eloise said nothing, allowing the thick silence to drip through Rachel.

22
JAKOB

The rain pelted the ghetto the following week, making the German soldiers meaner, if that was even possible. They didn't like having to march us to the factory each morning in the rain and mud and showed that displeasure, tripping the older men so that they fell face first into the mud and, when they had difficulty getting back up, kicking them back into the mud and laughing, saying, "Now they are truly filthy Jews!"

We heard of no further deaths from the typhus, or thwarted escape attempts. But when we were forced to disrobe at the showers for the lice disinfectant, the effects of the lack of food were starkly visible. Surely we had known that each of us was losing weight. Some who had been fat before laughed about it, calling our dwindling piece of bread and watery soup their "special diet" that they planned to trademark after the war and make millions. Gallows humor, my mother called it. Because we saw each other every day, thinning faces were not really noticed. Seeing each other without clothing revealed what ghetto life had been doing to us, and it frightened me. How much more weight could we lose and still be human beings, which, of course, we already weren't. Ask any German.

Returning to our apartment after it had been fumigated, I

checked feverishly for the book I'd hidden, fearing it might have been taken during the Germans' scouring of our room. *The Golem* and I had become good friends since being forced out of our home. I'd read Meyrink's book over and over, yet I still looked forward to a page or two whenever I could get it in, that is, when we got back from the factory with enough light left in the day to make reading possible. There were few comforts in our lives these days, so when I found the book underneath the loose floorboard in our room where I'd placed it, I was almost as excited as if I'd been given a bowl of soup with a whole potato in it and a large portion of bread to boot!

The days trod on, one after the other just as my father, my mother, and I did on our way to our places of work. Had there been enough food, were there no Germans tormenting us for no reason other than to alleviate the boredom they, too, must have felt, it would have been an acceptable way to live out the war. Of course, there was the film of grief and despair that hung over our heads since Mila's death. Matka, more than Father or me, was deteriorating. At first, we worried she was also infected with typhus, but the rash did not appear. Father believed it was her heart.

"Matka's heart is broken, Jakob," he confided to me, and I understood.

I tried to bring Matka news from the factory that might help heal her heart. Uplifting news, like the birth of a baby. But such a thing only made the film darker, as she, of course, had lost a child. Father had also lost a daughter and I a sister, but the bond of mother and child was stronger than we had understood. With nothing else to distract her, my mother dwelled on Mila's death, and her dwelling dragged her to depths we uninitiated men could only guess at (I had begun to think of myself in this place as a man, as random hairs had begun sprouting all over my body and I was given responsibilities greater than a boy could have managed).

The following day, as we were once again accompanied to

the factory, I witnessed a scene I wish never to have witnessed. As we passed through the barrier at the boundary of the ghetto, German and Polish soldiers checked our work passes and made us count out loud. It was sometimes confusing as there were two lines, and they required the numbering to be consecutive, so you had to be on your toes, paying close attention. If you were the one to mess up the count, you would be punished and, depending upon the day and the mood of the German officer, it could be a simple reprimand or a rifle butt to your groin. Bullets were generally saved for more serious acts, as I understood they were being rationed.

That day as we passed through, the count was forty-three. When we arrived at the factory, there was always another count. This time, the count was forty-four.

"Well, well," the German captain seemed almost amused by the discrepancy. "We began with forty-three Jewish vermin, and now we have forty-four. I know rats procreate rapidly, but I was not aware they could do so asexually." He and the other soldiers laughed. "What, you Jews don't find me funny? How about this: there are only two reasons I know of that we could have forty-four instead of forty-three. One, a mistake was made at the barrier." He turned to his second-in-command. "*Herr Leutnant* Schultz, did you make a mistake in the count at the barrier?"

"No, *mein Herr Kapitän*." The lieutenant clicked his boots together and saluted as he said this.

"*Herr Leutnant* Schultz," the Kapitän continued, "did anyone else make a mistake in the count at the barrier?"

"No, *mein Herr Kapitän*."

"Well, isn't this a mystery? There is only one other reason I can think of that the count would be greater. Smaller could be many reasons. A Jew could have dropped dead on the way or perhaps decided to take a little nap in the woods. But greater? No, the only reason is that one of you is an escapee *returning* to the ghetto. What, you ask? Why would anyone do that? Perhaps you found the accommodations in the ghetto better than outside. Or you missed the food. Who can know? What I do know is that if the Jewish pig who joined us outside the ghetto barrier does not step forward, I will begin shooting at random until he does."

The Kapitän allowed a few minutes for what he had said to sink in. We looked at each other, wondering who would be the one to snitch on his brother. We all knew Abraham had joined the march just outside the barrier and that he had escaped only a few days before. This was not the first time one of us who had escaped later returned. If your safe house failed, you would not make it outside the ghetto. Abraham thought he had a place on the Aryan side of town, a former Christian neighbor who was willing to take him in, but when he arrived, he was turned away. There'd been a recent search on their block, and a neighbor harboring a Jew had been shot on the spot, along with the Jew. Abraham's former neighbor was too frightened to accept him.

"So, nothing?" the Kapitän asked and, turning to one of the other soldiers, handed him his own pistol, saying, "Take mine, so you don't have to account for the use of your bullets." Turning to us, the Kapitän winked and said, "The paperwork is outrageous."

Abraham then stepped forward, good man that he was. Although in his thirties, he did not yet have a wife or children. His own parents, he hoped, were safe in France, having moved there with his twin brother and family almost ten years ago now. They had begged him to come a few years back when fears began mounting about Germany's aggression toward Jews. But he hadn't. After stepping forward, Abraham looked the Kapitän in the eye, hoping to see something human there. The Kapitän said nothing, just raised his hand in a signal to the soldier with the gun. Seconds later, a bullet pierced Abraham's head, and he dropped to the ground. In a sane world, many of us would have rushed to Abraham's side, if nothing else, to hold him in our arms, so he knew, on his path to eternity, that he had been loved, that his community cared for him. To have this, too, stripped from us, this human surge of compassion, was almost too much. Abraham ben Moises was left on the ground where he had fallen. On the way home that evening, four of us were ordered to pick him up by his arms and legs and carry him back to the ghetto so he could be dropped in the street where all could see him and learn what happens to disobedient Jews.

Abraham ben Moises remained stinking in the street for weeks. Every time we were lined up to march to the factory, we had to pass him. I saw that most of us avoided looking at him, but one could not avoid the stench. Matka was particularly angry—at the German soldiers, our Christian neighbors who collaborated with them, at Abraham for returning, and at God, most of all at God Himself, who not only allowed Abraham to be shot but countenanced this desecration of his corpse. And then, of course, there was always the lingering complaint against God for taking our Mila.

Abraham may have been the final straw that moved my parents to action. What if that had been me in the street, they asked themselves the night Abraham had finally been removed? Even the German soldiers had begun complaining and so rounded up some Jews to dig a hole in which to bury him outside the ghetto. We heard that the gravediggers had dug the hole too large and, as a result, were themselves shot and kicked into the hole so that their work should not have been wasted.

What if it *had* been me ... or would *someday* be me? I, too, was preoccupied with those thoughts. We had kept our spirits up, imagining that the war could not last much longer. Always *not much longer*. But the more evil and death we witnessed, the more the last drops of optimism dripped from us as honey from a honey jar, the closer we came to that state we could not talk about, when hope would be entirely drained from us, taking with it our humanity. I still prayed to God to be saved, but no longer knew what He wanted in return. He had my faith, yet that was not enough. He had my obedience, yet that was not enough. If sacrifices were what He wanted, He had my sister and so many more of His people. Yet all of it was not enough. What could I give that would be enough? What could any of us give?

Matka spoke with Uncle Nat about getting me out of the ghetto. I was not privy to those conversations, but I could imagine the mix of desire and pain that would have crept into her voice—the desire to save me and the fear of losing me. A choice no mother should have to make. He told her about a doctor in the Infectious Diseases Hospital. He would make inquiries and said that was all he could do and did not want to know anything more about plans for my escape, should they solidify. The lessons of the ghetto were painful and long-lasting: keep your head in the sand and you had a better chance of survival.

We, too, had heard of this doctor, Dr B., but because we had heard, we were suspicious. What if we went to him and it was a trap? What if the truth was that he did not help in escapes but reported those who contacted him, who were promptly taken out of the ghetto and shot? Or perhaps he reported to the Germans only after the escape had been put into motion so that the Jew would be shot believing in the imminent joy of freedom. What were the chances that there was truly one who retained, in these terrible times and in this terrible place, the compassion and bravery necessary to help a Jew? Truth in the ghetto was slippery, and trust nearly impossible.

Yet trust we had to muster. Tata volunteered for a detail to go to the hospital and carry out the most recently deceased.

It was dangerous, as we knew he would also be part of the detail digging the grave and never knew when a German might have a *twitchy* finger and add to the corpses. But Tata hoped this would give him a chance to talk with Dr. B. I had not yet consented to being the cause for so much risk, but I could not bear to take away what little hope my parents still had. It seemed to lift their spirits that there might be a minuscule chance of saving their remaining child. I left the next day on my own for the factory while Tata headed to the hospital.

I got back to the apartment before Tata, and both Matka and I were questioning whether we had sent him to his death. I realized I was not ready to be the man of the family and prayed as ardently as I could that he would return. An hour or so later, Tata walked into our apartment, smiling.

"Yetta, come here and give your best guy a kiss," Tata spoke teasingly. He was obviously in high spirits.

"Sol! Jakob is right here!" As if Tata didn't know that. I've noticed that females don't seem to get teasing.

"So he is, so he is. That's good, as I have news. Sit. Both of you. Sit and listen. I was able to speak with Dr. B. When we got to the hospital, I didn't know what I was going to do to find him or how I was going to get away. But it all must have been part of Yahweh's plan, as the doctor was the one who met us and took us to a room where our unfortunate had been placed. As we began carrying bodies downstairs, I tripped and hurt my ankle."

"My Sol! Oh no! How will you be able to work with an injured ankle?" I knew what Matka was thinking. We received a stipend for our work, small though it was, and without it, and without the meal at the factory, Tata would become weak with hunger, catch an illness, and die. Matka tended toward worst-case scenarios these days, but who could blame her?

"Yetta, listen, just listen and let your mind rest. When I tripped, the doctor took me aside to tend to my ankle. That, of course, gave me the opportunity to talk with him. I was very scared, but I could see his heart, that it was not black like some others working with the Germans. I told him of our situation, the loss of our Mila, and our hopes for Jakob, and he said he would help us! In one week's time, Jakob must pretend to be very sick. I am to bring him to the hospital, where the doctor himself will admit him. He will have a plan in place, but we are to ask no questions, and we must have said our goodbyes before reaching the hospital's doors. It will be the last time we see each other."

At this, I could see the tears on Matka's cheeks, but her words were strong, without waver, words I will never forget: "This war will have cost me both my children. I will hold on to the fact that one still walks the ground of this sweet earth. For that reason I will be able to do as the doctor says. For that reason alone I will give thanks to God."

I was less sanguine. *We are to ask no questions.* To me there was something foreboding in those words. But perhaps he simply meant he had no time for handholding. We could accept his help on his terms ... or not. I would have to go along, though I could feel tears also welling up in my eyes. Now that I had a chance of escape, the familiarity of the ghetto, the nearness of my parents, even the known evils were like comforting arms, and the unknown, though it included freedom, was a frightening phantom.

23

SARIAH

Sariah did not have much time. There had to be a way to avert the course of action set in motion by the Senhora. Think, Sariah, think. There is a way; there must be a way. Baruch is my child. How do I exist without him?

Ana had attempted to remove Baruch from Sariah's arms after telling her he would be sent to the priest to be placed with a good family, but Sariah had not allowed it, squeezing Baruch so tightly he began to shriek. "I'll kill him before allowing you to take him from me," Sariah shouted with the adrenaline of the moment and to make herself heard over Baruch's crying.

Ana was surprised at how calm she felt. She stepped toward Sariah and placed her hand on Baruch's face, wiping away his tears. "Shhh, shhh, little one. You will be alright. Sariah, loosen your grip and give him your breast to stop his cries." Sariah did as she was told. Baruch settled onto her breast once again and suckled into a peaceful slumber in minutes.

"You will not kill your son, Sariah. We both know that. Don't make me take steps to force your cooperation. Were the

Inquisition to learn that I caught you practicing Judaism in secret, you would be taken to their cells, and Baruch, well, who knows what they would do with a bastard Jewish child."

"But it is not true, Senhora. You know it is not true! Would you truly lie in front of your Christian God?"

"Don't you mean *our* Christian God, Sariah? The Inquisition torturers would surely notice such a simple slip of the tongue. You can be certain that I would do almost anything so that my husband's son is far from our world and so that I could be certain Baruch, or whatever his new name will be, will never know his true father."

Ana asked for Baruch to be placed in her arms. "It is the only way, Sariah, that you can know your son is safe; there is no other."

Sariah knew she had lost, and so began bargaining. "Please, Ana, please may I at least be told where he will be so that I can know for myself that he is safe."

"Dear Sariah, if I were to tell you, even if I knew, which I don't, you would try to see him. You can't tell me you wouldn't because I know, were it I, I'd do everything in my power to see my child. You may think me a monster right now, but I am truly trying to do the right thing for us all. But no more talk. The decision has been made and must now be carried out. Hand me the little one."

Sariah thought to pray to Christ, but Baruch was being sent to a Christian family. Christ had no incentive to support her appeal over the interests of such a family. She could pray to the Jewish God, but she was even less certain to be on good terms with Him, having abandoned her faith since leaving Portugal and having had nothing to do with the Jewish community here. Except for Lina.

At the thought of Lina, Sariah's heart lifted a little. She felt that strange, small flutter in her stomach. That is where she would go. Ruefully, she handed Baruch to Ana, first kissing the rose birthmark on his cheek, feeling the silky softness of him, inhaling his baby freshness, while silently vowing to find him one day so she could know what path God had in mind for him when He allowed this conception, for she believed there had to be a reason that only God—whichever God—knew.

24
RACHEL

After the conversation in the garden, Eloise gave Rachel her time, entering her room quietly to tend to her needs—bringing her food, changing her sheets and towels, removing the mostly untouched trays of food. Sometimes Eloise would stand at the window and look out at the cemetery, all the gnarled, sprawling tree branches upon which Children were hanging and underneath which some of the older Children were reading books, before she stealthily left.

One day, Rachel stopped her and spoke.

"I would like to speak with Inés again, Eloise. May we go to the cemetery today?"

"Of course," Eloise quickly replied, pleased with the request and not wanting to give Rachel any time to reconsider. "It is a beautiful, sunny day and would do us both good. I'll give you a chance to eat and dress and return in thirty minutes."

As they walked together in silence, Rachel, deep in thought, Eloise took in the scent of honeysuckle, plucking a single bloom from a bush heavy with blossoms and sucking its liquid. Reaching the cemetery entrance, Eloise opened the gate and led Rachel past the front row of smaller markers to the larger tombs toward the back.

"The cemetery is so beautifully kept," Rachel remarked, almost wistfully. "Inés must spend a lot of time here."

"I do," Inés responded, having just come out of the Leblanc tomb. Eloise knew she would have been chatting with the cousins Myrtle and Michael Leblanc, who had died together following a mishap while climbing Mt. Aconcagua in Argentina.

Rachel, startled, turned, and looked at Inés, wondering how she could have appeared so suddenly. She must have been completely in her head, she thought, though at that very moment Rachel felt unable to think at all, the numbness and accompanying fog that set in after learning of David's death having only partially lifted. Blessed numbness, soothing balm that allowed her time to accept having so suddenly become a childless mother.

"She does that," grumbled Eloise, though she followed that complaint with a hug. "How are you, sister?"

"Well, thank you, sister. Busy as always." She turned to Rachel. "It is wonderful to see you again, Rachel. Tell me, what can I help you with?"

Her stupor lifting, Rachel answered, "I wanted to speak with you, Inés."

"Yes, I know. I'm so sorry to hear of your loss, my dear."

Which loss, Rachel thought. Eloise jumped in nervously, "Let's go sit and chat. Come this way." Eloise led the way past the exedra with its circular, high-backed benches made of stone that decorated the very center of the cemetery where Inés often gathered the Children for lessons and sharing time.

Rachel walked with the sisters, her mind now buzzing with questions. Who were these sisters? They seemed unearthly, and sometimes it felt as though Inés heard her thoughts.

"You know already that Eloise and I are sisters," Inés answered Rachel's unspoken question. In fact, we have many more sisters and brothers. Perhaps Eloise has mentioned the Keepers to you."

Rachel shook her head no as Inés gave Eloise a piercing look.

"Eloise and I belong to an ancient community called The Keepers of Story, who have prepared many special individuals to become Story Tellers. The lineage of Tellers is a great one—from ancient times, Homer, Sappho, and Ovid, to more recent, Nawal el Saadawi, James Baldwin, and Irène Némirovsky, to name only a few. But of course, each place and each time has its storytellers. You are chosen to become one."

"And yes, we will talk about David," Inés continued, though Rachel had said nothing. "But first, you must do something for us. In this life of inevitable pain, each loss allows us to make a choice—to hide from the pain, adopting mask on top of mask so that we can no longer recognize ourselves, or stand with dignity and open hearts and go where the pain leads. You have asked about the stones. Here is your answer."

Inés took a stone out of her apron pocket and handed it to Rachel, this time with the herbs that would unlock the story within. With that, Eloise and Inés allowed Rachel her privacy on the bench directly underneath the Oldest Oak covered in Spanish moss and Resurrection fern.

Inés, hear my tale. I, Michael Stephen Katz, was working with my father and mother in our family hardware store, preparing to close for the Sabbath, when four men entered the shop. My father called out that we would be locking up in ten minutes. I looked out from the stockroom where I was putting away boxes of nails and screws we had received that day and saw the four men, none of whom I'd seen before, looking down the aisles. Seeing no one else in the store, one of them went back to the front door and bolted it. At that point, I dropped a box of screws that made a loud clatter and rolled out onto the floor in the back of the store. My father, who was tired after a long day and even longer week, yelled at me to be more careful.

"Hurry, my clumsy son, and pick them all up, or we'll be late for lighting the Sabbath candles."

It was then I could see the burliest of the men—and they were all large—signal to the other three. Each took out a gun and yelled at my mother, father, and me to stay exactly where we were or be shot. Had we only known the outcome, we might have fought back, but we were still naïve. Even with all we had already heard about Jews disappearing, we believed in the goodness of others. What we couldn't believe was that we could be hunted down just because we were Jews.

My father told us to obey whatever the men told us, still believing it was a robbery. He spoke to them, saying, "Here is the cash register key. Take whatever you want and go. We will not get in your way."

But, of course, they were not after the money. One of the men grabbed my mother as my father yelled, "Take your hands off her! Harm her and you'll be sorry." I could see the man holding my mother look back at my father as if he were a pestering fly, raise his gun, and shoot him in the head. As the gun went off, my mother shook loose, screaming, and ran towards my father. Another of the marauding men raised his gun and shot my mother in the chest.

I was so stunned I couldn't speak or move. I'd always wondered how I might act under such circumstances. It's not that I was anxious to obey; I simply couldn't move. Two of them grabbed my arms and pulled me out the back door to the alley where they had parked a car. As I was thrown into the trunk, I didn't think of escaping. When my wits returned, I thought only of revenge. It seemed like we drove for hours as I was bounced against the rough interior trunk walls, leaving me bruised everywhere, but I knew when we stopped and I was let out of the trunk, where I was, and that it could have been at

most thirty minutes. We were at the solid waste treatment fa-
cility just outside town.

Immediately, they tied my hands and feet, and I was put
into a burlap sack. I found my voice and began screaming. One
of them hit me, and I lost consciousness. I remember nothing
more until waking up here, in the cemetery.

The Children's Chorus: God allows men and women to
choose evil. But that the shop should open the next weekend
with new owners, and no one speaks out! How is this to be
understood?

Rachel returned to her room with Eloise, again in silence. At
the door, Rachel told Eloise she wasn't hungry and would skip
dinner. Eloise didn't object, leaving Rachel to consider what
must be strange facts to absorb. Before closing the door behind her, Eloise said only, "I am close by if you need me. Don't
hesitate to call for me."

How could Rachel understand what she had just experienced? Who was Michael Katz? How could she know his story?
As she tried to remember, she realized she didn't know if she
had heard it or just thought it. Had there been a voice? She
couldn't remember one ... but how else could it have been
communicated to her? And what were those herbs? What special powers did they have? What *was* this new world? All of it
made her feel dizzy. Fuzzy around the edges. She had to admit,
though—it wasn't boring. For the first time in a long time, she
found herself paying attention. Wondering. A Story Teller?
And the dreams? Each time she had one, whether about Jakob
or Sariah, she felt their worlds more familiar. Did they play a
part in this frustrating puzzle?

She walked toward the open window and sat at her desk,

allowing the fluttering coolness to bathe her, gazing out at colonies and colonies of stars that, as she relaxed into the expanse of the evening sky, conscious only of her breath and the heavens, drew her through millennia, through the stars' lives, to other times and other civilizations whose people beheld the same dazzling expanse. How many Michael Katzes have there been? How many Davids? How many mothers, their eyes drawn to the heavens for comfort and wisdom, shed similar tears and asked the identical, unanswerable question: Why my child?

It was dusk, and soldiers suddenly filled cobblestone streets. Rachel watched as two of them entered a store and came out with a man, his wife, and a baby. In his hand, one of the soldiers held a tiny dreidel carved from wood. His power was frightening, and the man and his wife reacted accordingly.

"No, no!" pleaded the woman, holding the baby who, feeling his mother's fear, was beginning to cry. "Please, we are faithful Christians."

The soldiers only laughed. Rachel wanted to step in and relieve the tension of the situation, beg for their forbearance, but could only watch as one soldier grabbed the man by the arm and another the woman, causing her to lose her grip and scream, "Wait, my baby, my baby is going to fall." The soldier let the mother go, grabbed the baby, walked over to the shop holding the baby by his feet, and swung him into the shop's stone wall.

She wanted to look away. She had to look away but couldn't. She saw the blood on the stone and watched the mother fall to the ground in anguish. She ran to the baby lying still on the ground, picked him up, and cradled him in her arms, feeling the wet stickiness of the blood on her uncovered arms. She looked upon his face, miraculously unblemished but for a birthmark in the shape of an almost perfect rose, and shut his eyes.

A burning sensation brought her back to the present. Disoriented and in tears, she jumped up from her chair and ran to the bathroom. She knelt in front of the toilet, waiting for the vomit to come, willing it to burst forth, to flush out the bile, the pure evil of what she had just seen. But she couldn't force it from her body—had to live with it—though how could she?

She stood up, walked over to the sink, and looked in the mirror. A second face looked back at her from the mirror and she screamed but, turning around, saw no one. The face belonged to a man with brown hair and a scar across the bridge of his nose. She'd never forget that smirk, the wry upturn of his lower lip. Not a smile. No, it was a statement: "Watch for me; I'm coming for you."

Rachel looked into the mirror again, prepared to be defiant, but he was no longer there. Emptied of everything but her image, the mirror revealed to her, as if rearranging letters that had never made sense, the birthmark hidden beneath her hair, just below and behind her right ear. Small, almost unnoticeable, yet unmistakable. A rose.

Rachel showered but could still feel the baby's horrifying stickiness. She put on her pajamas and slipped under the bedcovers, afraid to fall asleep, afraid to dream, but too exhausted to fight it.

25
JAKOB

I awoke sweating. The weather had turned warmer, but that was not the reason.

It seemed my body was responding to the power of suggestion; I was supposed to be ill, to have a fever, and it appeared that I was, that I did. Today, I would be leaving the ghetto, leaving my parents, forever. It had to be forever, for I had seen that once outside the ghetto, returning carried unacceptable consequences. I still wasn't sure I wanted to go through with the plans for escape, especially not knowing what those plans really were. I'd spent the past week sleeping poorly as I imagined numerous scenarios ... all of which resulted in a bullet to my head.

Before I could arise, Tata and Matka were by my side. Together, we grasped each other's hands and prayed for the last time, announcing our faith in the One God who looks out for His people. Our eyes were closed, yet I knew the tears I felt on my hand were more than mine alone. Matka would not make it harder on me by being emotional, but she could not keep those few tears during the praise of God from falling. I couldn't know what she was thinking, but hopefully, someday, I would be a father and would understand the courage it took for her to give up her remaining child.

"We must hurry, Jakob. But remember, you are ill. Matka has made a small pack with food we have been saving for the past week to send with you. We will say nothing to anyone other than you are very ill and, if anyone asks, I will speak and say I am taking you to the hospital. When we arrive, you will do everything the doctor instructs you to do. In a few days' time, we'll announce your death. After the war is over, we will, God willing, find each other and rejoice in family and give thanks to the God of Abraham, Isaac, and Jacob for His mercy. If that is not to be, if we are to die in this ghetto, we will die with gratitude in our hearts for your freedom and for the knowledge that you will recite the Kaddish for your parents."

I tried not looking up while Tata was saying this. I couldn't allow myself to absorb the reality of these last moments together. I had to hide all my emotions deep inside, or I wouldn't be able to do what we were planning to do. I gave Matka a kiss and allowed Tata to put his arms around my shoulders to help me, sick in my heart if nowhere else, on the walk to the hospital. Our neighbors watched as Tata held me up, saw my tears and my red cheeks, and could think only one thing: this family has been abandoned by God. These poor parents will lose both their children.

As we arrived at the doors of the hospital, we were greeted by a nurse who went to find Dr. B., instructing us to sit on the front steps and wait. I took in the world around me, aware that I would never see it in the same way again. While a prisoner, the sky always seemed to be grey, the buildings grey, the ground grey, the pallor of our skin grey. Color had been stripped from this world. How had the Germans accomplished that? The only color I would remember was the red of the blood spilled by my brothers and sisters in strife and the blue of my sister's lips as she lay dying.

Soon Dr. B. arrived, recognized my father, placed a hand on my forehead, and said to the nurse, "Take this boy to my office so I may examine him; I will be there shortly." Tata looked at me and, with a flick of his head, motioned for me to leave him. He turned and headed back to Matka. That quickly, I knew what it felt to be an orphan.

I had been in the doctor's office only long enough to make a brief survey of my surroundings. There was a desk with an abundance of papers on it, a chair, and an examination table. The hospital was not large, and I presumed each space had to suffer multiple uses, not unlike our own apartment. Dr. B. opened the door, walked in, and hurriedly shut the door behind him.

"We will not have much time. You must listen very carefully and do exactly as I tell you." The doctor's eyes looked exceedingly tired. I imagine he'd seen much suffering. What would it be like to be a doctor whose only role was to speed the movement of bodies from a ward to a mass grave? He continued, "Let me see the pack you brought with you."

He took the pack that had been stowed underneath my clothing, which was tied to my body with strips of cloth and removed some of the food to make room for items he added to the pack. At first, I was angry! My parents had sacrificed to provide that food for me. But then he explained, "Here are two packs of cigarettes." He broke into a half smile seeing my surprise as he stowed them in my pack. "They are not for you. You will use them to bribe others to help you. You will have to use your wits if your escape is to be successful." He took out a knife from an instrument drawer in the examination table. Adding it to the pack he said only, "This will be the only weapon you will have. I hope you will not have to use it." He rewrapped the pack around my torso and gave the final instructions.

"I will report that you entered the hospital on this day suffering, like your sister, from the typhus, that the disease was too far along to do anything, and you died in my office. We will wait until the end of the day at which time I will have a worker carry your body to a cart filled with the day's dead, and you will be taken along with them to be buried."

At this I flinched, fearing being buried alive! But the doctor placed a soothing hand on my arm. "Don't be afraid. These graves are not covered with dirt until the morning, when those who have died overnight have been added. Nevertheless, there is danger involved. The worker bringing your body to the cart will know you are alive. Him you can trust, but no one else. Once you are in the cart you must not give yourself away. You cannot move a muscle, not to scratch an itch, not to cough, not to cover your nose to escape the stench. After you have been dumped in the grave," he stopped, looking at me almost apologetically at having to use such stark language, "you must wait until dark and only then climb out. Head directly for the woods. There are farmhouses at the far end where you can seek help. Be very careful. This will be the most dangerous part of your journey, as there are German soldiers throughout the woods looking for Jewish escapees. That is a lot to remember, I know. Prepare yourself."

As he walked out, I heard Dr.B. utter under his breath, "May this damned war end before we are all its victims."

Sitting in the doctor's office, I was filled with fear. I jumped when I heard footsteps outside the door. I jumped at the sound of a mouse scurrying across the floor. I played out scenarios in my head as I considered the doctor's words and trembled at the risk I was taking. The doctor wouldn't be able to save me if I were found out at any point on the way to the pit. He would deny having been involved. And if I couldn't stop shaking now, how would I be able to remain completely still in the pile of bodies? Was it too late to run out of the office and return to the flat? Imagining Matka's and Tata's eyes as I walked into our room answered that question for me. I couldn't disappoint them now. I knew they were only able to continue knowing they could pray to God for my safety at the beginning, middle, and end of each day. Without the hope of my escape, the hope of not having to live with the very real fears of an aborted lineage, they would be lost. My escape meant more to them than to me.

Perhaps I dozed, for the door flung open and I had to catch myself from falling out of the chair. A very tall man spoke quietly to me, telling me everything had been prepared. He would carry me out of the office on his shoulder and place me with others on a hospital cart. He would do his best to cover me with other dead bodies so that if I moved, I would not be noticed, but once we left the building, we would be thrown onto a wagon that would take us to the pit. That would be the most dangerous part, and he would try to distract the soldiers while the loading occurred. I must be vigilant not to make any sound even if hurt during the loading. Once again, he would arrange the bodies so I was mostly hidden. The last danger would be the unloading at the pit. He would not be there to assist in any way at that point.

Having finished his instructions to me, he pressed into my hand a crust of bread and some potato, and said only, "Godspeed." Then he picked me up, carrying me over his shoulder. I kept my eyes closed both as the easier way to appear dead but also so I wouldn't see the corpses in the cart on whom I'd been thrown. I tried to stiffen my arms and legs a bit to approximate rigor mortis, though such extreme impersonation was likely not necessary. Who of the living is comfortable lingering among the dead?

The stench was not as bad as the odor of bodies left decomposing in the street for weeks. I surprised myself at my steadiness of heart and mind. My fears proved to be worse than this reality. I remember when I was younger, Tata would tell me that God would be with me in all perils, and fear of the future was a form of faithlessness.

Suddenly, the cart lurched forward, and I could feel that we were being rolled through the ghetto streets to the pit outside the gate. The uneven, rocky ground shifted the corpses constantly, and I worried what would happen if the cart overturned. I could also hear the factory workers returning for the day, the guards admonishing them—*Schnell!*—and then, as we passed each other, one returning to the ghetto, the other escaping it, the guards joking that one day the factory workers would be taking the same trip as those of us in the cart. I imagined my father among them. I wished I could call out to him; I wished with all my heart that he could know I was in that very cart, very much alive.

At last, the wheels stilled, and soldiers began shouting orders to those, most certainly weak, hungry, and frightened Jews, who had pushed the carts through the streets of the ghetto. Carts tilted, and we were all dumped into what was newly dug ground. I tumbled as awkwardly as I imagined a dead body might, knowing my life depended on the authenticity of my performance. I must have done well as I was not discovered. Real fright gripped me as I heard the loud volley of shots and felt the tremor as the fresh bodies of those who had carted us here were added to our world of tangled limbs, branches, and roots, and I imagined all of us, dead and dying, connected by shared waves of energy rippling through the growing stillness of this eternal hell.

I waited what felt like days but what was more likely only hours to fight my way out of the pit. I should have been disgusted by what I was doing, climbing heedlessly on faces and breasts and all manner of body parts. I was learning that disgust had its bounds in this previously unimaginable world of unbounded horror and was reserved for only the most profane of acts, though I could not imagine what those might be, the threshold between acceptable and unacceptable horror constantly moving as I learned to bear incomprehensible evil.

I peered beyond the top of the pit, seeing no one in the

blackness of night. I climbed out and ran from the lip of the pit to a wooded area outside the city. I had never been good in races at school, but then I hadn't the thin build and motivation I had now. It felt as though I flew over the uneven terrain in the sight only of God (I prayed) and arrived in a wooded area, throwing myself to the ground at the base of a tree.

There I sat, hearing nothing, though we had all heard in the ghetto that soldiers roamed the area outside the city at all hours looking for what they called "ghetto leakage." I lumbered further into the woods and away from both the ghetto and the surrounding city until I found some bushes that I could burrow into and made a bed of leaves where I felt safe for the moment. I was certain I would never fall asleep under such circumstances but had only begun my prayers when I lost consciousness.

I had no idea how long I'd been sleeping when I was awakened by what sounded like the braying of a donkey. If only it had been so. The voices I heard next were clear, so near were they. I was, thanks be to God, completely hidden within the bushes and so could watch the horror as it unfurled.

"Ah, a little Jewish boy out in the woods looking for Grandmother's house, is it?" This from the German soldier who had at gunpoint a boy, skinny and in rags, who could have been no older than I.

"I—I—I am not a Jew," the boy stammered. "I—I live in a farmhouse just on the other side of these woods."

"Oh, is that so," the soldier spoke placatingly. "Well then, tell me, what is your name, and what are the names of your parents?"

The boy stammered again but began to gain confidence in the fact that he had not immediately been shot. "I a—am Friedrich. I don't live with my parents; they were killed last year. The neighbors took me in."

"There are so many kind people in Poland. Perhaps I will move here after the war." I became angry with the German's tone as I knew he was leading this poor boy on, though to what end I did not like to imagine.

"Well, I believe you, of course. I can tell you would not lie, but I have orders and would get in real trouble if I didn't follow them. You wouldn't like me to get in trouble now, would you little ... Friedrich?"

The boy simply shook his head, looking down at the ground. The German had placed his rifle against a tree.

"So, Friedrich, my orders are to have any boy found in the woods drop his pants and show his uncircumcised penis. You would have no problem doing that for me, would you?"

At this, I saw the boy's shoulders fall. I was surprised not to hear him cry. Instead, he seemed to become almost more confident. Perhaps it was the inevitability of what would come next. Knowing his fate brought with it a courage. Even in my hiding place, I could understand. I watched as the young boy's fingers deftly untied the rope holding up pants that may have once fit but no longer, looked up into the German's face with undisguised defiance, and let his pants drop.

The German broke into a big grin, reached forward, and flicked the boy's circumcised penis with his forefinger. The Jewish boy remained rigid, waiting for the soldier to pick up his rifle and shoot. He was ready to leave this world, believing that God would be with him; this he relied upon for his strength. But as I remained hidden among the scraggly bushes, skin torn in spots by the sharp branches, I saw the German take out his knife and, to my eternal shame, watched and listened as he said, "It appears your Jew doctor did not complete the task at hand. Let me help." With that, he sliced off the boy's penis.

I gagged but somehow found the wherewithal to remain silent. The boy could no longer contain his tears, so great was his pain. He fell to the ground, his hands covering his wound, and pleaded, "Please kill me! Please, I'm begging you, shoot me!" The soldier walked away, saying, "I won't waste the bullet. You won't last long, filthy Jew-boy. Don't worry."

This was it; the threshold crossed.

Before I gathered the courage to leave my place of hiding, the mutilated boy's sobbing had stopped. I prayed to the Almighty alternately for the boy's healing and his release, knowing I would not want to remain on this earth in the same condition. When I crawled over to him, I could see that God the All Merciful had taken him. Though not a relative, I said *Kaddish*; who knows if he had a male relative still alive to do so.

Returning to the bush where I had hidden overnight, I grabbed my sack and looked for a farmhouse where I might be received. I couldn't get out of my mind the scene I had just witnessed. I had seen cruelty before, but not pure evil. In what world did people, did brothers, treat each other so? As much as I tried to wipe the image from my mind, the knife flashed before my eyes again and again, and each time I reached down to my own genitals, wincing in imagined pain. By a stroke of luck, for I was no more valuable to God than any other, I had not been found. Had I been found, and my penis exposed, I realized I could have experienced the same fate as Friedrich. Again, I gagged at the slicing and wondered how God, who was omnipotent, could allow such a thing.

It was then that it occurred to me. I remembered jokes during gym about Jewish boys: "They cover their head on top but leave their head below bare!" It bothered my friend Janusz enough that he researched and found a way to reverse a circumcision. We'd never tried it, as it seemed barbaric and painful, but then, we never *had* to. The idea was to stretch the loose skin of the penis so that it would naturally cover the head and use string to keep it from retracting. According to Janusz, over time the skin cells would create adhesions keeping the new skin in place. Now. Now, could I do it? I might be able to live a normal life like other Polish boys through the remainder of the war if it worked.

The thick woods were quiet except for scrub jays, the meanest of birds, appropriate for this place and time. I hoped I had put enough distance from the ghetto that soldiers were not patrolling here, though I knew not to let my guard down. I found a place to sit while I cut the rope holding up my pants, unraveled it to create thinner strands that I could more easily manipulate, then pulled down my pants to just above my knees. I worked quickly, making a slip knot on one end of the string, and, without giving myself time to question what I was doing—would God consider this act a violation of the covenant with him?—or the pain it would cause, I pulled at the loose skin so that it extended beyond my penis head, placed the slip knot around it, and pulled it tight while leaving a small opening for peeing. It took a few attempts and some dexterity, but soon enough, it appeared to stay in place. I raised my pants, retied the rope around my waist, and searched for a farmhouse.

Nearing a village, I assumed patrols would increase and so became even more cautious. Whenever I heard a noise, I scrambled quickly into a bush. As a result, I was scratched and bruised all over and could feel the friction of the string around my penis scraping the skin. This caused a hot, burning pain, but I believed the abrasions would enhance the creation of adhesions, and so I was almost cheered by the pain. It didn't take long to find a good spot where I lay down to sleep through the darkness, wrapping my thin coat around me for the cooler dark hours of the night, hoping I would not be plagued by nightmares of Friedrich's fate.

Next I knew, the sun, and not a nightmare, woke me. As I stood up, brushing leaves and sticks from my clothing, a wave of pain rose from my groin. I also had to pee, which, given the pain, frightened me. Pulling my pants down, I looked and saw that the string had rubbed my penis raw, leaving a red, swollen, bloody patch where it was tied to me. Just touching myself almost made me scream, but still, I had to pee, so I took care in directing the stream, then wiped myself with my shirt. There was nothing to do but pull up my pants and walk.

The sun beat down, causing perspiration to gather in the creases of my skin. As cool as I had been during the night, just so was my warmth during the day. I ate the last piece of bread before heading out and knew I needed to find some water to replace what the sun leached from my body. I tried to pick up my pace but became dizzy and weak. It was then that, almost like an oasis, I saw a farmhouse. Approaching it, I could see chickens, two goats, and a cow in a pen, but would I be welcomed, or would the farmer turn me over to German soldiers? For every Polish resister, there were two Polish collaborators. I had come so far, so many had sacrificed to get me here that I felt a responsibility to be careful, to know these were good people. As it turned out, I had no choice. My strength abandoned me as I tripped and fainted on the steps to their porch.

When I came to, I was on a sofa inside the front room of the small farmhouse. From the couch I could see family pictures on a table next to the door: a couple and a young boy in one, and the same boy, older, milking a goat and looking back at the camera with a huge smile on his face in another. Pillows embroidered with hearts sat on the chair across from me. As I surveyed the room, a man with greying hair entered. I tried to raise myself to be ready to bolt if I needed to but found I could not easily do so and groaned with the effort.

"Stay down," advised the man. "You haven't the strength to move about. Don't worry; we are no danger to you." He handed me a glass of water. "Here, drink this slowly; I'm sure you're parched." I took the glass gratefully and drank deeply.

A woman entered the room with a bowl and washcloth, placing them on a small table next to the couch where I was still lying, then moved a wooden stool close to it. She wet the washcloth, asking, "May I wash you off a bit? It will make you feel better." At my nod, she wiped my face first, then lay the cool cloth on my forehead and asked, "Are you hurt anywhere?"

How could I answer that? I was fine except for my penis, which I feared had become infected the pain was so great. "Thank you for the cool cloth. I am tired, is all."

"I will get more cloths, then, and some bread and jam if you are able to eat."

"Thank you, that would be wonderful." I hadn't had much food since beginning this journey and hadn't had jam since ... well, for a very long time. The thought of the sugary sweetness distracted me for a moment from the potentially dangerous situation I found myself in. As the woman went into what I guessed was the kitchen, the man, who had been standing nearby, sat in the chair across from me.

"I am Wilhelm, and my wife is Helga. What is your name?"

"Jakob."

"It's good to meet you, Jakob. These are not the times to be wandering by yourself in the countryside. How did you happen to come here?"

I didn't know whether I could trust this Wilhelm or not ... but what choice did I have? I decided to put myself in God's hands and tell him my story. Wilhelm was quietly attentive throughout. When I mentioned the Rabbi's death, he looked pained himself. When I told him of losing our home, he lowered his eyes as though feeling shame for what was being practiced upon our people. And when I told him of Mila, he swore under his breath. Finally, I told him the story of my escape with the help of the doctor. I did not yet mention the barbarity I had witnessed in the forest and did not know if I would ever be able to.

"I am sorry for all you have had to endure, Jakob," he responded when I had finished. "These times are an aberration, I like to think, in God's plan for us all, and all we can do is act according to our principles, keeping God in our sights. But not all can do that. May I ask ... how old are you?"

"Sixteen," I responded. "Or maybe seventeen."

Wilhelm reached over for the photo of the young man milking the goat. "This is our grandson, Peter. He is sixteen now." He looked to be inspecting the photo for something but soon raised his eyes and said only, "We have not heard from him in months. The Germans came through here and took him away to serve in the army. He was able to get two letters to us before they stopped. Each night we pray that he is well." He put the photo down and changed the subject, but I could tell worry over his grandson's fate dominated his thoughts, as I imagined my fate occupied my mother's and father's.

"Let me ask while Helga is in the other room, as your hesitation made me think you were uncomfortable talking about injuries in front of her, though perhaps I am wrong. Are you injured? You are perspiring, and it is not hot in the house."

I was grateful for his question, as I worried about my injury and had not wished to bring it to the attention of his wife. "Yes. I am afraid I may have an infection."

"Let me see," he spoke slowly but with an earnestness that conveyed his concern.

"Please, you cannot tell anyone," I pleaded with him as I untied the rope holding up my pants and exposed my groin. I looked down at my penis and cried out at the sight. It was swollen and reddish-purple with apple-green ooze coming from visible sores. The string was intact, making it obvious, I thought, what I had been trying to accomplish.

"Dear Jakob, what have you done? What could make you do such a thing?" Wilhelm asked this without expecting me to answer. "Stay still and try not to cry out. First, we will have to remove the string that is cutting into your skin."

He wielded a small penknife to cut through the string, but the sight of it in the proximity of my groin reminded me of what I had seen in the woods, and I attempted to cover my penis with my hands, touching it by accident and could not help a small scream. Immediately, Helga came running into the room. Wilhelm grabbed her by the arm, leading her back into the hall where I could hear him telling her what I had done. He returned quickly and said only, "Helga will come with clean bandages and help dress your wound. You will not shrink from her."

After the dressing, Wilhelm gave me a small glass of home-made spirits and told me to sleep, which I did, momentarily relieved to have a roof over my head and people to care for me who didn't seem to mind that I was a Jew.

26
THE CHILDREN'S CHORUS

But then, we are all more alike than different.

27
SARIAH

Ana had not given Sariah much time to pack her things and leave. Sariah moved about as in a haze. Beyond the loss of Baruch, which pain was the greatest she couldn't grasp. The loss of her relationship with the girls? She was not even allowed a goodbye, though she supposed that was wise and in the girls' best interest. She was being forced out into a world she had no knowledge of, though she had been given some money to help her when she found a place to settle. Ana had arranged for Sariah to spend her first days as a servant for the priest in a neighboring town, who had been instructed to direct Sariah to help in Lima after a time of transition. And Ana had taught Sariah how to bind her breasts to help her milk dry up. Sariah was most confused about how she should feel towards Ana. Ana had saved her and fought to bring Sariah to Peru. How could Sariah hate that person? But could she love that person and hate the person who stole her baby from her? The conflicting feelings burned a hole in her soul.

The Senhora arranged for a carriage to take Sariah, along with the suitcase containing all the belongings she had in this world, which included the blanket Lina had sent for Baruch embroidered with delicate multicolored flowers, to the home of Padre Dominguez, a few hours' trip from Arequipa in the direction of Lima. Sariah was reminded of the journey from the port to the Pessoa home, a longer ride when all were tormented with fears of the unknown. Then she was mourning too many losses, so many she couldn't imagine there could yet be others in her life. But here she was, mourning again. If there was a God at all, He must be uncaring and narcissistic. Who else would require daily devotion and, in return, allow the pains she had borne?

They arrived at the estate of the Padre, a large two-story stone home surrounded by grape vines and olive trees. Sariah carried her case out of the carriage on her own and walked to the front steps of the home. Having heard the carriage wheels, the Padre had sent a servant to meet her. Miguel took the suitcase from her hands and introduced himself.

"Welcome, Señorita. I am Miguel, the Padre's handyman. I do most of the manual labor around the estate."

Sariah found her voice. "It is good to meet you, Señor Miguel."

"There is no need to call me señor."

"And no need to call me señorita. I am Sariah."

Miguel was middle-aged, with long curly brown hair, a pot belly, and a beard hiding a winsome face. He looked to be quite strong, but Sariah could also see a kindness in his eyes and hoped she would not have to fear him.

"As it will be, then. Sariah." Miguel had looked her over briefly and found her to be comely. The Padre had not said much about her, just that she would be spending a short time with them recovering after delivering a stillborn child. He had warned both servants, Miguel and his wife Rosa, not to mention the birth as Sariah had left that life behind.

"Let us go in. You must be very tired. I will take you to the guest room. Rosa, my wife and the Padre's housemaid, has set a tray with some food in there for you. You may eat or sleep as you wish. Tomorrow you will meet the Padre at breakfast in the dining room. He eats at nine am." Miguel hesitated a moment, then said, "We are happy to have you here with us, Sariah."

So began the next stop of Sariah's journey. And though Miguel seemed pleasant and the estate itself would likely be called beautiful, Sariah could not open herself to a curiosity that required an engagement with life. Whatever her journey might be, and wherever it would take her was, at this, one of her lowest moments, of no interest to her.

The next morning, Sariah made her way to the dining room where the Padre was already seated with a breakfast of bread, olives harvested from the estate, and cheese that Sariah learned Rosa made of milk from the goats the estate raised on the property.

"Good morning, Sariah," ventured the Padre. "I hope you found your bed to be comfortable."

Sariah curtsied and thanked the Padre for his hospitality.

"Of course, my child. I am happy to share the bounty that Christ has provided us, and especially for one in need. It is our duty to do so. Just so you know, Martín and Ana spoke well of you. They were both so sorry for the stillbirth you experienced. Let me add my condolences as well. None of us knows the reasons for the sufferings we must endure in this life. But we know we are loved by Christ and that the reasons will one day be made known to us. Now that is the last we shall speak of it. Come sit with me, my child. Are you hungry?"

Sariah was shocked by the word "stillbirth." She could not, of course, contradict what Ana had said, though she dearly wanted to. On the other hand, perhaps that was the best way to look at things now. Baruch was, indeed, dead to her, wasn't he? No! Her entire being burst with denial. Her heart could not abide that path. She would meet him again. She *had* to.

Regaining her composure, she replied, "Thank you, Padre. Rosa provided me with a wonderful plate of food last night. I am not yet hungry again."

"You will come to love Rosa's kitchen skills—and Rosa her-self—during whatever time you will be spending with us here. To the point, you are welcome for as long as you are contrib-uting to the well-being of the estate. We can use another hand around here to relieve Rosa of some of her chores. Talk with her. She will assign you your duties. And if you have any spir-itual needs, I want you to feel that you can come to me with them. I understand your situation as a New Christian and am available to you if you ever have questions. Of course, you will be expected to attend church and serve Christ as you promised to do when you were baptized. But I am speaking too long. Go, go! You will likely find Rosa in the kitchen now."

Sariah got up from her chair, curtsied again, said thank you, and hurried into the kitchen, anxious to meet this Rosa whom she hoped would become her friend.

Rosa was sitting at the kitchen table having her own breakfast of cheese and bread when Sariah entered. "Good morning, Sariah. I am Rosa, the Padre's housekeeper. I am very happy to meet you."

Sariah was uncertain how to act and so curtsied again. "Good morning. Miguel told me you prepared the meal for me when I arrived. I am very grateful. It was a long, arduous day, and I was very happy to have a bite to eat before I went to bed."

"But, of course, Sariah. And you certainly don't need to curtsy; save that for the Padre, though I believe, in time, he will also tell you it is unnecessary. We are very informal here. In the church, it is entirely different, and we often must re-member to pay him the respect he is due in the house of God. But now, sit down and tell me more about yourself before we talk of your duties. Here, have some bread and cheese. Would you also like a cup of tea?"

Sariah took the chair next to Rosa, already enchanted by her long, almost black braids pinned on top of her head, her dark skin, and deeply piercing brown eyes.

"My stomach is still recovering from the bumpy trip. Perhaps I should have waited last night before gobbling down the delicious meal you left for me. It's better that I don't add more to what is already troubling it."

"I am drinking an *emoliente* tea, which is very good for many things, including digestion. It is the toasted barley. The horsetail is also good for ulcers, though you are young and that is not likely the cause of your indigestion. Here," Rosa urged, "have a cup."

Rosa's knowledge of unfamiliar herbs excited Sariah. On the carriage ride to the estate, Sariah had played in her mind with how she would make a living once she left the Padre's estate. All she knew were herbs, but those she was most familiar with came from Spain, Portugal, and worlds to the east. To learn what was near would be very helpful. She took a sip of the *emoliente* and smiled. It tasted very much like a tea her mother would make.

"I am happy to see you smile," Rosa said. "It is good, is it not?"

"It reminds me of my home in Lisbon," Sariah answered. Her smile left as she remembered she no longer had a home in Lisbon. Or anywhere. It was too much, and she began to cry. Rosa pulled her chair closer to put her arm around Sariah.

"Tell me all you have held within, little one," Rosa spoke with a voice so soft and sweet. Sariah wondered that there were no children about, as Rosa's manner was of a practiced mother.

Sariah told Rosa of her life in Lisbon, of the joys of working in the shop with her father selling herbs, and of the fears of the Inquisition soldiers, even though her family had converted and were faithful Christians—this part she felt she had to fabricate. Telling of the deaths of her father and baby brother and the loss of her mother caused new tears to fall, and Rosa touched her hand with compassion. Sariah couldn't remember her own mother's hands touching hers in that way. Sariah also told of her gratitude to Senhora Pessoa for rescuing her from a dangerous future in Lisbon and told of the long and difficult travels with the Pessoa family to Peru.

"Whatever happened to your mother?" Rosa asked softly.

"She disappeared. I have never known, but she was broken by the events of that day."

"But that must have hurt you, little one. To have your mother abandon you even during such horror. *Especially* during such horror."

Was that a question? If so, it was one Sariah was incapable of answering. Sometimes, she believed, to continue putting one foot in front of the other required a purposeful blindness. In many ways, all of Sariah's senses had failed her since that day. The sounds of birds chirping, the smell and taste of fresh oranges bursting open on her tongue; she could not remember these things at all during the two years she had been with Ana and Martín. Until Baruch. *His* fresh baby scent, the feel of his soft cheek against her body as he nursed. These things she hoped never to forget.

Sariah continued, speaking only briefly of the circumstances causing her to leave the Pessoa home, never mentioning the rape and the birth of the second Baruch. Sariah felt drawn to telling more of the truth of her life to Rosa but could not yet wholly trust her.

Rosa listened without speaking. And even when Sariah finished, Rosa simply brushed Sariah's cheek with her hand. There would be time for more, but now Rosa had to explain to Sariah her duties around the Padre's estate.

Sariah accompanied Rosa to the market each week. They were able to take the donkey, Terco, with them. All donkeys were stubborn, Sariah supposed, but this one particularly merited his name. It was fortunate that the market was not terribly far, as Terco's obstinacy increased as the day grew longer and his pack heavier.

Sariah loved market days for the slow, quiet time it gave her with Rosa and for the opportunity to pick not only Rosa's brain but the wisdom of herbalists with whom they would speak at the market. Sariah was told by many that she had a natural affinity for herbs and could become a great healer if she applied herself. They also cautioned her, though, as healing only in the name of Christ was allowed, and even then, it could be dangerous. One healer, a Señora Esmeralda, told the story of a doctor who, even with his degree, was punished when his ministrations to a wealthy patrón's wife, who had bled too much during childbirth, weakening her so that she was unable to fight off the infection that set in days later, were unsuccessful. The doctor was exhorted to apply leeches and empty the poor mother of bad blood, but he knew that she had already lost too much blood and treated her instead with propolis and garlic to improve her body's ability to attack the infection. When she, at last, was blessedly relieved of her suffering and died, the patrón was distraught. In his grief, he blamed the doctor and accused him of being a tool of the devil. A worthy, Christian doctor would have saved her, he was certain. The last anyone heard of the doctor, he had been thrown in prison and left there to die. Señora Esmeralda followed this up with a warning closer to home.

"You are a Jewess, are you not?" she asked Sariah.

Sariah wondered how she could have known but replied quickly, "I am a New Christian. A faithful Christian."

"Yes, yes, of course. You can make those claims all you want, but the fact is that if you become a healer and you once fail in healing, the first accusation you will hear is that you failed because you are not a faithful follower of Christ. You cannot outrun your Jewish blood, you know. I know because I have Roma blood. Jews and the Roma—we share a similar heritage. We are the hunted and the outcast. Though we may try to fit in, it is important to remember that, at any moment, the acceptance we believe we have won by our good actions will be ripped from us. We were both born for loss. I can see in your eyes that you already know this."

"Come, Sariah, it is getting late," Rosa grabbed Sariah by the arm as she spoke. "We must start home before the sun goes down. Thank you, Señora, for your advice, but Christ will be with all of us in our travails if we are faithful. Good day."

As they tightened their purchases on Terco's back with the rope they had brought, Rosa whispered to Sariah, "Do not heed Esmeralda. She has had a difficult life and is bitter. She does not open her heart to Christ and, therefore, is not touched by his grace. But you have, so you have nothing to worry about."

Sariah appreciated Rosa's words but knew in her heart the truth of Señora Esmeralda's.

Before Sariah knew it, she had been at the Padre's for three months. Though Baruch was never far from her mind, the orderly routine of life on the estate with Miguel, Rosa, and the Padre had a beneficial effect on her. In the beginning, she would awaken from a nightmare not knowing where she was. Her screams would bring Rosa to her bed, where she would hold her until Sariah was able to return to sleep. Rosa never asked what frightened Sariah so, and Sariah never told her of the rape, though she replayed it in nightmares all too often. Even three months later, Sariah was fearful of trusting anyone. She had once trusted Ana, and it had cost her Baruch. The Padre heard the screams, too, and asked Rosa if there was anything he could do. Did Sariah need a blessing? He knew she would be reluctant to come to him and ask for one.

Later that day, when Rosa was at the market with Miguel along to help in purchasing a goat, the Padre took advantage of the solitude to call Sariah into the parlor. Perhaps she would be more open to discussing what was frightening her if no others were there.

"Sariah, my child, come sit next to me. I would like to have a talk with you."

Immediately, Sariah froze. It was in a parlor like the Padre's that Sariah's greatest shame had occurred. She took a deep breath, as Rosa had taught her to do when she was afraid and said a silent prayer to the Christian God for her safety. The Padre had never given her reason to be afraid before, she reminded herself. He was a man of God; she could trust him. But she couldn't. Even Miguel, with his soft, kind eyes, frightened her. There was only one man in her life whom she had trusted, and he had been taken from her in a single moment of violence. But that wasn't true, was it? Her father had not been taken from her; he had *killed himself*. He had abandoned her over his grief at the death of his blessed son. Why was she just realizing the anger she felt at him? Was there no man anywhere she could trust?

Sariah walked into the parlor and sat on a chair across from the Padre, but he motioned to the settee cushion next to him. "Sit here where I can hear you better, child." She got up and sat next to him, though crowding the edge of the settee.

The Padre could see that she was nervous and tried to speak to her comfortingly. "My child, are you happy here?"

Sariah answered, "Yes, Padre."

"I am glad, as I know both Miguel and Rosa enjoy your company and have said you are a hard and willing worker."

"Thank you, Padre."

"But I worry that you are not as comfortable with the situation as are we. I am aware that you have nightmares. Would you like to talk about them with me?"

Sariah hesitated for just a moment. The Padre was kind, but something in her was so taut; she did not want to risk opening a door behind which there was so much pain. She answered, "No," and could get nothing more to come from her mouth.

In a moment of sincere compassion for the hardships of her life that seemed to be following her like the fleas on stubborn old Terco, the Padre reached out his hand and placed it on Sariah's arm. Feeling his touch, Sariah screamed, pulled her arm away, jumped up and tried to run out of the room, knocking over a vase of flowers as she bumped into the coffee table. She was surprised at the magnitude of her fear. Her heart raced, sending a message she had no ability to counter: Get away from that man!

"Sariah! What is wrong? Where are you going? Please speak your heart to me!" the old priest begged.

Sariah heard only her name, so quickly had she picked herself up and run out of the room. Behind her she yelled, "Stay away from me!"

———

Sariah left the estate with few words. Rosa and Miguel, who had been so very kind to her, could not understand what had happened. Nevertheless, they packed some food for Sariah's journey away from them, to where they were not told. Sariah herself did not know until her feet chose a path back to Arequipa, back to Lina. Lina would have counseled her against coming back, but Sariah had no choice now. As her thoughts drifted to Lina, the tickle in her stomach returned. Lina, with her dark golden curls and small mouth.

Sleeping in the bushes away from the main road, wrapped in a light blanket, Sariah took longer than she expected to make it back to Arequipa, requiring her to scavenge for food along the way, and drink from farm troughs. With some trepidation as she arrived, she walked through the town to get to the home of Lina's family. It was mid-morning, yet the cobblestone streets were already filled with people. Sariah knew she would shock Lina and her family, arriving, disheveled, on their doorstep with no notice, but again, she had no choice. She sighed, exasperated at having to explain so much away with the phrase "had no choice." Would the day ever come when choice was hers?

The sun was overhead when she arrived at Lina's, excited, frightened, and completely at the mercy of their charity. It was Lina who opened the door. She hesitated a beat before grabbing Sariah by the upper arms and kissing her on the cheek. Perplexed, she asked, "Sariah! What are you doing here?"

Sariah could not tell if she was welcome or not. Lina's reception was less warm than she had expected. She responded, searching the ground with her eyes, "I ran away. You are the only person in the entire world I know and whose help I hope is still available to me."

Sariah laid it all out in one quick burst, as it had been welling up within her over the journey from the estate. Then she was silent and looked up, waiting for the invitation to come into the parlor or the kitchen or *anywhere* to sit with Lina and, casually, over a cup of cold milk and warm bread perhaps, sitting side by side on the sofa, discuss the future.

Still, Lina hesitated but, at last, asked Sariah into the parlor. There they sat together on the comfortably overstuffed sofa that was covered by a beautiful blanket expertly embroidered in flowers like the one Lina had made for Baruch. Remembering this, tears appeared in Sariah's eyes. Lina responded with compassion, reaching out and taking Sariah's hand to comfort her. The softness in Lina's eyes that Sariah had been longing for emboldened her to draw closer and, without thinking, place a tentative kiss on Lina's lips. Immediately, Lina pulled away and Sariah, not understanding the urge to kiss Lina, began to apologize. "Please forgive me, Lina.

I didn't mean anything ..."

Lina interrupted her, defusing the awkward moment. "It is, of course, wonderful to see you, Sariah. Daniel and I have wondered how you were faring. Surely you didn't walk from the estate! You must be hungry and tired. Come to the kitchen and we can fetch you a lunch. There's an empty room where you can take a nap and join us for dinner refreshed. There, all will be interested in hearing your story."

Sariah thanked Lina, promising herself she would not again make the mistake of assuming Lina felt the same as she.

Sariah fell fast asleep after eating a substantial lunch of bread, olives, oranges, and jerky. Lina told her just to rest, and she would come for her when it was time for dinner. Sariah awoke and waited in the room for Lina to come, gazing out the window while sitting at a little wooden table with a flower-filled glass vase on it. But she must have awoken early as it had been some time and Lina had still not come to the room. Bored, she arose and ventured out of the room, walking quietly down the stairs to see if she could help in the dinner preparation. Hearing voices from the darkened parlor, Sariah moved closer to the closed parlor doors and listened to the familiar rhythms of prayer. But these were not Christian prayers. Sariah heard the mention of "Sabbath lights" and knew immediately, as she had intoned the same prayers herself while living with her family in Portugal. It must be Friday! It's the Jewish Sabbath, and they are praying over the candles. But no! It is forbidden! How could they risk such a thing? She quickly and quietly withdrew and climbed the stairs back to the room in which she had been sleeping. Lina must find her there; she didn't want her to realize she knew their secret.

An hour later, when Lina knocked at her door for dinner, Sariah had fallen back asleep.

The bright morning sun woke Sariah the next day. When she realized she had slept through dinner and the promised discussion with Lina and her family, she was mortified. What must they think of her! More than anything she looked forward to telling Lina everything about her circumstances and, even more, to inquiring about Baruch. Perhaps Lina knew something of where her son had been sent. Was there a chance Sariah could see him much sooner than she could have anticipated? Might he still know her smell? With these thoughts, her mood changed from fearful to joyful. Oh, what a beautiful day this was! Her trek had borne fruit!

A knock on the door interrupted her reverie. "Who is it?" she called out.

"It's me, Lina. Are you dressed? Can you come down for lunch?"

"Oh, no!" Sariah's mortification returned. She hurried to open the door, asking, "Have I slept through breakfast?"

Lina laughed. "Breakfast *and* dinner. How tired you must have been! Don't worry. I'm glad you were comfortable resting here." She gave Sariah a peck on the cheek as if to say, all is forgiven. We are friends, and friends can share intimacies *within bounds.* "Daniel returned home for lunch. Come join us."

"I'll just be a moment," Sariah said, taking a minute to wash her face and pin up her hair before following Lina downstairs.

Lina led Sariah into the kitchen where Daniel sat at the table awaiting his lunch. Seeing Sariah, he stood up and greeted her, "Good afternoon, Sariah. I hope you are feeling well today."

"Thank you, Daniel, I am. Please forgive me for last night. I hope you were not all waiting for me to come down for too long."

"No, of course not. We were happy you were able to rest well." Daniel pulled out a chair for Sariah and then sat down himself as Lina went to the oven to take out the freshly baked bread for their lunch.

Returning to the table with their lunch, Lina set it down first in front of Sariah and then sat at the table. She began, "We have heard what happened with Baruch, Sariah. We have no child"—she looked over at Daniel with a palpable sadness—"so we can only imagine the immense suffering you have been forced to endure. I just want you to know how much I, we both, wish life had not been so unforgiving of you."

Sariah had been ready to tell her story, to seek comfort at the feet of an old friend and a new one but was startled out of her vulnerability by what she had just heard. "Unforgiving of you." What had Lina meant? For what did Sariah require forgiveness? Lina knew that she had been raped, that Baruch's conception was not her fault, if *fault* could even be a term applied to the miracle of a child's birth.

"Have I done something for which I need forgiveness?"

Lina looked over at Daniel again, who looked at the floor to avoid her eyes but answered for her. "Of course not, Sariah. You are blameless for Baruch's birth. God is the granter of life, and every life is valuable in His sight."

Sariah listened closely, beginning to understand. Lina was not referring to his birth; she was referring to how he would be raised. That he would not be raised a Jew. This was a delicate topic but one she could not avoid.

"I understand. I witnessed the Sabbath candle lighting last night. You believe I have abandoned my faith, and you are probably right. The Jewish God has done nothing but send suffering to my family. I honestly don't understand your fidelity."

Lina was not hurt by Sariah's words. She prodded gently, "Tell me, Sariah, how would your father respond to those sentiments? He who had the right to complain as much as anyone. Do you not believe that, in taking his life, he believed he was going to God?"

Sariah could not fathom what Lina had just said. How

could she know how her father felt at the moment of his death? In Sariah's eyes, her father had not sacrificed his life to be with God but to spite God. He could as easily have been saying, "You have taken my only son, and so I will remove myself, your once-servant, from this life and from serving you." But she did not say this. Lina and Daniel were all she had left, and she could not risk alienating them.

"Let us not talk of my father ... nor of Baruch. Except ..." Sariah could not lose this opportunity to ask about Baruch's whereabouts, "have you heard or seen anything of him?"

Daniel again spoke for Lina. "We know only that he has been sent to a wealthy Christian family in Lima who had no children of their own. He will not suffer, Sariah." He could not help goading her with his next statement, "And for that, you can thank God. Whether you thank the Jewish God or the Christian God. It appears Baruch, though that is surely no longer his name, will have rights to petition both."

Sariah again felt their lack of understanding. Daniel continued, "We wish you well, Sariah, but we cannot provide you a home as we once thought we could. The Pessoa family has put out word that anyone providing you a home would be accused as backsliding Jews. As you saw, this is a threat they could make good on against us and against many other New Christian families here. We will provide you clothing, food and some money but must ask you to leave in the morning. I suggest you head to Lima, where you may find work and a community that is able to help. I hope you will not continue to turn your back on your heritage, Sariah. No one can know God's mind except to know He is all-loving. We trust you will not share what you have seen."

Sariah no longer had it in her to beg. Lina had not looked up.

Daniel saw Sariah to the door the following morning, providing her with a pack filled with food and two containers of water. He told her he'd arranged for her travel in a wagon carrying goods for sale in Lima and gave her the name of the shop in town where the wagon would be found.

"They'll be waiting for you, but will not wait for too long, so you should not tarry getting there." He handed her a pouch with some coins. "Lina asked that I give you this. You must know that she loves you and is heartbroken that things have ended like this. Stay well, Sariah. Godspeed."

Sariah accepted the pouch and pack and walked away. She couldn't muster words of thanks, fearing what might come out of her mouth if she opened it. Her anger was a mix of feeling betrayed and something else, something she had yet to come to terms with.

Walking towards the town, Sariah relived all that had happened since coming to Peru, and though she tried to push away thoughts of Baruch, she could not. She remembered his sweet baby smell, holding him in her arms, the softness of his cheek against her breast, gazing at his rose-shaped birthmark as he suckled until she had to pull him off when her nipples became too sore, such a vivacious imbiber of life he seemed to be! She felt behind her ear where her own birthmark hid as she clambered through an overgrown patch of weeds. She could never forget him anyway, but this cemented their bond.

Sariah felt she had not tarried, but when she arrived at the proper shop, she was chastised. "Where have you been?" questioned the merchant. "We would not have waited upon you much longer. Jump in the back and settle in. The journey will be long. There is a blanket back there for the evening hours. I have been told to drop you off at the market before unloading our wares."

Sariah climbed up without help and made herself as comfortable as possible among piles of pots and pans and sheared lamb's wool. The lanolin smell was thick, and she looked forward to the cooler temperature when the sun went down. The heaviness of the load lessened the sway of the wagon, allowing her some comfort in which to consider what she would do upon arriving in Lima. She knew she would have to put the past entirely behind her if she were to have any future. Still, the question nagged at her: Who in the entire world would care if she died?

The trip went by more quickly than she'd imagined, as she slept and, while awake, spent much of the time in her memories, choosing the good over the bad as if fortifying herself for the time ahead. Arriving in Lima, she was dropped off at the edge of a large square that served as a market. She climbed out of the wagon, and without as much as a *goodbye*, the driver left her.

The day was cloudless and warm, the cobblestone streets covered in a sticky substance attracting flies. Sariah waved them away as she walked, taking in the atmosphere of the big city. At first glance, Lima reminded Sariah of Lisbon, large and bustling, with ships unloading cargo and carts filled with goods from faraway ports. She remembered her father's trips and the goods he would return with that became her job to weigh, bottle, and shelve. As she walked further, she was drawn towards the many stalls of fruits and vegetables surrounded by throngs of people and animals, dogs hoping for dropped scraps, and a colorful bird shooed away by a shopkeeper. The similarities quelled some of her fears, though the uncertainty of where she would sleep that night reignited them. The relative safety of an alleyway beckoned Sariah, promising a few moments at least for her to orient herself to her new home.

Shouts suddenly accosted her from out of nowhere. Turning in the direction of the clamor, Sariah saw a great crowd surging from the direction she had just traveled, moving as if a roiling creek past her toward the center of the square, where she could now see there were wooden posts installed in the middle of what looked like straw baskets. They resembled, she thought, a male organ pointing toward the heavens. How she wished God would come down from the heavens and destroy those poles. How she wished all men were robbed of that weapon. The thought was accompanied by guilt, however, for she had had a father and a brother and a son. All gone.

Sariah remained in the alley, seeking safety in anonymity and in the shadows. She watched as soldiers marched in columns of three ahead of four men and two women that she could count who were tied by the hands, bare-footed, with ragged clothing, prodded by rifles. These prisoners, she realized, were being marched to the posts where they would be tied, and their punishments carried out. She had heard of such events but never witnessed one. They would be burned alive, the burnings carried out by the Inquisition against heretics.

Sariah was frightened by the spectacle and would have disappeared on the periphery had her arm not been grabbed, pulling her forward toward the crowd. She was preparing to yell out, to resist, when a voice spoke in her ear, "You must be new here; follow my lead. It's very dangerous to fall back during the Auto-de-Fé." Sariah saw that it was a woman older than she who had grabbed her, dressed simply, her hair covered with a beautifully embroidered headscarf in reds and blues and golds. "Take my hand and follow me."

The boldness of the woman inspired confidence, compelling Sariah to obey. They pushed through the crowd and settled themselves squarely in the middle among many who were yelling and jeering—"Heretics!" "Burn the sins out of them!" The crowd noise allowed Sariah to question the woman.

"What are these people's sins that they are to be tortured like this?"

Turning to Sariah, the woman said, "You must not say such things to anyone. They would not call this torture but the judgment required by God to allow these sinners to enter heaven's gates. Stay close to me, and when it's over, we can walk to my shop where we can talk in safety."

Sariah had no desire to remain there, didn't want to see what so many others had gathered not just to watch, but to celebrate. The crowd was hungry for gore, growing quiet only when a priest appeared to lead the crowd in paternosters while the sinners were prepared. All six were stripped naked, revealing evidence of their time with the Inquisitors—bruises in a mélange of colors, evidence of broken bones that had not been set, a grey pallidness of skin that had not seen the sun for too long. Sariah was surprised to see the grey pubic hair of one of the women. Did they have no respect for elders? She wished to turn away, but every time she tried, she was nudged by the woman who had forced her into the middle of this unholy crowd. Soldiers were stationed throughout the crowd, watching for evidence of heretical sympathies.

Finished with the prayers, the priest moved from the front, and a quartet began to play hymns, presumably for the benefit of the sinners as their souls were relinquished to Christ to do with as He deemed just. Sariah saw that some of the sinners were strangled by garrotes prior to burning, while others were not so mercifully treated. As the fagots were lit with flaming torches, the crowd reacted with a rising tumult in a symphonic concurrence.

Immediately after the screams subsided, the crowd dispersed. The bodies would not be removed for as long as a week to fulfill their role as warnings to other heretics and backsliders, whether Jewish, Muslim, Roma, or natives. Sariah followed the woman back to her shop a few blocks from the spectacle. She gasped upon seeing it—a shop selling herbs and soaps! Sariah grabbed the woman's arm, wanting to tell her of her father's shop in Lisbon, but instead remembered the need for caution and drew back her hand, offering only, "Thank you for your help. I am Sariah."

"I am María," the woman responded, unlocking the door that bore a *Closed* sign and motioning Sariah inside. "All shops will be closed for the rest of the afternoon. They always are after an Auto-de-Fé," she explained. "It seems we are to reflect upon what we have seen. You will be safe here. Wait for me here a moment, and I'll get us cups of tea."

As María strode to the back room of the shop, Sariah took in the familiar sights—different-sized jars with herbs of various colors and textures, all artistically arranged and labeled. She felt as if time had doubled back upon itself in so many ways. First Baruch, lost to her twice, now the shop, appearing again as if resurrected. What she didn't know was whether this warp was one from heaven, whether it would offer her sustenance or more suffering.

María returned with two cups of tea and sat with Sariah on an old, plush, green couch in a corner of the shop.

"Have you had *emoliente* before?" Maria asked. Sariah took a sip and nodded appreciatively.

"There are various versions, depending upon the combination of herbs that are in the mix. The most common ingredient is flax seed, which helps with colon issues. Alfalfa leaves are sometimes used to purify the urinary tract, blood, and liver, and other herbs, like chamomile or lemongrass, can be beneficial because of their anxiety-calming benefits and soothing flavor."

Sariah listened intently before asking, "How is it that you know so much about these herbs and their medicinal uses?"

"I am married to a doctor who has taught me much. The shop is his, but I am the one who runs it."

Sariah shrank at the thought of María's husband entering the shop at any moment. María, seeing her reaction, reassured her, "My husband is much older than I and ill. He is unable to visit patients any longer, though they often come to our home upstairs where he can speak with them and tell them what herbs they should take to heal. As a woman, this is the only way I would be allowed to run the store. But now, tell me, what has brought you here to Lima?"

Sariah told a version of her life that she would prefer to have been the truth, for there was no one to call her liar, no one to deny her the reality she felt she was due. She left out the most unjust parts. In her tale, she was not a Jew, Inquisition soldiers had not made her an orphan, she had not been raped, and her son had not been taken from her. Yes, she had come from Lisbon, where her family also sold herbs, but her mother had died, and to explain why Sariah had not remained in Lisbon, she created a stepmother who did not like having her around. She had left to pursue a living in Peru as a nanny but, upon arriving in Lima, had been notified that she was no longer needed. She had just received that news when María came upon her in the market. Sariah told this story with no hesitation, as though it were true. Perhaps she even began to believe it herself.

María questioned who the family was who had abandoned her here in Lima, but Sariah could not tell her, of course, and said only that she did not believe it would be proper to expose their name under the circumstances. She wanted to put it behind her and look only to the future.

"But Sariah, what future do you think there can be for a woman alone in Lima?" questioned María, taken aback at Sariah's naïveté. "Come stay with us for the time being as you figure out what your next steps will be. Juan, my husband, will enjoy the company. Though he is ill with an exceedingly painful case of gout, he finds any diversion from the pains to be quite welcome. You will like him, I promise. And this way, we can get to know each other better."

As she said this, María stood up and, before taking Sariah's empty teacup, briefly but warmly placed her hand on Sariah's arm. "We have no children, and it can sometimes be a little lonely in the evenings with Juan spending more and more time sleeping."

28
RACHEL

Rachel spent more time in the garden, where she sat beneath the willow tree on an old iron bench, its back plaited with long-stemmed flowers and painted over in white. She would bring a book or her sketching pad or simply sit and watch the complex worlds around her performing in alternating spotlights of sun as if circus rings. Today she watched spider webs woven from blade of grass to blade of grass, threads catching the early-morning dew, providing the rising sun a playground of prismatic delights.

She tried to will away the returning despair. So tired. She wept every night for David, for her mother and father, and, yes, even Henry, and awakened each morning diminished, as though each tear were a drop of blood. What is this world? Earlier, Rachel had spoken these very words with great intensity; now they were uttered with weariness. She might as well have been living in an existentialist novel, where she could as easily have been a talking cockroach as a human being. She was going to say, "as a wife, a daughter, or a mother," but she was no longer any of those, was she.

Soon enough, Eloise walked into the garden, bringing two

glasses of sweetened iced tea with lemon. She particularly enjoyed the opposites of sweet and tart. Too much of one or the other and the tea was ruined. She took pride in the fact that she had mastered the combination. Sitting down next to Rachel, she handed her the glass.

Rachel took a sip. "Thank you, Eloise, that's perfect," she said.

Eloise beamed. "You're welcome, Rachel. What a glorious day it is today, though the humidity hints at rain, I believe. How was your rest?"

"Good, thank you. But, to tell you the truth, I've been having these strange dreams. They feel so familiar, and I don't know why. In one, a baby was smashed against a stone wall by some soldiers." Rachel shivered. "Why would I dream something so dark?"

Eloise had been waiting for this moment. "We can learn many things from whatever we may call these sights outside of our everyday experience of reality. I think of dreams as invitations—outward to a larger world and inward to our heart."

"These days I feel as though all I do is collect puzzle pieces and store them away for a time when that one missing piece appears, the one piece that is the key to it all, the one that completes the puzzle. I wonder how I'll know when I've found that piece."

"I don't know," Eloise hesitated a moment. "Maybe you don't need to know that now, though. Maybe just having the faith that when it appears you *will* know is enough."

They sipped their tea in silence until Rachel did her best to stifle a yawn, then laughed and said, "Well, maybe I need to take a walk before this drowsiness overtakes me and I sleep all my problems away, as enticing as that may sound. Would you like to join me for a walk in the cemetery?" Rachel asked this of Eloise, hoping she'd say yes. Since hearing the story of Michael Katz, she hadn't mustered the courage to return, afraid another blow to her already disordered sense of reality might widen the newly emerged crack and cause the entire facade within which she had lived all her life to crumble. Then what would she do?

Entering the cemetery, Eloise and Rachel could hear a violin playing a happy tune. Ambling toward the music, they arrived at the exedra and found the Children sitting in a circle engrossed in the playing of one of the Ancestors. In fact, Eloise recounted to Rachel, it was Auntie May, who had been quite the musician in her day. Just a few days earlier, Rachel would not have been able to wrap her head around the truth growing within her as if she had swallowed an acorn that was extending its roots. A cemetery in which the dead were alive!

One of the Children saw them enter and blurted out, "Oh look! A visitor!" and jumped up to greet her, almost knocking into her before restraining himself.

"That's our little Markus," Eloise remarked. "We try to teach manners, but ..."

Many of the other Children followed Markus' lead once they saw that Rachel was welcoming of them. Auntie May put aside her violin a bit grudgingly and trudged off to her tomb. A few of the Ancestors hung about, interested in Rachel and how she would react to this world for which her rational mind had no vocabulary. For her part, Rachel did her best to shed her natural skepticism. Eloise marveled at the progress Rachel was making and wished Inés had been there to see it.

The Children gathered around Rachel, asking question after question: "Do you know my mother, Pearl?" "How many Children do you have?" "What's your favorite fairy tale? Oh, please tell us one!" It wasn't until Inés finally appeared that the Children dispersed and allowed Rachel, Eloise, and Inés to chat in some privacy.

"Visitors are a rarity, Rachel. As you can imagine. Please forgive the Children if they were a bit ... exuberant," Inés explained. "Really, Eloise," she gently scolded, "you should have told me you were going to come by."

"Oh, please, Inés, don't blame Eloise. It was my fault. I felt the need to get out and talked Eloise into it. In any event, it was a treat to hear the violin and to meet the Children."

"I am happy for that, Rachel," Inés said. "You will find the Children at times charming and at times nuisances. But I have just defined *children*, haven't I!" Becoming more serious, she asked, "Do you have anything you'd like to talk about after your experience here a few days ago?" She was, of course, referring to the stone and Michael Katz's story.

"Yes." Rachel hesitated. "I don't really know where to begin. I have so many questions. But I guess I wonder most if the story was real. And the pile of stones ... do they contain other stories? Are they all real?"

Inés's eyes crinkled in a half smile, half grimace. "There are, indeed, many stories locked in the stones. You can hear them because you have been chosen and prepared to hear them. I can't tell you what is real and what isn't, but you will know by learning to trust yourself." She saw bewilderment in Rachel's eyes and said only, "We each have the wisdom of the universe within us. Now, Eloise, can you help me with the Children's lesson today? Let's gather them over by the fountain and let Rachel have some moments alone."

As they left, Rachel wandered along the cemetery paths. It could have been any cemetery anywhere now. A ponderous silence engulfed it, broken by the occasional chirp of a bird or scurrying of a squirrel.

Though she believed she'd been wandering aimlessly, she saw she'd returned to the pile of stones. She sat on the bench under the Oldest Oak and yielding to her curiosity, reached down to pick up the stone nearest her. Impulsively, she rubbed it with herb residue from her sweater pocket and heard: "Inés, hear my story. I, David Phillip Latter-Reid ..."

Recognizing her son's voice, Rachel threw down the stone as if it burned her hand. She would not hear it! Not his! Not yet. Please, she thought, let me pretend just a little longer that the last tether to my old life has not been cut. A branch cracked as the Oldest Oak registered her wish.

***

Before Henry could leave, the Righteous came for him. Why would they not? David had put a bullseye on his mother's and father's backs when he joined the Resistance. It had just been a matter of time before being discovered. Had David known that? If he had, how could he have endangered them, too? If he hadn't, how could he be so naïve?

Henry remembered the conversations he and Rachel had had about having children. They'd discussed many things. He remembered her asking, "What kind of a world is this to bring up a child?" And "Am I selfless enough to put my child before myself?" Henry had added to the pile of pick-up sticks, asking, "Do we trust that we have the wisdom to teach a child what they needed to know to thrive?" The more questions they added, the more perilous the balance of the pile until the sticks all came tumbling down, and they decided against children. Nevertheless, five years after they'd married, with a mind of his own, David had been born. And with a mind of his own, David had left the earth and now perhaps would take with him both parents.

Henry was doing his best to avert that outcome. He'd done what he could, with David's help, to keep Rachel safe. He'd assented to Maura running the gallery alone for a while— "How long, Henry?" she'd asked. He didn't answer but saw the glimmer in her eye as she gloated at her good luck. Now he would finish what little packing he could afford to do within the time he had and hurry to the light rail station. No, Henry thought while stuffing important papers and books into his briefcase, he could never regret having brought David into this world, even if the effect of that was the loss of his life. Being a father had taught him more about love than being a husband had. He thought it may have something to do with that little bit of self he and Rachel had refused to share with the other. That wall that thickened over time.

Grabbing his large suitcase, his briefcase, and his umbrella, Henry took a final look around the house, doing all he could to consign it to memory, the good and bad memories of the average marriage, before heading into the garage. Henry opened the back door of his car, placed the bags on the seat, got in, and simultaneously turned on the engine and pressed the button to open the garage door. Looking in his rearview mirror to back out of the garage, Henry saw he was too late.

"Take him to cell number eight," he heard through the heavy cloth bag that had been placed over his head at the same time his hands had been tied behind his back. Trying to speak had only resulted in blows from a club of some kind, so he quietly consented to his imprisonment.

"Tie him to the chair and leave him there." Henry heard the orders, presumably from a superior officer to a junior. "The doctor is busy but will come to greet you as soon as he can." This must have been to him. "Did you hear me, Jewish pig?"

"I'm not Jewish!" Henry cried out.

The reply came in the form of blows to his back and shoulder. "You don't open your mouth unless asked a question."

"But you *did* ask …" The blows returned, along with laughter, until Henry heard door hinges squeak, followed by silence.

He had no idea how long he'd been in the cell before hearing the door open, followed by, "So, this is the father of one of our most illustrious Jews. I can't tell you what an honor this is." Henry remained silent, having learned well.

"Come now, you can talk to me." The speaker walked

closer to Henry and removed the stifling bag over his head. "So good to meet you. Henry, isn't it? Henry Reid? Father of David Latter-Reid? Well, wait a minute. You *were* his father is more appropriate, I suppose. David being dead, that is. I know you Jews are very attuned to language."

Henry kept his eyes to the ground in front of him. He didn't even want to see this vermin, this ... what? How dare he speak of David's death so cavalierly? Did he have no children, no loved ones himself, to understand the pain?

"You may think of me as your rabbi. I am here to receive your confession and to learn of the whereabouts of your wife, Rachel."

Henry looked about him, and seeing no soldiers and no bats, he spoke. "I have no rabbi. I'm not a Jew. And I've nothing to confess."

He heard laughter. "Oh, you have things to confess, alright, and I'm happy to be whoever you need me to be to receive your confession. Why, I could even put on a clerical cassock and collar if you'd prefer. And you can call me Dr. Kurtz. For what we have in mind for you, a doctor is much more fitting."

Henry knew he wouldn't last long under torture. He wondered what David had suffered and how he'd stayed strong, as he must have, or they'd already know where Rachel was.

"Now, Henry, the soldiers will be back in a minute to undress you and strap you to the table." Dr. Kurtz looked at David's father and knew this one would break easily. After so many interrogations, so many tortures, the signs were easy to read. The doctor could almost guess to the minute when they'd break.

He walked out of the room and motioned for the two guards to come in. As they passed him, he turned to the first one, handed him some cash, and said, "Put me down for four minutes."

The doctor lost his bet, as Henry gave Rachel up before the

first electric shock to his testicles. All he'd had to do was turn on the cattle prod at a low voltage and touch Henry on the arm. Not even two minutes. Henry told the entire story of how he and David had hidden Rachel, of the house, of Eloise, of the cemetery, all the names he knew and some he made up to provide a more realistic and juicier tale. In return, Henry was promised his safety and release when Rachel was found. Much more important to have the mother, the doctor thought. Her blood is the carrier.

"You'll take us to her tomorrow," Dr. Kurtz told Henry after he'd been allowed to dress. "And stay in this cell tonight," he said, pointing to a metal cot without bedding. "Sleep well."

Before leaving for Rachel's, Henry had provided an address, but the Righteous had been unable to find it on their digital map of the city. The warning came with a blow to his left knee that was placed to avoid breaking a bone while achieving the pain desired. "If you're lying to us, you can expect to return here for some lengthy interrogation sessions."

"No, I swear to you that's where she is. I'll take you there, I promise!" Henry hated himself for his cowardice, had always resented Rachel for recognizing it in him. The knowledge lit a fuse of anger that was not easy to snuff out.

They took two cars. One had Henry, Dr. Kurtz, and two soldiers, and the other, three soldiers and room for Rachel. Henry provided the directions. He'd been to the mansion many times since bringing Rachel there. Each time cowardice and guilt jousted for prime time. It was certainly true that Henry wished to protect Rachel, that the mansion was for her safety, but he couldn't deny it was also for his peace of mind. Henry needed to know he didn't have to worry about what Rachel might do if she found out about his earlier dalliance with Maura, or, worse, about Maura usurping Rachel's role at the gallery. Coward, coward, coward.

Henry looked out the window and saw the turn approaching. "Here," he called out, "it will be just up ahead on the right, next to the cemetery." Both cars turned where Henry had advised. Henry watched for the mansion that was partially hidden by two oaks, some bushes, and a creole tomato garden that Eloise had planted ... but didn't see it. Were they on the wrong block? Had he been distracted?

"Mr. Reid," Dr. Kurtz inquired sternly, "where is it?"

Henry answered with the stutter that sometimes returned from his elementary school years when he was under stress. "I must have m-m-missed the turn."

"Hmmm," Dr. Kurtz responded. "Well, where should we go? And please get hold of yourself. We have no time for your stuttering."

This, of course, didn't help at all, but Henry took three deep breaths, as he'd been taught those many years ago, before replying, "Take a right here and then another right." Henry looked at the street signs and saw they weren't familiar at all. What had happened? They drove for another few minutes before Henry brought them right back to the first spot. "It h—has to be here! I know it was here," he cried out, understanding the danger of his situation. But not only was the house not there, neither was the cemetery.

Dr. Kurtz placed a hand on Henry's injured knee and squeezed, evoking a gasp from Henry's mouth. "You wouldn't be playing games with us, would you, Henry? You do know that would be ... unwise? Buildings and cemeteries don't just disappear." Of course Henry knew that. Or thought he knew that. Yet ...

The doctor continued, "But I like games. How about this one? We'll return to the cell and continue your interrogation until you decide to tell us where your wife *really* is, and I'll allow you to join in on the betting of how long it will take before you pass out. How does that sound? Fair enough?"

Henry didn't know what *fair* or *unfair* were, terms that no longer applied to his reality. Where was that blasted house?

29
JAKOB

While I was dozing on the sofa in the great room, covered lightly by a blanket Helga had knitted for Peter, I could hear Wilhelm and Helga talking in the kitchen about what they should do.

"You've heard the same stories I have, Helga. The Germans are vicious with those who aid runaway Jews. Remember the group of villagers around Ciepielów who were burned alive merely for providing food to a Jew? That the burned included an 8-year-old girl in all her innocence cannot be forgiven ... nor can it be ignored."

"I know," Helga responded. "I know, Wilhelm. I also know we are charged by Christ with helping our neighbors. Is it for us to decide who is our neighbor and who is not?"

"If only it were that simple," Wilhelm sighed. "Tell me this: if we risk our lives, to whom would our own, our Peter, have when he returns? Could we rely on another to care for him in our absence?"

Wilhelm continued. "And what about the entire barnful of Poles who were set on fire in Rekówka, including families we knew, the Obuchiewicz and Kowalski families? What was gained by their attempts to follow Christ's charge? Not only were they killed, but the Jews they were hiding were also killed. It is an unwinnable situation. What is the point of putting ourselves at such risk? I could never forgive myself if you were killed or if our actions threatened harm to Peter."

A moment passed before she answered. "I admit that I'm afraid, Wilhelm. We would be stupid not to be afraid. But if I live my life now in fear, then I believe the Germans have already won. I can't give them a victory they don't deserve and that I, with all my heart, hope they will be denied. This boy was led to our doorstep. Perhaps it is a test. Or perhaps there is no reason at all. I no longer know the patterns of this universe. I can only act from my heart, and my heart says that either way, whether a test or a random occurrence, I know what I must do. My dear husband, whose heart I know and have loved for all these years, you, too, know what we must do."

They discussed my fate, believing I slept. There was a storeroom down some stairs next to the kitchen that they would empty and make into a room for me. The trick would be hiding it so when the Germans came, as they regularly did, looking for runaways, they would not be able to find me.

"I can create a wall with a hidden door out of some old barn wood," Wilhelm said to Helga, "and cover it with shelving for your bottling and storage items." With the task in mind, Wilhelm began to make his peace with the decision. I could see them through the kitchen doorway standing, and almost shyly embracing as they sealed this solemn vow, this decision to keep me safe. I wondered if they might have believed I was sent to their care in the place of the boy they hoped was being cared for by another in Christ's name.

When Wilhelm and Helga first invited me to stay with them, the bands that had been pressing against my chest preventing

it from expanding with my breath, loosened. For a brief moment, I could breathe freely. Then they told me I would live in
a room behind a hidden door, a room with little light, in complete solitude, and the tightness returned. I was, of course,
grateful but also scared. But then, those were descriptions of
everyday life since the Germans invaded. In fact, I can't remember a single day—not one—since the invasion of Poland
that I had not woken scared yet grateful to be alive. Some days,
I woke also determined and hopeful, but not every day, though
I had been taught to begin and end each day in gratitude to
God, the Almighty. You'd think it would be easier now, when
simply to awaken was fodder for gratitude, and perhaps had I
no memory, it would be. But thanking God for a life of hardship was not easy, whereas before, the complaints against God
were trivial and easier to overcome. Having seen what I had
seen, what no one should ever see, gratitude was more difficult.

To enter my very own room, something I had not had
since ... before, one had to remove a sack of beans from shelving Wilhelm had constructed to cover the entry in order to reveal a latch that allowed the shelving to be moved, the opening
to the room bared. The latch was locked for additional security. The interior had been stocked with an oil lamp that I was
warned to use sparingly as the supply of oil was, as with everything else during the war, low. I also could use it only after
the dinner hour, when Germans were less likely to be patrolling. There were two rectangular vents near the ceiling that
filtered some daylight through so that, depending upon the
angle of the sun and the presence or absence of clouds, I could
see during the day without the need for a lamp. They had fur-
nished my room with a small desk and chair, along with a
horsehair cushion and blankets that would serve as my bed,
as well as providing a pan for my waste. I began to think of
myself as a fugitive from the law, prepared to protect himself
and his bounty in the event he was found. But the fantasy lost

its allure entirely when memory claimed the present for its own.

Wilhelm stopped in daily to bring food, empty my pan, and provide clean cloths and a soothing salve for my wound. I was grateful the abrasions were healing and I could begin to pee without having to cover my mouth to muffle screams of pain. When I finally gathered the courage to look down at my penis, I was surprised to see that it looked the same. I believe I thought the device I had rigged had worked, that this pain was the result of the circumcision's reversal, but likely I had not let the experiment work long enough. I was still, to all who cared to look, a Jew.

While Helga and Wilhelm took care of my physical needs, for which I was grateful, I was plagued with long hours alone with little to do. They were attentive to these needs, too, sharing with me books from their library. Wilhelm was particularly interested in Russian history, and I had access to the books he'd had to hide in the storeroom with me lest the Germans find them, about Peter the Great and the Russian Empire, Alexander II, and the 1917 Russian Revolution's overthrow of the monarchy. Helga preferred fiction, books I'd seen in my own home back when the world hadn't turned upside down. Sometimes they were a welcome break from the thick history books, but they were also reminders of my family, and of my sister's death, of a world that did not exist any longer and, for all I knew, would never again.

It was then that my mind drifted to *The Golem*, the book that had engaged me in the comparatively carefree days of my youth, and I began to fantasize about Rabbi Judah Loew's creation of a golem as a weapon against those who persecuted the Jewish community in sixteenth and seventeenth century Prague.

In the divided city of Prague at that time, Jews were targeted as infidels and outsiders and were treated poorly as all outsiders are. A young Jewish girl, returning to the Jewish quarter with supplies for the Passover seder, came upon a gap in the rocks while running her fingers along the wall separating the Jewish quarter from the larger city. Looking inside the gap, she saw a bundle that, upon inspection, contained a dead, uncircumcised baby boy. Not knowing what to do, she took the bundled baby, no larger than a brick, and placed it in her shopping bag. Traumatized, she went first to her mother and showed her what she had found. Knowing the danger, the mother brought her trembling daughter and the bundle to the Rabbi with the news that it had begun again.

Rabbi Loew understood as soon as he saw the baby, as it had happened before—a stillborn Christian child, placed within the wall of the Jewish Quarter to implicate the Jews in his death. Stillborn Christian babies who were ripped from their parents' arms and brought, even unbaptized, to serve as indictments against the Jews.

Fearing the uprising and murders this event would incite, Rabbi Loew acted quickly. He first had his assistant bring the child to a trusted Christian friend, a priest who would provide the child a baptism and thus ensure his passage to God according to the Christian faith. It was the least the Rabbi could do for the infant. Next, he proceeded with the plan he had been formulating for just such an occasion. What the Jewish community needed was a soldier, one who could protect them from situations of potential harm such as this one. The Rabbi had been preparing for many years to be sufficiently wise and worthy of God's blessing in this endeavor. He created this warrior from mud, according to the dictates of Kabbalah: a golem who would live as a man but was no man and who would be put away when his purpose had been fulfilled.

I wondered. Here I was, no good to anyone, too many hours in the day with nothing to do. What if I dedicated myself to study and prayer to improve my character and become more worthy? Perhaps I could make a golem that could end this war.

30
SARIAH

Meeting Juan was a surprise for Sariah. He seemed much older than María, but she had expected that, given María's description of him. What she had not expected was his humor and good-naturedness. Sariah's own father, may his memory be for a blessing, was a good man and a good Jew but could not have been called good-natured. He had been too stiff, too proper, too rule-bound—which is perhaps what made him a good Jew. Sariah did not often reflect on her heritage, but when she did, it always seemed so severe. How many times had she been found wanting for having been lax with the rules of the Sabbath, for example? Why should she be enamored of a religion that so often sought out her deficiencies to dwell on them?

Juan, on the other hand, spoke only kindly to her. When María first introduced them, he had her sit by the large stuffed armchair where he spent so much of his time, his affected limb resting on a footstool nearby, and begged her to tell him of the world outside Lima. Sariah indulged him, finding great satisfaction in telling him of her father's store that so reminded her of his own. Once again, having learned caution, she left out any reference to her family's background. Sariah nevertheless drank in Juan's interest, answering questions that he posed concerning what kinds of herbs they sold, from where her father obtained them, and whether she had any training in the use of medicinal herbs. At the end of the hour's interview, Juan gave his blessing for her to stay with them.

Together one morning, some weeks later, María and Sariah entered Juan's study with his breakfast tray and a pot of coffee to last the morning hours. As they were leaving, Juan stopped them, saying, "I have been thinking, my little bees, about Sariah's future; please sit down a moment before you head down to the shop." There was a loveseat across from Juan's chair where María and Sariah settled. Sariah felt an anxious cramping in her stomach and a tightness in her chest, the physical reaction to reminders that she controlled nothing in her life.

He continued, speaking to them both but directing himself to Sariah. "You have a special talent, Sariah, for herbs, not just for the selling of them, but for understanding and using them. Your knowledge already equals my María's, and hers is beyond the ordinary." At this, he looked over with kind and grateful eyes to María, who bowed her head appropriately. "No false modesty, María. You know your talents and how much I value them." María looked up with a grin, and Sariah caught the wink Juan sent in María's direction. He continued, "But for what I am going to suggest, I cannot spare María. Sariah, I want you to be my apprentice, to learn all that I know about the science of medicinal herbs. To provide for the good people of Lima in my stead when I can no longer do so."

María started to interrupt with protestations of health and long life for Juan until he stopped her. "Now, now, María. Since when have we ever been less than honest with each other? I am failing and I know it. We must plan for the future. Sariah's future is now part of that planning if she might be well-disposed. There is one thing that we must prepare immediately for my plan to work. These are no times for women to be out in the world alone. The only women doing so are either widows or witches, neither of whom have easy lives, if they have lives at all." This was a reference to the burning of witches by the Inquisition, which extended its interest in protecting the Catholic religion to various threats, including heresy, magic, miracles that were not Christ-centric, and individualism. Presumably witchcraft fell into one of these. "I will get to the point," Juan continued. "Sariah, you must be a man for our plan to work."

Sariah flinched at this, looking over at María with an expression that imparted her deepest feeling at the moment—that Juan must have lost his mind! How could she say this, though? She next looked at Juan, expecting to see a twinkle in his eyes and a grin on his face, but saw neither. He was serious! Before Sariah could respond, María spoke for her.

"Dear husband, you are overworked. We must not allow so many visits. Did you not sleep well last night? Perhaps I should stay home today. The shop can remain closed one day."

Juan smiled at last, but not the smile his little "bees" expected. He was making no joke but *was* amused by the way both Sariah and María had taken his suggestion.

"I see that you fear for my mind. I have not lost it ... yet. Hear me out. Sariah is unknown in Lima now. It would not be difficult if she would cut her hair, bind her breasts, and wear men's clothing, for her to be taken as a man. This will open doors that could otherwise not be opened, at least not without legitimate fears. What do you say, Sariah?"

But again, María spoke first. "Juan, that is asking too much! At least for today. Let Sariah live with this thought for a bit, and we can speak of it again later."

Sariah began to speak but was interrupted by Juan. "She can have some time, my dove. One day, Sariah, to become used to the thought of becoming a man. Think on it ... and tomorrow morning you can give your answer. If you agree, we will begin your apprenticeship at once. What would a good name be? Ignacio? Hortensio?"

Sariah knew immediately that she could answer Juan's offer. To María's surprise, but not her own, she said, "I will accept your offer, Juan, with gratitude." She looked over at María so María would know she was not only comfortable but happy with this turn of events and announced, "Tomorrow morning, I will be known by all others as Simon."

María, though unconvinced that what they were planning was right, helped Sariah in becoming a man. Sariah sat on a stool in the kitchen, her hands clasped tightly in her lap. María could not tell if her posture was indicative of resoluteness or fright. As she brought the scissors up to Sariah's long dark curls, she hesitated, giving Sariah a chance to change her mind, but Sariah made no sound, no movement, showed no aversion to the first step that would put into motion the renunciation of her God-given gender.

"Your hair is so thick, Sariah. It may take some time to give it a good cut."

"Don't be afraid, María. I'm not. I am grateful to Juan for his advice and his wisdom, and I look forward to learning from him." She, too, hesitated, worrying that María might be jealous of her. "I hope you are comfortable with this path as well. I am as grateful to you as to your husband for giving me this new life."

"Of course. I am happy for you. I saw something special from the moment I set eyes on you, and I'm not surprised that Juan also saw that quality. For your young years, your eyes show a wisdom, whether born of inheritance or gained through experience. You will make a fine healer. Now," she said as she walked around the chair to face Sariah directly, snipping at her bangs and looking into her eyes. "Let us see what a handsome man you are going to make!"

After finishing the cut, María left the room and returned with a looking glass for Sariah. "Here, how did I do?"

Sariah brought the looking glass to eye level with excitement and looked with wonder at the visage returning her gaze. A beautiful boy looked back at her, and for perhaps the first time in her life, Sariah felt as if she truly belonged in this world. She took the torn bedsheet that María had brought with her into the kitchen. Turning away from María, she removed her blouse shyly and tore the bedsheet into strips that she used to bind her breasts tightly as she had done when they had been engorged with no baby to drink from them. Now Sariah felt as if she belonged in this new body.

Turning toward Maria, she asked, "What do you think? Will this work?"

María was amazed at the transformation. "Let me get you some new clothing tomorrow from a friend, and we will bring you to Juan for his opinion. I believe he will be surprised."

The next morning, María brought home the clothing and gave it to Sariah, who asked her to go to Juan while she dressed, where she would meet them in just a few minutes. Sariah was nervous she might not be able to pull off the disguise, but when she looked at herself in the mirror with her short hair, hat, bound breasts, and dark pants with a white shirt and embroidered vest, she saw the image of her father. She headed to Juan's room with confidence and pride. When had she last felt proud? Not since seeing Baruch for the first time, and every time thereafter. But she could not go down that rabbit hole now. Juan's door was open, but she knocked, nevertheless.

"Come in, Sariah," Juan called to her in his soft baritone. Both Juan and María turned their heads to look at her in amazement. This was no woman; Sariah had indeed become Simon. Sariah drank in their eyes and hoped she could do for them someday what they had done for her: allowed her to find her truth.

"You are ready now," said Juan from his chair, his ailing leg up on a stool. "Tomorrow, we have two appointments, one an ingrown nail and the other a belly complaint. I will introduce you as my assistant, newly arrived in Lima from the countryside. All of that is true. Before tonight, I would have said the only lie would be in presenting you as Simon, but now I am happy to say I do not have to lie at all. We will meet in my office at ten in the morning. Welcome to your new life. You must remember that, in our home, we will call you Sariah; with others, you will be Simon." Juan reached out to hold María's hand. "María and I are so happy to have you with us."

———————

In the first years, Juan and Sariah had little time for conversation that did not touch on their work. Even so, after the last patient on a busy day, the flu season having begun, Juan was in the mood to talk. As Sariah put away the herb jars and cleaned the ointment bowls, Juan spoke of the town's impending Easter celebration, how it was one of the times he wished he and María had a child as they were so full of innocent expectation, their joy infusing the town with a gleam singular to that time.

"I, too, love this season," Sariah contributed. "Growing up in Lisbon, my parents did not allow me to participate in the Easter procession to the church, but I was able to sneak away and watch from behind the bakery. Oh, how I wanted to join in"—here Sariah glanced at Juan with a mischievous grin—"but I was ever the obedient child."

"But why wouldn't your parents allow you to participate?" Juan asked her.

Sariah responded with the truth that she hadn't yet shared with him, though she had with María and had forced her to swear not to tell Juan. Now, however, she felt comfortable enough and trusting enough to say, "Because we were Jews."

Sitting on a chair in his office, so weary from the long day that he had allowed Sariah to do all the cleaning up, Juan said nothing. Minutes passed as she wondered if he had fallen asleep. Finally, she could take it no longer and said loudly, "You must have something to say. I just told you I was a Jew."

Juan responded, "So you did. And by God, I wondered how long it would take you to tell me."

Surprised, Sariah countered, "But how could you know? María promised not to tell you!"

"She didn't tell me, though now I have more about which to wonder. Why you would tell her and not me," he laughed.

"So, you are not angry with me?" Sariah ventured.

"Why should I be angry? You have done everything I have asked of you since becoming a part of this household. You are a great help to me and a quick learner. You are a loyal friend to María and have provided no reason for either of us to have concern. And you have accompanied us to church each Sunday, out of respect for our beliefs, if not your own."

"I have attended church for so long I no longer know what I believe," Sariah responded truthfully. "If there has been a constant in this life of mine, it has been that I know I can rely on no single path, for the minute I find myself on one, whether one I chose myself or one chosen for me, it is ripped out from under my feet. As far as being a Jew, it has cost me everything more than once."

Juan studied her from his chair with saddened eyes. Though a devout Christian himself, he did not support the Inquisition's attitudes or methods. He had seen too many burnings and was too aware of the tortures inflicted upon everyday folk who had the misfortune of misstating their beliefs in front of the wrong person. Nevertheless, his faith was everything to him, and so he responded, "Religion is important, Sariah. One *must* look to God, regardless of the prayer one uses. But family is also important. You must discern for yourself how to make both work in your life."

Sariah was grateful for Juan's words, grateful for the twists in her life that had brought her here. She answered, "I no longer have family, Juan, except for a son taken from me as a baby. I wonder if you and María might consider me a part of yours?"

Sariah lowered her head at the memory of her losses and of her son, almost as if in prayer, though she did not know what prayers to say. Her parents' God had allowed Baruch to be taken from her. To recite the *Shema*, glorifying that God, would be a lie. The Christian God had allowed her rape, then did nothing to punish her rapist. Neither could she pronounce the Lord's Prayer in good conscience. But no God could erase from her memory her flesh and blood.

Juan's heart ached to hear of Sariah's loss. "I am sorry to hear this, Sariah. If your son is alive, may you yet be returned to each other. God is loving and just."

Sariah did not know if there was a God who was loving or just. She did know that she prayed daily to her memory of a God she believed was out there somewhere, that Baruch was well. And she knew if she were ever to encounter Baruch again, she would know him and would hope to embrace him in her life.

"But, of course, you are already part of our family," answered Juan as they went to clean up for the dinner their loving wife and sister, María, had prepared.

As the years passed and Juan's ability to tend to patients was circumscribed to fewer and fewer hours due to his aging and ailing body, Sariah ascended from junior doctor to doctor. Her study with Juan, her access to a large medical library, and her own predisposition toward helping others propelled her into a role she had never dreamed for herself. These were the happiest years of her life, all of it due to María and Juan.

Nevertheless, Sariah's happiness hid in the corner at times, fearing that monster guilt that visited more often than she liked. How could she be happy when her happiness came because of Juan's declining health? How could she be happy when she didn't know the fate of her son? Though she thought of Baruch every day, would another mother have found a single drop of happiness having lost her son? Was there something wrong with her?

There was yet another guilt, one she least wished to acknowledge. She had never been questioned about her gender, though there were those who surely wondered why, as Simon, she hadn't chosen a wife, but to any who asked, and there were those who offered their daughters—if only they had known—Sariah was quick to point out that she was too busy now, with the doctor's dwindling health, to spare even a moment for courting. The guilt most plaguing her began at some hour she could not pinpoint, but somewhere along the way, when she realized that the feelings she had experienced with Lina had returned. That churning of the stomach, the familiar butterflies. But she had not heard anything of Lina or her family for many years. It was a torch Sariah believed she had laid down long ago. No, the butterflies were no longer for Lina.

It was María who kept the numerous balls in the air for all of them. In the earlier years, Sariah spent much time in the shop with her, and there they were able to share stories about their lives and their desires. They became best of friends, talking about everything when there were quiet hours and working in tandem when the shop was busy, as if they always knew what the other would do next. Was there ever a lingering of a hand on hand or a gaze that revealed something more than friend-ship? If there had been, surely gossip would have erupted:

"Have you seen María and Simon, Dr. Juan's assistant, eye-ing each other in the shop? Something is going on, I tell you."

"Yes, but of course, it was inevitable. Dr. Juan is getting older, and María is becoming only more beautiful."

But neither Sariah nor María had heard any of these things. Their innocence was a shield, protecting and blinding them.

Only lately, now that Sariah was spending less and less time at the shop as she had to fill in for Juan, had her desire become more insistent. Sariah knew that María and Juan no longer shared the same bedroom. Still, she didn't know if Ma-ría could be open to a relationship with her. Though she was, in her mind and heart, Simon, María knew the truth. And in all the time they had spent together, they had never discussed love between women as anything other than sisterly. Sariah knew that María loved her, but could she *love* her?

One afternoon, when the shop had shuttered for siesta and Juan was asleep, Sariah went into the kitchen where María was cutting vegetables for an evening stew. Sariah engaged María in conversation about the husband of one of their pa-tients, who had been caught *in flagrante delicto* with a neigh-bor while his wife was recovering from childbirth.

"Can you imagine him literally caught with his pants down?" laughed Sariah.

"Oh, that's too wicked of you, Sariah," María began, and Sariah worried she had gone too far, that the easy joking María and she had enjoyed in the years of keeping shop together had faded with time. María continued, "Perhaps I could imagine it if he were ten years younger and without the hairy buttocks that I am now trying to get out of my head!" They both giggled at that vision, reconnecting in easy banter.

"Here, Sariah, take a knife and chop these vegetables. I be-lieve they are helping Juan regain some strength."

Sariah knew better but didn't know how to tell María that his path would not be one of quick, or even lingering, recovery. Juan would live for some years yet but would not regain strength. Sariah took the knife María handed her, stood next to her at the kitchen table, and began chopping yuca root.

"I have noticed, María," Sariah began this conversation slowly, with some trepidation. She had run through it many times in her mind, the outcome different each time. She could do no more than hope for a happy one. "I have noticed that you and Juan no longer share a bedroom." That was all. The question "why?" would be too much.

María put down her knife and stood there, looking at the kitchen table as if counting the sections of tomato she had been slicing for some complex formula. When she looked up at Sariah, there were tears in her eyes, and she couldn't speak. It wasn't desire that propelled Sariah but a longing to quell whatever pain María was feeling that made her put her arms around María and hold her tightly, whispering in her ear, "It's okay, María, whatever it is, it's okay." María wiped the tears from her eyes and pulled away to explain.

"I know Juan will not live a long life. I would prefer to be in the bedroom with him to provide what solace I can in the time he has left. It is he who asked for the room alone so that he can prepare himself to die." Having gotten all the way to the last phrase without tears, at *so he can prepare himself to die,* Sariah's tears joined María's own newly flowing ones, and they held each other in their mutual grief.

31
RACHEL

Rachel returned to her room, her palm retaining the burning imprint of the stone containing David's story. She climbed into bed without changing her clothing and pulled the quilt over her head, physically and emotionally exhausted. She lay there motionless except for the movement of her palm rubbing rhythmically against her thigh as if to wipe away the evidence of David's death, or perhaps wishing to summon a genie, knowing the three wishes she would utter: "Give me back my son. Give me back my son. Give me back my son." Then she slept.

"Mom," came the first whisper that sounded more like a breeze lazing through the curtains into the room. Again, "Mom." This time the breeze brushing against her cheek. With the third "Mom," Rachel sat up in her bed, startled. As she left her bed to cross the room and close the window through which she'd heard an owl's cry, she saw him. "He's here!" What joy she felt at seeing her son alive! But as the fog of sleep cleared and the shock of his presence settled, confusion exchanged places with joy. He was David, yet he wasn't. His body was ... flimsy. Insubstantial. Instinctively she tried to grab him and hold the thick, black mat of his hair to her breast, but he stopped her.

"We're not allowed to touch, Mom. But we can talk. I know this is confusing. Please bear with me. Sit."

Rachel stumbled to her desk, sitting before testing her ability to speak. "David," she uttered. It was a susurration more than anything else, fearing that saying his name aloud might cause this vision to go away. Was he real? Was he alive? Was he dead? How was she seeing him? Too many questions playing "Ring Around the Rosie" in her head, chanting, "Ashes, ashes, we all fall down."

David spoke again, dreaded words. "Mom, you must listen as I tell you the story of my death."

Rachel shuddered at David's command.

"No! I don't want to know. I'm not strong enough to know. I can't do this!"

"But you can, Mom. I know you can. It's important, as you must write it for others. Trust in my knowledge of your strength if you cannot yet trust in your own."

So he began the wretched tale.

Not long after Dad and I made sure you were safe, he and I parted again, and I continued my work with the Resistance.

Sitting in her desk chair, Rachel shifted while David paced nearby.

I was working with Eli and a group of others to avenge Caroline's death and remove the physician whom we learned had tortured and killed her. It required another of us to work from the inside.

Rachel couldn't restrain the sob that escaped her lips, guessing what he would say next, but she remained otherwise silent and still, quivering, unable to take her eyes off him, as if the path of her vision were a rope binding him to her. David looked at her with such sorrow, his eyes revealing how much he wished to spare her this pain, the pain of knowing how her only son had suffered.

I volunteered to allow myself to be kidnapped. We released

false information that we knew would get back to the Right-
eous, suggesting another bombing, this time at a headquarters.
I went there at the day and time of the supposed bombing with
materials that could be used in making an explosive, and was
arrested. They took me to the same place we knew Caroline had
been kept, a location where Resistance members were held.

Rachel couldn't keep her silence, a question burning
through her. "But how, David, how did you think you could do
anything from within? Surely they had searched you so that
you could bring nothing in that you could use to harm anyone."

"There are many things you don't know about these times,
Mom, and about what goes on in the Interrogatorium. It's not
important for you to know, but I can tell you there is a network
within, and my role was to communicate with the network to
provide the time and location of my tortures, which would allow them to know where the doctor was, information necessary to enact our plans for justice."

After I was put in one of the rooms—perhaps the very room
in which Caroline died—tied to a cold chair and handcuffed, the
doctor who'd been described to me, brown hair with a jagged
scar across the bridge of his nose, entered and spoke to me.

"Well, David, I hear you wanted to bomb a building that
would have resulted in the killing of many innocent people. Is
that true? Such a nice-looking young man to harbor such evil
intent. What? No response? No denial? Doctor, I had no inten-
tion to harm anyone? Doctor, please don't hurt me; I'm inno-
cent? I hear those denials all day, every day. Go ahead. I'll give
you your chance to convince me to spare you."

The Children's Chorus: Speak, David, speak!

"You're right, doctor," I responded while sitting as straight
as I could, though to do so bent my shoulder painfully because
of the way my hands had been handcuffed behind the steel

chair. "I intended harm. But the harm I intended had nothing to do with innocent people. The innocent people are those you and the Righteous murder each day in your bid to rid our society of anyone different from you."

The Children's Chorus: No, not that, David! Speak of your innocence!

"Oh my, oh my. I see I have a reckless one here. One who cares nothing for his welfare, I presume. Well, we can change that. Brave words are usually caught in the throat when the throat is cut, as the old saying goes. Or perhaps I made that one up. Ah well, it doesn't matter."

That session was brief, but at the end, when he thought I was unconscious, the doctor told those who arrived to carry me back to my cell and to bring me to the same room again in two days at five pm, giving my wounds time to heal as well as giving time for fear to well up in me. I was able to send that information to the Resistance through avenues you should not know. Back in my cell, I catalogued my injuries and tried to think only of Caroline, of her bravery, and of the certain justice we would obtain in two days' time.

The two days in my cell passed with no remarkable incident. I didn't eat, using the time to fast and pray that I might be able to hold out and that we might be successful. At five pm on the second day, I was brought to the doctor again. Though I wished to show strength, I knew the guards who grabbed me by each arm could feel my trembling. They treated me almost gently, and I thought of the wives and children they likely had at home. I tried to feel no hatred for the guards as they deposited me in the room, removed my clothing, strapped me to a table, and walked silently out. I saved all my hostility for the doctor, whose sorrows and suffering I actively desired.

I worried as I lay there for what seemed like forever, knowing that the plan couldn't be enacted until the guards changed at six pm, at which time the Resistance would have replaced one of the regular guards with an implant of our own. For a full hour, I would have to endure whatever the doctor planned for this session so that I could keep him in the room.

"David, David, my son," the doctor said upon entering just moments later, "I see we will get to chat once again. Please forgive the chill in the room, but soon you will not notice it, I promise."

The doctor pulled a metal tray closer and emptied onto it an assortment of implements that made a loud clang as they were being arranged. I turned my head to look away, but the doctor intervened, grasping my head and turning it so I was looking directly at the tray.

"Now, now, David. Surely you want to see where we're headed. Aren't you Jews intent upon truth? Isn't there a Talmudic saying that goes something like, 'Truth is the seal of the Holy One?' You see, I know quite a bit about your people. Much of it I've learned in here, though, so I suppose its verity is suspect."

Saying that, the doctor grasped what looked like a surgical knife. "Now, David, once again, can you tell me all who were involved in planning the bombing episode in which you have found yourself implicated?" As he asked that question, he grabbed my hand and pinned my little finger to the table. Holding the knife near my finger, he repeated the question. "Come now, David, I asked you a question. You're being rude. Must I quote scripture to you? 'Stand up in the presence of the aged, show respect for the elderly ...' That's from your Leviticus. Though I hate to call myself 'elderly,' I suppose to you I may, nevertheless, seem so. Ah, the perspective of youth. So skewed."

"No! I can't hear any more," Rachel interjected, jumping up and running towards the door. "My son, my flesh and blood! How can you expect me to listen to this?" In the entirety of his telling, she hadn't looked away from him, reveling in the perfection of his appearance, absorbed by his dark curls and broad shoulders. But now, she broke eye contact with him, even praying he would disappear. She looked at the door, then looked back toward the window where she had seen him, expecting him to be gone, but he was still there. He looked at her with eyes full of compassion.

"I'm almost done. There are a few more things you must know. I'll leave out the details of the tortures, but not what I learned from them before my death."

Before we were able to obtain our justice, and we did, though the Doctor escaped with his life, I endured pain greater than I had ever before experienced. There were moments I lost sense of who and where I was. I discovered that with enough torture, identity is broken down. I learned that the pattern I had accepted from childhood—if I am good, nothing bad will happen to me—was false. As the pain pushed me further and further into a place I didn't recognize, I wondered—if I could no longer count on that pattern, who did I become? Who was I—who am I now? Is there something shared between the person who believed and the one who continues forward?

Though listening, at that moment Rachel could understand only the pain her son had experienced and asked angrily, "But why didn't you tell them what they wanted to know, David? Why didn't you try to save your life?"

David answered quietly but firmly. He had once felt the anger that was coursing through his mother but had found his answers. "Saving myself was never an option. This is a totalitarian government we're fighting, and the defining characteristic of the totalitarian mind is that it needs clarity and order. There are no good Jews and bad Jews, some worth saving and some not. There are only Jews, and they are enemies of the republic. There are no half-Jews or quarter-Jews. There are only Jews. I was a dead man when I was kidnapped and knew it. We all know it. Jews occupy a role in history. I don't say 'occupied,' but 'occupy,' for it continues. There are periods of dormancy, but we know that Jews as irritants, that which must be washed out, is eternal. The only question, *the only question*, is when. What does it mean to be the Chosen People? You might say we were *chosen* to be persecuted and to suffer.

"How, then, should we act in the moments of persecution? Do we fight back, or are we docile in accepting our deaths? There is a third choice: when they come for us again, as they always will, do we cast off our heritage entirely? That is, do we deny who we are? That's the question we each must struggle with. Including you, Mom."

It was April, and the colors and smells of spring were all at-witter in the cemetery, preparing for their coming out fiesta. The Children danced and played, taking advantage of the good weather and high spirits that always accompany the cycle of rebirth. They'd been promised a story hour by Inés later in the day, and the excitement of gathering as a community for a story they hoped would have a King David destroying a Goliath overwhelmed their senses so that, had any seen them and not known, there might have been a shaking of heads and a wagging of fingers at what could have appeared to look like drunkenness. Yes! The Children were inebriated! But with no substance other than the sense of anticipation.

As the Children frolicked, playing hide and seek among the gravestones and tombs, Inés and Eloise sat on the bench beneath the Oldest Oak enjoying an afternoon tea and discussing the stones.

"I've been wanting to share something, sister. The thing is," Eloise said, starting and stopping a few times as she gathered her thoughts. "The thing is ... the important point to get across to Rachel is ... I mean to say, what we most want her to understand is—"

"Oh come, come, Eloise," interrupted Inés, "spit it out!"

"Yes, I'm sorry, sister. It's just that ... well, I mean, it's difficult ... that is to say—"

"Do let me help, then," Inés spoke with some impatience, as she knew story hour would be upon them in no time at all. "You have seen Rachel with the stones and want to talk about how we can help her better understand their importance ... how we can relay what they represent, the Children's pasts and their unlived futures ... or rather..."

"You see, sister, it is not so easy after all!" Eloise harrumphed triumphantly.

"Yes, yes, Eloise. It's my turn to apologize. Best perhaps to point to another who has written poignantly about what I believe you are trying to say. Walk with me for a moment to Uncle Hymie's family tomb, where I believe he will have this book."

As Eloise and Inés walked, they heard the Children playing but also could hear the singing of the crickets and katydids mixed with the sonorous snoring of napping Ancestors. "Oh, I do hope Uncle Hymie isn't sleeping," worried Eloise. Inés unlocked the tomb and called for Uncle Hymie as she and Eloise entered the beautifully attired front room, which Inés knew led to a large library.

"Welcome, welcome, sisters," shouted Uncle Hymie, who was a bit hard of hearing. "To what do I owe the honor of this visit?"

"I am looking for a particular book," Inés ventured. "A story by Elie Wiesel entitled *The Judges*. Might you have a copy?"

"Oh yes, of course. I just read for the one-thousand-thirty-second time one of his other works. Wonderful Story Teller, that one. Terrible the preparation he had to endure. I remember when—"

Inés had to interrupt him. "I'm sorry, Uncle Hymie, but we're in a hurry."

"Yes, yes. Of course, of course. I'll go find it for you."

Uncle Hymie returned shortly with the book, gave it to Inés, and told her to keep it as long as she liked. "They're here to be read, aren't they? A book can't be a witness if it isn't read."

Inés and Eloise thanked the uncle and returned to the bench underneath the Oldest Oak. There it took no time for Inés to find the passage she wished to share, as she had read it herself many times over many years:

I'm on a mission ... My purpose is to take charge of the future that our dead children leave behind. At midnight I go to the Wall and talk to the Lord. I implore Him not to squander these young lives that have yet to have been lived, nor these joys prematurely cut short, but to offer them to those who need them: the sick, the wounded, the invalids, people in despair.

"Oh, that's perfect!" exclaimed Eloise. "Yes, sister, that is exactly what I was trying to say. There is such a connection between the stories that the stones protect and the future. In fact, I think stories are really living things that exist in our bones, always looking for a path out into the world. If we are silent, that is, if we shackle our memories, that silence becomes an enemy, betraying the persistent, living, throbbing message we carry within. We must find our stories and tell them, knowing that as we do, we create the pathways for generations to see through the too-many-silences and recapture what is theirs, what is ours, what is in the bones of the world."

Inés sat there saying nothing for a moment before blurting out, "Sister, I am stunned! I had no idea you could be so poetic."

Eloise beamed.

32
THE CHILDREN'S CHORUS

Our silence must always make way for our stories.

33
JAKOB

A pounding on a door woke me, followed by the polite but sharp command, *Öffnen Sie die Tür!* I knew this meant German soldiers were here to search the premises. They'd come twice since I'd been here, and each time my heart did flip-flops. As Wilhelm went to answer the door, Helga came and knocked to let me know the Germans were there ... as if I couldn't hear them. But, of course, it was a reminder that if I could hear them, they could very well hear me, so I became silent as a mouse.

The day before, Wilhelm had told me the story of the death of Peter's parents. It had been many months—I guessed—since Wilhelm and Helga had taken me in, and I still had no idea what had happened to Peter's parents. As he told the story, I heard both Wilhelm's pride and his suffering. His son, Józef, and his wife had been in charge of a cell of Polish resistance fighters. Wilhelm did not recount the details but told me that in a single day, each and every fighter, including his son, had given their lives for our Polish motherland, and Józef's wife had been taken away and never heard of again. So it was that Peter came to live with them in the countryside. Helga and Wilhelm's grief was assuaged as they focused on parenting once again, until that day when the German soldiers came and took Peter away to serve in the German army. That day, too, I imagine, German soldiers had pounded on the door with the same command. Each time they came to search, the echo must have been profound. It made me wish for justice not just for the Jews but for Wilhelm and Helga, too.

Sitting as still as possible and trying to hold off the insistence of my bladder, I listened intently to hear the conversation in the house, growing louder and softer as they traversed the small interior of the home.

"*Herr Leutnant*, tell me how the war effort is going," I could hear Wilhelm making conversation.

"Well, *Herr* Baer. In fact, we have received information that it should be over very soon in a victorious flourish."

"May it be so, *Herr Leutnant*. May it be so. It would be wonderful to have our Peter back home."

"Ah, yes. Your grandson, wasn't it? Taken with heels dragging, I understand. There are some cowards, I suppose, who do not understand the honor that is theirs in participating in the war efforts of our *Führer*."

Wilhelm I knew must have had to bite his tongue to keep silent at the accusation and besmirching of Peter's name.

The lieutenant continued, "The story has circulated around the town how your Peter cursed our great *Führer* even as he was being given the high honor to fight at the Russian front."

That Peter had been sent to the Russian front, I knew, was news to Wilhelm. He and Helga believed Peter was still with the German army somewhere in Poland. I imagined how Wilhelm's heart must have sunk at the information.

"Is *this* your Peter?" asked the lieutenant. He must have been talking about the photo on the small table in the hallway by the kitchen. "I see now why he would be afraid to serve. A little girly-looking, wouldn't you say?"

Next, I heard a scuffle as an incensed Wilhelm must have

rushed toward the Lieutenant, and then a loud thump. I heard the lieutenant utter, "Swine," before he gathered his soldiers and tromped out the door, kicking over the morning's tub of churned butter as he did so.

Helga waited five minutes or so to make sure the soldiers were not returning before she came to my door, opened it, and asked me to come into the living room to watch over Wilhelm, who had been pistol-whipped by the lieutenant and was bleeding from the head, while she went to fetch a doctor. "It will take only a half hour to return. I will speak loudly when we approach the house. You must listen for us and hurry back to your room before we enter the house. Can you do that, Jakob?" I nodded, but when I saw Wilhelm, still lying on the floor with blood covering the rag that Helga had tied around his head, my heart leaped with the fear that he might be dead.

Helga saw my fear and said, "Wilhelm will live, Jakob, don't worry. But he will need stitches to stop the bleeding. When he is more alert, would you help him to the sofa (the same sofa-hospital bed on which I had lain when I first came to the home) and sit with him? Do not give him any water, even if he asks for it. I will return as quickly as I can." Helga hurried to the door but turned around just before walking through it and said, "Thank you, Jakob. It is a blessing to have you with us." And she hurried away.

I helped Wilhelm to the sofa and laid him there as he was too weak to move about much on his own. I looked down on him, his head bandage completely soaked, and prayed that God the Eternal Father would watch over him and make him well. And I prayed even harder that I could be a force of justice for all who suffered at the hand of oppressors.

And in the Ghetto: a chamber, a room to which no one can find an entrance, and a shadowy being that lives there, occasionally feeling its way through the streets to sow terror and panic among men. That, I decided, would be the beginning. I stole it from *The Golem.* It was a scary tale that, even with all I've seen, I can't get out of my head. The thought of the golem's power and his existence in the shadows. That there could be one to frighten others as I've been frightened! That is power! But I realized it wasn't just power I was seeking—though would anyone judge me if it were—but justice! Justice for all the wrongs I'd seen, all the wrongs poured out upon the oppressed of the world for the past ten years! But why do I stop there? One hundred years! One thousand years!

In the dark of my room, with the pencil and paper provided by my generous protectors, I was ready to create a golem. But I hoped not to start from mud, as Rabbi Judah Loew, the Maharal of Prague in the late sixteenth century, had. He went to the riverbank in Prague and fashioned a man out of clay, bringing him to life using kabbalistic teachings from the *Sefer HaYitzirah.* I was aware that the golem he created and used to protect the Jews from their Christian neighbors, who held them responsible for all manner of mishaps naturally occurring, he had also buried in the attic of the Prague Synagogue. I wondered. What if his golem, his Yossel, was merely sleeping? Could I awaken him and have him do my bidding?

"But why would you wish to awaken my Yossel?" The whiny voice belonged to Rabbi Loew, who was sitting on a chair in the room before me with his legs crossed, pulling at his long, black beard. On his head was a strange fur hat that he did not remove the entire length of his visit.

Startled, I responded, "Oh! Pardon me, Rabbi Loew. I had no idea ..."

"Exactly," he retorted. "You have no idea and no sense! Yossel was a good golem for a time, but God will only allow what God will allow, and God required Yossel be put away."

"I understand," I answered, though I was pretty certain I didn't. "But wouldn't God allow the use of Yossel's form one more time to provide justice for His Chosen People?"

"Ah, so are we _____ to talk about being the 'Chosen People?' What could that possibly mean?" He stopped to uncross his legs and place a hand on each knee, forcing him to lean forward a bit. "I knew if I were being 'chosen' for the kind of suffering to which we Jews have been subjected, I would simply say 'no, thank you, but thanks anyway,' and walk out of the land of Canaan. Part the sea for me? 'No, thank you.' Create for me the Ner Tamid so I can work my body to the bone repairing Your synagogue in only eight days? 'No, thank you.' And here's a good one. Have Moses carry the Ten Commandments down from Mt. Sinai so I, and all my heritage, can be consumed with guilt for generations upon generations? 'No, thank you.'"

I couldn't believe my ears. "But you're a rabbi! And that's blasphemy!" I exclaimed.

"Blasphemy, shlasphemy," was his rabbinic answer. Then he continued. "And anyway, you say you believe God would allow the use of Yossel's form one more time? Who are you to believe? You are just some snotty-nosed kid inside a dank wall space hiding from Nazis with nothing else to do but write tales about superhero Jewish monsters."

"That's not true!" I exclaimed a bit too loudly. "I have an important task to perform and require the services of a golem to do so. If I can't use your Yossel, I'll find another way."

"My, my, you young ones give up so easily. I can't stop you ... you're the author of the tale. Go ahead and see if I care. But I must warn you: Be careful calling forth that which you do not understand and cannot control. Okay, there, I said what I came to say. Perhaps I'll return; perhaps not."

With that, he disappeared, though slowly, as I watched his black robe melt into the blackness of the room, and then his black beard, until I saw no more of him except a hand on his fur hat, holding fast lest it be lost in his travels.

Raising Yossel had not been as difficult as Rabbi Loew had made it seem. It was really a simple task of adding an aleph to the mem and tav on Yossel's forehead so that the word *emet*, "truth," was formed, and with that, he was once again alive! I imagined he would have the wings of a bat and the dark frown of something angry. Surely a golem would be angry! In fact, I decided to rename him Orlok, thinking it appropriate. As it turned out, Orlok was not angry but happy to be alive and grateful for my intervention. I expected only grunts and groans, but he was so verbal I had to take extraordinary steps to silence him, writing that his vocal cords had been injured by the rope Christians had tied around his neck in an effort to drag him out of the city.

"But that didn't happen," he squawked.

"If I wrote it happened, then it happened," I chastised him.

"But if I cannot speak, I am limited. I must have 'the word' at my behest. For God created the world, and He called it good. I must be able to call things by their name. All holiness requires it."

How could I respond to that? And so, I allowed Orlok to speak, hoping I would not regret it. Nevertheless, I had to remove one faculty from him lest he be too close to human, an affront to God the Creator, so I took away his eyes, that he would not have to see what I had seen, that which should never be seen. With these words, I recreated him, "You shall have no eyes, to protect you from viewing the carnage, but will move about as does a bat." Then I fell asleep, consumed with even more worry than usual.

Soon enough, though, the Rabbi appeared again, pushing a bony finger into my side to awaken me. "Ouch!" I tried to whisper, as I had been warned several times by Wilhelm. "That hurt!"

"Of course it hurt," Rabbi Loew replied. "It was meant to hurt. How else was I to waken you?"

"But why waken me? I had just fallen into a deep sleep and was dreaming of my mother."

"May her name be for a blessing," the Rabbi intoned.

I stopped in my tracks. "Are you saying she's dead?" I could barely utter the question.

"No, idiot! I am saying she is deserving of great respect, as are all mothers. How would I know if she is dead or alive? I'm not God."

He was right. He was very obviously far from being God.

"Why are you here, Rabbi? What was so important you had to wake me up?"

"Do I need a reason? Do you have such a tight schedule that you worry about not getting enough sleep at night? What are you doing tomorrow? Eating some bread and cheese? Drinking some goat milk if you're lucky? Shitting in your pot? I have important matters to discuss with you. About my Yossel."

"You mean about Orlok."

"Whatever. Why do you want a golem, anyway? He can be very difficult, you know. It's like having a mountain-sized baby, the things he doesn't understand, the desires he has but can't fulfill."

"I need Orlok to provide justice for our people and for others."

"And who might these 'others' be?"

I didn't think the Rabbi would understand, but I tried anyway. I explained to him how the German lieutenant had taunted Wilhelm, then physically harmed him. I wanted justice for Wilhelm, too. I wanted Orlok to kill the lieutenant!

The Rabbi scratched his head underneath his hat, then folded his arms across his black-robed body before speaking. "And what of this lieutenant's wife? His two children?" (How did he know?) "If he is killed, who will care for them when this war is over? They will suffer for their husband and father. And in their suffering, isn't it likely that they will wish others to suffer? Might they not carry the grudge to another generation ... and another, and another? Mighty is the hand that is stayed." Saying this, the Rabbi dropped both hands to his lap and appeared to be looking them over, turning them this way and that, searching either for their might or perhaps the lice lingering from his head-scratching.

Continuing, he said, "Is it really justice you want, anyway, or revenge? They aren't the same, you know."

I retorted, quoting the bible to a rabbi, "Exodus calls for absolute justice. An eye for an eye, a tooth for a tooth. That is what I want."

Rabbi Loew answered, "Justice is complicated, my son, just as the human condition is. Absolute justice forces the innocent to suffer. Vengeance in the name of justice has a long history."

At this, Orlok, whom I thought to be asleep, jumped in. "*If we could read the secret history of our enemies, we should find in each person's life sorrow and suffering enough to disarm all hostility.*" Then he turned over and went back to sleep.

Rabbi Loew explained, "Ours is not the only suffering. If all we do is act to avenge the causes of suffering, we are lost."

I agreed to think on it but was unconvinced that inaction was the better course.

34
SARIAH

For a spell, Juan seemed to get better. His recovery brought joy into the home again, for he was a good man, and both María and Sariah relied on his many kindnesses to lift their days. But. Such a large and complicated *but.* In the time Juan had been almost totally bedridden, María had turned to Sariah more and more for support, both emotional and physical. And as happens when two individuals rely on each other for almost, if not completely, everything, they seemed to fall in love.

For the first time in her life, Sariah felt a certainty about who she was. She was María's lover, and that was all that mattered. Was she Sariah or Simon? Who cared! Was she a Christian or a Jew? Why should it matter? She was *in love!*

It was more complicated for María. Though she felt stirrings, she knew who Simon really was—*he* was Sariah. María had been taught that such love was an abomination in the sight of God. How could she betray not just Juan but God Himself? It would be too much, but somehow, in the everyday interactions with Sariah, it had not seemed so: hands touching as they took hold of the corners of starched white bedsheets and meeting in the middle for folding; her wrist held as a cut finger from the knife blade that slipped while slicing carrots for the day's supper was wrapped; her sweat wiped from her brow as she stood over a boiling pot. A touch of hands, of hand on wrist, hand on forehead, became a touch of cheeks, of breasts, and then, well.

It all came to a head one day as Juan surprised them, entering the kitchen when they thought him asleep. María was sitting on Sariah's lap with her blouse open as Sariah fondled her breast with her right hand. It was only fortunate that Juan could not see her left. Occupied, neither heard him until he was well into the room. The extent of his surprise at first slowed Juan's mind and silenced his tongue, allowing María and Sariah the chance to disentangle, though not to inveigle him into believing an innocent explanation to what he saw. Coming to himself, Juan waved them each to a chair—separate chairs—and found his tongue.

"I take responsibility for this occurrence," Juan began. "I will not ask if it is the first or one of many. That does not matter. I drew you, María, onto this path; it is my fault. I was the one who suggested Sariah pose as a male, and posing as a male, she became one in your sight, opening the door for acts that our times disapprove of. I cannot say it will always be so in the eyes of God, as I am neither His priest nor prophet. But I don't believe intercourse is for procreation alone, and if not for that ..." Juan stopped for a moment, watching closely to determine their attitudes. He saw no defiance in either but pain and fear in them both. María's pain that she had transgressed against her husband at all, whether with a male or female, thereby hurting him, and Sariah's that she had sullied María's honor in the eyes of her husband. Each feared the consequences of their actions, though in this perhaps differently. María feared losing her husband's love and respect, recognizing only now that she could not live without those precious gifts. Sariah must have feared the same somewhere in her soul but at that moment feared only losing María.

Juan continued. "Because I will not condemn either of you

does not mean that others will not. We cannot continue as we have before. To save your reputations"—Juan cut Sariah off, knowing she was about to say her reputation meant nothing to her—"I must send you away, Sariah." He looked over at María whose countenance revealed such a sadness mixed with the contrition she felt that he almost couldn't continue. He thought back to that miraculous day they married. He had believed he would never find a wife, especially as he grew older and older without one. But they had found each other, and he, at least, knew he'd been saved. That feeling introduced into his soul such a joy that he spent all his time, when not tending to patients, acting upon his marriage vows to take care of María and make her days happy. Now he knew he must choose which of those two vows he would honor.

"I will investigate the matter and inquire about a position for you with the Inquisition Office, Sariah. I am aware they are looking for a doctor to tend the heretics within the walls of their prison. It is a place you could do good. Now go to your room and allow me to talk with my wife. We will discuss details later."

Sariah began to walk out of the kitchen, wanting to flee but also wanting to explain. She hadn't intended it to come to this. She didn't understand her own yearnings. It was only in their house, with the two of them, that she felt real. She would prefer killing herself to living without them—either of them. But she said nothing, feeling God was justified this time in forcing upon her another rejection.

35
RACHEL

Rachel spent the days after hearing David's story attempting both to forget it and memorize it. It was more than she could bear, but it was a link to her son, and so she held it near, feeling, at times, as if the pain were becoming almost too sweet. Finally, she felt ready to emerge from the cocoon of self-pity and anger in which she had wrapped herself and dressed to go outside, grabbing her sketchpad before going to look for Eloise, whom she knew would likely be in the kitchen preparing lunch.

"Do you have time, Eloise, to walk with me to the cemetery? I'd like to be outside for a bit."

"Of course, Rachel. Just give me a moment to wash my hands. I am so happy you would like to enjoy the sun today. You know vitamin D is integral to increasing the serotonin levels in our blood."

On the short walk to the cemetery, Rachel replayed in her head the conversation she'd had with David about what it meant to be a Jew. She knew she had never *really* been a Jew, though she understood that as the daughter of Jewish parents, she was one. She had gone to a synagogue until she was confirmed and had never returned until David had been born.

Then, more for her mother than any affinity with the faith, Rachel had taken David to Sunday School and to high holiday services at the synagogue. After that, Rachel moored herself with her artistic and literary preoccupations, eschewing matters of faith and ancestry. But now, she wondered. What strength flowed through her veins because of her genealogy? Not just what did she owe *to* it, but what did she get *from* it? Was Judaism something she could toss out like a pair of pants too loose at the waist and too gathered at the crotch?

Reaching the cemetery gate, Rachel thanked Eloise and walked over to the bench beneath the Oldest Oak, seeing one or two of the Children hiding behind headstones as she passed, pretending to ignore her. They'd been told by Inés to keep their distance and knew better, from the tone of her voice, to test her orders. The rough surface of the bench was cool to the touch in the shade of the tall oak though it was a warm day, and with the humidity, Rachel could feel the sweat on her back soaking through her blouse. She sat, placing the pad next to her, and for the first few moments, just sat with her eyes closed, taking in the scents of magnolia, the songs of the birds, and the wind's breath through the old oak's branches. Just as she imagined the oak whispering of longevity and patience, filling her with a soothing calm, she heard him, David's voice, softly prodding, "Mom. How are you?"

Opening her eyes, she saw her beautiful boy again. "David!" Not certain of protocol—or of his substantiality—she reached her hand closer to his but then retracted it. David remained silent for a moment as Rachel enjoyed his nearness. Then he began.

"I wanted to see if you had any questions after our last conversation. I imagine it's all so strange." His brown eyes glowed with a compassion she'd not really noticed before.

Rachel had decided long ago—or at least long ago since arriving at the room, and at the cemetery, and meeting Eloise and Inés, and learning of the Children and the stones and the

Ancestors, and having the dreams that felt so intimate—that she could question everything all at once, or allow time to have its effect, wearing away entrenched certainties the way water creates new channels in the riverbed, allowing for a more gentle shift in attitude. She answered David, "I love just sitting here with you."

David nodded approvingly and waited.

There was so much she wanted to know, so much she should have known, she thought, and didn't.

"I do have questions. I can't let go of why you refused the path of compromise that might have saved your life. I've been thinking since our talk that passivity and silence need not be seen as fear ... they can be a tactic."

David hoped to be a help to his mother and was as grateful as she that they had this time to say things they'd never shared. He answered with a passion Rachel had never heard in him before.

"The rationale for silence is irrelevant, Mom; the result is always the same. Silence emboldens. Silence tips the scale of morality in ways that make living within the silence impossible. Historically, silence is judged with contempt because, in retrospect, we always believe the outcome would have been different had we spoken up, had we resisted. History looks at Jews with scorn and calls us fearful and so aware of our own faults that we must acknowledge our persecution is fair and moral. Our silence is our indictment: we *must be* the subhumans we are accused of being, or we would speak up. Which is worse? The horrors perpetrated upon the Jews throughout history, or our silence? Jacobo Timerman wrote about this after his thirty-month imprisonment in the Argentinian prisons of the Dirty War, questioning Jewish silence and Jewish resolve."

Rachel took this all in, marveling at the assertiveness and

philosophical bent she had never fully recognized in him, before forming her question, "But isn't that the epitome of antisemitism? To blame the victim?"

"As a Jew," David answered, "he had a right to do this, to question without the motive of blame, but with the hope of learning."

Rachel had never had such conversations with her son. Why hadn't she, she now wondered. He had grown up without her noticing, had developed strong feelings and a sense of commitment that she herself never had.

"I acknowledge," David continued, "that silence can be of value at times, as providing a gap, a time for feelings and thoughts to mature, like wine aging in a barrel. But inevitably, the gap must give way to revolutionary action, when silence is no longer a virtue, but is a capitulation to fear and an abettor of continuing tragedy."

Rachel was not certain of this, still fearing the idea of "revolutionary action" and its cost in lives lost. Like the Children. Like her own son. But she listened to his voice, its timbre echoing in her head deliciously long after they'd parted.

36
SARIAH

Sariah had been working in the Inquisition prison in the center of Lima for only a few weeks when she met Rodrigo Jacobo de Simon, a prisoner accused of heresy and considered especially dangerous because of his previous position in the *conversos* community in Lima. Rodrigo had been in the prison for six months when Sariah arrived and was one of the first patients she attended. He'd returned from an interrogation in which he'd been hung from a rafter in the torture cellar by the wrists, tied together behind his back, and left there for half a day. Such a position often resulted in displacement of the shoulder socket and was particularly painful, as torture methods go.

Sariah had come to quietly accept her lot after leaving María and Juan, each of whom had wished her well upon her departure, though distanced themselves from her of necessity. If she could have, her dignity would have required her to return the money Juan pressed into her palm as she left, but she needed it to pay for a small cottage within walking distance of the prison.

Sariah's first week in her new home pained her. Everything ate at her sense of self; nothing was a comfort, not even the honey tea she had enjoyed with María daily in the kitchen. María. That name she would have to forget. But she tried to remind herself she had overcome so much to arrive at this point.

Visiting Rodrigo for the first time, Sariah was surprised at how young he was. Though his brown curls touching his shoulders had not been washed for too long, and his dark eyes revealed deep swaths of pain and suffering, he would be called handsome. As Sariah, dressed as Simon, tended to him, they talked.

"Tell me about yourself, Rodrigo," Sariah uttered, attempting to distract him from the painful procedure of putting his shoulder back into its joint. If it stayed in place, she would know the tendons had not been stretched too far. If it did not, she would wrap his upper arm tightly to his body and put him in a sling while they waited for the tendons to heal. Surgery was not an option, as prisoners were expected to incur bodily damage. "How is it you ended up in here?"

Rodrigo would have been wise to be cautious, as the Inquisitors used many techniques to discover the secrets of the prisoners, including planting informants as doctors. But there was something about Sariah that was soft and innocent, that put others at ease. In any event, Rodrigo had abandoned any attempt at masking his identity. He was tired of being false, as Sariah would soon hear.

"I have been imprisoned for being a *Crypto-Jew,* the name assigned to those who are false Christians. But, in fact, I am no *Crypto-Jew.* I don't say that to avoid torture, as do others. But I ask you, how could I be both Jew and *Crypto-Jew* at the same time? I am a Jew. I don't deny it."

Sariah was shocked by this utterance. To be a Jew was heresy. Unrepenting, he would be burned at the stake. Yet there was a strength about his demeanor, broken in body though he was. Something about the bold statement of his truth.

"How were ———————— you discovered?" she asked, probing further, "I assume you know the Lord's Prayer. Why did you not recite it for them?" Sariah was overcome with anger at his refusal to fight for himself, for his life. "Do you have a family? Aren't you concerned for them?"

Rodrigo laughed. Even during the pain, he let out not a scream but a hearty laugh. "So many questions, and I don't even know your name!"

Sariah blushed at having been called out for such impropriety. "I am Simon," she responded. "I have been trained by Dr. Juan, who you may know, in the practice of medicine."

"Indeed, I have heard of him. He has a reputation as a good doctor and a good man, one who would even service Jews when he was well. You must be the doctor who attended little Hani when he fell ill. I have also heard good things about you. I was told you could have reported the family for celebrating the Passover seder but did not. May I ask why you did not?"

Sariah was taken aback at first, frightened at the personal direction the conversation was taking, but answered, "Why would I report them? Then I would be accused of aiding Jews and likely be your cellmate rather than your doctor."

"Ah," responded Rodrigo. "Good answer. Yet I believe there is more to it than that. But then, we will have time to learn more about each other." A grin followed the grimace that appeared as Sariah tied his arm to his chest, where it would have to remain for some time as it healed. "I am tired. Thank you for your assistance, Dr. Simon. I look forward to our next conversation, though I hope you will not be tending to my injuries while we speak."

Sariah let out a nervous laugh and knocked at the cell door to be let out. As she looked behind when the door opened, she saw Rodrigo, a genuine smile lingering.

Brother Bartólome had been visiting Rodrigo for months with the sincere intent to encourage him to recant and truly accept Christianity. So many in their black robes with their covered heads and deep-set eyes, their lips in omnipresent snarls, resorted to trickery to obtain confessions. They began by attempting to create a bond: I am here to help you, but you must first help me. These words were softly and soothingly pronounced, accompanied by a touch on the arm or the back, an attempt to inject a sense of humanity into the relationship, for a relationship it was, though it changed with more suddenness and frequency than young love. This bond was intended to create a desire on the part of the accused to say what the Inquisitor wished. So, the hope was, the Inquisitor would lead, the accused follow.

Brother Bartólome was not this kind of Inquisitor. He took a real interest in Rodrigo, found him to be a soul worth saving—though, of course, all souls were in the eyes of God, he reminded himself. He also knew the limits of torture. Under torture, a man might say what the Inquisitor wanted, though it be not the truth. He had had many a conversation with his Brother Inquisitors in which they would claim, "Torture is a necessity as it opens the heart and the mouth." To which Brother Bartólome answered, "Torture is a necessity only for the destruction of a man. A necessity to obtain your truth, not his." Even he had to be careful with these views, though, as they were not the views of the Grand Inquisitor.

Rodrigo, for his part, looked forward to his discussions with Brother Bartólome, not just for the diversion from his struggles with solitude but because they were often a test of his beliefs, a chance both to teach and to learn. Hearing the footsteps coming down the hall that day, Rodrigo hoped they belonged to Brother Bartólome. The key clanged in the metal lock, and the heavy door opened, scraping the dirt floor as it did so. Rodrigo saw a smiling face beneath the black hood and said, "Welcome, dear brother."

"How are you faring, my brother?" Brother Bartólome responded.

Seeing Bartólome's eyes landing on his own arm as he asked the question, Rodrigo responded, "Well in spirit. Not too badly in body," and produced a grin.

Brother Bartólome took a seat on a wooden chair that had been placed at a writing table Rodrigo had earned over his time at the Inquisition's prison. He placed a small red apple on the table for Rodrigo sitting opposite him. A special treat.

"That I am happy to hear. I bring you news from your wife. She is well, as are your two sons, and wishes only to have you back with them."

Such news pained Rodrigo, as he knew of only one way to return to them alive, and that he was not willing to do. He knew Brother Bartólome did not intend him this pain, that he sincerely wished for Rodrigo to be back with his family. Brother Bartólome began that day's discussion.

"Let us begin the day's discussion with truth. I have found you to be a reasonable man, one who values truth. I cannot help but be plagued by your misunderstanding of it, for I do not believe it is willful derision that leads you astray. You do understand there can only be one truth, for it is in the very nature of truth to be absolute."

Rodrigo sat at the table with his face resting in the hand of his good arm, leaning his elbow on the table as he looked into the eyes of Bartólome across from him and silently listened to his argument.

"The one truth is that which Christ offers us. Such a blessing to know this! How could it be otherwise? If we gauged truth only by numbers, would Christianity not be persuasive? Such freedom we are offered, and all we must do is accept it! Once again, I implore you, can you not accept the opportunity Christ offers of eternal life with him?"

Rodrigo saw the sincere desire with which the Brother accented his speech, his hands placed with open palms in front of his body, legs uncrossed, spread wide to support his slim physique wrapped in its heavy robe, in a position of complete openness and vulnerability, his hood dropped, revealing an unfurrowed brow and clear eyes.

Every fiber of Rodrigo wished to bring Brother Bartólome happiness but knew the best he could do was offer a robust conversation and a worthy opponent.

"Let us take this apple, for which I thank you," Rodrigo began in response. "Here on this table, out of the sunlight, it is a dark red. But if we move it to this spot," Rodrigo said as he moved the apple some centimeters to a sliver of sunlight coming through the cell's barred window, "where the sun can shine on it, it is a lighter shade of red, and it can be seen that it has a dark bruise. Further, if you and I were each to take a bite, we would experience different levels of sweetness or tartness based upon what we had eaten or drunk before tasting the apple. Yet we both call it apple and believe its qualities to be universal. The apple you experience is unique to you, and the same apple I experience is unique to me. Multiply that by humanity and what, then, is truth? What, the truth of our own lives? What, God's truth?"

Brother Bartólome shook his head in disappointment and fear. He was happy he had discouraged Brother León from joining him in this meeting with Rodrigo. He could imagine the intercourse that would have followed: "I told you he has the tongue of the devil. His arguments will cause even you to question God's truth! No more of this! He has proven he is a danger to all observant Christians, and therefore the fire is his destiny."

No, Brother Bartólome would continue his discussions alone.

37
JAKOB

I had made little progress in putting Orlok to his work as I had seen neither Helga nor Wilhelm for two days, something that had never occurred before. What if something had happened to them? I worried, and worrying, could not put pen to paper, though what else was there to do? What if they had been taken away by German soldiers and I had been left to die, unable to leave this room to discover my fate? Or what if at any moment I would feel the lick of the flames as the Germans burned down the home of enemies of the German state?

"It's beginning to stink in here, you know," came the voice of Rabbi Loew. Here he was again, sitting in the chair he had moved across the room to the furthest point from my chamber pot. "Perhaps an appropriate task for your Orlok would be to empty your shitpot. He may not be able to see it, but he can surely follow his nose."

"Shhh," I begged him. "There may be Germans here."

"Nah," the Rabbi countered. "There are no Jerries, though they were here yesterday ... or the day before. They took your Wilhelm and Helga away. Not sure if they're coming back."

"But, but—that's horrible," I spluttered. "What will I do? How will I eat? Is it safe for me to go find food?"

"I see, I see," observed the Rabbi. "Quite concerned for the well-being of your patrons, aren't you?"

I'd been rightly upbraided. Of course I hoped they were okay. I saw now, though, that I might have less time than I imagined. I couldn't let Orlok rest any longer. It was time to put him into action.

"Never mind," I said to the Rabbi, to whom I wouldn't apologize. After all, he had waited at least one day, maybe two, before telling me Wilhelm and Helga had been taken. What help was he?

"I can be of great assistance," Rabbi Loew contradicted me. "I allowed you to co-opt my Yossel, didn't I? That you haven't yet put him to any use isn't my fault. Perhaps there is a strain of laziness in your genes?"

I knew better than to get into an argument. I hadn't the time to waste. I wrote, "And so Orlok was sent on his task, to stalk the forest during the darkest nights, when the moon was obscured by thick clouds and the night sounds were heavy in the air. To find the exposed necks of German soldiers, throbbing with the strong Aryan blood of which they were so proud. To strike, suck, and drink his fill. Orlok would take the life of the *szkop* and make of him, reborn, a vampire soldier for the golem army of the Jews! For every German life Orlok took, a vampire golem would be born! This, in obedience to the first of the 613 commandments of the Torah, *'Be fruitful and multiply and fill the land and conquer it, and you shall rule over the fish of the sea and the birds of the sky, and all the animals that move upon the earth.'*"

"Whoa, whoa, whoa," the Rabbi interrupted to question the turn of my story. "Whoa. What right have you to make of my Yossel a vampire golem?"

I piled on. "And it is in the night, like any other vampire, that Orlok will strike, and strike, and strike, creating not one vampire golem for each German soldier, but two. No, make it three! And only when all war is over will he rest."

The Rabbi shook his head, holding his hand to his hat that was wobbling a bit from the shaking, and muttered something about the excesses of youth. Suddenly, Orlok sat up in the corner of the room and spoke.

"You have awakened me from my sleep of sleeps for what? To give voice to your pains and strike back at those who have caused them? I was not created for vengeance, but for justice." Orlok turned his head to look at the Rabbi as he spoke this. "To be Jewish is to respect justice and fairness. What you ask of me is neither."

"What can you know of justice or vengeance?" Jakob retorted. "To me, they are the same. I look to God and see the father who put into his son's hands a slingshot by which he could smite his enemy. I see his eyes and see the power of his anger."

Orlok interrupted. "And I see my God's eyes and find there only patience and the capacity for joy."

The Rabbi walked over to Orlok and endearingly rubbed his hand over Orlok's bald head, whispering in his ear, "I always knew you had a good head on you."

To Jakob, the Rabbi said, "It is a good lesson my Yossel introduces. How will the actions that you require of him contribute to justice? If he follows your commands, how will the end be anything but continuing darkness? Doesn't hate beget hate, and war beget war? If so, when will war ever end? Will night's darkness never give way to day? Will your Orlok be forever doomed to slink through the city until *his* thirst, but not yours, is slaked? You may find that the paradox of vengeance is that it does not free you. Instead, it makes you dependent upon those who have harmed you through your belief that it is only their torment that will allow you release from your pain."

Jakob looked up from his writing and saw the room was empty. Nevertheless, he answered the Rabbi, "When this war is over, and the next and the next, and Jews no longer fear persecution, that is when we will all be brothers and sisters, and then, and only then, may my Orlok rest."

On the third day, Helga and Wilhelm returned. I was lying on my bed, my hunger growing stronger but still wary of emerging from hiding when I heard the familiar *tap, tap-tap, tap*, and both Helga and Wilhelm entered the small space. Happily, I greeted them, thankful to God that they were alive but also that the Rabbi and Orlok were not there when they arrived, as I had not yet determined how I would be able to explain them.

Helga spoke first, with emotion. "Oh, Jakob! Please forgive us! You must be wondering why we left you for so long without food or water!" She came closer as if to give me a hug, but I stopped her.

"Please, don't come in further. This room must smell horrible to you, though I have become accustomed to it," I made sure to add so she would not think me ungrateful.

Wilhelm, in the meantime, put down a pitcher of water and walked over to the chamber pot to empty it outside. While he was away, Helga began to explain that they had been taken by the Germans for questioning.

"But I knew that," I responded. "I was only worried the damned szkopi might hurt you. Please tell me they didn't," I pleaded.

Wilhelm had returned to hear my statement. I saw them exchange looks before Wilhelm said, "But how could you have known where we were?"

How was I to respond? It appeared the time had arrived for my introduction of the Rabbi, at the very least. Orlok might be too much for them. So, I answered, "The Rabbi of Prague, Rabbi Loew, saw that you had been taken and told me. But he didn't know if you would return or not. I am afraid to admit I was as frightened for myself as for you. Please forgive me my selfishness." Should I say more? Likely not, I decided.

They looked at each other again but said nothing about the Rabbi. Helga excused herself to prepare a small meal for me while Wilhelm sat with me and told me what had happened at the German camp office.

"It seems a Jewish family of four was found hiding in the barn of a farm some four hundred kilometers away. We had not heard yet, though this kind of news usually travels quickly. Because of this, the Germans have been rounding up all the farmers in the area, one by one, and interrogating them. I believe they wanted to frighten us more than anything else, as Helga and I were not treated badly. After they questioned us in very general terms, we were allowed to return."

"What happened to the Jewish family that was found?" I had to ask, though I wasn't sure I wanted to know. I could see that Wilhelm also did not want to address that elephant in the room. But he had always been honest with me and so answered.

"They were locked in the barn, which was then set on fire." He'd lowered his head as he spoke that horrific sentence.

I didn't have to ask if any had survived. He hadn't mentioned the farmer and his family, though, so I asked, "And the farmer, what did they do to him and his family?"

He hesitated. "I don't wish to say," he replied. He looked up and could see that I would not accept that answer, and so he continued. "Before the barn door was closed and barred, the farmer and his family were thrown into the barn and told they deserved the same fate as the swine they'd been hiding; that swine attracted its own kind."

His tears flowed as he let loose a burden that had been on his heart. "The littlest girl was only three. How could such inhumanity exist on this beautiful earth? An innocent three-year-old? We were being given a warning but were never asked directly if we were hiding any Jews. I suppose they knew we'd be unlikely to divulge if we were after having heard the sure consequence of such a forbidden act. I don't know why I'm telling you this, except perhaps to confess that I don't know what I would do if given a choice by the Germans to expose you or have our farmhouse burned down. I am ashamed to tell you that." Wilhelm lowered his head into his hands and sobbed.

I reached over to him, placing my hands on his. "Please don't be ashamed," I whispered.

Helga returned with a small piece of bread, some cheese, and a blessed glass of milk. More, I could not have eaten or drunk. They said their goodnights and left the room.

On their way to the kitchen, I could hear Wilhelm say, "The boy is losing his mind in that room. I pray that our Lord may soften the Germans' hearts that this war may end quickly. I don't know if Jakob can survive much longer."

And even softer, I heard Helga add, "Can any of us?"

38
SARIAH

Fifteen years passed with Sariah still treating the bruised and beaten, the victims of hatred clothed in the vestments of love. She had witnessed such suffering in the name of one religion or the other that she wondered at a God who would sow such confusion and refuse to lead the way directly to Him. She went cell to cell, experiencing the same in each—filth, rats, the stench of the unhealthy body's waste, battered skeletons and weary, broken minds.

But for Rodrigo she might have succumbed to the dreary pallor of this prison herself. It had all begun to weigh on her so heavily that she let her guard down. It began one day in his cell, as Sariah once again had bandages to apply. This time the thumbnail on Rodrigo's right hand. When she walked into his cell, she saw his left hand grasping his right, holding it aloft, as he grimaced. Sariah, who had not become accustomed to the violence, could not help but let out a cry when she saw the smashed thumb.

Seeing Sariah's distress, Rodrigo attempted to lighten the atmosphere, saying "I seem to have misplaced a thumbnail. Perhaps you could help me find it?" In his pain, he flashed a half grin.

Quietly feigning a calm, Sariah had him sit on his mat while she prepared a salve to apply. She walked over, sat on the mat next to him as Rodrigo offered his battered hand, applied the salve, and bandaged the wound.

"I included some drops of juice from a grated mandrake root, so it should begin to feel better soon," Sariah explained. "I will have to redress this each day for the next four days, and then we will see if more will be necessary for it to heal well." She stood up, gathering her things to head to the next cell.

"Thank you, Simon. You treat me as well as would my own mother." Another twinkle and slight grin, which Sariah ignored. She had not forgotten what it was to be "mother." Not a single day went by that she did not think of Baruch, wonder where he was, and who called him family.

"Stay a moment, Simon. Tell me, now that we have known each other for so long—whatever time means in this place—what is the sadness I see in your eyes each day? What is it you bring with you when you come to care for us all as you do?"

On another day, Sariah might have resisted, but she was so tired. Slowly, carefully, she chose the words to explain. "I *am* you. I am your neighbor and your neighbor's neighbor and the neighbors next to him. I am an outcast, as are you all, and even more than you all. I am tired and wish so mightily to belong somewhere and to have some hope of being loved for who I am." That was as far as she would go for the moment. Had Rodrigo not been listening well, he would have missed the confessions.

Rodrigo studied her intently. What could he say? Was now the time? "I don't wish to belittle your pain, as I can see it is very real. But there is a place for you, Simon. None of us is an outsider when we open our hearts to God. He calls us to him, and to the service of others, in subtle ways. *Shema, Yisrael.*"

Sariah turned from him, not wanting him to see as she whispered the rest of the prayer, "... *Adonai Elohenu, Adonai Echaud.*" She did remember, and it called to her still. Turning around, Sariah sat again on the chair by the desk.

"You have heard His call," he continued. "You may resist, but ultimately you must honor that which is inside you. There is no other way."

"How can I know what is inside me?" Sariah asked. "So many times I have thought I tasted joy, the joy of feeling at one with the world. Each time the source of that joy was ripped from me and, once again, I was alone, cast out, lost. I had to abandon what I thought was inside me to stay alive. Now I don't know if anything is left."

Rodrigo stood, walked over, knelt next to her, and took Sariah's hand in his good hand. "What is inside is never truly lost, Simon. Or whatever your name is." As she began to pull her hand away, Rodrigo mollified her, "Don't worry, I have no sway with anyone. Your truths are yours to keep or yours to share. But I have learned that in sharing, the heart grows."

"Do others know?" Sariah asked him.

"Know what? That you are a woman, or that you are a Jew? They are too wrapped up in their individual circumstances to pay much attention to others, though I try to help them see otherwise. And you have nothing to fear from me, Simon. I have resisted torture for so long their only attempts are when they have an Inquisition official to impress."

He continued. "If you will allow it, I can help you understand much about your heritage that you see as your enemy. You cannot live in such a way. It will eat at your soul until there is nothing left, and you are an outsider, not just with others, but an outsider to yourself. There is a community that waits to embrace you, a community that is, granted, human, and being human, sins against each other. Nevertheless, a shared history and culture bind us in ways we could never be bound to Christians. Let me guide you back to it."

Sariah wanted nothing more than to find comfort, to be accepted for herself, for all the parts that seemed unacceptable. If Rodrigo could help, she would submit to him. But she had a question.

"You have been a leader in the Jewish community is what I have heard, Rodrigo. What keeps *you* from returning to them if you are as committed to them as you say? You would be released if you would simply recant publicly, if not privately."

Rodrigo's answer was quick. "To do so would require that I split myself in two, one side authentic, the other a lie. The two could never survive together. I am afraid that either way, whether I tell the truth and die as a heretic, or lie and die a spiritual death, death awaits ... as, of course, it does for us all."

Sariah couldn't let it go at that. She asked, "But if a Jew tells a lie in order to prevent torture or death, whom should we judge—the Jew or the world that would force such a lie from his lips?"

Sariah had been at the scene of an Auto-de-Fé once before when she'd first come to Lima. When she saw the soldiers leading natives carrying the large posts and the wagons of straw as she walked from her small cottage to the market, she feared for Rodrigo. After filling her market bag, she hurried home to fetch her herbs and bandages and left for the Inquisition prison to discover Rodrigo's fate.

Sariah's heart thumped loudly in her chest as she waited for Rodrigo's heavy prison door to be opened for her. "Señor Simon," a guard called out. "Have you heard of the Auto-de-Fé tomorrow? Thanks be to God for His goodness in providing these heretics a chance to enter His heavenly home."

"Yes, Pedro, thanks be to God," echoed Sariah. Hoping to prepare herself before seeing Rodrigo, she asked Pedro if he knew which of the prisoners were to be *saved* tomorrow. Was Rodrigo one of them?

"Not that scoundrel, Señor. They are saving him for something special, I believe. He has plagued the Brothers for such a long time."

Sariah was relieved to hear Rodrigo had time left. Perhaps she could yet influence his fate. She thanked Pedro, who then let her into Rodrigo's cell, saying, "I will await your knock."

As she entered, she found Rodrigo facing the small window in his cell, though he could not see through it without pulling a chair over and climbing onto it. Just then, he was simply standing there, in such deep thought, he did not seem to hear her enter. Sariah stood at the door for a few minutes until Rodrigo turned around and addressed her.

"Simon. I did not expect you today."

"I did not expect to come here today," she responded.

"Yet you are here, so there is a reason. Tell me what is in your heart."

Sariah hesitated. If he did not know about the Auto-de-Fé, should she tell him? It would be a worry she could spare him. But it was too late for that. She was there, and he needed to know.

"I was at the market and saw the approach of soldiers who were accompanying those bringing the makings of an Auto-de-Fé into the town. I feared for you."

"So that is it," Rodrigo sighed. "And I feared for you, that it was something worse than an Auto-de-Fé."

"But what could be worse than being burned at the stake for committing sins that are not sins?" Sariah asked.

"Sit down with me," Rodrigo invited, pointing to the chairs at the small table, directing Sariah to the one nearest the door. "And let us talk. There is much that can be worse. You know this."

Sariah sat, bowing her head. She *didn't* know. Physical pain and suffering brought her great fear. There were times, alone in her cottage at night, trying to get to sleep, that her entire body would tremble, tremble in such a way she couldn't control it as she remembered the pain of her rape. Sariah wondered, too, at the pain her brother had felt when his head had been broken open or the pain her father felt when impaled. At least their deaths had been quick, their pain not prolonged. She looked up at Rodrigo and answered angrily.

"*I don't know.* I don't. What is worse than flames lapping at innocent skin? What is worse than smelling the burning of one's own flesh? Of appearing naked before all?" That, of course, frightened her as much as pain itself, as she would be unmasked. Townspeople would see breasts where they expected none. See emptiness where they expected more.

"The fire of the Auto-de-Fé is no different than the tortures endured here in the prison," Rodrigo explained. "There are ways to manage. Understanding that suffering is a part of this life is a beginning."

Anger rose in Sariah again. Hadn't she suffered enough to know that it was a part of life?

"But *why* suffering, Rodrigo? Don't just tell me it exists; I want to know why. What merciful God requires it?"

"Listen to me. Look at me and truly hear what I say. The heart can be opened in many ways, but you will never avoid suffering. It is a part of this world, of past worlds and future worlds. It is in your very bones—so much so that even if you believe you do not suffer, you suffer. But in between the moments of suffering are gaps: The hungry young boy hurling himself through a field to chase after a ball; for those moments, his hunger does not exist. The elderly woman whose legs ache after years of work in the fields, remembering the moment she first held her daughter and mimicking the child's innocent smile without knowing it. In each of these small moments, we taste the joy and freedom that triumphs over suffering.

"You will learn, too, that it is enough to know you are not alone in your suffering ... that others have suffered, do suffer, and their living—and dying—in the face of suffering has created a pattern for us to follow. They did it, so I can, too. And from whom else to learn suffering's lessons than the Jews?"

As he spoke these words, Sariah looked at Rodrigo's broken body, the scars and badly healed fractures causing his limbs to turn in ways that should not be possible. She heard outside the barred window the clopping of horses' hooves on the cobblestone streets, each carrying, she knew, dignitaries invited to witness the fire, to praise the God whose ego would be fed by the suffering of so-called heretics.

39
RACHEL

Rachel sat at her desk, looking out the window at the cemetery and remembering her conversation with David. "With David," she marveled, still questioning how that could be but unwilling to question so far as to undermine its possibility, as she lived for more conversations with him. The cemetery was dark, but she could still see the bench beneath the Oldest Oak and imagined the two of them sitting and talking as if all were well and normal in the world. How far this world had swerved from *well* and *normal* was still unnerving to her.

They'd parted without a word of how and when they would speak again, and there was so much she still needed to understand. So much she felt David could help her understand. Looming largest were questions of "why me?" Why have I been selected for all these losses, for all this suffering? But how could she stop at "me" when she now knew about the Children, about David, and about those in her dreams who also suffered? Was it all connected in some grand plan by a malevolent god, for who would impose such suffering with beneficent intent?

When Eloise brought her a soft-boiled egg and pomegranate juice later in the morning, Rachel asked again to go to the cemetery. She didn't know if her conversation with David should be kept secret or not, but she so wanted to tell Eloise to have someone with whom to share both the joy and the discomfiting strangeness.

"Oh, let's do," Eloise jumped at Rachel's suggestion. "In fact, I was going to the cemetery myself today for Sharing Time with the Children. It is something Inés schedules once a week—have I told you before?—to provide some degree of structure to their lives. Structure, you know, can be essential to mental health." Rachel did know but wondered if, being dead, the Children's minds responded to stimuli in the same way as when alive.

As they walked the short path to the graveyard, Eloise stomped on a pecan shell on the ground, picked it up, and tore out pieces of fresh pecan that she shared. Rachel was reminded of walks to elementary school and the trouble she'd get into for being late because she'd found pecans on the ground and stopped to fill her pockets and savor the sweet meat. Memories of her own childhood reminded her of the Children and their lost childhoods.

Eloise opened the gate, and as they walked inside, they could see they were already late, as there were no Children running about the graveyard paths, no rope skipping or games of capture the flag. They hurried to the exedra, where the lessons occurred, the best place to settle the Children and maintain their attention. Sidling toward the rear so they could hide next to a large Camellia bush, they saw they had not succeeded, catching a wicked glance from Inés, a silent rebuke for arriving late. Inés was in the middle of a lesson that involved the South African activist Desmond Tutu as an introduction to Sharing Time.

"Archbishop Tutu," Inés was saying, after answering one of the Children's questions about what an archbishop was, "often introduced African culture this way: 'In Africa, when you ask someone *How are you?* the reply you get is in the plural even when you are speaking to one person. A man might say, *We are well* or *We are not well.* He himself may be quite well, but his grandmother is not well, and so he is not well either.'"

The Children looked up at Inés with baffled faces, so she tried another tack.

"Jameson, are you well?" she asked of a twelve-year-old, whom she most hoped would have understood.

"We are not well," he responded.

Grateful for his answer, Inés continued, "And why not?"

"Because our mother suffers."

Inés paused, then directed, "Thank you, Jameson. Will you be the leader for the rest of Sharing Time? I must attend to matters with Auntie Eloise."

Inés walked over to Eloise and Rachel, motioning them to follow her through the cemetery, speaking as they walked. "Rachel, tell me how you are doing. I noticed you sat for quite a while yesterday on the bench beneath the Oldest Oak."

Rachel wondered if all Inés and Eloise did with their time was spy on her; they seemed to know her movements so intimately. Nevertheless, without irritation, she responded, "Yes, in fact, I hoped to speak with you and Eloise about that." For a moment, Rachel feared they would think her crazy—they who spoke daily with dead Children—but asked slyly, "Could you see with whom I was speaking?"

They could, but this was a delicate matter, and neither wished to speak out of turn. Eloise was silent, deferring to Inés, as she almost always did.

"We could see, and we could not see," answered Inés, speaking, seemingly always, in riddles.

Rachel was more direct, watching for their reaction. "It was David."

"Oh," Eloise remarked noncommittally, brushing an ant off her leg.

"He spoke to me of his death and then promised to meet me here now and again so we could discuss questions I might have."

"Ahh," Inés also reacted casually, readjusting the scarf around her shoulders as if a cold breeze had just arisen.

"Is that all either of you can say?" Rachel charged, turning an angry eye first on one and then the other. "I tell you my dead son is appearing to me, and you say, 'Oh' and 'Ahh'?"

"But what do you expect us to say," Inés countered. "You must know we would not be surprised. We're happy for you, of course, and believe you'll benefit from the encounters. But," here Inés touched Rachel's hand, "you should know it cannot be always. Now, we must return to Sharing Time before it devolves into such a rowdiness that it disturbs the Ancestors."

As the sisters walked in the opposite direction, Rachel could hear evidence of sparring. She paid no attention, as she was filled with the anticipation of seeing David. She sat under the Oldest Oak and rested there, trying to settle her fast-beating heart and to forget the warning "it cannot be always." In no time, David appeared.

"Mom."

Again, that word. The one that made her question her own substance. Mother or not-mother? Once-mother? Former-mother? Oh, but she felt still-mother!

"David! I wasn't certain you'd really be here." Rachel paused, catching her breath. "I have so many questions I don't even know where to start. I've been thinking since our last meeting about your affinity for your Jewish heritage and wondered how you came by it."

David had wanted to move more slowly into these waters, but here they were already, and he hoped his mother could tread long enough to grow comfortable with the current, to allow it to carry her along rather than continue to fight against it.

"Do you remember, Mom, when I told you about the boy Eli and I had seen surrounded by a crowd? The boy who set himself on fire to protest the atrocities of the government and the Righteous? Who had already been subjected to hideous torture and was now willingly choosing something even more extreme, hoping to inspire the rest of us to fight back? It was such a desperate, brave act. Something flipped in me then. Others might say what the boy did was reckless and ineffective. But it wasn't. If I was the only one touched, it wasn't ineffective. It was at that moment that I connected to the suffering of my ancestors in a very real way. I could *see* them being tortured through the years. I could *hear* their screams as piercing as those I heard right in front of me. For the first time I got a taste, a real taste of what it meant to treasure something enough to sacrifice for it. Until that moment, I'd been doing nothing more than pretending to be Jewish, nothing more than playing at being a revolutionary."

David wondered if it was time to talk about the Holocaust, always the elephant in the room when it came to discussing the experience of being Jewish. Their time was short, so he decided to jump in.

"We have so much to learn, as Jews, from history. Just a century ago six million Jews were annihilated. It's easy to think of the Holocaust as something that happened to a people as a whole. Anonymous. The threat of anonymity is that it escapes moral vision. It's too easy to look away. A single person's terror and misfortune, on the other hand, captures our moral imagination and holds it fast. That's what I felt in the presence of the boy on fire. My moral imagination was burning with him."

Rachel believed she could feel what David had felt as he spoke; the importance of the individual story.

David continued, "With the Nazis themselves, it's easy to look past individual responsibility. But remembering a machine is made of individual parts forces us to look more closely at the people who made condemning decisions every second of every day: the guard who chose to pull the trigger, the bureaucrat who chose into which pile a name should go, the neighbor all too willing to rat out a hiding Jew. Everything that happened, happened because of one person's decision. It's a reminder that each of us plays a role in either choosing to support or choosing to abort the status quo."

Rachel listened, marveling at David's certainty and maturity. Here was a boy with only one Jewish parent—non-practicing at that—yet so certain of his faith. She, on the other hand, wondered why her ancestry had never been valuable to her. Why she had always *chosen* to hide her heritage when so many of her ancestors had been *forced* to. Was it to gain acceptance in a Christian world? Was it to avoid creating discomfort in others who would have to deal with her difference? What a horrible thing that would be, to abandon her ancestry to make others comfortable.

"I haven't your faith, David. I'm afraid there's a part of me that tires of the differing certainties and longs for a more inclusive connectedness. But unlike you, I assess blame to my heritage for hiding in differences."

David responded gently. "I understand, Mom, but I would ask, doesn't that pit you against you? Must it always be one or the other? Can you really disavow who you are that easily?"

40
THE CHILDREN'S CHORUS

You may resist, but ultimately you must honor that which is inside you.

41
JAKOB

It wasn't long after Helga and Wilhelm had returned from their questioning by the Germans that I heard shouts and pounding on the door, what sounded like an entire platoon of soldiers back to harass my dear benefactors. I kept very still, aware, again, that if I could hear them, they might also hear me.

"Let us in!" I heard though the words were in Polish, not German. "We're not here to harm you."

Wilhelm opened the front door and I heard him say, "Who are you and what do you want from us?"

It must not have been German soldiers, for he would have recognized them. But then, who could it have been?

"We're not commissioned soldiers, but we are fighting the Germans for all of Poland and for the world beyond Poland. We're camped nearby and have come to ask for food and supplies to help us make it through another week."

Helga had come to the door, though I'm certain Wilhelm would have tried to prevent this. Nevertheless, I heard her say, "We have nothing to spare. You must know it!"

"We're not asking for your entire store, just enough for our band of thirty to make it through another week. Then we will move on and seek help from another. This we promise."

Surprisingly, I didn't hear the tromping of boots inside the house. Were these polite brigands? That there could be such a thing in this world amazed me.

"But why should you be amazed, my son?" The Rabbi had joined me at a very inopportune time. "War can make of men both immoral and moral actors. It is not the external circumstance alone that creates character, but internal wisdom and goodness ... or lack of it."

"Shhhh," I warned him. "Now isn't the time for sermons. We could be overheard. These would-be thieves may be polite, but I'm certain their arms are deadly all the same. And you and I are not supposed to be here."

"Speak for yourself," the Rabbi interjected with some ardor. "I can be anywhere I wish ... if that were not already apparent to you."

"We would like to come in and see for ourselves what you have to share. We promise to take only what we need." Both the Rabbi and I were silent as we listened to this most unusual approach. "But be certain that if you cannot find it in your hearts to share willingly, we will not decline to use force. We are mice in a corner, and the cat has our hole in his view. We Jews have always been thus."

"What?" I exclaimed, though in a whisper, to the Rabbi.

"Yes, yes. I could have told you," answered the Rabbi. "They are Jews who have found a way to escape the camps and fight for the freedom of all. May God bless their efforts."

"But how are they different from the Germans who raid the farms around here? How can they target Poles when they themselves know the vulnerability of innocence?"

The Rabbi fiddled with his beard before answering. "*Innocence* is a word that doesn't belong in this world anymore," he sighed. "Even we Jews are not innocent. Of what are we guilty, you ask? Of much but not what you think. We are guilty not of defending ourselves, as these brigands are doing, but of not defending ourselves. That is our guilt. That is what we will be praying to our God for forgiveness on Yom Kippur. For not killing more. New commandments must be written. And because we cannot wait for another Moses, we must write them ourselves."

While listening to the Rabbi's monologue, I could also hear the band of Jews enter the house and leave it, carrying, I supposed, bags of flour, potatoes, and some smoked meat. I only hoped they had not made off with any butter. I took a moment to thank God they had not searched the house, as much of the food was stored in my little habitat. I wondered, though, what would have happened had they searched and found me. Would they have forced me to join them? Would I have wanted to? I turned to the Rabbi to pursue these thoughts with him, but I saw only his arm as it disappeared to join the rest of his body.

Moments later, Wilhelm came to the door, tapped, and entered. Immediately I apologized, anguished that it had been Jews to have caused him further pain. "Please forgive them, Wilhelm," I pleaded. "They must have been desperate." Though I quickly added, "But that is no excuse."

Wilhelm put his arms around me in a hug, something that did not often happen. "It is alright, Jakob. You are safe. We are safe. We have food. We can share this good fortune with others. Let us hope our small offering will be of some use to them in their fight for freedom, a freedom we may all share in."

The raid by my Jewish brothers and sisters angered me. How were we to enlist the sympathy, the support, of non-Jewish Poles when we made of them victims, too? Wilhelm's magnanimity cheered me, but still, I worried and realized I must do all I could to hasten the end of the war so that everyone's suffering might end.

Again, that night Orlok took to the forest, searching out hidden bands of Germans. One German in particular he searched for: one who was widely known for taking the manhood of Jewish boys and leaving them to die horribly. Lacking eyes, Orlok relied on his other well-developed senses, listening for the pleading, searching for the scent of blood and shit. How he longed to kill that one and enlist his three vampire brothers in the army that would, by its mere numbers, overwhelm the Germans.

"I am happy to hear you say 'overwhelm' and not murder, which, as you must know, is forbidden by God." The Rabbi was back, sitting in the air as the second chair held my lunch while I was using the table to write. "Thou shalt not commit murder. Sixth commandment. Remember?"

Annoyed, I responded, "Of course I remember. Tell the Germans!"

"I have. They don't seem to understand Yiddish. Though it surprises me—it's so close to German."

I kept writing. The Rabbi wasn't going to get me off track again. *In the darkest part of the forest, Orlok came upon the scene he'd been looking for.*

"Wait, wait," the Rabbi interrupted. "If you're going to go down that road, at least be consistent. What does it matter that it was the 'darkest part of the forest?' Orlok is blind. It's all darkness to him. And I know it's not meant to be literal, but it feels a bit sloppy to me to say a blind vampire was 'looking' for something. Can't you find another word?"

"So now you're a literary critic?" I didn't want to engage him, but I couldn't help myself when he was criticizing my writing. "You put on and take off hats like nobody's business." As I said this, he removed the kippah on his head and replaced it with the large, ornamental hat he'd been wearing earlier.

From the corner of the room came another voice. "Now that we're having a discussion, I must add that I don't relish continuing this bloodthirsty path."

I looked there and saw my Orlok standing, partially bent over so that his head did not strike the ceiling. "Excuse me?" I spluttered. I was tiring of these challenges. "You what?"

Orlok rephrased. "I don't want to keep sucking blood. I believe it's beneath my dignity."

The Rabbi jumped in. "I created my Yossel out of clay in the form of a human being, just as God created mankind in his own image, 'in the image of God he created them; male and female he created them.' That's Genesis 1:27, in case you've forgotten. Nowhere does it mention vampires, by the way."

Now they were ganging up on me. I retorted, "The golem's purpose is to protect the security and future of the Jewish community. That's what Orlok is doing. His form is irrelevant. Besides, the vampire has an exalted history in Jewish literature." To Orlok, I said, "You should be proud."

Hearing no response from Rabbi or golem, I continued.

"Anyway, your purpose is also to be my companion in this dank place." I vented. "I miss my family, playing ball on the streets with my friends, studying in school. I miss so much. I can't take this any longer!"

"But you would impose suffering on me to avoid suffering for yourself? You are right that sorrow is not meant to be borne alone. I, too, spent much time in seclusion." Saying this, Orlok shot a withering glance at the Rabbi. "There were times I wished I had never been born. But that would be a rebuke of God and His will. A sacrilege. Better that I remember this:

Know that joy is rare, more difficult, and more beautiful than sadness. Once you make this all-important discovery, you must embrace joy as a moral obligation."

In the corner of his eye, Jakob sees the Rabbi, a proud father's smile on his face. "My Yossel, you have been reading great literature, I see."

Orlok bowed his head in humility. "You must do what you were born to do. You must be who you were born to be. That much is true." Speaking to me, he said, "You are a Jew. You must *be* a Jew. What that means is yours to discover. I am a golem. I, too, must obey the law of my creation, which is subject to interpretation, as are all laws."

Had I created the first literary golem, the first vampire golem, or the first lawyer golem?

"He is wise, this golem of mine, don't you think?" asked the Rabbi.

"He's mine!" I exclaimed, loud enough that both Rabbi and golem pressed a finger to their lips and said, "Shhhhh," in unison.

Rather than argue further, I continued writing. *And Orlok, having found the evildoer, flung himself upon him and relished breaking his neck as he pierced the filthy, pimpled skin with his fangs and drank and drank and drank, then watched as three vampires rose from the dead body. In the meantime, the dying, mutilated young boy looked on. Who can say whether his last moments were spent in the pain inflicted by the German or in fear of the loss of his sanity?*

42
SARIAH

Rodrigo had just returned to his cell after visiting Emanuel, something the guards allowed him, knowing he was the Jewish equivalent of a Father Confessor, assuming there must be one even for such a God-forsaken faith, and so merited privileges others did not have. Emanuel's cell was smaller than Rodrigo's by half and was an inner cell, meaning it hadn't even the narrow, barred window providing the slivers of light that Rodrigo felt blessed with on cloudless days. Rodrigo struggled with feeling blessed, as such emotions often relied upon another's misfortune. He tried not to think in such dualities, for he knew them to be false. What were good/evil, life/death, really? All he knew, or wanted to know, was love. Even hate, an oft-paired duality to love, was an imposter, repackaged insecurity and fear.

Only minutes after returning to his cell and laying down for a rest, evidence he was becoming weaker—the toll of his imprisonment—Rodrigo could hear the clang of the key in the door's lock. Brother Bartólome entered, and Rodrigo, tired though he was, jumped up for the greeting.

"I am sorry to disturb you, my brother," Bartólome uttered, "but I have come to discuss important matters with you." The Inquisitor hesitated in revealing that his superiors were weary of Rodrigo's recalcitrance and would not give Bartólome much longer to work with him, so he began his visit with a discussion of other prisoners he would like Rodrigo's help with.

Finally, Rodrigo asked, "What would you really like to talk about?" when the well had dried following the discussion of others.

Bartólome displayed a weak smile, a recognition that he could never fool Rodrigo. He had stayed up most of the night reading through the scriptures, attempting to find anything that might be useful in breaking through Rodrigo's hardheartedness, and was tired.

"I have been thinking about the similarities between your faith and mine and wished to discuss this with you."

"I always look forward to our discussions, Bartólome, for I find you a worthy debater."

"And I, you, Rodrigo. But we must go beyond debating. Things become more serious for you. I pray that our Lord and Savior will touch your heart," he said with a sincerity that spoke to who he was.

"I was reading this last night in John:

> In the beginning was the Word, and the Word was with God, and the Word was God ... And the Word was made flesh, and dwelt among us, and we beheld his glory, the glory as of the only begotten of the Father, full of grace and truth.

"It is clear that our savior Jesus Christ is the Word. But here, now, I must stretch a bit. I am aware that for the Jews, the Torah is also considered the Word of God. Is it so far-fetched to imagine that our Jesus Christ is the name given to the Word of God of your Torah? Could you not accept Christ on that level?"

It did not take long for Rodrigo to structure his answer as

he thought of his study of Kabbalah. "It is not only 'the Word,'" he answered, "but words, and even individual letters, that are precious to the Jews because of their potential for creation and destruction both. In the second century, Rabbi Meir, a teacher of the Mishnah, wrote of this." Rodrigo walked over to a stack of books on the floor of his cell, found the one he was looking for, and read from a dog-eared page, *When I went to Rabbi Ishmael, he asked me: My son, what is your occupation? I answered: I am a scribe of the Torah. And he said to me: My son, be careful in your work, for it is the work of God; if you omit a single letter, or write a letter too many, you will destroy the whole world ...*

"This creative force of words and letters, equal to the creative force of God, has a correlative, and that is the power to destroy. Is this what you want me to discuss with your Inquisitors? You believe *this* will save my life?"

Bartólome was not to be deterred. Ignoring most of what he had just heard, he struck on the one concept he believed he could sell to his Brothers. "But if you acknowledge the power of *your* Word to create, can you not see in the Gospel of John this power at work? Can you not at the very least speak to these similarities when questioned? Can you do that for me so I do not have to feel I have failed in attempting to save your life?" His impassioned plea, he realized with disappointment, was for himself perhaps even more than it was for Rodrigo, and he was ashamed.

"I can," Rodrigo answered, "but there is a question that roots out the very core of our differences, and that question will always betray a Jew to his captors." Rodrigo said this while looking Bartólome directly in the eyes.

Still confident in Rodrigo's intellectual abilities, his inherent ability to parse and repackage truths, Bartólome retorted, "But we have agreed that Christians and Jews believe in the divinity of the Word, so that our differences may be explained simply in the naming of the divinity. If that is so, what is the question you believe cannot be finessed?"

Rodrigo sighed deeply, disagreeing with his brother but not wishing to cause him distress. They could have talked of more, of the fact that both religions believed in a Creator, and both, giving leeway to the weaknesses of men, wished to create good, kindhearted, and spiritual people. Instead, Rodrigo answered Bartólome's endgame request. "The question is this: 'Do you accept Christ as the Messiah?' I cannot, as the letters for the name of the Messiah have not yet been arranged, the Messiah having not yet arrived."

What was this damned Kabbalah double-talk? Bartólome's weariness overwhelmed him, yet he tried once more, saying, "You must give me something, *something* to bring to them that will abate their hunger for your life."

"I have no desire for death, my brother. Tell me what I could say, though, that would not require my inauthenticity."

Bartólome's shoulders slumped, a sign he knew it was over. "You and your damned authenticity." The quiet complaint leaked from a tired Inquisitor, who knew this would lead to Rodrigo's end.

On her way to the market, Sariah was distracted, thinking about Baruch and where he might be.

"Excuse me," said a man who'd been walking ahead of Sariah and, in stopping to pick up a coin, caused her to bump into him. He was wearing the *sanbenito*, a tunic that identified its wearer as a heretic, most often a Jew who'd been found guilty by the Inquisition of practicing Judaism in secret. If they confessed—under torture—and repented—more torture—they were spared the fire but forced to wear the tunic as a symbol of disgrace.

Sariah nodded at the man but knew not to engage with

him in public. Those who spoke with heretics invited the Inquisition's interest. Nevertheless, she could not help being curious about the man's story, how he had come to the tattoo of this garment. The man continued to walk in front of her but turned into an alley. Courting danger—but what did she have to lose?—Sariah followed him.

"Excuse me. Um, excuse me," Sariah spoke up. "I would talk with you now that we are hidden from probing eyes."

The heretic stopped and looked Sariah up and down. "Who are you and what do you want? Though you may not see the eyes watching, I can promise you they are everywhere. What is your purpose that would cause you to take such a risk?"

Sariah didn't know how to answer him. What did she want from him?

"I wish only to talk with you for a moment." She pointed to a bench at the end of the alley with a balustraded back that had once likely existed in a wealthy cleric's home but was now abandoned and left in an alley. "Will you rest with me there and answer a question I have?"

It was such a bold request that the heretic was taken aback. Either this was an Inquisition spy or an imbecile. Either way, he felt he had little to lose. Though he'd saved his life by denying his practice of Judaism, were he to forfeit his life, it would matter not to him now. He was torn in two, his interior life warring with his exterior, and didn't know how much longer he could remain in the fight. So, he answered, "It depends on the question, my lord, but I will sit with you if you desire it."

"Please, there is no need to address me as 'my lord.' I am Simon. What is your name?" Sariah began.

"Avraham. Avraham Meir," the heretic answered.

"Tell me, Señor Meir, how it is you have come to wear the *sanbenito*. I am a doctor who works in the Inquisition prison and wish to understand more about what motivates your people to cling to a God that has so obviously forsaken them."

Avraham was an old man with a short white beard and a bent back, missing teeth, and did not seem to have the use of his left hand. Had he lived an arduous physical life that left him debilitated thus? He responded quietly but kindly to Sariah's question.

"I, too, am ... or was a doctor. But as you can see, I am in no condition to continue as such."

Sariah was surprised. Though she, of all, should have known better the effects torture could have on the human body. She remained silent to encourage Avraham's story.

"I will share my story and hope that it may help others. If you choose to use it against me, it is the will of God.

I left Spain as a young boy, forced out with my family when the crown disavowed the very Jews from whom it received much of its support in both gold and goodwill. This was the first time I realized I was hated not for who I was but for with whom I associated. We first went to Portugal, where my father, also a doctor, was imprisoned. I knew then that his actions contributed to his imprisonment. Though he was a Jew, had he simply not *practiced* Judaism, he would not have been imprisoned. This was a difference I would remember.

My older siblings, as I was the middle of five and younger by seven years, arranged for the family to take a boat to Peru, where a Jewish community was still allowed. But the Spanish Inquisition followed close behind. They were relentless in their desire to wipe all Jews from the earth. You might have thought I would wish to distance myself from a religion that seemed to be cursed, but I did not. In fact, within, I felt the desire to share the strength and certitude of youth with my community, to buoy them and sustain them in times of hardship. To bring them to the understanding to which I had come, that life without community, without principles, was empty.

I was able to maintain a quiet medical practice in the Ayacucho region, where I tended to a small Jewish community and also to the natives _____ for many years. I believe now I must have been reported by a traveling cleric, who heard from the natives of my medical prowess. He came to my home one night, where I now lived with my wife and my own son, and asked me to treat him for a disease that I knew could only have a sexual origin. When I inquired with whom he had been since the symptoms of the disease had first appeared so that he could bring them some of the medicine with which I had treated him, he became incensed at what I was implying. Not long after, the Inquisition came for me.

If I have a regret, I suppose it is that I married at all and that I had a son. 'Why,' you ask? Would I truly ask God to reverse what others would deem great good fortune? It is because I was forced to abandon my own faith, my community, and my very identity to save them. Had I refused to recant, we would all have faced the flames of judgment on this earth together. I could choose those flames for myself but could not for my loved ones."

Sariah could be silent no longer, his story speaking to her as if meant just for her. "Where is your family now, Dr. Meir?"

"I do not know. Yet I wear the *sanbenito* and walk about in a city trying to be as true to myself as I can, within the confines of my betrayal, which is what the *sanbenito* reminds me each day that I put it on. To others, it is a symbol that I practiced Judaism unlawfully but have since recanted. To me, it is a symbol of my submission. Submission. Betrayal. They are the same."

Sariah placed her hand on Avraham's for just a moment. A touch forbidden by the *sanbenito*. She looked around, stood up, and said, "I will remember." Dr. Meir sat there, resting, as a stray dog approached, looking for a scrap of food.

Visiting Rodrigo the next day, Sariah recounted to him her meeting with Avraham Meir.

"I met a Jew wearing a *sanbenito* yesterday. Something made me engage with him, and I heard the story of his condemnation."

"Did you learn this man's name?"

"He was a doctor. Avraham something. I'm afraid I was nervous and not paying as close attention as I might otherwise have."

Quickly, Rodrigo interjected, "Dr. Avraham Meir, then."

Sariah looked up at Rodrigo with surprise. "That's it. How did you know?"

"Does it surprise you that we take care even of our outcasts? Especially our outcasts? We are discreet, but a Jew can never truly abandon his people. The time will come when the one thing that remains is his ... or her ... connection to their heritage."

Sariah took Rodrigo's hand to check the healing of his injuries as she said, "I took his hand like this. We were in an alley, but I suppose we could have been watched."

"It was not wise of you," Rodrigo responded, "but I understand your desire to provide comfort. It is something you are good at."

Sariah soaked in the praise that she did not often receive. "I asked him to tell his story, which you likely already know, and when he was finished, I was grateful and, again, angry. Forgive me, Rodrigo, for laying this all on you, but I am weary of being angry all the time."

"Anger is not something we can live with for long without experiencing its corrosive effects. It may help to talk about this anger. Tell me."

"But we have spoken before of the suffering that God allows in this world. You have told me to hold my anger, but I cannot! This Dr. Meir suffered greatly and continues to suffer. He endured torture, as you do, and the loss of his family, as you have, yet neither of you expresses anger. How can that be?"

"I am not superhuman, nor is the Avraham I have met, but I will not speak for him. Perhaps you can ask him yourself another time. Speaking for myself, yes, I experience anger. What I have learned, though, what I know, is that holding on to anger gets me nowhere. There is a Rodrigo who reacts to the environment around him, and one who seeks to create the environment around him. I hope it is the Rodrigo who creates who is the stronger. I pray to God that He may make me so."

Sariah took this in, but Rodrigo could see she wasn't satisfied and asked, "Why that look, Simon, as if you have indigestion?"

Sariah laughed a small, quiet laugh. "I cannot fool you, can I, Rodrigo? You know me too well."

"And you, me. One of the blessings of my imprisonment has been these conversations with you."

Sariah nodded in affirmation. "You are right; there is something in what you said that does not sit well with me."

"Then tell me," Rodrigo said after Sariah had been quiet, trying on her argument in her head before sharing it.

"You talk of praying to God ... often. I can see that you obtain some measure of comfort from Him. But how can I learn to trust the God who has brought me such pain?"

"Be careful cultivating bitterness, Simon; it is an acid that will eat through your soul," Rodrigo warned.

"Why should I not be bitter? God took from me my mother, father, and baby brother. He took from me my son. He made me an outcast in love, giving me desires and then refusing to allow them to be satisfied."

Rodrigo countered softly, "He also gave you intelligence, compassion, and a community that would welcome you if you would only allow it. He did not give you suffering, but allowed you to suffer, knowing suffering itself is a gift, not to be sought, but to be used, nevertheless, to teach the soul what it must learn for the path into eternity."

Sariah would not yet be swayed. "What do I care if He *gave* suffering or if He *allowed* it? Is not the result the same? The God who allows Jews and the Roma and Muslims to be burned for their beliefs is as culpable as a God who struck them down with His own hand." Sariah repeated the question that haunted her waking hours and her nightmares. "How do I learn to trust such a God?"

Rodrigo was anxious that he answer this one question to her satisfaction. "To put it slightly differently, Simon, I believe your question is 'Is God worthy of trust?' The answer will be different depending upon whom you ask, their circumstances, but most of all, their faith. You have lost much and attribute that loss to God. I, too, have lost much: my freedom, my family, and my community ... but I do not attribute that to God but to those who have misinterpreted God's commands.

"What makes God trustworthy, ultimately, is our free will. He is constrained to act according to certain laws, meaning we are all allowed to choose, but there are consequences to our actions from which He cannot save us. Both the good and the bad that occur in the world are a result of choices, whether ours or someone else's, now or in the past. Though seemingly unjust, it must be thus, for *had we no choice, we would be mere puppets on strings*, and I refuse to believe that. Therefore, I do not blame God, nor do I mistrust Him."

Sariah listened and wished for Rodrigo's confidence.

43
THE CHILDREN'S CHORUS

Our free will is both boon and bane.

44
RACHEL

Rachel paced the room, suddenly feeling like a trapped tiger. How long had she been there? What did the world look like ... outside? Where was Henry? What had happened to the gallery? Between the dreams, the Children, the visits with David ... she longed for a tether to reality!

"Will you come to the cemetery Friday? The Children are preparing a play and are so hoping you'll attend," invited Eloise when she brought Rachel's breakfast.

"Of course, Eloise."

But then, changing the subject quickly, Rachel trod on what she thought might be delicate ice. "I don't know that I need permission ... nevertheless, I want to be honest with you and Inés, as you may be all I have left of family on this earth." (She had no idea where to assign David.) "I feel like I am losing more and more of myself here." (Or, Eloise would like to have added but did not, you are gaining. Widen your perspective!) "I need a connection to who I was before. To know there was a before. Some days it seems I live in a bubble of timelessness, which I know can't be true—or at least, I'm not ready to accept that truth. I'll be discreet, but I need to know what's happening outside, what has happened to Henry and to the gallery, the dangers from which I am in hiding."

Eloise interrupted, "It is *too* dangerous. You are still being hunted. You are safe here ..."

"But why am I safe here?" Rachel retorted impatiently. "They could find me here if they wished as well as anywhere else in the city. In fact, how have they *not* appeared here to take me away?"

"I can only say you are safe here. More you would have to ask Inés."

"You've said yourself that Inés speaks in riddles. Riddles, secrets, and madness! I'm tired of it all. I'll be taking a streetcar into the city tomorrow."

"Oh dear. Oh dear," was all Eloise could utter.

"She's threatening to leave the safety the Keepers have created for her and go into the city." Eloise had hurried over to the cemetery after her conversation with Rachel, saying aloud, "Oh dear, oh dear," over and over, turning a head or two. "She wants to visit the gallery."

Inés sat Eloise down to calm her, then responded. "Then you must let her."

"But it's dangerous! If they find her, they'll torture and kill her! All our work will be for naught!"

Inés was the older sister for a reason. Her wisdom was relied upon by so many, not the least of whom was her baby sister. "We must grant her the same free will that God gives to all, Eloise. She must find her own path. She must make her own choices. We can warn her of the danger, but the decision is hers to make."

Eloise listened, silently shaking her head as though fighting with herself, before responding, "You are right. But it's so hard ..."

"Of course it is difficult," Inés acknowledged, sighing and

straightening her back, stretching out the kinks of very old age. "If it were not, would we grow at all?"

Sitting on the streetcar, something she hadn't done since her college days, Rachel opened the window, smelled the inner city's scent, and looked out at the people and buildings appearing postcard-like along the tracks. It was such a unique city, with its lush foliage and classical style mixed with a certain indescribable whimsy, all so much easier to see from an open streetcar. Rachel was happy recapturing moments from a world she missed, from a world she realized she'd not appreciated enough.

With the gallery less than a full block away, though, the danger she courted coursed through Rachel, pushing her heart to the bottom of her stomach, and causing her head to spin in ever-faster circles. A panic attack was near. She exited the streetcar and looked for a bench to sit on to collect herself before deciding what to do next. Deep breaths. One, two, three, four, five, six, seven ...

Oh my God! It was Maura, her arm through a man's—not Henry's!—walking out of the gallery in her direction. Rachel kept her head down, and Maura walked right past her, not seeming to even notice her! How dare she, Rachel thought. But how dare she ... what? What was the end to that sentence? How dare she walk right past Rachel without apology? How dare she steal the gallery from her family? How dare she live a normal life when Rachel's was anything *but*?

After the near-encounter, Rachel took the opportunity that presented itself to see what had happened to the gallery, walking toward it, all the while looking back in Maura's direction to make sure she hadn't turned around. The coast was clear. Isn't that what they wrote in those noir detective novels? But this was no fiction; the danger was all too real.

Rachel almost walked right past the gallery, not recognizing the storefront with the name in large gold lettering announcing a welcome to Maura's Arthouse. A double "How dare she!"

As Rachel walked in, the door chimed the first measure of "God Bless America." The gallery was empty except for a salesclerk.

"May I help you?" he asked. The clerk was in his twenties and could have been one of David's friends.

"No ... no, thank you. I just wanted to browse." Then Rachel decided to take advantage of the opportunity and continued, "I'd been in here a year or two ago, and it looked so different." She scanned the "art" on the walls, almost all paintings or photos of religious or military objects and was silent.

"Oh yes," the salesclerk responded. "There was a change in ownership. The previous owners were Jews, you know."

Rachel swallowed hard to keep from saying something she shouldn't. "Yes, I'd heard," came out of her mouth. "I wonder what happened to them."

"Oh, you know. Whatever happens. What they deserve."

She wanted to ask this ... this kid, *what do you know about what people deserve?* But, of course, she couldn't.

"The owner may know more. She'll be back any minute."

Rachel's heart lurched as she thought of what might happen if Maura found her in the store.

"I'm afraid I can't stay," she said as she turned to leave.

The clerk asked as Rachel almost ran out the door, "Who may I say came calling?"

"No one, really," Rachel replied, then couldn't help herself. "Just another deserving Jew." She hurried out the door, bumping into a man walking into the gallery who was wearing a tan trench coat, overdressed for the light rain and warm weather expected.

"Pardon me," he said as Rachel rushed by. Rachel's good manners got the best of her as she turned to say, "No, my fault." Their eyes met, and as Rachel saw his face, the face from the mirror with the scar across its nose, she turned again and hurried away.

Fast-walking down the street, the brief encounter swimming in her head, Rachel saw a woman at the corner just ahead of her, looking in her direction. The woman briefly stared at Rachel, then broke into a smile as if she knew her and walked toward her.

"Here," the unknown woman whispered as she came closer, "come with me into this tearoom, won't you? We must talk, and it will be safer in here."

Rachel resisted but knew she ought not linger on the street. The man, whom she knew must be David's torturer from David's description of him, would put two and two together soon, if he hadn't already, and realize she was David's mother. Still, could she trust *this* woman?

"Do I know you?" Rachel asked.

"I am a Keeper, and you are in danger. There is a man with a scar across his nose who wishes you harm. You must not let him find you."

"But he's already found me," Rachel responded. "How do you know about him? How do you know I'm in danger?"

"Come with me. Hurry. He'll have the street blockaded when he realizes you're here."

The woman took Rachel's arm and pulled her past a homeless man with his dog, sleeping under the shade of a store awning in mid-day. Rachel could see armored vehicles beginning to amass ahead and began to be truly frightened. Was this woman part of the citizen militia, delivering her to them? She tried to pull away and run to the other end of the street, but it, too, was filling with approaching military vehicles. Rachel stopped in her tracks, her legs refusing of their own accord to move her in any direction. It was at that point the woman said to her pointedly but not unkindly, "You can follow me to safety or remain here and be captured. The choice is yours."

With only a split second to decide, as Rachel could see soldiers pouring out of the armored vehicles and heading in her direction, she allowed herself to be pulled along. Soldiers were only seconds away, and Rachel could see in her head the smirk on the face of the man in the mirror when the woman whisked her into an alley, spoke in a language unfamiliar to Rachel, and in doing so, seemed to have made the alley invisible to others, as the soldiers ran right past it. Rachel could not see them but could still hear them shouting: "She was right here! Where could she have gone?" and "Dr. Kurtz will have our hides!"

The alley led to a street Rachel didn't recognize, though she wondered how that could be, as this was the neighborhood she'd worked in for most of her life. She knew its corners intimately, but as she looked around, she saw nothing familiar. Suddenly she was walking on cobblestone streets past low buildings made of stone, dogs loose everywhere.

"I know this is strange for you, Rachel, but come with me. A family awaits you."

45
JAKOB

I was sitting at the kitchen table of my childhood home in Radom. The Germans had not yet invaded our city, desecrated the temple, or killed our rabbi. I knew this as our rabbi was also at the table. There was a discussion about the Torah. I heard my father speak of *hamavdil bein kodesh lekhol*, the One who separates the holy from the mundane, and heard him ask our rabbi how it was that we as Jews could continue to strive for the holy when the mundane was so all-pervasive and crushing. The rabbi answered, "But that is true for all places and all periods of time. What is 'mundane' changes, but it is always a diversion from the holy. Study is the key. God has given us many wise teachers. We must study their words and puzzle over them. We must struggle! We were not promised our path would be easy but that we would be provided that which was necessary to fulfill our role as God's Chosen People. In the struggle, there is both honor and fulfillment."

The scene changed, and I saw my mother and father kneeling in front of a long trench, with others on either side of them. Shots rang out (it is, in reality, the Germans outside the farm shooting one of the pigs to bring back to camp) and I knew my parents had not survived the ghetto.

I was now utterly alone.

46
SARIAH

Rodrigo felt the drain of the years in the very depths of his soul. He'd tried to be the leader he thought all expected of him his entire life. Especially God. But now he knew he could not remain in this world much longer. He was tired. He was spent. And for the first time in a long time, he was angry and frightened. He tried to pinpoint the anger and knew it was both at God and at himself. Weakness in his body was spreading to his spirit, and he was frightened that, at the end, all he felt he'd accomplished would come to naught in a sudden loss of composure. He was most afraid of losing the certainty he'd had his entire life of a loving universe. Despite his circumstances. Despite all the evidence.

It was while in this dark mood that he heard the iron key in the heavy cell door and looked up as Brother Bartólome entered, himself looking broken. Rodrigo stood to greet him as they had grown accustomed to greeting—an embrace, before Bartólome spoke.

"Please sit, my brother. We must talk."

"I haven't the energy to spar with you today, Bartólome. My soul is heavy. Please forgive me."

Bartólome looked at the cell floor, seemingly unable to

look directly at Rodrigo. "My brother, Rodrigo. By the end of this visit, it will be I seeking your forgiveness."

Rodrigo could see Bartólome was distressed and wished he could make whatever it was his brother had to say easier for him. As always, concern for another brought Rodrigo out of his own darkness as he considered the difficulties of life for all.

"What is it, brother? What troubles you so?" Rodrigo inquired.

"I can hide nothing from you, Rodrigo. Neither my solicitude nor my anger. Today I bring both into this cell with me. I have come to tell you that I could no longer protect you from my Inquisition brothers." Bartólome looked up into Rodrigo's eyes as he said, "You have been sentenced to be burned at the stake at the next Auto-de-Fé." Bartólome's voice shook as he said the dreaded words, and Rodrigo could see tears falling down his cheeks.

"My dear brother, do not cry for me. I have known my end was predetermined. Without you, I would have had much less time. I am ready." As Rodrigo said this, he knew it to be true.

"And that is why I am angry." Bartólome's tears stopped as his eyes clenched shut and his brow knitted. Opening his eyes, he reached over to Rodrigo and slapped his face with his open hand. "How dare you give up! Because you were unwilling to compromise in even the smallest way, you have brought this upon yourself. You have spoken grandiose words about sincerity, about concern for the Jewish community here in Peru, about your love for all of humanity, but I call all that lies! You care only about yourself and your so-called authenticity. If you cared about others, you would *be* there with them! You would *be* a father to your children, a husband to your wife, and a leader of your people. Instead, you choose to hide in this cell where there are few demands on you. You can teach those around you, but you have the impact here of a gnat compared to the impact you could have in the greater world. Yes, I am angry! I am angry that I befriended you only to suffer from your self-centeredness, for that's what it really is."

Bartólome realized he had gone on longer than he intended and stopped suddenly, taking a few long, restful breaths.

"I apologize, my brother," he said softly. "I was unaware how angry I was and how much I loved you. I must ask you one more time. Why not recant? Let your family enjoy your protection once again, or are you hardened to their plight? Consider whether your resistance that you call authenticity is so tinged with pride that you are unable to change direction."

Rodrigo wished with all his heart he could have given Bartólome what he desired. And what he himself desired. Of course he wanted his freedom! What wouldn't he have given to hold his sweet Mira in his arms, to cup the cheeks of his two sons and cover them in his kisses? He couldn't expect Bartólome to understand why he could not simply say, "Jesus Christ is my Lord and Savior, and I repent of my recalcitrance in this acknowledgment." Some days he didn't understand why himself. But those were the bad days. In his heart he knew what he had to do.

"I am unable to do as you wish, Bartólome. Think what you will, but know that I have loved you and have valued our relationship. I have one request if that can be given me. Would you allow Simon a final visit?"

Bartólome stood, head bowed, and walked towards the door. Reaching it, he knocked for it to be opened to him, turning to Rodrigo before leaving.

"I will do as you ask." He walked out but looked back just as the door was closing behind him. Pushing it open a crack, he said, "Do not expect me to be there when your sentence is carried out. I cannot." He repeated almost inaudibly, "I cannot," turned, and slowly walked away, looking like a father who had lost his own beloved son.

Rodrigo sat in the silence of his cell after Bartólome left, allowing himself to feel the heights and depths of the emotion echoing within. He desperately wished to feel God's approbation but also chastened himself for the need. He sat on the floor in a corner of the cell, his bony legs crossed, the nearness of the walls adopting the fibrous comfort of a blanket, closed his eyes, and gave himself over to silence. Though he could hear the scratching of rats, though he could glean the scream of a fellow prisoner being tortured, those were white noise for the focusing of his being on the pure silence that was God.

It was in this silence that Rodrigo knew he must prepare. Language had failed him in his conversation with Bartólome, as it must always. He could not capture the sorrow of never seeing his family again in this life. He could not capture the joy he experienced in celebrating the Sabbath, the incandescence of the candles as they were lit, Mira's face that always shone as she waved her hands over the candles and recited the blessings. Those were a reality lost to him now and forevermore. The stab of pain he felt at this realization surprised him in its intensity and caused him to question whether his attachment to reality would hinder his resolve to live a life true to its very end.

When there came a knock at Sariah's door, she first thought to hide ... but where? No one visited her. A knock could bring only bad news. She answered, but by the time she opened the door, no one was there. Under a stone, though, was a piece of parchment on which a note had been written. Picking it up, she read, "You have been requested to attend to the prisoner, Rodrigo Jacobo de Simon. Please come to the Inquisition prison immediately." It was signed by Brother Bartólome, the

Inquisition priest Sariah knew to be honest and a protector of Rodrigo.

All Sariah could think was that Rodrigo at least had to be alive. She would not have been asked to appear just to see Rodrigo's dead body, and so she was heartened. Nevertheless, on the walk to the prison—a trip she had made so many times she no longer noticed anything along the way, her mind wandering and considering the horrors that lay ahead of her on any single day—she felt the insistent tug of doom, appearing in her mind as a dark and empty pit devoid of hope.

It was in that mood that Sariah asked the guard to open the door to Rodrigo's cell and walked in. Rodrigo was sitting motionless on the floor, still with crossed legs and eyes closed. He seemed, again, not to hear Sariah enter. Not wishing to disturb the peace he was so obviously feeling from the calm appearance of his face, pale and drawn though it was from years of poor nutrition and his current fast, Sariah pulled a chair toward her and sat to await Rodrigo's attention. The chair scraped along the stone floor, making a screeching noise that roused Rodrigo from his quiet.

"Simon," Rodrigo said after opening his eyes, "It pleases me to see you. So Bartólome sent for you? Did he alert you to the reason for my request?"

Sariah answered, "I have not seen Brother Bartólome in person but received a message from him at my house."

"Good, good, please sit down," Rodrigo responded absent-mindedly, failing to notice that she was already sitting. He took a seat on the chair across from her but remained silent.

When Sariah's curiosity could quell itself no longer, she asked, "What is it, Rodrigo? Why have you called me here?"

"Yes. Yes," Rodrigo began, but in beginning, was unable to continue. Sariah had never seen him like this. He was always so resolute, so attentive to others. Now it was as if he were in a different world.

"Sariah," he began again.

"It is Simon," Sariah countered. Though she had told him her birth name, Rodrigo had never used it, aware that it would put her in danger.

"Yes. Yes. Simon. Please forgive me. My heart is in a place of honesty, but I do not desire to endanger you."

"What is it, Rodrigo? What is going on?"

"I have something to share with you and two requests. Well, three requests. The first is that whatever I say, you remain calm." He looked at her in a way he had never before, in a way that spoke to Sariah of the importance of the next words that would come from his lips.

The request frightened Sariah, but she assented. Rodrigo continued.

"I have been sentenced. I will be burned at the stake at the Auto-de-Fé to occur next month." He looked hard at Sariah, his eyes pleading that she accept this news with equanimity.

Sariah gulped, but that was all. She checked her emotions and asked, "And your other requests?"

Rodrigo knew then that the faith he had in Sariah had not been misplaced. He continued. "I must get the news to Mira, but I do not want to do it through the usual avenues. Will you go to her? You will like her; she is a strong woman, like you." Sariah began to interject that he must remember she was masquerading as a man, but Rodrigo did not allow it. "It is a great compliment to you both. Allow me that."

Sariah nodded, then asked, "But how will I find her?"

"Find Avraham where you met him before; he will be your guide." Rodrigo hesitated a moment, then added, "I know you will, but I must ask you anyway ... Please be gentle with Mira. She is strong, but she has suffered a great deal in my absence."

Sariah was glad Rodrigo recognized that fact. There were times she'd found herself growing angry with him for what she saw as indulgent self-importance that cost so many others so much. But she would never have told him that.

"And the third request?" Sariah pushed on before her

emotions could catch up.

"The third is more difficult to talk about but is, in many ways, the most important." Rodrigo stood up with effort and began pacing, looking at the floor as he spoke. "In the Jewish faith, as you must know, circumcision is required for a male to enter into the covenant with God. It is so important a mitzvah that it is one of only two commandments for which the punishment of karet, or being cut off, is applied if it is not fulfilled."

Sariah knew this already, as she had asked her mother when her brother was circumcised why they must cause Baruch such pain. Rodrigo stopped pacing and looked over in Sariah's direction to make sure she was listening.

"What you could not know is that when I was born, my parents, fearing for my life more than for my relationship with God, did not have me circumcised so that I would not bear that certain sign of my Jewish heritage." Now he looked directly at Sariah. "I must be circumcised before meeting God. To fail in this would mean my expulsion from His kingdom."

"Why are you telling me this, Rodrigo?" Sariah asked, fearing his response.

"I am unable to perform my own circumcision." He stopped, then walked over to his chair, sat down, and looked into Sariah's eyes, which were just now beginning to tear. "You must do it for me."

Sariah sat and closed her eyes as tears pooled, then fell down her cheeks, dripping onto her shirt. It was all too much. This request, a request too far. Rodrigo was placing great faith in her, and for that, a part of her swelled with pride. But the things he was asking were hard. Were they too hard, though? She didn't want to understand, but she did and knew she owed him these requests and more. He had been her friend and teacher, as he was to so many. But he had also allowed only Sariah to see all sides of him: his great strength and spirituality, but also his humanity, and it was in seeing the human side of Rodrigo that she felt most blessed, that she felt encouraged that she, too, could do more, could be more. She told him she would do what she could. Having already been chastised for being careless in speaking with Avraham in public, she would have to be careful but would discuss the details with Avraham, who had likely performed many circumcisions.

"If I may, Simon, there is one last thing I would ask. Will you continue my lessons with my fellow prisoners when I am gone? It is important they understand they can withstand torture by training their minds to leave their bodies. Though the body exists in time, the consciousness that perceives it does not. You have the ability to minister to the others. While doing so, you must teach this."

Then, lowering his eyes for a moment before raising them to look directly into Sariah's heart, he added, "Deep within, you know perhaps more than us all that suffering cannot rob us of joy. They cannot take joy from us; they can only deepen it."

Fear interrupted the flow of atoms that would carry that message to Sariah's heart. Instead, she whispered, "But I would be imprisoned for teaching thus."

Rodrigo asked in response, "Are you not imprisoned now?"

At this, Sariah's tears grew. "I don't know how I will live without you, Rodrigo," Sariah spoke in between gulps of air as she sobbed harder than she had in years.

"But why weep?" Rodrigo asked. "I am here. And when I am not here, I will be here. Where is it you think I could go?"

The assignments Rodrigo had given Sariah were a blessing. Though she questioned whether she was up to them, they kept her from falling into a deep sadness as she anticipated yet another loss. As it was, she had no time for sadness. Key to accomplishing what Rodrigo had asked of her was getting in touch with Avraham Meir.

She prepared herself by praying, as Rodrigo had taught her. Though her message would be difficult to share, she was almost in high spirits as she walked with intention down the cobblestone streets, past the many vendors yelling to get her attention. Another day, she'd have stopped for oranges or for her favorite fig jam. Today, she was on a mission.

Suddenly, out of the corner of her eye, Sariah saw the bright yellow of the *sanbenito* with the red saltire. At the same time she saw Avraham, he saw her and waved for Sariah to follow him to the alley in which they had previously met. There they sat once again, each more confident and less cautious than before.

"Avraham," Sariah began, "I have come to seek your assistance."

"I know wherefore you have come, Simon, as I have received a message from Rodrigo. I am to take you to Mira, which I am most happy to do."

"Did Rodrigo explain more?" Sariah wondered if he knew of the sentencing.

"He did not. When they occur, our messages are, of necessity, brief, as the chance for interception is high."

Sariah wondered if she should tell him of Rodrigo's sentence but decided it would dishonor Mira for Avraham to know before Rodrigo's wife. She would tell him after, before the Inquisition had the opportunity to spread the word themselves, as they often did, using these occasions to encourage Jews to recant.

"Come then; we can start now if you are ready," Avraham urged, "though we must be careful and walk where others are not likely to see us. Their home is some distance; you will stay there the night." Sariah had not taken this into account and was reticent but relented.

Along the way, Avraham talked further of his life and what he had given up to remain a faithful Jew in the sight of God while still protecting his family.

"I would do it again," he told Sariah, referring to the circumstances that led to his wearing the *sanbenito*. "I was imprisoned with my only child, my son. I cannot tell you how difficult it was to hear my son's screams when he was being tortured." He stopped for a moment as a sob rose from its deep hiding before continuing, knowing the story must be shared. "We were imprisoned in the same cell, and when he was returned to it after they had tortured him, he would try so hard to pretend it had been nothing. He understood the pain I felt was greater for him than for myself. Nevertheless, I knew he was growing weaker over the weeks. Finally, during an interrogation, I was offered the opportunity to save my son. If I would recant, I would be allowed to wear the *sanbenito*, and he would be set free. I prayed to God that He would understand my betrayal. Would He not do the same for his children?"

Sariah's heart softened hearing Avraham's story. "Is your son with you here?"

Avraham continued walking but kept his face down so Sariah could not see the tears. "He died shortly after we were released. I believe now they knew he had contracted pneumonia and thus used the ploy of his release to their advantage."

"I am sorry, Avraham," Sariah offered, knowing that was not enough, desiring to embrace him to share the comfort of a beating heart but knowing she could not.

"And your wife? Were you able to reunite with her?"

"I did for a short while, but she died not long after my son. Her heart had been broken, and I believe she wanted only to rejoin him in God. I do not blame her. I have learned not to blame the Inquisitors, either, thanks to Rodrigo. His example has been a blessing not just to me but to the entire Jewish community here. And you will see that his Mira, and his two boys,

Rodrigo and Levi, are also revered."

They continued in silence, Sariah reflecting that the sorrows Avraham had experienced in his life were equal to hers, yet he seemed reconciled in a way that made her feel small. In time, they arrived at the home of Rodrigo and Mira. Avraham led Sariah to the front door and knocked on it. It was opened by a tall, beautiful woman with long dark curls and the deepest brown eyes.

"Good day, Mira," Avraham said in greeting. "I would like you to meet Simon, who is new to our community and has come to meet you and pay his respects."

"Of course, Avraham, Simon. Do come in."

Sariah realized it would be inappropriate for Mira to accept her into the house as a man unless Avraham were to remain with them, yet she needed to be alone with her. So she began, "Please excuse me for the disguise, Mira. My name is not Simon, but Sariah. I am a woman." Sariah looked at Avraham to see the surprise he would register, but there was none. Was she that transparent to all?

"Yes, I have known but have told no one," Avraham assured her. "I must leave now, but I will come tomorrow with a cart, and we will make the return trip in style," he promised, smiling.

"I am grateful to you, Avraham," Sariah replied and entered Mira and Rodrigo's home.

Inside, they were immediately accosted by Rodrigo's sons. Mira excused herself and brought them into the kitchen where she gave them some milk and sent them outside so she and Sariah could talk. She then prepared a tray of food and brought it out to Sariah.

"Thank you, Mira. May I call you that?" As Mira nodded her head in assent, Sariah looked down into her lap shyly.

Mira spoke first. "Tell me how you have come to this town, Sariah. Where are you from?"

Sariah began the long story that led to her becoming a doctor in practice, leaving out her work in the Inquisition prisons.
When she finished, Mira said, "You have been prepared for
great things, Sariah. I am sorry for all you have suffered, but
your suffering has brought you to us. For that, I hope you will
be grateful."

"Us?" Sariah asked. "Who is 'us'?"

"Your God. Your brothers and sisters. Your community.
This is where you belong. Tonight, I will take you to meet others who have had experiences like yours, if you will allow me.
And tomorrow, before you leave, we will go to Davida's home
where there are women gathering to bake challah for the Sabbath."

Sariah felt the pull of Mira's words, of a friend and a community that might accept her as she was. But there was more
to tell, and until she had, she could not raise her hopes.

"I would like that," Sariah began. "But first, I have more to
tell you." Then she hesitated, afraid to announce what she had
been sent to announce. Afraid her words would disturb the
delicate balance of the day. Enjoying her time with Mira. Self-
ishly desirous of some normalcy.

"Please continue, Sariah," Mira encouraged. "I am listening. You have nothing to fear."

"I am afraid only for you, Mira," Sariah answered, "for the
pain that I bring to your home and to your community. For
that, I am truly sorry." Again, Sariah looked down into her lap,
not shyly this time, but sorrowfully.

"You are speaking in riddles, Sariah. Please tell me your
news."

Sariah remembered Rodrigo's wish that she be gentle. But
how to present news such as this gently? "I told you that I have
been practicing as a doctor. It is for that reason I have had to
camouflage myself as a man." She continued, "What I did not
say is I have been working in the Inquisition prisons."

Hearing this news, Mira's heart raced, but she said nothing. She had spent every night praying this moment would not come. She'd prayed to God to help her understand Rodrigo's heart, to understand his need to act in accordance with his conscience even though it had caused him to betray his own family, his choice leaving them without his succor. She had struggled with when a betrayal is just and when it is not. Yet now that the moment of his ultimate betrayal had arrived, she felt a calm come over her. It was she who took Sariah's hand, understanding how difficult the news would be to share, and asked simply, "Rodrigo?"

Tears once again fell down Sariah's cheeks as she shook her head and quietly said, "Yes." And understanding the words that would be most difficult to say need not be said, Sariah responded only, "It will be within the month."

"You are brave to bring this news to me, Sariah. I am happy to have learned it from you. Thank you."

They sat then, hands still interlocked, crying.

The trip back to the city with Avraham was both too long and too short. The instructions he had for her about performing a circumcision were frightening. Sariah had not performed any surgery before and particularly feared this one as she knew Rodrigo would eschew the opium-soaked sponge she could otherwise use to lessen the pain. But she was happy to talk about something, anything other than the sorrow she'd left behind in Rodrigo's home and in his community. Spending time with Mira, she understood everything she had been told about her. Warmth and security emanated from her, as well as a quiet confidence about who she was and what her role was in the community to which she belonged.

Meeting Davida and the other women who joined them in baking the challah spoke deeply to Sariah's being. Memories returned of days before all the suffering, before her mother and father lost their only son and their will to live. She began to understand that she had allowed her anger to build within her since that time, the anger that her own parents had not wanted to remain alive for *her*. That she was not enough. Would never be enough. But that narrative was untrue, or, at least, she now believed there could be a different ending to that story.

47
RACHEL

Dr. Kurtz returned to Henry's cell shortly after having seen Rachel, even more convinced now that Henry was lying and was hiding Rachel. How else could she be eluding him? He had to give Henry some credit, though. He didn't believe himself capable of such love. To go through the tortures Henry had without divulging Rachel's whereabouts? No, he wasn't capable of that. He loved his wife, loved his two children even more. (After all, Susan was getting older and seemed to have become bored with him. And though he wasn't sure he could really blame her, he did.) He'd applied the tools of torture, listened to the screams until, ultimately, Henry passed out. Dr. Kurtz knew in his inner heart that he would not have lasted even as long as Henry, which was why he supposed he'd yet to win a single lottery.

The doctor had Henry's cell door opened quietly so he might surprise him. He relished this visit in which he could put an end to all Henry's protestations of ignorance. What joy it gave him to imagine Henry's resistance giving way in the face of facts impossible to refute.

"Henry. Henry!" the doctor repeated his name loudly, as Henry appeared to be sleeping. But he could not awaken him, and as he felt for his pulse, it was so weak he could barely feel it. His anger rose. "No! You will not take this from me! You who had it all but married a Jew and added a Jewish child to the world. Wake up! I have seen your Rachel. Don't you understand? You can no longer keep her safe from me! Now you must tell me where to find her. No more lies!"

Dr. Kurtz was yelling so loudly that two guards appeared in the room. The doctor leveled his rage at them. "I will have your heads for this!" he screamed. "Where have you been? How could you have let this happen? Your prisoner is near death! Pick him up and take him to the treatment room. Hurry!"

The doctor followed them to the treatment room and readied some instruments as they placed Henry on the gurney. "Now leave. I have work to do," he ordered, turning his back to the door as they left and intermittently pounding and massaging Henry's chest to regulate his fading heartbeat. After some time—long enough for the doctor to curse Henry for the pain in his arms—Henry's eyes fluttered, and he began coming to. The doctor felt an almost orgasmic rush, the preceding all having been a form of foreplay. In control again, he spoke softly to the still weakened body on the gurney.

"Now, Henry. I hope you're doing well. Don't answer. Don't waste your breath. I have more important questions for you." He watched Henry's face closely. This was the crucial point, his reaction to the information the doctor was about to reveal. "I saw your Rachel today, lovely lass that she is."

Henry's lips moved slightly, but no sound came from them. His eyes fluttered again, but he seemed too weak to keep them open.

"You seem interested. Yes, yes, yes. I understand even better your efforts to keep her safe, to hide her from us. She really is quite a catch. For a Jewess, that is."

Still no sound from Henry.

"So, you've been telling a little white lie, haven't you? Taking us to a house that didn't exist. Forcing us to search for a cemetery. Such an imagination you have, Henry. It could be a tale by Edgar Allen Poe! Really, when this is all done you should become a writer! But now. Now. It's time for you to stop playing games with us. Now you know that we know."

A weak cough came from Henry's chest. What he was thinking was anyone's guess. If he'd had the strength, would he have joined the doctor in the search again for Rachel ... now that he knew she was leaving the confines of what could only have been a magically protected environment? (God protect him from such a belief, but what choice did he have?) Spittle dripped from his mouth.

Dr. Kurtz realized then that Henry had won. He was past the point of being able to defend Rachel ... or betray her. The doctor usually felt he knew when to stop the tortures, when the body was at that equilibrium between optimum suffering and death. But this time his calculations had failed him. And in failing him, he had lost the chance at Rachel. He could be angry, but then, he thought, he still had Henry. Hoping Henry could hear him, the doctor taunted, "You are my second-place prize, Henry. Satisfying? No. But I believe even less satisfying for you."

As they walked further, Rachel took in the smells of citrus and tobacco and, she noticed, as they walked past an open cart, of fetid cheeses.

"Where are we?" she inquired of her savior. Or captor? "And how do you know my name?"

"Inés and Eloise told you of the Society of the Keepers of Story, to which I also belong. But we don't have much time. Please follow me."

They hurried to a small stone house and knocked on the

door. Knock, knock-knock, knock. Immediately they were invited in, and Rachel was introduced to a woman—Mira—and her two sons. The Keeper pulled Mira aside and whispered to her before returning to Rachel and telling her she would be safe there. Then, she disappeared before Rachel ever knew her name.

Mira took Rachel's hand and led her to a chair at the kitchen table. It was Friday, and the sun was disappearing into the earth. The older son, Rodrigo, went to the kitchen windows and shut the shades tightly while the younger took out candles and placed them on the table.

Mira spoke first, welcoming Rachel to their home and inviting her to celebrate the Sabbath with them. "We are happy to share our many blessings with you and to thank God for all that He has done for us now and throughout time."

Lighting the candles, Mira waved her hands over the flames three times and then covered her eyes while reciting the Sabbath blessing. Just as she finished, a light shone directly outside the curtained windows. Mira quickly but solemnly put her finger to her lips to signal Rachel to be quiet and pulled her down to the floor with the others. Young Rodrigo grabbed the candles in a practiced manner and carefully brought them under the table with him.

The light lingered for a moment or two, then passed, but they all remained under the table, silent, for some time afterward. Finally, Mira gave the sign, Rodrigo returned the candles to the table, and they all took their chairs again. Turning to Rachel, she explained, "We celebrate the Sabbath with great risk as, if we were discovered, we would be jailed. From time to time, the Inquisition sends its soldiers to look for those celebrating the Sabbath." She spoke softly but with confidence. Her dark eyes were kind, her arm resting on her son's. "Don't be afraid. We have been through this many times and are very careful. There will always be risk, but strengthening our connection with God and each other is worth the risk. These are difficult times, but what times are not?" She smiled, and Rachel returned the smile, feeling a great warmth, a mysterious bond to these people she didn't know but who seemed so familiar to her.

During the meal, Rachel kept mostly silent, listening to the happy chatter around her, as if they weren't hunted, as if they were blessed with the happiest of lives. She knew this place somehow, knew this Mira, and knew she was safe—no, more than safe. Knew she was home. She felt the ember of Judaism she had carried within all her life rekindling. After the meal, she and Mira found a quiet spot in the living area to sit and talk.

"You know," Mira began slowly, "we have known each other before. You were a doctor and a leader within the Jewish community here in Peru."

Rachel suddenly realized with amazement, "But you are speaking about Sariah!"

"I am. Even then you were being prepared to tell stories of great suffering, having yourself experienced such suffering and having born the precious scars of each experience."

Rachel knew the dreams had been familiar. She had wondered at the fact that she kept returning to them as if each had been the story of someone's life. So they were! They were hers! She wondered, what had they taught her? The question was more to herself than to Mira, more of a searching within, the first inkling of the rearranging puzzle pieces.

Then, to Mira, "I remember your husband, Rodrigo. What a challenge I must have been for him."

"Yet he loved you so, as did I."

Rachel looked into Mira's eyes, so full of honesty and love. "Rodrigo said to Sariah once that she must honor what was inside her, there was no other way. I don't know what I understood then, but I'm beginning to understand now."

Mira reached out for Rachel's hand, saying, "I am only sorry that you have had to suffer the loss of yet another son.

While I lost my husband in this life—it is not the same. I would never wish for the pain of losing either of my boys."

Ah, David. This memory tore at Rachel's heart. She had lost her parents and a brother as Sariah, and a son before she'd ever really known him. Her heart told her that what Mira said was true. Losing a child brought with it the greatest suffering. At that moment, all she wanted was to see David again. Would that be allowed her? If not, there was nothing to return to, her entire family dead except Henry—but he might as well be dead, having already abandoned her.

"May I stay here with you, Mira? Would the Keepers allow it? Must I return?"

"I am afraid you must, Rachel. You know now that you have a task for which you have been prepared. A task so important it has taken centuries for your preparation. But there will be danger in returning. The Keepers can keep you safe only in the cemetery, mansion, and the alleyway portal between the worlds. You will return through that portal and must make your way through the world in which you are hunted back to the cemetery."

Then Rachel remembered Dr. Kurtz, and a heat rose through her body. How could such a man be allowed to live in the world after his sins against so many—especially against her own son? The anger burned through her, anger she had been afraid to feel before but now threatened to overwhelm her.

"But how will I be able to return to the cemetery safely?"

"You have your strength, your wisdom, and an intuition honed through many lives. I will also give you a pistol, but I would counsel you to use it only if there is no recourse. For this one night, though, let us talk of other, simpler things. The morning will be upon us all too soon and with it, the time for your departure."

After minutes or hours, Mira took Rachel's hand and

brought her to a bedroom, where she took a quilt with delicate, multicolored embroidered flowers from a chair and wrapped it tightly around her, inviting her to lie down on the bed. For the first time in longer than she could remember, Rachel felt completely safe. Soft intonations escaped Mira's lips as she, with bowed head, prayed for Rachel's safety and for her safe return home. Emotional and physical exhaustion overtook Rachel, and she fell immediately into a deep, restful sleep.

48
JAKOB

Orlok, large and sleek as he was, glided through the forest in the dark of the night as does a bat, unseeing but with powers greater even than sight. With nary a crackle of dead leaves nor of dry branches on the ground, he searched out his victims one at a time.

That night Jakob had already written into existence one hundred twenty vampires for Orlok's army, but it was just the beginning of another long evening. He had extra incentive now, the deaths of too many piling up: his parents Sol and Yetta, his sister Mila, Adam and Marta Behrman with their children, Mr. and Mrs. Markus, Uncle Nat, and the blessed Rabbi of Holy Name, just to begin.

With his acolytes in tow, Orlok stealthily approached a band of sleeping Germans, taking one of the guards on watch and lapping at his blood like a hungry, mongrel dog—

"No, no, no!" interrupted the Rabbi. "That is all wrong. You cannot compare my Yossel to a 'mongrel'!"

I stopped, stunned by the Rabbi's criticism, and annoyed that my most important scene thus far had been interrupted. "What do you mean by that?" I asked the Rabbi, though loath to encourage his further interference.

"It is how the Germans refer to Jews and all they consider to be less than pure Aryans. Have you not been paying attention? I would suggest not using the term 'mongrel,' even for a dog. But while we are on the subject, I must tell you my Yossel is losing patience ..."

"Orlok! It's Orlok! And *his* patience is irrelevant. *I* create his patience or his impatience! He is *my* creation ... or re-creation." I was becoming confused, and all this disruption was unhelpful.

"Yes, yes, I understand," the Rabbi conceded. "You wish to punish. Well, go ahead and punish. If you think it will bring back your mother or father, go ahead. But I believe deep within, you know better. I would appeal to that part of you, on behalf of my Yossel, who is tired and finding it increasingly difficult to swallow all the blood you are forcing him to drink, but I appeal to you also on behalf of all Jews. We are not, as a people, bloodthirsty. You play into Hitler's trope of Jews as creatures draining the blood from the German Volk. You are making of my Yossel a realization of Hitler's terrible metaphor!"

All I could think to respond was, "Blah, blah, blah." So much for brilliant author. "You go on and on. I will no longer listen to you! Begone!" I waved my hand at him to shoo him away but, while doing so, knocked over the pitcher of milk Wilhelm had brought in that morning. I looked over at the Rabbi to scold him for causing me to waste my very precious milk, but he was gone. Here, gone, in, out ... I couldn't take much more of the Rabbi's shenanigans.

I slept and had a vision of my golem burning at the stake. He was naked and appeared to be in prayer as the flames lapped at his bare, stony skin. There was a crowd yelling words of condemnation that I couldn't decipher. I also saw faces in the crowd that looked away, unable to cheer on or

even watch such suffering. I screamed out loud, "You cannot

kill him that way! You may cause him to suffer, but he will rise like the phoenix and seek justice!" I woke myself up burning with the need for revenge. The next day, I prepared to apologize to Wilhelm and Helga for the mess I'd made, but they didn't visit. Nor did they the following day, or the day after that. Again it had been three days since I'd seen them or received food or drink, or since my pot had been emptied. I could hear no movement through the wall. There was no way to know what had happened ... when I would be remembered. Or if. I tried to eat the grain and potatoes stored in the wall with me, but without water, I could swallow neither.

More time passed until all I could do, all I wanted to do, was sleep. It was then that I realized I had to return to Orlok before I could no longer write, to set him loose upon the Germans in a final campaign that would break their backs. The numbers were growing. Orlok's army, if properly motivated, could achieve the ends I had set out for them, I was certain of it. Complete annihilation of the German army!

"You will not achieve this, my son," the Rabbi said softly, even kindly.

I was not surprised by the Rabbi's presence, but how was I now the Rabbi's son? After all his ridicule, his attempts to forestall my plans, to usurp my Orlok, he would now speak of me as "son?"

Softly, from the corner of the room: "He's mine."

Stage directions now? Was everything coming apart? I was even more committed. There were things I had to do, to accomplish, before ...

"The one thing you must accomplish is the destruction of my Yossel. I should have done it myself instead of leaving his body in the attic of the old synagogue to be reawakened one day for purposes that are not kosher. He was never meant to become a vampire golem, never meant ... mmmph."

I'd had to silence him, so I stuffed the Rabbi's tassels—may

God forgive me—into his mouth, and grabbed his robe, weakened though I was, causing him to twirl to the other side of the room like a lumpen ballerina until he disappeared. I returned to my writing.

Many months later, Wilhelm and Helga returned to the home they'd been forced to leave by the Germans. The war was over, but suffering was not. Food was in shorter supply than it had ever been, and their animals and land had not been cared for in the time they'd been imprisoned. In fact, as they walked toward their house for the first time after the war, they could see it had been raided.

The entire time they'd been gone, they'd worried about Jakob. How would he survive? They'd convinced themselves he would have found a way out of the room after realizing they were not returning. Hunger would have propelled him. A desire to live would have been his muse! So they reassured themselves in the face of their impotence.

The front door was ajar, and debris covered the floors. They went together straight to the door to the room in the wall. Turning the handle, Wilhelm was surprised it was still locked. He looked for the hidden key, but it wasn't there. They both took this as a good sign. Jakob must have left and locked the door behind him to protect the grain stored within. Such a good boy. So concerned for their welfare. Wilhelm went to the barn and found an ax. He brought it into the house, broke off the door handle with one great blow, and knocked in the door with his boot.

The stink was immediate and unrelenting. Jakob must not have emptied his pot when he escaped. Wilhelm held Helga back while he covered his mouth and nose with his arm and ventured further into the room to investigate.

The Children's Chorus: Stay away, Helga! This you should not see!

There, on the pallet, was Jakob's decaying body.

Wilhelm turned away and, in doing so, saw on the desk the manuscript Jakob had been writing while in his uncertain captivity. Wilhelm picked it up and took it with him out of the stultifying room. He closed the door behind him and took Helga's hand, leading her into the kitchen. There they sat in the two unbroken chairs at the table that leaned only slightly to one side, with the manuscript in front of them, and read:

To Matka, Tata, and Mila, who I was unable to save. I dedicate this story to your memories and pray that with my Orlok, I have been able to end this war and the suffering it has caused so many. I also dedicate this story to my benefactors, Helga and Wilhelm Baer, who also suffered pain and loss and without whom I would not have made it to this point.

There is one question that plagued me throughout the war that I wish I'd had the courage to ask. But I will ask it now.

Why?

If the Jewish people had been made aware of our sins against all who consider us unclean, Poles, Germans, Christians, and Muslims, we would surely have begged your forgiveness. Repentance is core not just to Christian theology but to Jewish theology as well. Yom Kippur, the Day of Atonement, is the holiest day of our year. We are all more alike than different! Please, please tell us then, why do you revile us so? Until I know the answer, I choose to live and die with my golem in the night.

And last, to my Orlok. May I spend eternities by your side as we continue to fight against evil and injustice in our battle against the enemies of the Jews.

More Helga and Wilhelm could not read. Later. Right now, they knew they needed to mourn all their losses and consider their culpability before they could face the new beginning that lay ahead of them while awaiting the return, God willing, of Peter.

49
SARIAH

When she arrived at her house, Brother Bartólome was at her door, awaiting her.

"I don't mean to frighten you, Simon. I have come on Rodrigo's behalf. No one can ever know that we have met in this way. I owe Rodrigo much and wish I could do more to save his life and his soul. It seems I have failed in accomplishing both." The priest appeared haggard and empty to Sariah. She had seen him many times at the prison and had always enjoyed seeing him, the one priest who brought hope rather than hopelessness into the prison cells.

Bartólome continued. "Rodrigo has spoken to me of his wish, and I am here to escort you to his cell that you may accomplish it." Sariah followed the priest to the prison with the tools Avraham had lent her in hand.

When she returned, having performed the circumcision with such skill that Rodrigo, even in great pain, had praised and thanked her, she fell upon her bed in the greatest weariness she had felt in a long while. As blessed sleep approached, Sariah closed her eyes and saw little Baruch's hand around her finger, the rose birthmark on his face. She heard Rodrigo's words, "Our grief is a moment in time and repeated through-out centuries or even eons, its power is finite and connected to fear, whereas love is infinite, an opening to freedom."

She slept soundly, dreamlessly, and awoke the next morning refreshed. Then she remembered the Auto-de-Fé.

In his cell, Rodrigo gritted his teeth against the pain that felt heavy to him; but his heart was light. He'd accomplished all on this earth for which he believed he'd existed, except for his death. He'd loved and served his God, the father of Abraham, Isaac, and Jacob, and his people. He'd married and had children who would be well-raised within the covenant by his sweet wife, Mira. Mira. He had missed her. But he'd chosen well and knew she'd continue her leadership within the Jewish community as she had done since his imprisonment.

And what of Sariah? He knew in the deepest parts of him that Almighty God had sent her to him, or him to her, to reignite within her the flame of Judaism and return her to her community, where she would become a leader equal in ability and stature to Mira.

Rodrigo had just learned that the Auto-de-Fé during which he would accomplish his death would be in two days' time, as there was some fear there would be an attempt to free him. What the Inquisition didn't know was that he looked forward to his death, the completion of which would free him. He had spent more and more time meditating to prepare himself, to know the afterlife. Its mystery perplexed him, though he felt certain it existed. The God of his fathers was a loving God. It followed from that premise that there had to be another world. The existence of evil could not have been allowed otherwise. To argue differently would require he believe in an amoral God, and this Rodrigo could not do.

He began the final preparations for his death. Others in

the prison wished to visit him, to say goodbye. Instead, Rodrigo asked the guard to share a message that he sent his blessings to all but must prepare himself without interruption. He was content with his sentence. The guards also wished to honor him, for he had always been kind to them, even in his days of greatest pain. They brought him special meals, greater than they ate themselves, bringing from their homes jams and fresh fruits and home-baked breads. Rodrigo thanked them and asked that they distribute the food to the rest of the prisoners. He would fast until his end. He sat on the floor in his cell and meditated to prepare himself as the sounds of a Children's Choir wafted through the air.

The day arrived, and the noise accompanying the arrival of the soldiers and the crowd that had been gathered to cheer the burning of a heretic greeted Sariah's ears after a sleepless night. She had not returned to Mira, knowing she would be using this time to prepare herself, her children, and her community for their father and holy one's death. Word had certainly reached her of his contentment with his death, which Sariah hoped would be some comfort. Sariah herself felt no comfort at all. Until awakening that day, she had not known if she would attend the Auto-de-Fé, but when she heard the ruckus as the procession passed through the streets by her house, the crowd's shouting and condemning of the supposed heretic, she knew she would be there to lift her prayers to the heavens in praise of Rodrigo's life, hoping her supplication would be heard above the din of the crowd. She owed him that and more.

Dressing in a simple long skirt and covering her head so she would not be recognized, Sariah walked alone to the square where the platform and stake had been erected. Her legs buckled, her entire body taken with shaking, and she realized this might be too difficult for her. Her ears were assailed by shouts as the crowd awaited Rodrigo's arrival: "Christ killer!" "Child sodomizer!" "Dirty Jew heretic!" She wanted to shout back, "You don't know him! You don't understand! He is love itself!" Instead, she remained silent and, as if there were no crowd around her at all, lifted her eyes to the heavens and prayed, prayed harder than she ever had before, that Rodrigo would be rewarded, that the Jewish community to which she had been introduced so recently, would be healed, and find its inner strength.

The crowd became restless, chanting now for Rodrigo to appear after an hour of waiting and listening to minor officials berate all Jews, heathens, witches, and the like. Sariah knew it would not start until the Inquisition priest appeared to speak to the crowd and to Rodrigo. Suddenly, Sariah looked to her side and saw Mira walking toward her with forceful steps. As she approached her, Mira put her arms around Sariah's shoulder and pulled her in tight, then walked with her away from the crowd, away from the spectacle. At the same time, a priest in Inquisition robes, with a birthmark in the shape of an elongated rose on his cheek, walked by and looked directly at Sariah before continuing to the front to begin his practiced tirade.

50
RACHEL

The next morning came too quickly as Rachel remembered and savored the feeling of safety and belonging she'd experienced as Sariah in this close Jewish community. Mira accompanied her to the alleyway portal. As they arrived, Mira put her arms around Rachel and slipped a gun into her jacket pocket, whispering, "It is loaded, Rachel; all you will have to do is pull the trigger. God willing, you will have no need for it. Be very careful." She kissed her on the cheek, turned, and walked away.

Rachel wanted to shout after her: "Don't leave me! I'm afraid! I can't do this!" She knew, though, what Mira's response would be because she was Rodrigo's wife, and she knew what Rodrigo would have said to Sariah: "Call on your God for strength and you will find it. Nothing is denied the faithful." Was she faithful enough, though?

She felt in her pocket for the pistol and stepped into the alley.

Walking quickly past the barking dogs nipping at her feet, Rachel slowed her steps as she approached the end of the alley. The rapid beating of her heart was so loud she was certain, were there danger awaiting outside the portal, it would give her away before her footfall did. She tightened her grip around the handle of the gun, ready to pull it out if she had to. She'd not had practice shooting, but remembering the face in the mirror, the smirk, she knew she'd be ready.

Bright sun shone at the exit. All she could hear was the usual bustle of commerce, encouraging her to sidle into the sunlight. Rachel put on the shawl Mira had given her to tie over her hair so she wouldn't be recognized and tightened it so it would not come loose if she had to run.

She saw that the armored vehicles were no longer there. In their place, however, police had amassed along the narrow street, watching the comings and goings. Taking her time to survey the scene and plan her next steps, Rachel saw what she had most hoped, or most feared, to see. There, just outside the gallery, talking with an officer. There *he* was. She was too far away to see his face but knew him from his trench coat in the warm air and his swagger. She was certain; it was Kurtz.

What next? Praying her disguise would protect her, Rachel walked with slow, deliberate steps both to avoid unwanted attention and to mask her fear, taking a side alley with which she was familiar, one that led to another alley used for deliveries to the businesses along the street. She walked in the alley toward the gallery, praying she would not be noticed. Several delivery men and women carrying packages to the numerous businesses walked by her with just a glance. Each glance delivered a blow as Rachel didn't know if one of the workers might grab her and bring her to Kurtz, recognizing her from her many years at the gallery. The conflict of wanting and not wanting to see Kurtz almost paralyzed her. *Watch for me; I'm coming for you.* No, she thought. It isn't I who must fear you, but now you who must fear me. *I* am coming for *you.*

She walked more briskly, knowing what she wanted to do. She would enter the gallery from the alley door and casually walk through the shop to the front door. She would open it, look Kurtz in the eye, and say nothing before shooting him in the face. The face that had smirked at her in the mirror. The face that had been the last sight of too many. Who would blame her for the murder of such a man? And if she were caught? Well, then, she would know her last act had balanced the scales, had avenged so many. Emboldening adrenaline coursed through her.

Suddenly she stopped, not out of fear, but because she heard a voice. A whiny, familiar voice. Rachel quickly turned around, looking behind her, but saw no one. *You may find that the paradox of vengeance is that it does not free you. Instead, it makes you dependent upon those who have harmed you through your belief that it is only their torment that will allow you release from your pain.* At the same moment, she saw someone exit the back door of the gallery, and startled, disoriented, she heard another voice. *To be Jewish is to respect justice and fairness.*

She had no time to listen to voices, real or imagined. There was danger wherever she looked, wherever her next steps might take her. Before moving at all, the back door of the gallery opened, and stopping just short of Rachel was a single person. The man in the trench coat. Kurtz. For a moment, they looked at each other, each surprised at the luck of their meeting. Kurtz pulled a cigarette out of his coat pocket and offered one to Rachel.

"Well, well. So good to see you, Rachel. I was just stepping out for a quiet, unobserved smoke, but I guess you now know my little secret. Please don't tell my wife; I promised her I'd quit."

Rachel stared at him with white-hot hatred. The light banter was the ultimate in inhumanity. She grasped the gun in her pocket and pulled it out, pointing it at that face. That hideous face. She didn't want to imagine how he had smiled at David while sending him to his death.

"Oh, I see now where David must have gotten his criminal tendencies. Really, do you plan to kill me? Your people have already tried and failed. Such ineptness. You do know that murder is against the law?"

What Rachel knew was that she didn't have much time. At any moment, Kurtz could call out to the police, who might just be feet away, and she'd be a dead woman. But she was frozen. She could neither talk nor pull the trigger. Something held her back. Something at war with her hatred. Still pointing the gun at his face, Rachel looked into Kurtz's eyes and saw a blankness. There was no humanity there. Just pull the trigger! In the second she had before all would be lost, Rachel remembered a young boy living in untenable conditions in the midst of a horrible war, the descent from a desire for justice into vengeance. She pulled the trigger.

Kurtz fell to the ground grabbing his leg, shouting curses at Rachel as she ran and ran and ran until she was far away from the business district, far away from Dr. Kurtz, far away from the feelings of ugly vengeance. Yes, she'd hurt him, but she knew her God could forgive her that; knew Kurtz had deserved worse.

Now she wanted only to see David.

51
THE CHILDREN'S CHORUS

There is no quick path through suffering. One must stumble over anger and its call to vengeance, weariness, and its call to slumber.

52
RACHEL

Rachel hurried back to the cemetery and banged on the heavy gate. "Let me in! Let me in!" Inés opened the gate, stepping aside as Rachel rushed past her. There was no time for explanations. Rachel had to find David! Had to see him again! Had to tell him how much she would miss him. How much she cherished who he was, his strength of will, his sense of commitment, his love for others. Though she wanted most to feel his strong arms around her, that being denied her, she wanted at least to tell him she would always love him.

Rachel thought then of Sariah's feelings for Rodrigo, the great love Sariah had felt that caused her to ask, "How will I live without you?"

Finding her way to the bench under the Oldest Oak—David's bench—Rachel crumpled at its base, praying for his presence, hoping against hope he would come and talk with her again. *Just one more time*, she looked up into the tree's canopy, begging. The Oak's leaves, cupping droplets from the morning rain, stretched out to the very edges of their lamina, unfurling, allowing the watery tears to fall onto Rachel's neck.

How will I live without you? Sariah's words, echoing.

On the wings of the breeze through the Oldest Oak's leaves

came the answer.

But where do you think I can go?

———

The Children, with help from the Ancestors, had prepared a scene they'd adapted from *The Graveyard Book* by Neil Gaiman. That scene where Nobody Owens—Bod, to his friends—with his friend Scarlett, meets the Sleer in the grave-yard, and the Sleer tries to scare them away with a ghostly projection. Rachel had been invited and was seated by the stage, completely taken with the creativity of the Children as they used a flashlight and hand gestures to create the ghostly projection and had dressed up one of the, well, larger Ances-tors to play the Sleer. It was both funny and frightening, ex-actly as Rachel imagined the author had intended.

She was seated in between Inés and Eloise, and after the play was over, the three of them congratulated the Children and walked over to David's bench to sit and talk.

"You know, I suppose, that I will no longer be able to visit with David," Rachel began.

Inés and Eloise checked with each other, then nodded at Rachel. "Yes," Eloise spoke first. "We know," added Inés.

"I suppose it would have been too much to ask to have been prepared a bit for that," Rachel said but then relented, recognizing there were more important things to talk about.

"We're sorry," the sisters chimed almost in unison.

"It doesn't matter now," Rachel continued. "I wanted to talk with you about my ... preparation. That is what I've heard you speak of before, isn't it?"

She grinned at the sisters' looks of surprise as they realized Rachel had been aware of their planning.

"Yes." Again, together.

"Is that all you can say now?" Rachel asked with pretend

annoyance.

"No, it isn't," Inés replied, rising to the bait. "We have been waiting, though, to see what *you* are ready to talk about. We've waited for so much to come together. Each of us, Eloise and myself, and many more through time, has had a role in guiding you to this place, this time. But there are just a few more things to share with you before our roles have been fulfilled. It has been said that profound sorrows are not meant to be borne alone. Here in the cemetery, the Children have us. They have the Ancestors. They have each other. We share the suffering and thereby make it bearable."

The Children's Chorus: God help us bear our suffering well.

"Their stories must never be forgotten. It is the path all descendants will walk into their futures. And you will be the one to tell their stories, Rachel. Do you feel ready?"

Rachel sat with her eyes closed, feeling for her response. "This is what I understand," she answered after moments of silence.

"There is no single note to suffering. It is a symphony of harmonies and dissonances that, in its crescendos and its diminuendos, can break open the heart's vault and unveil the path to freedom and joy. David said to me once, 'Mom, you hide in your mind sometimes. Trust your heart.' I no longer want to run from who I am. My soul teems with Judaism's great heritage of storytellers: Marcos Aguinis, Aharon Appelfeld, Paul Auster, Louis Begley, Simon Bellow, Chloe Benjamin, Michael Chabon, Leonard Cohen, E. L. Doctorow, Nathan Englander, Myla Goldberg, Allegra Goodman, Nadine Gordimer, David Grossman, Lillian Hellman, Theodor Herzl, Eugène Ionesco, Rachel Kadish, Franz Kafka, Imre Kertész, Nicole Krauss, Tony Kushner, Primo Levi, Norman Mailer, Bernard Malamud, David Mamet, Osip Mandelstam, Arthur Miller, Rachel Nagelberg, Irène Némirovsky, Amos Oz, Cynthia Ozick, Grace Paley, Dorothy Parker, Boris Pasternak, S.J.

Perelman, Robert Pinsky, Harold Pinter, Chaim Potok, Marcel Proust, Philip Roth, Nathalie Sarraute, Maurice Sendak, Isaac Bashevis Singer, Gertrude Stein, Tom Stoppard, Lyudmila Ulitskaya, Ayelet Waldman, Elie Wiesel.

"I could go on and on. It's a heritage of which I'm proud and one I wish with all my heart to contribute to. I've lived a surface life too long, hiding from myself. Time doesn't lend itself well to the lukewarm. I'm ready."

53
THE CHILDREN'S STORIES

Days later, I returned to the cemetery, met by the Children, dressed in their best clothing and in high spirits, the older ones twirling with the younger ones in their arms so that they looked and sounded like dervishes. They'd come to hear a story and knew *they* were the stars. I sat among them on David's bench, and with one of the Oldest Oak's branches resting on my shoulder, I opened the notebook in my lap and began.

"Let me tell you the story of lives unlived. Lives rife with pain and sadness, wisdom and joy. So it is for all sufferings. It begins in a cemetery."

The Children sat quietly, eyes on Rachel, rapt.

ACKNOWLEDGMENTS

I am indebted to the following books and authors for insight into different times, traditions, and truths: *The Golem* by Gustav Meyrink, *The Night Trilogy* by Elie Wiesel, *The Rise of the Inquisition* by Juan Marcos Bejarano Gutierrez, *Snow in August* by Pete Hamill, *The Lima Inquisition* by Ana E. Schaposchnik, *Against the Inquisition* by Marcos Aguinis, *Prisoner without a Name Cell without a Number* by Jacobo Timerman, *The Golem Redux* by Elizabeth R. Baer, *By Light of Hidden Candles* by Daniella Levy, *The Last Jew* by Noah Gordon, *Clara's War: One Girl's Story of Survival* by Clara Kramer, and *On the Kabbalah and Its Symbolism* by Gershom Scholem.

To all the novelists I read while writing *The Bones* whose influence is, likely, apparent, my gratitude and apologies.

Most of all, thank you to good readers and listeners Carly Fetzer, Jessica Fetzer, Scott Fetzer, Rick Anderson, and Marie Fishman for their comments and never-ending encouragement. And to all family and friends who offered unconditional support throughout years of writing, please know of my love and gratitude. I am particularly grateful to have had the opportunity to read a draft to my blind mother after she came to live with us and before she died nine months later. A special thank you to Rick for his wisdom, cheerleading, and love—*In spite of ourselves, we'll end up a' sittin' on a rainbow.* And though he wasn't there to provide his brilliant and gentle editing, David is always in my head and heart as I write.

ABOUT ATMOSPHERE PRESS

Atmosphere Press is an independent, full-service publisher for excellent books in all genres and for all audiences. Learn more about what we do at atmospherepress.com.

We encourage you to check out some of Atmosphere's latest releases, which are available at Amazon.com and via order from your local bookstore:

Icarus Never Flew 'Round Here, by Matt Edwards
COMFREY, WYOMING: Maiden Voyage, by Daphne Birkmeyer
The Chimera Wolf, by P.A. Power
Umbilical, by Jane Kay
The Two-Blood Lion, by Nick Westfield
Shogun of the Heavens: The Fall of Immortals, by I.D.G. Curry
Hot Air Rising, by Matthew Taylor
30 Summers, by A.S. Randall
Delilah Recovered, by Amelia Estelle Dellos
A Prophecy in Ash, by Julie Zantopoulos
The Killer Half, by JB Blake
Ocean Lessons, by Karen Lethlean
Unrealized Fantasies, by Marilyn Whitehorse
The Mayari Chronicles: Initium, by Karen McClain
Squeeze Plays, by Jeffrey Marshall
JADA: Just Another Dead Animal, by James Morris
Hart Street and Main: Metamorphosis, by Tabitha Sprunger
Karma One, by Colleen Hollis
Ndalla's World, by Beth Franz
Adonai, by Arman Isayan
The Journey, by Khozem Poonawala
Stolen Lives, by Dee Arianne Rockwood
Waiting 'Round to Die, by Chris Grant

ABOUT THE AUTHOR

Betsy L Ross is a writer, filmmaker, and happily retired attorney. She has published nonfiction, poetry, book reviews, and wrote/directed the documentary *Looking for David*, available on Amazon Prime. *The Bones of the World* is her first novel.

CPSIA information can be obtained
at www.ICGtesting.com
Printed in the USA
BVHW071958120323
659887BV00002B/12